THE KEY OF SKELETON PEAK

THE KEY OF SKELETON PEAK

LEGENDS OF THE LOST CAUSES

BOOK 3

BRAD MCLELLAND & LOUIS SYLVESTER

HENRY HOLT AND COMPANY

NEW YORK

Henry Holt and Company, *Publishers since 1866*
Henry Holt® is a registered trademark of Macmillan Publishing Group, LLC
120 Broadway, New York, NY 10271 • mackids.com

Library of Congress Cataloging-in-Publication Data

Names: McLelland, Brad, author. | Sylvester, Louis, author.
Title: The key of Skeleton Peak / Brad McLelland & Louis Sylvester.
Description: First edition. | New York : Henry Holt and Company, 2020. |
 Series: Legends of the Lost Causes ; book 3 | Summary: Ever in pursuit of
 justice and revenge for their killed families, Keech Blackwood and his
 fellow orphans travel to Skeleton Peak to retrieve a magical object that
 could help Reverend Rose return to his full, villainous strength.
Identifiers: LCCN 2019019764 | ISBN 9781250124364 (hardcover)
Subjects: | CYAC: Adventure and adventurers—Fiction. | Magic—Fiction. |
 Supernatural—Fiction. | Robbers and outlaws—Fiction. | Orphans—Fiction.
 | Revenge—Fiction. | West (U.S.)—History—1848-1860—Fiction.
Classification: LCC PZ7.1.M4628 Ke 2020 | DDC [Fic]—dc23
LC record available at https://lccn.loc.gov/2019019764

Our books may be purchased in bulk for promotional, educational, or business use. Please
contact your local bookseller or the Macmillan Corporate and Premium Sales Department
at (800) 221-7945 ext. 5442 or by email at MacmillanSpecialMarkets@macmillan.com.

First edition, 2020 / Designed by Liz Dresner
Printed in the United States of America by LSC Communications, Harrisonburg, Virginia

10 9 8 7 6 5 4 3 2 1

This one is for Jim,
My mentor, first writing partner, kindred spirit, brother.
Thanks for always being there, Jimbo. A faithful friend is a sturdy shelter.
—B.M.

For my father, Lou,
Who has supported me in my endeavors and given me space to imagine.
—L.S.

PART ONE

ON THE
SANTA FE TRAIL

FEBRUARY 1856

MIGUEL ON THE MOUNTAIN ROUTE

For eighty-five days, Miguel Herrera rode on Chantico's weary back.

He knew the count well; using his special bone-handled knife, he'd been scoring the days into his saddle since embarking from eastern Kansas. His riding companion let him keep the big knife, provided he be a "good boy."

Miguel wore his hat pulled low and his blue bandana high to keep the swirling frost off his cheeks. He traveled in silence, following the small man through the shallow foothills of western Kansas Territory and into the Rocky Mountains. Bitter winds colder than the worst Missouri winter blew down the canyon passes. Miguel felt as if his fingers would turn to icicles despite his thick gloves.

"These storms will keep curious eyes out of the canyons where we're headed," his companion said. With the heavy snow flurries threatening to bury them, the Mountain Route they were climbing portended avalanches and impassable ice walls.

When he was a little kid, Miguel's mother had told him

frightful bedtime stories about Shifters and *fantasmas*, but she had never told him tales about unnatural weather. Miguel knew well the cruelty of a hard winter, but this was something different, something fiendish and calculating. Perhaps he was seeing what his old Spanish Bible had called *los últimos días*, or the last days. *Pray when you see fearful things*, his mother had once said. *Make the Sign of the Cross, Miguel, and your faith will spare you.*

But Miguel felt no such salvation.

Peering up at the white peaks rising high on each side, Miguel marveled at the size of the Rockies. Having once roamed across the southern rise of the Appalachians in Alabama with his *amigo* Frank Bishop, he'd thought he knew mountains, but these peaks towered with such majesty that they seemed to scrape the sky itself.

As the horses lumbered up the snow-choked path, Miguel's callous chaperone pointed. "Let's stop for the night in that clearing."

Reining Chantico to a halt, Miguel dismounted.

The small man hopped off his own pony, a knock-kneed gelding he had rustled from a lonely farmer in December. "Fetch us some supper. We still have a few days before we reach the Peak, and our beans and bacon are mostly gone."

Miguel moved off into the woods to search for small game. He scanned the drift for prints, watching for signs of a passing rabbit. He kept his long blade in hand. In Missouri, Bishop had said it was a magical blade that would someday kill "the Eye."

Not long after, the one-eyed Bad Whiskey Nelson, *El Ojo*, had killed Bishop in an Arkansas prison. Miguel thought he'd discovered the knife's intended target, but when he thrust it into *El Ojo*'s chest at Bone Ridge Cemetery, the blade did nothing. Only the silver charms and the Reverend Rose's devil birds were able to stop the fiend once and for all.

But now Miguel had *new* plans for the knife. Once he found his opportunity, he would rid the world of his vicious traveling partner.

After fetching a jackrabbit for grub, Miguel fed and watered the two ponies. He muttered kind words to his palomino, asking forgiveness for riding her so hard.

"Enough messing around with those nags. Fetch my saddlebag." After brushing away snow to clear a spot, the small man leaned against a fallen cottonwood tree. He peeled off his ragged hat, revealing a mangy tonsure of gray hair. "Then build up a fire. My feet are cold."

The stolen gelding carried a few saddlebags, but Miguel knew his captor desired a special bundle tucked inside a small leather pouch. Miguel unhooked the bag and carried it over. "Here," he muttered, setting the bag in the fellow's hands.

The man pulled the bag close. "Here . . . what?"

Miguel clenched his teeth. "Here, *sir.*"

"That's better. Now, since you and I have become old pals, go ahead and speak my name." The man's satisfied grin melted into a malignant frown. "I insist."

Miguel had no desire to speak his captor's name. He preferred to think of his infernal companion as *el diablito*, small in stature but possessed by evil. He had first met the desperado in Arkansas, locked inside a *cárcel* called Barrenpoint, the accursed prison where *El Ojo* had killed Frank Bishop. Even then the small man had forced terrible orders upon Miguel. Yet he knew better than to resist a direct command. "*Coward*," Miguel said. "Your name's Coward."

"Good boy, *Cutter*. Now get that fire built." Coward turned his attention to the bag on his lap, shooing Miguel away with a dismissive wave.

Snow-frosted firs crowded the surrounding hills, and powdery drifts blanketed the ground. Miguel stomped through brittle, knee-high brush, hunting for wood dry enough to serve as tinder. He emptied the firewood into a pile, placed a few stones in a circle inside the clearing, and set about laying their campfire.

As he worked, Miguel scratched at the charred mark on his forehead—the devilish product of Coward's ambush in November, not long after the Lost Causes had returned from Bonfire Crossing. Miguel had wandered into the woods to be alone and failed to notice Coward lurking in the brush. When the man suddenly emerged, Miguel drew his blade. He landed one lucky jab before the desperado knocked him out with his mystical cough, a strange but potent power the man possessed.

Miguel awoke to discover that his flesh had been branded with the Devil's mark, a gruesome scar maiming his forehead. The wound hadn't taken but a few days to heal, but now he couldn't help scratching at the foul thing.

While he stoked the welcome fire, Miguel noticed Coward removing the tied canvas bundle from inside his saddlebag. The man loosed a twine knot on the bundle and opened the wrap, revealing a small silver box. Strange etchings lined every inch of the metal—inscriptions Miguel had seen before on a pair of amulet shards worn by his two friends. One of those shards, the one Keech Blackwood had carried, jutted from the pocket of Coward's frock coat even now. But Coward cared little for the shard; what he desired lay inside the chest.

Resting the silver box on his knees, Coward ran his fingers across the grooves, then lifted the box lid.

From where he stood on the opposite side of the campfire, Miguel felt a whisper of sour air caress his face. Twilight shadows shifted around them, despite the glow of the fire.

The small black rock resting inside the chest seemed to hum, not as a sound that could be heard with the ears, but as a vibration that pinched the nerves. Eldritch fumes drifted up from the box's corners. Thin tendrils of raven smoke waved in the breeze but never seemed to dissipate. The stone was no larger than a fist, its surface jagged like that of a rock found in a field. Yet the darkness painting it appeared to *move*, as though thousands of tiny, swarming spiders covered it.

Coward breathed in, sniffing the object in the box. He wielded another curious sort of magic, this *diablito*: His bizarrely powerful nostrils could track a scent from miles away or sniff out the deepest secrets of a person's mind. Yet every night when Coward snorted in the fumes of the ancient relic, he couldn't seem to inhale enough to satisfy his craving.

Miguel backed away from the Char Stone. The artifact was cursed. And somehow alive. He felt it calling to him. Not in a voice he heard, but with a whittling gnaw deep in his gut. At night, his dreams were haunted by images of writhing things creeping under his skin. More than once, he'd woken from a fretful sleep, a scream dying on his lips. If Miguel had his druthers, he would destroy the Stone and forget it even existed.

But Coward obsessed over it. He saw the Stone as a talisman

he could wield. "It's beautiful," he said. "Pure power. The Prime in material form." He hovered his hand a few inches above its black surface, as if tempted to graze the Stone with the tip of his finger, but he resisted—as he did every night.

The silver box snapped shut.

Miguel said nothing. Long ago he'd learned that when Coward spoke about the Char Stone, he was not seeking conversation. He was basking in the promise of powers to come.

Hunkering down in his thick fur and blanket, Miguel pulled his hat over his brow. Though the Devil's mark forbade any hope of escape, he often retreated to secret hollows in his mind where the power of the dark brand couldn't touch him. Where he could envision his best friend, John Wesley, who reminded him so much of Bishop. John was Edgar Doyle's son, a clumsy kid but a fierce fighter. Miguel had lost him to the Chamelia, the creature that had stalked the boy at the command of Big Ben Loving. John Wesley had been scratched, infected, turned into a monster. The last time Miguel saw his friend, John had dashed off into the Kansas woods to join the Chamelia and adapt to life as a Shifter. Miguel's final words to the boy had been, *Remember, no matter where you go, you're one of us. You're a* Lost Cause.

Miguel reached into his coat and touched the brim of John Wesley's wrinkled and warped *sombrero*, a bullet-torn hat made of yellow straw. He had carried the hat since the Chamelia's first attack at Mercy Mission, and though John was gone, Miguel couldn't bring himself to throw it away. Sometimes when Coward slept, Miguel would stroke the hat's ragged brim. No sooner would his fingers graze the straw than he would hear John's whisper in his head, undeniably sharp and clear: *Don't fret, Cutter; I'm exactly where I need to be. Someday, I'll find ya again. Keep your eyes and ears open.*

Miguel always felt better, gripping the hat and hearing John Wesley's voice. But he doubted he would ever see John again, or any of the other Lost Causes. Coward owned his soul now. They were tethered by the Devil's mark that Cutter despised but couldn't escape.

"Soon we'll reach Ignatio," Coward said, his voice yanking Miguel from his buried thoughts. "We'll find the Key and take the Fang back from Red Jeffreys. Once we have the relics, you and I will take them on a final journey."

"To the Palace of the Thunders," Miguel said.

"Yes. And once there, we'll free the Master."

A shiver coursed down Miguel's spine. "What'll happen when we reach him, Coward?"

The small man smiled. "The Reverend will emerge in his full glory, and this world will tremble at the sight."

3 September 1833

The skeleton holds the key.

—R.J.

CHAPTER 1

THE SCARECROW

Keech Blackwood lay flat in the deep snow, watching the hunched figure down in the pasture wobble in the blizzard wind. His trailmates, Duck Embry and Quinn Revels, waited to his left and right, unmoving, buttoned up against the cold. Over the shriek of the winter squall, Quinn steadily sang his peculiar *Odyssey* tune—the melody his aunt Ruth had taught him long ago while fleeing Tennessee. The song worked as an incantation that concealed the group, placing them inside a mystical bubble of sorts that obscured all signs of the young riders, even their horses' hoofprints. It was a trick Quinn had picked up from the man who'd betrayed them, a fellow who went by two names: Edgar Doyle and Red Jeffreys.

"The wind's gonna knock it over," said Duck, her words muffled behind her scarf.

"No, it'll hold." The February freeze pummeled the otter-fur coverings over Keech's ears, so he couldn't hear much except for the wheeze of the Kansas plain. But Quinn's hum still drifted through the blurry noise, filling Keech's bones with comfort.

"I hope you're right," Duck muttered. "I don't want to go down there again."

"It'll hold. Trust me."

"What if they don't show?"

"They're getting antsy." Keech glanced up at the sky. "They'll show."

The trio's position atop the bluff offered the best view of the pasture and the shuddering scarecrow. But what Keech had in mind was not to *scare* crows. Far from it. The makeshift figure perched in the field was intended to lure them out of the sky.

"Something feels wrong," Duck said.

The girl's concerns held plenty of merit, but since losing her brother, Nat, to the explosion in Wisdom, when Big Ben Loving had come to wreak havoc, she'd been second-guessing her own grit. Sometimes loss did that to a person. Keech had struggled with his own doubts after losing his entire family, including his beloved pony, Felix. He wanted to find the right words to reassure her, but all he managed was a cursory nod.

"We're wasting our time up here," she continued. "If this plan don't work, we may never get to save Cutter."

"Or Auntie Ruth," interjected Quinn, interrupting his *Odyssey* tune long enough to speak. Quinn's aunt had been hauled out of Wisdom in November, after the Reverend Rose's devilish brood, the Big Snake, had seized control of the town. All they knew about Ruth's predicament was that she'd been taken somewhere west in a wagon train, along with any other surviving townsfolk.

And based on the original trail Keech had found, Cutter and his captor, Coward, were headed in the same direction, likely planning to marshal with Rose's crew.

"Everything's gonna work." Keech gestured to the clouds. "The crows will come."

They had noticed the Reverend's dark birds on their trail the morning of Christmas Eve, the same day Keech turned fourteen. Duck had spotted a large flock circling the prairie north of the Moonlight River; the creatures were searching, on the hunt. Instead of celebrating Keech's birthday, the Lost Causes spent the day hidden away in a snow trench, watching the turbulent skies.

Though Quinn had continued to conceal their movements with his magical song ever since, it seemed it would be only a matter of time before they made a mistake. If Rose caught a glimpse of their horses or a telltale boot track in the snow, he would send his gruesome birds to tear them limb from limb.

Thanks to Edgar Doyle's betrayal after Bonfire Crossing, they had no silver amulet shards to defeat monsters, or mystical Fang of Barachiel to heal wounds. All they were carrying on their long ride to Hook's Fort, the place they were headed in search of a trapper named McCarty, were bucketfuls of dumb luck.

Sometimes that luck paid off when they crossed friendly paths on the trail. One day, for example, they met a group of Pawnee travelers headed south, their horses pulling flat carts full of pelts. The party had spotted the Lost Causes hunkered down in the drifts while Quinn was resting his throat. The horsemen had sent over a pair of scouts to make sure the trio was okay, and the encounter resulted in a pleasant meal of pemmican and dried squash.

But Keech knew such luck couldn't last forever. As Pa Abner

used to tell him and Sam, *You can ride a streak of fortune for days, maybe months, but it will eventually peter out.*

The afternoon's merciless gale picked up, scattering hard snow over the plain and battering the beleaguered scarecrow. "I'm telling you, the wind's gonna blow it over," Duck said.

"It won't. I drove that pole down myself," Keech said, a speck of doubt lodged in his throat.

The scruffy scarecrow wore a brown buffalo pelt hung over a T-shaped post, and the ragged bowler hat on top was almost identical to Keech's. They had discovered the robe and hat, along with a few other useful items, inside a broken-down wagon some unfortunate traveler had abandoned on the trail. The idea of taking things that didn't belong to them hadn't sat well at first, but after watching the deserted wagon for a few hours and seeing no one return, the young riders decided to gather up the provisions and chalk up the occasion to more good luck.

As the scarecrow took a beating from the hateful flurry, Keech prayed the Reverend's birds would arrive. He studied the landscape and felt energy gathering in his mind, a buzz tingling his fingertips. He was ready. The plan would work.

"My lips are about to fall off," said Quinn, pausing his incantation again. "Let's find a ditch somewhere and hole up. The animals are tired." The horses waited below the bluff—Duck's pony, Irving; John Wesley's old nag, Lightnin'; and Hector, the cremello stallion. Keech's steed had once belonged to Milos Horner, the Enforcer who died in Wisdom. If Quinn stopped humming for more than a minute, the horses would lose their enchanted shroud and reappear, along with their prints, as if emerging from a dense fog.

"Hold your position," Keech said, scanning the white skies.

Rubbing the cold off his lips, Quinn resumed his tune, this time adding a few words: "*Ol' Ulysses saw the cities of men, and he knew their thoughts . . . On the ocean he suffered many pains within his heart . . .*"

The heavy curtain of snow grew thicker, obscuring the scarecrow. "Duck, fetch the spyglass, would ya? I can't see anything down there," Keech said.

Duck's gloved hand fumbled toward the pocket of her coat. She withdrew a small brass telescope, one of the items they had collected from the forsaken wagon. Duck rubbed a smudge off the telescope's lens, then peeked at the pasture below the bluff. "Dang it all, Keech, the scarecrow fell down," she grumbled.

"Lemme see." Keech took the scope. Sure enough, the winter wind had blown the scarecrow onto its side. The buffalo pelt flapped against the gusts, and there was no sign of the bowler hat. A hot flush of embarrassment burned Keech's cheeks. "I thought it would stand, but this wind's furious. I'll head down and fix it."

Quinn stopped humming. "I'll go down, too. I can hide us." He moved to grab the object lying beside him, a sturdy war ax he'd fashioned from maple wood and stone flint. Being handy at toolmaking, Quinn had designed the weapon to match the formidable war club that Strong Heart, the young Osage Protector, had used at Bonfire Crossing to battle the Chamelia.

"Hang on; I just thought of something," Keech said. The scarecrow must not have fooled the crows, but if he went down to the pasture unconcealed, they would spot their prey and hopefully emerge. Handing the spyglass back to Duck, he raised up to his knees. "That scarecrow was a test of their smarts more than anything."

"What do you mean?" asked Quinn.

"We wanted to see if the crows would take the bait, right? But I reckon the Reverend Rose can see right through a dumb scarecrow. I'm sick of waiting. I'm going down there. No more hiding. Not this time."

Quinn looked surprised. "You're gonna let them spot you?"

"Keech, don't you even think about it," Duck said.

But Keech was already tromping down the bluff to reach the pasture. These past few months, Keech had been doing more than simply hunkering down. He'd been working to collect the energies Doyle had taught him to harness, what he called his *focus*. He had used his focus to destroy one of the Reverend's crows at Bonfire Crossing. Now was his chance to prove his practice was enough to finish off the remaining devils. "Y'all stay right there," Keech called, his long deerskin pelt fluttering around him. "I'm gonna go kill me some crows."

As soon as Keech reached the pasture, the barbaric wind stripped the hat off his head and sent it tumbling across the untouched snow. He cursed his luck and kicked after it, but the constant gusts pushed the bowler beyond his reach. Pouncing, he trapped the hat's brim under his boot. Dusting the snow off, he pushed the bowler back onto his brow.

Something dark and furry appeared at the corner of his vision. Keech spun to find he was standing near the fallen scarecrow. The buffalo hide flapped against the post, which had cracked from rot. The bowler he'd nailed to the top was missing, lost in the whiteout.

With a resigned sigh, Keech looked toward the sky.

Three massive crows flew above, not fifty feet from Keech's head. One of the creatures squawked a furious *Ack!*

They dived for him.

CHAPTER 2
ONSLAUGHT OF THE CROWS

High above, several other crows glided across the dappled sky. Keech counted at least seven of them circling, holding back, keeping their distance while the closer trio advanced. A solid strategy. If he proved too capable, they could report to Rose and prepare a stronger ambush farther up the trail. The best Keech could hope to accomplish would be to hold off the attackers without revealing too many of his newfound tricks.

He dashed across the open field, high-stepping through snow mounds. No way would he lead them to Duck and Quinn, who were still hidden on the bluff by Quinn's protective song. Instead, he aimed for a small gully that cut through the pasture.

Aside from the furious wind and the snowy putter of his own steps, there was no sound around him. The birds swooped down in silence. Keech dared a glance over his shoulder and nearly screamed when he saw the lead crow less than two feet away.

Keech sprang to his right. The bird zoomed at his face, and its carving-knife beak scored an instant line of pain across his cheek.

He landed sideways in the snow and threw an arm over his face, hoping to keep the outstretched claws away from his eyes.

The crows soared past him and spiraled to the left, circling for a second attack. In a piercing staccato, they squawked—*Ack! Ack! Ack!*—as if a frenzied bugle had signaled a bloodthirsty charge.

Keech pushed to his feet, slogged back toward the fallen scarecrow, and raised his fist to taunt the three birds. "You'll have to do better than that!"

Screeching in unison, the crows bombarded the field.

Keech grabbed the scarecrow's flapping buffalo pelt and tugged. The nails slipped out of the rotten post, and the pelt came loose. As he turned to face the oncoming attack, he spread the big fur out in front of him.

The first crow veered to his left, the second to his right, but the last continued straight for him. Keech tossed the pelt, and the heavy hide enveloped the squealing thing. It crashed headlong into the field, kicking up sprays of frost.

"Gotcha!" Keech shouted. He aimed his finger at the bundle and reached for his inner focus, but before he could awaken his destructive power, the second crow was upon him. Savage talons appeared before his face, ready to slash. He jumped back, narrowly avoiding the claws.

Razor-sharp barbs slashed across his ear as the first crow struck, slamming into the back of Keech's head. He tumbled forward, a spatter of his own blood marking the white powder. Keech flailed at the bird, punching wildly, till the crow climbed back into the air with a murderous squawk.

His mind dizzy with pain, Keech stood and stuttered forward, his boots slipping in the snow. A shredding noise struck his ears as the buffalo pelt tossed over the third bird ripped open. The crow wriggled out and shot back into the sky. Keech resumed his mad dash toward the ditch, lifting his knees high with each step, his heart raging inside his chest. Slick wetness trickled down his neck as he bled into his coat.

Rose's dark-winged trio circled him, cutting off his path.

Keech skidded to a halt. Gasping for breath, he waved his hands in circles, mimicking the motions Edgar Doyle had used to summon whirlwinds. Keech attempted the chant the Enforcer had murmured to accompany the motion, whispering as he moved his hands. Sure enough, the telltale buzzing of his focus stirred deep within him.

The frozen winds around Keech shifted. The gale blowing out of the north slipped past him and curved around his boots. Despite the distraction of his wounds, Keech felt a sense of calm growing inside him. He faced the approaching crows and whispered, "Come and get it."

A twisting gust pulled the snow into a whirlwind. Waving his hands, Keech felt the energy buzz ever stronger in his chest.

As he'd hoped, the three crows plunged smack-dab into the small twister.

Keech clenched his fist. "Take that!"

But in an instant, the birds burst out the other side of the flurry. The whirlwind of snow collapsed, dissipating like a puff of smoke.

Keech felt his focus extinguished just as the crows returned. They flew at his face, talons bared. He sprang away, throwing his arms over his head. A heavy weight landed on his back. He felt hooks dragging through his pelt and shredding his wool coat. A beak speared the flesh of his neck above his collar. Keech screamed into the snow.

Suddenly the weight lifted, and the sound of flapping wings touched his ears. Keech dared a peek and saw the monsters clambering back into the sky.

"Keech!"

Duck galloped across the pasture on Irving, hunkered low against the gale. Quinn sped beside her on Lightnin', holding his homemade ax. Hector raced along behind them without the need for a lead rope.

Rose's crows were still circling the area, screeching at the approach of the new riders, but they kept their distance. Pushing through the pain, Keech struggled to his feet.

As Duck neared, she said, "You're bleeding! Are you still kickin'?"

Keech's heart wouldn't stop thumping. "I couldn't get my focus to work. I'm a bit cut up, but I think I'm all right." He hobbled over to Hector and swung up into the saddle.

Quinn pointed his ax. "They're coming back."

The three crows plummeted toward the pasture, each aimed at a different rider.

"Back to the trees!" Keech yelled.

As they swiveled toward the bluff, a screeching bird flew in close, flashing a pair of gruesome talons. Gripping his saddle horn, Keech slid sideways till he was hanging low off Hector's side. The creature sailed past, missing him by an inch.

Upright in the saddle once more, Keech watched as Quinn hurled his ax at the second crow speeding toward them. The dull side of the sharpened flinthead bounced off the creature's midsection. The beast shrieked and flapped away, dipping to the left as though favoring a wing.

"Good throw!" Keech shouted.

"I need to get the ax back," Quinn called as he swiveled Lightnin' around.

Keech expected to see Duck still tearing along beside him. Instead, he spotted Irving galloping with an empty saddle.

Duck had been knocked to the ground. She was lying on her back, and a heavy black shape fluttered on her chest.

Furious cackles echoed down from the other two crows.

"Duck!" he yelled.

Resolution cemented Keech's mind. He was no longer thinking, no longer planning. He wanted the birds gone, nothing more. Feeling the warm surge of his inner energies gathering, he waved his hand across the sky, his palm brushing past where he saw the birds.

A shimmer of ice appeared overhead. The crows flew straight into the glacial curtain and stopped in midair. A split second later, two feathered balls of ice plunged toward the field. When they landed, their disfigured bodies shattered like glass into dozens of pieces.

Keech bounded off Hector's back. His mind was reeling, but he would sort out later what happened. Duck needed him now. He sprinted toward her, yelling her name—then stopped in his tracks.

The charcoal bird that had landed on her chest shuddered, then pitched over. Duck shoved it away with one elbow. She sneered. "Serves you right, you filthy gargoyle."

"I thought you were buzzard bait!" Keech said.

Quinn galloped up on Lightnin', his war ax back in hand. "What happened?"

Duck climbed to her feet and brushed clods of snow off her pelt. "I reckon I got in a pretty decent punch." She wiggled her gloved hand, wincing a little.

Quinn's mouth gaped. "You flattened that thing with a *punch*?"

"They ain't so tough," Duck said—but the sheer size of the dazed bird suggested otherwise. At the Home for Lost Causes, Keech and Sam had gotten a close glimpse of a crow perched on Bad Whiskey's shoulder. That creature had been a respectable size, but the one lying on the ground before them was much larger, more like a nasty vulture than a crow. The bird appeared too heavy to fly, but Keech knew it could ride the wind in a snap. The creature's long beak curved down in a crescent, and the talons were twisted and barbed.

The Lost Causes bent closer to inspect the thing—then jumped back in unison at the twitch of a wing. Snow was suddenly kicked up as black feathers thumped the ground.

"That critter's still alive!" Quinn raised his ax.

The creature tried to rise, found one of its wings mangled, and slumped. A burning eye flashed at the kids, and the hideous beak creaked open. Startling them all, a terrible voice crawled like a serpent from its throat.

"*Blackwooood*," the beast rasped. "*I've caught your scent.*"

Keech had heard that nightmarish voice before. On the night the Lost Causes battled Bad Whiskey in Bone Ridge, the Reverend Rose seized Whiskey's thrall body and spoke to Keech through the outlaw's mouth. The same sinister voice was speaking to Keech again, this time through the horrible crow. *"Your days are numbered like a shadow that passeth away."*

"Shut up!" Duck clutched her ears.

"I'm coming for you all."

"No you're not," Keech said. Pointing his finger at the creature, he opened his mouth to send the foul thing to its doom. For a second, he felt a small trickle of warmth sputter into his fingers, but then his focus energy fizzled away again.

A wicked laugh poured from the crow's black gullet.

Unexpectedly a phrase entered Keech's mind—a perplexing, ugly string of sounds that weren't quite words. He had discovered the phrase a few weeks ago while reading the journal Doyle had left behind in his pack. This particular entry was dated *10 January 1833*, and above the curious phrase Doyle had written five words: *Invocation to Disrupt Concentrated Energies.*

"Duck, Quinn, step back," Keech said.

Swapping puzzled glances, Duck and Quinn shuffled back as Keech moved in closer to the Reverend's crow. Peeling off one glove, he splayed his hand over the bird, like someone drawing warmth from a campfire.

"No-ge-phal-ul'-shogg," Keech muttered, pronouncing the strange invocation from Doyle's journal. The words tainted his tongue like curdled milk—a sign that he was dealing with an inhuman language, something unnatural—but as soon as he gave them voice, the crow on the ground ruptured in a flash. All that remained were charred feathers and tarlike gore.

Mouths agape, Duck and Quinn gazed at the remains of the destroyed creature.

"What did you say to it?" Duck asked.

Keech didn't quite know how to answer. A terrible feeling clawed in his gut, as if he'd swallowed a quart jar full of nasty medicine. Moving to slip his gloves back on, he realized his fingers were smoldering.

Quinn broke the silence, pointing at the snowbound sky. "The other crows are falling back. They sure didn't like that hex you spoke."

The distant flock was, indeed, drifting away, retreating into the white haze of the storm.

"Or they're done learning what they need to," Duck said. The sharp bite in her voice suggested she was deeply troubled.

"Let's go find somewhere to camp and get some rest," Keech said, shivering. "Come first light, we'll ride on to Hook's Fort and put this day behind us."

10 January 1833

Invocation to Disrupt Concentrated Energies—<u>Book of the Black Verse</u>, Stanza XVII

No-ge-phal-ul'-shogg

Note that the Reverend speaks with force upon the guttural "ge." To forget this vital emphasis will cause failure in the invocation. This phrase will beseech the doomed target to "return to the earth" or "return to the blood of the earth."

The invocation holds violent effect and will cause pure destruction.

—R.J.

CHAPTER 3
THE BOY AT THE DOOR

That evening, the Lost Causes huddled in a deserted, tumble-down shack, a lonely hovel they had stumbled across in a patch of cottonwoods north of the trail. Quinn built a fire in the hut's old fireplace while Duck brooded in the corner.

"What's got your dander up?" Keech asked.

Duck raised a stern finger in his direction. "Nat never would've put us in danger like you did back there. He'd have listened to the team about the scarecrow and not run off all topsy-turvy."

Shrugging, Keech said, "I just altered the plan a bit."

Quinn shook his head but continued placing wood onto the flames.

Duck said, "You exposed us. Now Rose can find us."

"No he can't." Except Keech knew better. Rose had said himself, *I've caught your scent.* "Quinn hid us again. We're back in the blind."

Duck's face scrunched in clear frustration. "We need you to be steady. We gotta work as a team to find this McCarty fella and learn what he knows."

Keech felt his teeth clench. "I *am* steady, Duck. And you're strong. We're a team. Don't forget what Milos Horner said before Friendly Williams shot him. He said we're *Enforcers*."

"He did not! He said, 'The Enforcers live on.' That's different. Don't start thinking you're as powerful as an Enforcer, 'cause that's gonna get us all killed."

"I don't think that," Keech insisted. "But you have to admit the Enforcers passed some kind of *power* on to us."

Duck's face turned even darker with anger. "Those words you spoke to kill the crow sounded unnatural, Keech. You shouldn't have said them. You don't know what you're dabbling in."

"They're *Doyle's* words. I found them in his journal. It's fine."

"Doyle told us he tapped a dark magic. Then he stole from us so he can resurrect his dead daughter." Duck's voice sounded weary as she spoke. "I don't aim to follow down his path."

Keech's temples pounded with a sudden headache. "You're going *gutless*."

Duck's fierce blue eyes turned as cold as ice.

Quinn held up his hands, a brace between the two. "Now, Keech, that ain't too cordial."

Though Keech was spitting mad, he did regret the accusation. The last time he'd spoken that way to an Embry, during a scuffle with Duck in the town of Whistler, Nat had put him on his rump. Keech knew Duck wouldn't hesitate to do the same.

"Oh, never mind," Duck snapped. "Getting you to listen is a fool's task."

Keech stomped over to the door. "I'm gonna go check on the ponies."

Duck shouted back, "Go on and do it then!"

As he slammed the door behind him, he heard Quinn's voice call after him. "Y'all need to work this out!"

"Let *her* work it out," Keech spat, hoping Duck had heard.

He plodded around the shack to the windbreak they had built to shelter the horses. Keech stood in the empty silence, and a disconcerting anger stirred inside him. The horses watched him with tired gazes, their bodies huddled together in the lean-to, their saddles and bridles still cinched in case the gang needed to ride out in a hurry. John Wesley's old gelding nickered.

"What?" Keech barked at the horse. "I did what I was supposed to. I killed the dang crows. What else does she expect?" When Lightnin' grumbled to his partners, Keech tossed up his hands. "*Felix* would understand." He knew he sounded foolish, speaking to a gelding about the beloved pony he'd lost, but he didn't care.

Plopping down on a snowy log pile, Keech took a few minutes to collect himself. He didn't enjoy being riled at Duck, but there was nothing for it. As Granny Nell once told the orphans, sometimes you had to let yourself feel the anger, so long as you didn't harm others with your vexations. Little Eugena had been a master at getting her dander up, but she dispelled all her rage when she played her brass bugle in the woods. At times, Robby's crooked hand left him feeling plenty resentful, so he purged all his scorn by building Patrick the finest toys.

But Bad Whiskey had taken his siblings away, so now Keech had to find the best way to channel his anger without punishing Duck.

Peeling off his gloves, Keech stared at his fingers, inspecting the knuckles, scrutinizing the fingertips that had smoldered like the barrel of a gun after firing a bullet. The same power Doyle had wielded lay inside, waiting under Keech's skin. Whatever that force was, it was different from his focus. It didn't grow slowly from within. The invocation from Doyle's journal, words taken from something called the *Book of the Black Verse*, had summoned power that was instant and effective.

The places where the crows had scratched Keech stung something awful. Wincing, he dabbed at the talon slashes on his cheek and ear, then the pecking wound on the back of his neck. If the Lost Causes still had the Fang of Barachiel, he could heal those wounds lickety-split. However, because Doyle had stolen the Fang, Keech would have to find regular old remedies for his injuries. In this case, cottonwood buds would do the trick. Despite the terrible chill, the trees still offered plenty of shoots to serve his needs.

Keech stripped a handful of buds off a few branches, bundled them in a cloth, and turned to walk back to the cabin.

Suddenly he glimpsed a shadow moving through the cottonwoods. Keech pivoted toward the movement. As he did, the cloth tumbled out of his hands, spilling the buds. The dark shape had vanished. The shadows lingering beyond the shack belonged only to the somber trees.

Keech waited like a stone, probing the cottonwoods for danger.

Truth be told, the gang's encounters with the Chamelia still haunted him. Gooseflesh rippled over Keech's arms as he envisioned the nightmarish Man Slayer closing in on the shack, baring its fangs, setting its claws to attack.

"Hello?" he said. The cottonwood boughs rattled in the wind. He pursed his lips to whistle for Duck and Quinn, but a rustling noise pulled his attention.

Powdery snow shook from the canopy and sugared the ground. Keech crept deeper into the woods, closer to the spot where he'd seen the shadow, and scoured the tangle of growth. The snow was undisturbed. No sign of prints from either animal or man.

A frigid breeze blustered through the spiderweb of branches. The wind must have rattled a tree limb. Nevertheless, one of Pa Abner's rules of survival spoke up in Keech's mind. *Don't let your guard down when you get a hunch. Listen to your gut, and learn what it wants to teach.* He stood in silence and waited. Nothing moved till another gust shook the cottonwoods, sending a fresh rain of frost fluttering to the ground. "Nothing out there," he muttered.

Satisfied, Keech scooped up all the cottonwood buds he could find in the snow. Then he hustled back to the shack.

Duck and Quinn were playing a card game on the dusty floor when he stepped inside. Their hats, coats, and pelts were drying by Quinn's fire, and Quinn was humming, his special tune hiding the shack in their magic bubble and concealing any hint of the fire's smoke outside. The game between the two was Old Maid, a game Keech had never found particularly enjoyable.

Quinn apparently noticed Keech's jitters and frowned. "Lordy, Keech, a ghost must've stumbled over your grave! Everything all right?"

"I thought I saw something in the woods. But it was just the wind blowing branches." Keech placed his bundle of buds on a flat stone next to the fire. When the resin softened, he mashed out the buds with Doyle's paring knife and applied the oily gum to his cuts—a sticky concoction Pa used to call "balm of Gilead."

Quinn reached to pull a card from Duck's hand.

"Careful, that's the Old Maid," Duck said with a smirk.

"Your bluff stinks to high heaven, Embry." Quinn grabbed the card and snickered when he examined it. He placed a pair of red fours on the floor, then resumed his hum.

Keech watched the game for a spell, feeling more and more wounded by Duck's accusations as the evening drew on. The forgotten shack boasted little in the way of comfort other than a forlorn rocking chair in the corner, shrouded with cobwebs and dust. He pulled the chair close to the battered front door and watched the frozen night unfold through crevices in the rotting walls.

"Keech, you wanna play Hearts?" asked Quinn.

Not a word stirred from Duck, but Keech noticed her giving him a sideways stare. "No, I'm keeping watch. Y'all go ahead."

Quinn said, "Riddle me this, then. I have two sides, but only one you care to see. Sometimes I bring you ruin, sometimes victory. What am I?"

Keech pondered for a second. "I give up, what?"

Quinn held up the queen of diamonds. "A playing card."

The boys shared a small laugh, then Quinn and Duck reshuffled.

Feeling the cold night creep closer, Keech huddled up in his deerskin pelt. A short while later, his trailmates put away the cards and curled up under their blankets. Duck soon fell to snoring, leaving Quinn to pass the time drawing stick figures in the dirt floor, something he did frequently on the Santa Fe whenever they went to ground. He started with a few crudely formed shapes on horseback, then added dozens of stick soldiers, drawing up a complex battle formation like the great Odysseus from the magical poem. But halfway through his mental battle, he, too, began to snore, leaving his stick figures to fight the night away in the dirt.

Keech reached into his coat pocket and pulled out Doyle's leatherbound journal. Before cracking open the book, he made sure Duck was sleeping. Bad dreams had been disturbing the girl for months. One time in eastern Kansas, Keech had even shared one with her—a dream about a massive cavern filled with terrible light. Tonight, though, her sleep seemed free of monsters and misery.

Convinced he was the only one still awake, Keech peeled open the journal and flipped through the pages.

Duck and Quinn had shown little interest in Doyle's writings. They knew the Enforcer once rode with the Reverend, but Keech didn't think they knew the true extent of that villainous partnership. Doyle had not only traveled with Rose; he had studied under him, penning several passages of the so-called Black Verse into his travel logs. Many pages of the book were devoted to Doyle's musings on the origins of the dark words, while other entries showed nothing but frustrated scribbles. On one page, Doyle had written the words *The Black Verse came not from Man* before concluding the entry with nonsense lines of turbulent scrawl. The gibberish seemed to indicate Doyle had lost all track of reality, so disjointed from the rest of the man's jottings that it didn't even contain a date. Keech suspected if Duck had read this madness, she would have insisted they burn the journal.

Keech could never let that happen. He was certain that somewhere in the Enforcer's record hid a clue that could help them destroy the Reverend. *To understand your enemies*, Pa Abner had once taught, *search for the method behind their actions*. Maybe Doyle had written about the *Key* they were supposed to find. They had been told this artifact was hidden in a place called the House of the Rabbit. Other than that, the Lost Causes had no idea what they were seeking; they knew only that locating it was vital. *You must hurry to find it first*, the Osage elder Buffalo Woman had said. *The Scorpion must not find it.*

So far, Keech's investigation of the journal had turned up nothing regarding the location of the House of the Rabbit. But there was one interesting note at the corner of a torn page. Beneath the date *3 September 1833*, Doyle had scratched the words *The skeleton holds the key.* The rest of the page had been ripped out of the book, along with several other complete pages before it. Perhaps the answers Keech sought had been removed at one point, but he would continue to scour the pages of the journal in search of more clues about this *skeleton*.

Keech rocked in the shack's old, forgotten chair, pondering the Ranger's writings. His head grew heavy, and he was starting to nod off when the snapping of frozen twigs near the shack jolted him awake. He sat upright, his heart hammering, his fists tightening.

Another twig snapped, this time closer.

At the fireside, Quinn and Duck continued their slumber, oblivious to the night noise. Keech tiptoed to the door, peeked through a gap between the rotten boards, saw nothing but darkness. He waited.

A boy's whisper infiltrated the cracks. *"Big Bad Wolf? Are you in there?"*

Staggering back, Keech almost tripped over the rocking chair. He caught his balance just before spilling backward.

Again, the faint voice blew through the wall's crevices. *"Come on out and talk."*

Keech slapped a hand over his mouth to keep from crying out.

A rapping of knuckles jittered the cabin door as softly as a windblown branch tapping a window. *"Please, Keech. It's me, the Rabbit! I need to talk to ya."*

The gentle knocking didn't stir Quinn or Duck. There could be only one explanation for what was happening. Though the world felt vivid and real, he must be dreaming.

Curious to discover where the fantasy led, Keech stepped toward the door and unlatched the hook. A heavy bluster of wind tried to drive the door wide open, but he caught the edge before it could crash against the shack's inside wall.

Standing in the snow was none other than Sam.

Keech jiggled his head, trying to jar himself awake, but the vision was too stubborn. *"Sam?"*

"Hey, big brother."

The boy looked exactly as he had the night Keech left him behind, the night Bad Whiskey descended on the orphanage. The knees of his trousers were ripped, and his boots were muddy like they used to get when he and Keech played together. He was even holding the lacebark limb they'd been using for their game of Grab the Musket before Bad Whiskey invaded their lives. Except now Sam was covered head to toe in a thin layer of blue frost, as if the night's chill had turned his skin to solid ice.

"Don't worry, dummy. I ain't a ghost or nothin'." Sam tittered.

Keech allowed himself a cautious laugh. "Am I dreaming?"

"You guessed it." The boy smirked. *"But listen, I got something real important to tell ya. Let's take a walk."*

"All right." Keech stepped out into the deep night; the chill instantly rattled his teeth. "I'm gonna turn into an icicle."

"Don't be a big baby. C'mon."

Keech followed Sam away from the shack and into the cottonwoods. Through recesses in the winter clouds, a vibrant moon shone down on the Great Plains, illuminating the snow-covered highway stretching off to the west.

They stopped shy of a snow-packed ditch, and Sam peeled off his hat—the same one Granny Nell had given him a few years back, the same one he'd been wearing when he ran into the burning Home for Lost Causes. He scratched the dandelion fluff of his hair, then slapped the hat back on. Flecks of ice chipped away from the brim.

"Do you recollect how Pa used to tell us to be true to our gut?" Sam asked. *"How we should always do what's right, even if everybody around us tells us not to. Remember?"*

Keech pulled his pelt and coat tighter. "Pa called it 'being true to your own whisper.' I miss him every day, Sam. Just like I miss you." Warm tears bubbled up as he thought back to all the spry summer days spent with his orphan brother on the banks of the Third Fork River. Sam would bring along his trusty Bible, the one Pa Abner had given him, and read aloud his favorite adventures from the Old Testament. *Ain't too many rip-roarin' sagas in the New Testament*, Sam would say. *You gotta turn to those older books, like Daniel and Joshua and Deuteronomy. Those boys knew how to spin a yarn.*

Keech wiped away his stray tears, which were already freezing on his cheek. "You wouldn't believe what I've gone through since I lost you, little brother. I found myself a pack of new trailmates. I faced down Bad Whiskey. We rode on to Wisdom, and—"

Sam held up his small hand. *"None of that matters. What matters is what's* about *to happen. There's a wagon team rollin' north of the Santa Fe, past Hook's Fort, that's in trouble. The Reverend Rose is sendin' a hard rabble after it. You can't let him take that wagon team, Keech. No matter what."*

"We're headed to Hook's Fort to find a trapper named McCarty," Keech said.

"Dandy. Get on to Hook's Fort, see what you can find. But save that wagon team. *Everything depends on it."*

"What do you mean 'everything'?"

"The whole thing, brother." Sam's unblemished face grew somber. *"If you don't save the wagons, you don't save the world."*

"Why in blazes would the world depend on a bunch of wagons?" Keech asked.

Blue moonlight glinted in Sam's eyes. *"Because they have what you're huntin'. The* key *to your mission."*

Keech's throat nearly closed in shock when he heard the word *key*. "That's what we're searching for! A key! But the Osage at Bonfire Crossing told us we're supposed to find it in the House of the Rabbit. You know, like your nickname."

Sam shrugged. *"I don't know nothin' about a house. But there's a special* key *tucked away in a lockbox in one of those wagons."*

Keech chewed over the new information. "Save a wagon team north of the Santa Fe. Fetch the Key from a lockbox. I'll do what I can."

Sam's cheeks lit up. *"That's the Big Bad Wolf I know."* The boy turned as if to walk away but stopped. "*One more thing.*" He gestured back toward the abandoned cabin. "*Your trailmates might try to talk you out of helpin'. They won't listen to reason. But you gotta convince them.*"

"Don't you worry about them," Keech said. "They'll do the right thing."

"*Maybe, maybe not.*" Sam held out his hand to Keech. "*I best go. I know you won't let me down.*"

Keech shook the younger boy's bare hand, and Sam's fingers pulsed a terrible chill straight into his glove. He figured his dream must be trying to wake him with cold sensations. Before he could wake up, Keech said, "See ya, Rabbit."

"*See ya later, Wolf.*" Sam turned and crossed the ditch, sinking into the night shadows.

Keech needed to say one more thing. "I'm sorry I left you alone!" he called out, but it was too late. The shadows of the Santa Fe Trail had swallowed Sam whole.

CHAPTER 4
HOOK'S FORT

Keech hurried back to the shack before the night air could freeze him through. After latching the door, he covered himself in blankets and shivered near the fire. When sleep finally came, Sam's icy face haunted him.

Before he knew it, the gossamer light of daybreak peeked through the hut's shabby walls, and Keech awakened, huddled on his side. Quinn's fire had diminished to coals and powdery ashes.

Keech sat up with a start, his breath creating clouds of mist in the frosty air. Heavy winds wheezed through the rickety wallboards. The top of Duck's head peeked out from under her blankets, and Quinn lay burrowed under quilts that muffled his snores. Keech clapped his stiff hands a few times to wake his partners. "Rise and shine, you two. We need to strike out soon."

As Duck and Quinn stirred, Keech unlatched the door and stepped outside to the horses. Hector and the ponies greeted him under the lean-to with a series of irritated huffs. The cold night had been hard on them. Keech patted the cremello stallion's muzzle. "Sorry, Heck. I reckon you want to get to a proper barn."

After they packed up the horses, Quinn asked Keech if he could borrow Doyle's carving knife. "I got an idea," Quinn said, a long piece of pine bark in his hand. Keech handed over the knife, and Quinn set to work. On the inside skin of the bark, he carved the phrase *Amicus fidelis protectio fortis*, Doyle's Latin phrase about friendship. Quinn propped the strip of bark, carved words facing out, against the shack's door. "Just in case Cutter rides through and needs to stop for shelter. He'll see we stopped here, too."

"We probably shouldn't leave a sign, what with the Reverend searching for us," Keech said.

Quinn handed the carving knife back. "I don't reckon Rose's gang knows any highfalutin words, so we'll be safe. Even if that fiend Coward sniffs me on the bark, it won't matter. I want Cutter to know we haven't given up on him. It's worth the risk."

Duck tilted her head at the sign. "I'd wager Cut's already ridden past here."

"Maybe he has, but maybe he hasn't. Anyhow, it's worth a try. I'd want to know my friends still cared," Quinn said.

Bundling up against the cold, the Lost Causes headed back to the Santa Fe Trail. They rode in silence, feeling too cold and sleepy to chat much. A gentle snow tumbled over the prairie, large flecks frosting over the tracks of earlier travelers.

As they traversed the endless miles, Keech found himself playing through the previous night's vivid dream. He couldn't figure out an easy way to tell Quinn and Duck about his strange experience without sounding foolish. They would surely laugh at him for saying they needed to save a wagon train because of a ghostly midnight visit. But Pa Abner had always told the orphans to pay close attention to their dreams. *Sometimes your night eyes will notice something your daytime eyes might've skipped*, he used to say. *Dreams can be a way to spot the true path you missed while awake and blinking at the sun.* Keech felt there was something important about his lost brother's mysterious words.

So he summoned his grit and told them about the vision.

Duck and Quinn listened in guarded silence as Keech recounted Sam's message.

Quinn asked, "You think the dream was talking about the wagon train that left out of Wisdom? The one holding Auntie Ruth and the other prisoners?"

"Maybe. Not sure," Keech said. "Sam didn't say which wagon team, only that we had to save it." He hesitated. "He also mentioned a *key*."

Duck's gaze turned suspicious. "What are you talking about?"

"He told me the wagons are carrying a special key tucked away in a lockbox."

"A key as in *the* Key?" Quinn asked.

Duck didn't seem convinced. "I ain't saying I don't believe you, Keech. I know the importance of a dream these days. But this wagon team business don't involve us finding McCarty or tracking down Aunt Ruth or Cutter. It doesn't point us to the House of the Rabbit. Seems your dream aims to make us lose sight of our mission."

"But our mission *includes* the Key," Keech pressed. "If we can get our hands on it, we're one step closer to stopping Rose."

Quinn said, "I dunno, Keech. Seems to me a proper vision would've given a trifle more information. Your dream feels more like a nice wish when you think about it."

"Not to me. It felt as real as you and me talking right now.

I think there is a wagon train out there, and it's in trouble." Keech shook his head in frustration. "Don't y'all think we have a responsibility to investigate? As deputies of the Law?"

"I think calling ourselves the Law might get us in trouble," Duck said.

Though Sheriff Turner deputized the Lost Causes in Bone Ridge, Keech noticed that the farther they traveled from Missouri, the less Duck seemed to believe in the solemn oath they had taken. And Quinn had been skeptical of their claim to be the Law in the first place.

Keech felt his blood begin to rise, but he stifled the anger. "Forget it."

They traveled on through the delicate snowfall. Duck kept peering at their back trail with a concerned frown, but Keech couldn't see any sign of movement behind them. The rolling plains seemed to merge into the winter clouds, erasing any distinction between earth and sky. "Something's got you spooked," he said.

Duck pulled Irving to a halt and drew the brass telescope out of her coat. Swiveling in her saddle, she scanned the horizon. After a moment, she compacted the glass and returned it to her pocket. "I can't see a thing."

"Please don't say the crows have found us," Quinn moaned.

"I thought I saw a rider, maybe two, in the distance. But maybe I didn't. I don't know."

"Do you reckon we're being followed?" Keech asked.

"This is the most traveled road in the whole territory," Quinn said. "We ain't the only ones riding it."

"Y'all just keep a close lookout," Duck said.

Farther west, the snow-clouded sky cleared a bit and the

Kansas plains dished up a mighty sight. The landscape broke into a series of tall, jagged ridges resembling giant teeth biting into the haze.

The Rocky Mountains.

"Would ya look at that," said Quinn. "Me and Auntie Ruth saw plenty of high hills in Tennessee and Arkansas, but I never saw anything that big."

They rode on toward the mountains, stopping once at a frozen creek to eat a light meal of cold bread and dried blueberries. After a few more hours of slow crossing over the foothills, the horses showed signs of fatigue. Keech was about to call for another short recess when Quinn cupped a hand over his brow and said, "Hold up." Squinting through the blurry snow, Quinn leaned over his saddle horn to fetch a better glimpse. "I think I see somebody."

Halting the horses, they stood still in the deep freeze. No one spoke.

To the north, a solitary rider shuffled across the snowpack, drifting like a spirit straight in their direction.

"Quinn, you might warm up those vocal cords, get ready to hide us," Duck said.

But before Quinn could start singing, the rider noticed them. "Hello the trail!" a deep voice called.

Keech grew tense when Quinn waved. "Don't!"

"He looks like a regular ol' traveler to me," Quinn said. "But if he tries something, break off and ride hard and I'll start my singing."

As the horseman drew closer, Keech noticed that the fellow was a dark-skinned man wearing several layers of thick gray hides. He rode a handsome pinto horse, and behind his cantle lay a dead deer, tied to the horse's rear. A smoothbore musket rested on the fellow's lap. The stranger moseyed up, stopped his mount, and tipped his hat. A mean white scar zigzagged across the man's forehead.

"Don't mean to interrupt your passage," the fellow said. "Just ridin' through. Got me a deer to skin 'fore the daylight passes."

Keech tipped his own hat. "No troubles, friend. We're happy to meet a kind soul on the Santa Fe."

The deer hunter said, "You best be careful thinkin' folks are kind before ya know. Not if you want to live long in the rough."

"Mighty good advice," Duck replied. "Say, mister, can you tell us if you spotted a fort nearby? Our horses are in terrible need of a stable."

The hunter hooked a thumb over his shoulder, indicating north. "You want Hook's Fort, back yonder. Last spot of civilization for fifty miles. They got a saloon with rooms to rent. North gate's closed up for winter, but you can enter 'round to the south."

Before the trio could push on, the hunter stopped them. "Hook's Fort is safe enough, but some of those folk can be a tad unfriendly. Watch yourselves. And *you*, son"—the hunter gestured at Quinn—"keep yourself low and your eyes open."

Quinn frowned at the man's words. "Don't you worry. I can take care of myself."

The fellow smiled. "What's your name, son?"

Quinn pushed himself up taller in the saddle. "Name's Quinn Revels, son of George and Hettie Revels." He added with a proud tone: "Tell everybody you come across."

The man's scarred face turned melancholy. "And are you safe, Quinn Revels?" The fellow peeked at Keech and Duck, then back at Quinn.

Quinn pondered a moment. "No, sir. But my friends and I are fighting to make it so."

A sympathetic kind of silence overtook the hunter as he wiped a gloved hand across his forehead. His eyes spoke of long days and haunted memories. "Some bright day, Mr. Revels, maybe you won't have to fight no more," he said. Then, clucking to his horse, the stranger disappeared up the path.

The young riders continued, pushing their mounts farther up the rutted highway till the landscape dipped into a northern valley. Quinn found them an easy path into the basin, and they veered off the Santa Fe Trail.

To the northwest, a speckling of black dots roamed the snowy flatlands, and Keech realized it was a massive herd of buffalo. The herd was slipping steadily past a dark shape atop one of the distant hills—the walls of a remote garrison. "I'd wager that's Hook's Fort," Keech said. "If a trigger-happy horseman happened to see the buffalo from the fort, he could fire off and start a bona fide stampede."

Quinn chuckled. "Well, let's hope that don't happen."

"We need a plan before we ride up," Duck said. "If this place is like Wisdom, overrun with outlaws and thralls, we'll be caught before we can sneeze."

"Don't forget; it may be crawling with slavers, too." Quinn's cautious frown spoke of longtime vigilance on the trail out of Tennessee with his aunt.

"We should scout first," Keech said.

They trotted toward a vantage point that looked out at the fort, a rectangular stronghold with gray block walls. Quinn hummed, hiding them from the garrison, as the horses labored up a long rise. A strong flurry swirled around them, reducing their sight, erasing the mountains and the west-moving buffalo, leaving only the fort in view.

Dismounting, the young riders huddled on their stomachs. They watched the fort's stone walls till Keech spotted a pair of armed men patrolling the eastern side.

"Think they're thralls?" he asked.

Duck peered through her spyglass. "They walk like normal men."

Part of Rose's mission involved taking down settlements in his path, as well as seizing military supplies to outfit his reanimated scum. But Hook's Fort didn't show the first sign of a thrall. Maybe Rose was leaving towns intact along major highways so as not to stir up the attention of the Law—at least till his dire army was fully assembled.

"Let's go in," Keech said, "but remember what that deer hunter said. Stay low, and watch one another's backs."

Mounting back up, they traveled down the slope and across a flat field toward the garrison. The high walls and the corner bastions reminded Keech of a medieval castle. Black cannon barrels peeked out of big loopholes, and a square blockhouse loomed over the north gate. Keech spotted a brass bell hanging over the gatehouse—the fort's emergency signal—and the thirty-one-star flag of the United States flapping on a pole.

As they approached the south gate, a pair of rugged herdsmen stared down at them from the parapet. The men bumped each other's elbows as the kids stepped up. One of them called down, "*Hola, niños.*"

"*Hola,*" Duck returned.

Seated on a stool near the gate, a bearded fellow cradled a steaming cup of coffee. A heavy fur cloak draped his shoulders, and a musket leaned against the wall. He lifted a bushy brow when he saw them. "Why, you're just a buncha little 'uns!"

Duck huffed. "We're seeking shelter. May we enter?"

The bearded man shrugged. "Long as you ain't carryin' firearms. We don't allow civilians to carry pistols and such around the fort. You can drop your lead chuckers in this here bin." He kicked the side of a large open crate full of shooting irons and a few rifles.

"We ain't armed," Duck said. She patted her pelt to show nothing concealed.

The guard shook his head. "What kind of fool lads are y'all to travel these plains without sidearms?" The man had clearly mistaken Duck for a boy, but no one corrected the fellow.

"Maybe we're smart enough we don't need them," Duck said.

The guard unlatched the crossbars. "In that case, welcome to Hook's Fort! Enjoy our hospitality."

They rode into a spacious plaza, a bustling square alive with commerce. Narrow streets extended from the center like the spokes of a crooked wheel. Mingling smells of moldy hay and chicken manure filled Keech's nostrils, but he didn't mind the odor.

Men and women of all backgrounds and colors milled about the plaza, chatting and laughing and grumbling at the cold. Snow-covered wagons sat along the edges of the square, many seemingly abandoned for the long winter. Keech tipped his hat to a group of dark-skinned mountain men loading supplies onto the backs of haggard mules. A few scruffy dogs roamed in a pack, nipping at one another's paws. Beneath the overhang of a tottery porch, a long-legged Texan bartered the price of a bison hide with a pair of Kiowa tribesmen.

"Folks here ain't so bad," Quinn said.

No sooner did he speak the words than a heavyset cowpuncher with a bulging stomach and a filthy goatee stepped out of the crowd. He bumped into Quinn's shoulder as he passed, catching Quinn off guard and spinning him about. The scruffy man kept walking but spat a few terrible curses back at Quinn.

"Hey!" Duck shouted at the man. "Watch where you're going!"

Quinn said, "Don't worry about it, Duck. We need to keep low, remember?"

But the cowpuncher was already twisting back around to face them. His pale features scrunched. "What'd you say?"

"I *said*—" Duck began, but Keech jumped in before she could finish.

"She said we best be on our way. Have a pleasant day."

The man glared at Duck, then tossed another scowl at Quinn before disappearing into the plaza.

Duck grimaced. "If we didn't have places to go, I'd set that fella straight on who he can shove."

Quinn clapped her on the back. "I'm sure you would. For now, though, I think that deer hunter on the trail was right. We best get outta sight, maybe head down an alley. They're too many folks milling about, and like Auntie Ruth says, rattlesnakes often wear human faces."

The Lost Causes passed a stumpy courthouse and a soldiers' barracks. A church steeple leaned in the breeze, and a few rows of tents housed a throng of pilgrims waiting out the winter. A water well sat in the center of the square, the circle of stones frozen over, and a gaunt man wearing a beaver cap plucked at a guitar with only two strings.

They turned down a side street named Broken Bit Alley and asked around for a farrier to tend the horses. "Then we can hunt down the trapper McCarty," Duck said. The fallen Enforcer Milos Horner hadn't given them any details about the fellow beyond his name, but surely someone in the fort would know something helpful.

As they rounded the corner, the dusty sounds of piano music filled Keech's ears, an old river tune he recognized as "Oh Shenandoah." The song wheezed out of a two-story building ahead, where a sign over the front door proclaimed:

TANGLEFOOT TAVERN

FARO TABLES ♣ FINE WHISKEY

AFFORDABLE RATES

"This must be the saloon," Quinn said, speaking over the noise of the piano and a hee-hawing mule nearby. "Maybe somebody inside can tell us where to find the trapper."

Suddenly the door to the Tanglefoot Tavern burst open, and out spilled an older woman clad in dark brown furs and batwing chaps. "*Oh Shenandoahhh, I long to see youuuu, away you rolling riverrrrr!*" the woman sang, off-key. She wore no hat, and the wild tangles of her curly red hair stuck to her forehead and cheeks in greasy clumps. Stumbling down the icy steps, she lost her balance and tumbled into the snow in front of Hector.

"Miss, are you all right?" Duck asked.

The tipsy woman cackled. "I been called a lot, tadpole, but I ain't heard 'Miss' in ages." She attempted to stand, gave up, and plopped back to the slushy ground. "Goodness, am I roostered!" she said, swiping dirty snow off her chaps.

"We're on the lookout for a trapper," Quinn said. "A fella who goes by McCarty."

The stranger rumpled her grimy face. "*Bah*," she spat, then raised two fingers to her mouth and whistled. "Achilles! Com'ere, boy!"

"Our mounts need attention," Duck said. "Could you point us to a farrier?"

Not bothering to answer, the woman searched the street. "Where is that dang mutt? I *tol'* him to wait here." She glanced at Keech. "Have *you* seen my dog?"

"I saw a few back in the square," Keech said.

The red-haired stranger pushed herself up onto wobbly feet. She staggered, pitched forward, and caught herself on a hitching post. She called out, "Achilles, where are ya, boy?" Then back to the young riders: "There's a livery stable at the end of Broken Bit. You'll find a farrier named Travis."

Duck tipped her hat. "Much obliged."

The young riders watched the woman disappear into the crowd. "That's funny," Quinn said.

"What?" Keech asked.

"Her dog's name is Achilles. That's the fella who fought Hector in *The Iliad*. Hector is your horse's name."

Keech pondered the coincidence, agreed it was interesting, then turned his thoughts back to the mission. "Let's go on to the stable."

Down the alley they passed several open stalls, most of them empty, the frigid winter days having driven the boot menders and harness-makers indoors. At the end of the path, the young riders found a livery stable built up against the fort's high wall. A sign on the door carried the farrier's symbol: a pair of crisscrossed hammers nestled inside an upside-down horseshoe.

They dismounted, and Duck banged a fist against the door. "Anybody there? Y'all open?"

The door creaked open, and a thick, sturdy woman with round cheekbones peeked out. She wiped her hands across her leather apron and gandered at the horses. "Those animals look run down," she muttered with a frown. "I can tend their shoes for ten cents a hoof. Dollar twenty for the lot."

"You must be Travis," Duck said.

The woman threw open the stable doors. "Bring 'em on in. I'll give 'em proper care."

A heavy wall of warmth greeted them as they stepped inside. Keech loosened his scarf and shrugged off his pelt.

A few lanterns set around the barn lit the chamber. Straw littered every inch of the floor, and a cast-iron stove blazed in the corner, the front grate open. Farrier tools rested atop a leather bag on the ground, and a black anvil sat nearby for shaping horseshoes. Narrow stalls lined the side walls, housing a number of uninterested horses.

Travis didn't bother to fetch their names, but she greeted their horses like old friends, allowing them to learn her scent. She watched the animals shift about. "I wonder if you youngsters understand how painful it can be for a pony to walk a trail without decent groomin'. That means daily hoof pickin' and work with a brush."

Keech frowned. "We brush them and clean their hooves near every day."

"Whatever the case, I'll need a few hours," Travis said.

Duck pursed her lips at Keech and Quinn. "Let's have a huddle."

The trio gathered in the corner, away from the farrier's ears. Keech said, "We can leave the ponies, but we need to keep aware of the time. I've got a bad feeling we're gonna squander our chance to save that wagon team and find the Key."

"Keech, I just don't know," said Quinn. "We should stick to the mission."

"I agree. Let's just fetch our supplies and ask around for McCarty," Duck told the boys. "We need to get a lead on this trapper. I reckon if we can find him, things will fall into place."

A cold surge of anger ran through Keech's veins. He hated being ignored, but he bit back his irritation. "Fine. Let's get moving, then."

6 November 1832

The Black Verse indicates a way to disarm without bloodshed, but the Reverend desires that we use the invocation of destruction against enemies instead. Without annihilation, the Reverend teaches, the enemy shall return. Even still, I have learned the more peaceful solution in battle, which is to use the phrase:

M'gah-ge-hye'thn—translated to mean, "Stop your attack."

I have not yet attempted this phrase, because I fear the slightest misspoken sound could prove fatal to my target. But in a case of extreme desperation, I may decide to employ the hex.

—R.J.

CHAPTER 5

WHISPERS IN THE ALLEY

Quinn volunteered to remain with the horses and help with the grooming to speed Travis along, while Duck and Keech agreed to find the fort's general store. There they could restock a few supplies and seek a direction for Milos Horner's trapper.

They returned in silence to the plaza, kicking through the muddy snow with each trudging step. "I feel like we live in an eternal blizzard," Keech noted. When Duck didn't respond, he scowled. "What's got under your bonnet?"

"Under *my* bonnet? You acted reckless yesterday. We were lucky not to get killed." She pointed to the scratches on Keech's face, ear, and neck. "And when I tried to talk to you about it, you ignored everything I said."

"I didn't ignore you. I disagreed. That's different. Sure, I got cut up a bit, but in the end, I beat those crows fair and square."

Duck frowned. "And now there's this wagon team business."

"It ain't *business*. I told you, it was a vision."

"I think it was just a dream this time. Nobody knows what's *gonna* happen."

"Maybe," Keech said. "And maybe you're wrong."

"Yeah? Well, maybe *you* are."

It didn't take long for them to find the general store. It was the largest business in the plaza, boasting a long front porch and a colorful sign that read TIPPETS' TRADE & SAVE. The shop owner, Mr. Tippets, was a mustached man with a round belly and a friendly disposition. He helped them gather provisions for the trail, collecting small burlap sacks full of feed and beans and other dried goods. "Let's stack all this near the door," Mr. Tippets said. "When you're ready to light out, hitch your ponies outside and I'll help ya load."

"I reckon running a shop like this, you get to know most everybody, right?" Duck asked.

Mr. Tippets chortled. "Anybody living within fifty miles any direction has shopped at Tippets' Trade & Save." He popped his suspenders with pride.

Keech said, "We're looking for somebody. A trapper. Name of McCarty."

A bitter frown crossed Mr. Tippets's face. "That old vagabond? Probably still beatin' about the fort somewhere, but that scoundrel keeps a low profile. Owes money to half the territory and ain't welcome 'round my store no more."

"So this gent could still be in the fort?" Keech asked.

The shop owner laughed. "*Gent*, he says. Do yourselves a favor an' forget McCarty. That filthy cheat ain't got nothin' to offer but trouble." Turning his back on the conversation, Mr. Tippets bent with a grunt and lifted a sack of shelled beans. "Let's get to stackin' these goods."

While Duck settled the final details of their transaction, Keech stepped out of the store. He groaned when he saw that the white haze over the sky had grown dark, portending another rotten blizzard. Feeling irritated with the whole world, he sat on a porch step.

A rambunctious cackle sounded down the nearest alley. Keech peeked around the corner. Three grimy, trailworn men stood in a circle, shooting the breeze and passing a flask back and forth. One fellow had a face that twitched like a rat's, and two bandoliers packed with bullets crisscrossed his chest. Another stood on bowed legs and wore an empty holster on his bony hip. All three roughriders had deeply tanned faces, features that were almost golden when the day's pale light shone on them.

"They'll be sittin' ducks," one of the men said, then chuckled. He lifted the flask to his lips and took a mighty swig, spilling the container's amber liquor onto his thick brown beard.

"I ain't sayin' you're wrong, Ian, but I'd still like to see for myself," the rat-faced fellow said. "I don't relish the idea of ridin' down on a mess of barkin' rifles."

"Don't you fret none. They won't be armed." The man called Ian drained the last of his whiskey and tossed the flask over his shoulder, where it landed in a pile of frozen, moldy hay. "I got myself a good look when they lit out this morn'. Five wagons packed high with goods and not a single musket. That train'll keep us stocked the rest of the winter."

The man with the empty holster slapped his knee. "Then let's collect our firearms and git to it! My hip's been feelin' mighty light."

"Not just yet." Ian held up a cautionary hand. "We gotta wait for Alfy. Way this snow's a-tumblin', we're gonna need his trackin' talent to find the wagons up in the mountains."

Keech could hardly believe what he was hearing. These bandits were planning to attack and rob a *wagon train*, just as Sam had promised. His dream vision was true after all! He shook with excitement, eager to share the development with Duck and Quinn.

A forceful hand tapped Keech's shoulder, jolting him to attention.

"What are you doing out here?" Duck asked.

"You scared me!" Realizing he'd been too loud, Keech glanced back down the alleyway. All three bandits were staring at him.

"We're ready to ride," Duck said, holding up a small piece of paper. "Mr. Tippets gave me a receipt. He said to present it before we light out." She followed Keech's worried gaze to the alley. "Who are *they*?"

Keech hoped the ruffians would dismiss them as nothing more than meaningless kids. "Nobody. Let's get out of here."

As soon as they were out of sight, he said to Duck, "Listen. I overheard those men talking about a wagon train. About chasing it down and robbing it."

Duck considered his words. "Keech, I don't like bad jokes."

"I wouldn't joke about this."

After pondering for a spell, Duck shook her head. "Sorry, but if they ain't helping us find McCarty or track down Cutter and Ruth, then they ain't none of our business."

"But they're gonna attack innocent people," Keech argued. "That bearded fella said five wagons and not a single musket. They'll wipe everyone out!"

"Then we oughta tell the authorities. The soldiers here could deal with such a scheme."

"We gotta help that team. It's vital that we do it." He tapped his chest. "It has to be *us*."

Duck hooked a thumb back toward the alley. "Didn't you see those fellas? They're covered in bullets! If we got in their way, they'd kill us dead."

"We're no pushovers, Duck. And Quinn could hide us. And I've got my focus."

"No, sir." Duck's face went from incredulous to offended. "You will *not* use your finger to explode people. Let's just report those men to the fort."

"You gotta believe me," Keech begged.

Duck gave him one more sharp look. "Keech, you know I dream about Nathaniel every night. I don't think I'll ever have a sleep where I don't. But if I was to say Nat told me to leave aside our mission and hunt down another whole gang, you'd say I've gotten confused."

Keech clutched his temples. "You haven't listened all morning. But don't forget the Moss farm, Duck. We both dreamed the *same thing*, remember? It felt different. It was something *real*." His voice was turning wild, as if he was on the verge of yelling, so he paused to take a calming breath. "Sam's visit wasn't just a normal dream; it was a *vision*. Those schemin' outlaws are confirmation. We have to listen. People's lives are at stake. And so is the Key."

Duck nibbled at her bottom lip. "Let's talk to Quinn, see what he thinks."

Keech slapped his knee in excitement. "Dandy. But if you both agree, we'll need to ride out soon. We can't let those bandits get too far."

"We'll see what Quinn thinks," Duck repeated.

They hurried back to Travis's stable. After Duck banged on the door a few times, Quinn opened up. He had stripped down to his shirt and trousers, and sweat covered his forehead and neck. "I ain't been this hot in six months. I love it in here," he said.

Travis was hard at work shoeing Irving. The farrier muttered easy words to the Fox Trotter, but her entire attention was focused on the tool in her hand.

"Y'all will never guess what I found out," Quinn said. "I told Miss Travis here about Cutter and Coward. She said she *saw* them. They came through Hook's Fort!"

Surprise shuddered through Keech like a lightning bolt. "Did Cut seem all right? Did Coward have him tied up?"

"I wondered the same thing, but Travis said they was riding side by side, like regular old partners. No ropes or threats to keep him in line, free to go as he pleased. I asked which way they headed after leaving the fort, but she didn't know."

Keech frowned. "Are you sure she saw the right pair?"

"Hey, kid, I'm standin' right here," Travis called out. "I can't imagine two other fellas fittin' their description. I saw 'em, sure enough."

Though Duck had been irritable all morning, true rage now flashed across the girl's features. "I *knew* there was something devious about Cutter! Remember how he wouldn't ever talk straight about Coward back in Wisdom?"

Quinn shook his head. "No way Cut would help those killers. Not a chance."

"Why not? Maybe deep down he's a bad seed."

"John Wesley didn't think so," Quinn said.

Duck momentarily dropped her head.

Keech refused to believe Cutter would betray them, but then again, he had never thought Edgar Doyle would forsake his son's own trailmates, either. "Maybe we've been too trusting, but I'm with Quinn on this one. Cut stood by us in Bone Ridge. He faced Bad Whiskey alone in the Floodwood cave, and he fought beside us at Bonfire Crossing. He's got a good heart."

Duck said, "Don't y'all forget, Cutter confessed he was holding back a secret from me and Nathaniel. He did something to our family but never would say what."

Quinn's face suggested he had no good answers or comfort to offer. "So what do y'all think we should do?" he asked.

Keech contemplated their ever-multiplying avenues. Track down Coward to retrieve the Char Stone. Find Cutter and investigate his motives. Save a wagon train from annihilation, and obtain this mysterious Key while doing so. Find a stranger named McCarty who might hold a crucial clue to stopping Rose. Track down Edgar Doyle to recover the Fang and the amulet shards. There were simply too many pieces in play, too many impossibilities.

A loud knock at the barn door interrupted Keech's thoughts.

"Somebody answer that," Travis said peevishly.

Quinn grabbed the door handle to pull it open. When he did, a brisk hand pushed against the door, shoving him back. A cold breeze blustered in, followed by a bedraggled woman. Keech recognized her as the redheaded drunkard outside the Tanglefoot Tavern. A bushy gray hound dog with floppy ears followed her. The dog inspected them, barked a couple of times, then trotted over to a horse trough and lapped up water. A thick black cord circled the hound's neck like a collar, and a flat leather pouch dangled from the cord, as though the mutt might be carrying his own treats.

Travis straightened at once. "What d'ya want, McCarty?"

All three young riders exchanged looks of pure shock.

"Hello yerself, Gail."

"You can't sleep here no more. The horses don't like yer stench."

Disregarding the farrier, the red-haired woman pushed the door shut, then turned her attention to Hector. She scratched the cream stallion's chin, whispered something in his ear, then turned to regard the Lost Causes. Scowling, she said, "Where is Warren Lynch, and what are you tadpoles doin' with his horse?"

CHAPTER 6
THE TRAPPER AND THE HOUND

The woman's inquiry about Lynch, the alias of Milos Horner, didn't even register at first. Keech was too flabbergasted that they were looking at McCarty, one of their primary objectives since embarking down the Santa Fe Trail. "*You're* the trapper?"

"We thought you'd be a fella!" Even as she spoke, Duck looked delighted that she was staring at a rugged woman, hardened by the elements and decked out in deerskin hides.

Quinn said, "Miss McCarty, we're sure tickled to see you."

"Whoa now," said the woman, holding up a grimy hand. "Y'all can cease with that 'Miss' hogwash. Now, answer my question. Where is Warren Lynch, and what are y'all doin' with Hector?" Slapping her hands on her hips, she stared at the Lost Causes. She didn't seem very tipsy anymore.

Keech said, "We met Lynch in a town called Wisdom, and he sent us here to find you."

They waited for McCarty to say something, but she simply

glared at them, her eyes so brown they looked like two dark buttons mashed into her face.

Nearby, Travis's hammer clacked and clanged against Irving's horseshoe. The farrier clearly didn't appreciate McCarty's presence, but she seemed far more engaged in the Fox Trotter's well-being than the business of a ragged stable drifter.

The floppy-eared hound finished drinking at the trough and trundled over to sit at Quinn's feet. He licked at the kid's fingers and was rewarded with a hearty scratch behind the ears.

"Lynch sent you to find me, huh?" McCarty finally asked.

"He said you could help us," Duck replied.

Keech knew they didn't have time to dally. The roughneck Ian and his brood were preparing to ride for the mountains in search of the wagon train. The Key was in trouble. Innocent lives were at stake. It was better to toss all their cards on the table and see how McCarty reacted. "Here's the thing. We know his real name was Milos Horner. And we know he was an Enforcer who once worked for a monster named Rose."

A peculiar expression crossed McCarty's dirt-smeared face—but her expression turned to something else when she heard Rose's name. Something like dread. "You said his name *was* Horner, not *is*. Did somethin' happen to him?"

"I sure hate to have to tell you this news, but he's dead, ma'am." Keech hung his head. "He was shot in the back on the streets of Wisdom."

"Gunned down by a hateful slaver," added Quinn.

McCarty took in the information with a sober face. After a long silence, she patted Hector on the neck and whispered something in the horse's ear. Keech thought he heard the words *stay strong*. The stallion's head bobbed up and down, as though he understood.

"I take it you and Horner were friends," Duck said to McCarty.

"We worked together for a time. A few months back, he lit out. Left me with"—McCarty's attention flashed over to the hound, Achilles—"a mighty unsavory dilemma. But tell me, how'd you end up with his horse?"

Keech said, "Mr. Horner had been taken prisoner in Wisdom, and the bad men who did it left his horse to perish in a wretched barn. We released the stallion to save his life. And he helped save ours."

Peering up from her anvil, Travis growled, "That heroic animal deserved a better treatment on the trail. His coat is a terrible muss."

Keech felt his cheeks heat up with shame.

"How did you know Mr. Horner?" Quinn asked McCarty as the woman's dog nuzzled his hand. Quinn tousled the animal's fur.

"We used to trap together along the Great Divide," McCarty said. "We traded pelts with the Ute and Shoshone. We made a good sum together."

The trapper's story didn't quite ring true to Keech. It was feasible she and Horner had once explored the Divide together, and traded with the tribes, but her tone sounded shifty and her gaze darted about the stable. "I'm awful sorry to give the news about Horner," he said, "but we're hoping you can tell us why he sent us in your direction."

"Sorry ya came all this way, tadpole, but I don't know nothin'."

"Before he died, he was fairly well adamant that we find *you*," Duck said.

McCarty shrugged. "A man facin' his final moment tends to say strange things."

Hoping a surprising shift in their questions would shake out some answers, Keech asked, "Have you ever heard of a place called the House of the Rabbit?"

The unexpected query worked like a charm. McCarty's face squinched up in clear consternation. "Nope. Never in my life."

Keech tossed a look at Quinn and Duck that said, *She's lying*. He continued to press McCarty, recollecting a strange phrase in Doyle's journal. "Do the words 'The skeleton holds the key' mean anything to you?"

McCarty shot a worried look at Travis, then glared at Keech. "You just forget about that," she said. "And while yer playin' pretend, I advise ya forget ever knowin' the name 'McCarty,' too." Then she waved a hasty farewell at Travis and made for the door. Her shaggy hound, Achilles, departed Quinn's side to run alongside her.

"Wait, don't go!" Duck said. "We still don't know what you're supposed to tell us."

Hauling open the door, McCarty turned, her pale face full of distress. "One piece of advice." Gusts from the alley blew through her matted red curls. "Forget you ever heard the name *Rose*. Go live yer lives in peace. That name will only lead to fiery perdition." McCarty slammed the stable door shut behind her, leaving the Lost Causes alone with Travis.

Rushing over, Quinn yanked the door back open. "Come back!" His voice echoed down the alley, but no answer returned. "She's gone," he said.

Travis feigned a spitting noise. "Good riddance. You kids don't need to concern yerselves with her. She's nothin' but hot air and tornado juice."

"That woman's my only lead to Auntie Ruth," Quinn said. "She knows something important, and I gotta follow." Pulling on his forage cap, he dashed out of the livery stable, the cold winds whipping in behind him.

Duck said to Keech, "He's right. McCarty's the only reason we're here. We'd be foolish to lose sight of her." She sprinted after Quinn and disappeared into the alley.

A feeling of profound unease threatened to drown Keech. Not only did his trailmates mistrust his word about the endangered wagon train, but their mission to find McCarty had led to a dead end.

Resigned, Keech sprinted out of the stable to follow Quinn and Duck. Back on Broken Bit Alley, he spotted Duck and Quinn hurrying down the snow-frosted corridor, heading toward the corner of the Tanglefoot Tavern and the Hook's Fort plaza. As he ran, Keech searched for a glimpse of McCarty's red curls, but she had disappeared.

Quinn and Duck stopped near the plaza and searched left and right. By the time Keech caught up to them, Quinn was shaking his head. Peddlers and passersby crowded the slush-packed square, threatening to confound any hope of spotting her.

A flash of ginger hair caught Keech's eye beyond the fort's stone well. "Over there!"

They took off, skidding over the slick plaza. An old man stopped in the middle of their path, pausing to light a cigar. Keech slipped on a mud patch, bumped into the man's back, and earned a grumpy snort. "Sorry!" he said, then resumed his jog. As they rounded the well, Keech caught another glimpse of dirty red hair next to a ragged dray horse.

Duck called out, "McCarty, wait!"

Keech clapped a hand down on the woman's shoulder.

A stubby man turned to regard him, his scruffy beard a deep red, his cheeks freckled and pink. The fellow shrugged off Keech's grip. "Hands off, bug, else I flatten yer nose!"

"Sorry! I thought you were somebody else."

They took another few minutes to roam the busy plaza, till Quinn said, "I swear she headed this direction. That lady's faster than greased lightnin'."

Duck pointed back toward the Tanglefoot Tavern, which had grown even more boisterous with afternoon chatter. "Maybe she headed back to the saloon."

They jogged back to the Tanglefoot. A lanky Texan—the fellow Keech had seen bartering with two Kiowa men when they first arrived—leaned over the tavern's second-story railing, his mouth full of tobacco chaw.

"Who are y'all kids after?"

"Red-haired woman, name of McCarty," said Duck.

The Texan hawked a brown gob of chaw into a brass spittoon. "And why are you bopeeps runnin' around huntin' down that trapper?"

Keech blinked up at the man. "You know McCarty?"

"Oh, I know her all right. When she ain't up in the mountains, she slinks around the fort lookin' for gut warmer."

"Any idea where she went, mister?" Duck asked the man.

The Texan's voice rumbled down from the balcony. "Y'all are set on findin' McCarty, huh?" The man pointed out across the plaza to the fort gates, which had again been pushed open to the snowbound prairie. "Then y'all might want to take a gander at *that*."

Following the fellow's gesture, Keech spotted McCarty's dog loping out of the fort, vanishing into the wilderness.

"There goes Achilles!" Duck said.

The Texan chortled. "That old mutt lives up in the mountains a small ways from here. He's probably followin' his master home."

Quinn held up a hand. "Are you saying McCarty already went through the gate?"

"She lit out not ten minutes ago, lookin' fit to be tied. Comes and goes like a whirlwind on the prairie, that one."

"But which way do we ride?" Duck asked.

Bending farther over the balcony, the Texan pointed beyond the fort's walls. "Y'all would do well to head *north*. Keep to the canyons for 'bout a day and a half. Then take the narrow pass known as the Suffering Bluffs. McCarty's place ain't too far after."

"Suffering Bluffs?" Quinn shivered. "That don't sound inviting."

"I wouldn't fret too much. It's just a spooky name for a gorge between two cliffs. Several years back, a pack of settlers tried to build a town on top of one of the rock faces, but a few buildings tumbled right over the edge. Travelers took to callin' the twin cliffs and the path between the Suffering Bluffs. Ain't nothin' to worry about there but a few timbers left behind on the path. Just ride with care, and watch yer steps. As long as the snowfall stays gentle, y'all should be able to follow her tracks."

"Thank you kindly, Mr.—" Duck paused to let the man give his name.

"Hamilton. Call me Hamilton."

Duck smiled at the fellow, then tapped the boys' shoulders. "Let's get the ponies loaded. We need to get riding *pronto*." She scurried off down the alley, and Quinn hurried after.

Keech turned back to address the Texan one more time. "Mr. Hamilton, would you happen to know if a wagon train left the fort this morning?"

Hamilton hawked into his spittoon. "One of the most foolish sights I ever did witness! Five wagons rolled out of here at the break of dawn. Those poor drays could barely pull them wagons through the drifts, but they was determined. Said their cargo couldn't wait, or some such. For the life of me, I can't imagine what would cause folks to drive a caravan north in the middle of winter. Ask me, that train'll end up stuck in a gulch and froze solid."

The news that the wagons were headed the same direction as Achilles was music to Keech's ears. He'd been worried his trailmates wouldn't back up Sam's plan, but now he could carry on with Quinn and Duck, searching for traces of McCarty, while also keeping a lookout for the wagons. Maybe he could still persuade his partners to follow Sam's counsel and rescue the train.

Keech doffed his hat. "Much obliged, Mr. Hamilton."

Tilting over the balcony, Hamilton said, "Just be careful, lad. You never know what could be waitin' 'round the bend. When darkness comes, it's always a fine idea to stick with yer partners. Work as two, succeed as one. Remember that."

Keech staggered. "What did you just say?" He had heard the

expression before; many times, as a matter of fact. Pa Abner had always used it.

"I said have a pleasant day." Tipping his own hat, Hamilton pushed off the railing and returned to the smoky ruckus of the Tanglefoot Tavern.

This morning Rowdy Bennett spotted a cottonmouth snake in a mud puddle upon our path. The company stopped, and Rowdy lifted his Hawken to dispatch the serpent. Before he could pull the trigger, the Reverend stopped him.

"We must take moments such as these to learn lessons," the Reverend said. He proceeded to teach from the <u>Book of the Black Verse</u>.

Stanza XXI—Invocation to Distort Natural Creations

Ahthro'don-'u-Ruyon

The complete translation for this phrase is unknown, but the Reverend believes the final utterance to mean "twist," a variance upon "distort."

The stanza's effect upon the cottonmouth was a terrible sight to behold. The snake coiled violently upon itself in the puddle, constricting into a rigid ball of brown and black. A monstrous hum warbled from the wind around us, then the reptile's curled body thickened in unnatural, pulse-like motions. The cottonmouth magnified in dimension, growing thrice the size of a normal serpent, overshadowing its tiny perch of mud and hissing as loudly as the crack of a pistol. The scaly horror uncoiled before us and focused two glowing red eyes upon our company. Rowdy fired a shot, but the pellets did nothing to the abomination but cause it to shriek in horrid rage.

When the Reverend was confident we had seen the verse's full potential, he shouted a minor alteration of the original stanza, Ahthro'don-'il-Yon, and the monstrous serpent returned to its normal size.

—R.J.

CHAPTER 7
The Vanishing Trail

Despite their pleas that Travis hurry, the farrier still required several more minutes to finish up her care of the animals. "If I don't do this right," she said, "you'll end up with lame horses and have to put 'em down. Then you won't have a ride a'tall."

Once Irving and Lightnin' were set to ride, Duck and Quinn headed off to Tippets's to load up their supplies. Keech waited in the barn as Travis finished up Hector's shoes. Keeping her focus on the stallion's hooves, she scolded Keech in a rough tone.

"You got to treat yer horse like part of yerself. *Better* even. A well-tended mount will save yer life in the deep wilderness." Travis finished pounding a nail and lowered Hector's hoof. "'Specially a fine stallion like Hector here. When you bring me a handsome steed so ragged, I want to bend you over my knee and spank ya."

"I understand, Miss Travis, but I need to ask you something," he said. "Before, when I mentioned the words *skeleton* and *key*, McCarty threw you a peculiar look, like you might know the meaning. Do you?"

The farrier set her hammer down. "McCarty's a private lady,

and her business is her own. But sometimes, when she catnaps in the barn, she jabbers in her sleep. A few months back, McCarty comes bangin' on my barn door. I offered her my cot, and no sooner did that woman hit the pillow, she commenced to kickin' up hay in a terrible fuss. Started shoutin' about a skeleton and devils from a *Dead Rift*. All that talk about monsters sure did spook me."

"A *Dead Rift*," Keech repeated with a shiver. He recalled a few months back when Cutter mentioned tales of monsters from his youth. *When I was a kid*, mi mamá *used to tell me stories at bedtime*, he had said. *The tales that scared me the most were about the Shifters from another world* . . .

Then later, after the team had met Doyle, the Ranger had spoken of Big Ben's Chamelia in eerily similar fashion. *A creature that crawled up into our world long ago*, the man had said.

And now there was this talk of something called a Dead Rift.

"Much obliged, Miss Travis," Keech said. "Have a good day."

He mulled over everything Travis had told him as he and Hector waited in the alley for Quinn and Duck. When the pair returned from Tippets's with their ponies loaded, Keech started to tell them what he'd learned, but Duck insisted they hurry to catch McCarty.

The moment they stepped out into the white expanse, the weather barreled down, pummeling their cheeks with furious cold. The plains drifted forever flat to the east, but to the north and west the ground bubbled and rolled into foothills and mountains. Spikes of granite and Douglas firs rose high against the sky.

"Time to search for the Suffering Bluffs," Quinn reminded them. "That Texan seemed pretty sure it's the way to McCarty's doorstep."

Two separate trails led away from Hook's Fort, scarring the otherwise pristine coat of snow that frosted the land. One run of tracks left by a horse and a dog—certain to belong to McCarty and Achilles—ran parallel to a series of deep wagon ruts and a crowd of hoofprints. Keech pointed out both trails. "That must be the wagon train. Looks like McCarty struck out in the same general direction."

Quinn started humming his *Odyssey* tune as they rode, blotting out their figures on the trail. For over two hours they followed the tracks, keeping silent except for Quinn's song. The wheel grooves from the wagon caravan trod a rough path along the slope of the hills, sometimes swerving around difficult terrain, but always holding the same northern direction as McCarty's passage. At one point, Keech suggested McCarty might be tracking the wagons, too, but no one responded.

Before long, the trio came to a low gulch full of dead brush. They stopped to inspect the caravan's migration around the deadfall. While they examined the passage, Keech caught sight of quick movement atop the next rise, a sudden blur of gray slipping over the edge of the hill. "Look!" he said. "I think I just saw Achilles!"

When they reached the top of the rise, sure enough, McCarty's hound was standing on a flat rock a few yards away, watching them, his bushy tail wagging to the rhythm of the wind.

"Is it my imagination, or is that dog *waiting* on us?" Quinn asked.

"Appears that way," Duck said.

As soon as their horses took the next step, Achilles leaped off his rocky platform and loped out of view again, vanishing behind a narrow spruce thicket in the distance.

By the time they reached the thicket, there was no sign of the hound. His paw prints showed a northwest track toward the mountains, but the critter himself was too fast and had slipped out of view.

Disappointed, the young riders forged on. When they reached a long, empty field, Duck stopped Irving.

"Fellas, we got a problem," she said.

Though Achilles's prints remained in the snow, McCarty's trail had disappeared. Her mount's hoofprints ended in the middle of the valley. Keech searched for some kind of sign—perhaps the woman had swept over the snow to obscure her movement—but other than the dog's prints, the snowpack appeared undisturbed.

"Where in blazes did she go?" Quinn said.

"Maybe she stepped through a magic door, like a bending tree," Keech suggested.

Duck glanced around. "We're in the middle of an empty field. No trees. Besides, the bending trees don't work no more, remember? Doyle and the elders sealed them for good."

"Then how do you suppose she made her trail vanish?" Quinn asked.

"I don't know, but I suspect McCarty ain't just some trapper," Duck said.

Keech had been thinking the same about McCarty, especially after her forceful words about Rose, but he'd been too irritated with Duck to bring it up. Till now. "I think I know why Horner sent us to McCarty. Horner wouldn't tell us to gather the artifacts and head to any old trapper. He knew the person would have to be trustworthy, but also somebody who knew things about Rose, important things."

"Are you saying you think McCarty's another *Enforcer*?" asked Quinn.

"An Enforcer named *O'Brien*." And now that the name was out, Keech realized he'd seen it written in Doyle's journal. He pulled the Ranger's book out of his coat and started flipping through the old pages. "It's in here somewhere." He turned to the entry dated *25 July 1832* and ran his finger down the page. "The Enforcers were ambushed by some bandits when two folks showed up to save them. Here it is." He tapped the page and read aloud:

"*The pair introduced themselves as Isaiah Raines and Em O'Brien . . . From the look of their partnership, the two are very close.*"

"*Em O'Brien*," Keech said. "At first, I assumed the name had to be short for *Emmett*, but now I'd wager it's short for *Emily*." After a brief silence, he tucked the journal back into his coat. "McCarty is O'Brien, the sixth Enforcer."

Duck and Quinn seemed momentarily stunned.

Doyle's writings claimed that Isaiah Raines and Em O'Brien had maintained a close partnership—yet never in Keech's life had Pa Abner ever mentioned such a woman. But according to Doyle's journal, Pa Abner and O'Brien had once saved the other men from a bandit attack up near Lake Superior, and the six had decided to travel together, becoming Enforcers for Rose not long after.

Quinn finally said, "Enforcer or no, we've lost her trail. We have no choice but to track the dog."

Keech agreed. "I say we head to the next rise, see where the ruts lead. The wagon trail's still following the same path. The caravan can't be too far. If we pick up the pace, maybe we can catch up to the dog and warn those folks. We can still do some *good*."

Duck nibbled at her bottom lip. "All right. Let's ride."

The trio resumed their northern trek, pushing the horses to a comfortable trot through the deep drifts. They tried to follow the trail left by McCarty's hound, but soon the searing, cold gusts that blew off the plains blotted out the dog's path.

"Dang it all; we'll never find him now," Duck spat.

As they ascended a steep grade, they saw a lowland bowl cut by a winding river. Hundreds of large brown animals roamed the valley floor, murmuring and meandering along each side of the water. The Lost Causes suspected they were looking at the same buffalo herd they had spotted near Hook's Fort. The shaggy brood covered nearly every inch of ground for at least half a mile in every direction.

"The wagon trail slips toward the river," Keech said. "Let's head down the slope, but be careful not to spook those buffalo."

"Achilles wouldn't have gone anywhere near that herd," Duck said.

"We'll find his trail again," Keech said.

They started down the embankment. When they rounded a large boulder, Keech spotted five large shapes rolling over the landscape to the west of the river. Covered wagons. "There they are!" he said.

Quinn huffed in disbelief. "Well, I'll be."

The lonely caravan struggled across the snowy expanse, the dray horses yoked to the tongues tromping at a turtle's speed. From all appearances, the drivers looked to be heading toward the nearby canyon.

Keech scanned the hills for any sign of Ian and his roughnecks. "The caravan's safe for now."

Duck pointed toward a cluster of fir trees along a nearby ridge. Fumbling a hand into her coat, she withdrew her spyglass. "Something's moving in those trees." She handed the scope to Quinn. "Y'all better see this."

Quinn scanned the tree line, wrinkled his brow, then handed the glass to Keech.

Less than a mile from the wagons, four mounted men were gathered on the ridge.

Duck sighed. "You were right, Keech. Sorry I didn't believe you."

"We need to send out some kind of warning," Quinn said. "Maybe the guards can hold them off with their rifles, least till they can reach cover."

Keech shook his head. "No guns on the wagons. One of the bandits said so himself. Besides, we're too far out to warn them. You two wait here." Flicking Hector's reins, he started back along the ridge, trotting toward the distant desperadoes.

"Not again!" Duck called out. "Keech, get back here!"

But Keech didn't stop. His instincts, his trust in faithful Sam, had proved right. He would continue to trust his gut to guide him to the end of this task. He released his reins as Hector moved over the ridge, realizing he didn't need to guide the stallion. Duck's warning shouts stopped. He glanced back and saw an empty hilltop, the snow as untouched as if it were freshly fallen. He knew, of course, his partners were still there, just concealed by Quinn's song. The fact that *he* could no longer see or hear them meant the concealment spell was no longer protecting him. He would have to be careful. If the bandits spotted him, they would surely draw down.

Keech's heart pounded as Hector ran. He searched for the bright heat living deep in his gut, the power that would spark and grow as he focused. A thrum of energy vibrated under his skin, a dizzying pulse that spiked at the base of his skull.

His *focus*. He was ready.

Keech held his hand out before him, his fingers fanned wide.

But the bandits were no longer bunched near the firs at the ridgetop. The four men were galloping down the hill, weapons drawn, headed straight for the caravan.

"Follow them, Heck!" Without missing a step, Hector leaned to the right. Within seconds Keech was tailing the bandits, a few hundred yards behind, but closing fast.

Remembering Doyle's hand motions in eastern Kansas, Keech waved his open palms in circles, working to summon a whirlwind. He aimed his focus at a patch of ground just ahead of the bushwhackers. *Discover the tune of the world*, he thought, drawing from the Enforcer's lessons. *Clear your mind of distractions.* The rugged bounce of Hector's gallop strained his concentration, but Keech refused to let anything break his focus. "Come on," he muttered. "*Come on.*"

Churning winds kicked up a wall of snow in front of the riders.

But the men didn't slow. Instead, they surged right through the bluster as if the frosty barrier were nothing more than a breeze. The bandits hooted and laughed, their spurs driving their bangtails down the hill faster yet.

"No!" Keech thought he'd found his focus, but for some reason the whirlwind had collapsed into a pitiful puff.

The bearded ruffian, Ian, shouted something to his gang, pulled his reins, and peeled away from the group. As the other three bandits continued their charge toward the wagons, Ian brought his horse to a standstill on the ridge. He lifted his revolver and aimed at Keech.

Keech heard a slug whiz past his head, then a loud crack rang across the valley. Anger washed over him. "No!" he cried again, pointing his finger at the shooting iron.

A blue sheen of frost encased the bandit's glove, and Ian's revolver turned to ice. The man flinched in surprise and dropped the frozen weapon into the drift. Shouting curses, he hopped off his horse and started digging in the snow to fetch the revolver.

Hector galloped straight at the bandit. "Take him down, Heck!" Keech yelled.

Squawking like a stunned bird, the bearded man lifted his pistol out of the snow. He took aim but the icy metal refused to fire. Hector charged the man. Ian tried to jump aside, but the stallion's massive shoulder smashed into him. The fellow's bootheels flipped up as he landed on his back in the snow.

Keech regarded the man in the snow only for a second, then pointed at the other three outlaws. "Their turn, Heck!"

Across the valley, one of the men turned, saw Keech, and called to the others. The gang veered toward a thick stand of junipers. A desperado holding a musket jumped off his mount and dropped to one knee like a soldier taking aim. As he sighted down the musket, the other two found cover behind the trees.

Keech prepared to yank at Hector's reins, hoping to pull the pony out of the musket's line of sight, but even as he fumbled for the straps, Hector seemed to read his intentions and bent his path away.

The digression was too late. A puff of smoke billowed from the man's musket, and a blink later a heavy hammer smashed into Keech's forearm, punting him off the saddle. The world tumbled around him, a bedlam of ice and fiery pain as he crashed into the snow.

CHAPTER 8
THE STAMPEDE

For a moment Keech thought he'd gone blind, but when he lifted his head, he realized the heavy snowpack had buried him. Hector slowed to a trot and circled back, but when Keech spotted the bandit reloading his musket, he yelled, "Run, Hector, get outta here!"

Blustering, Hector turned and raced away.

Keech raised up to his elbows but dropped when a screaming pain cascaded through his left forearm. A ragged hole poked through his coat sleeve. Wet darkness grew around the space.

"Not again," he muttered, remembering the time when Bad Whiskey's thralls, Scurvy and Bull, had nicked his arm with a musket shot at Floodwood. No matter; he had to push on and try to forget the ache.

He peered over the snow mound at the bandits. The kneeling man was packing his musket bore with a fresh lead ball.

The desperado with the musket aimed again. Keech ducked below the mound as musket fire cracked again.

A gruff voice echoed across the expanse. "Yer a goner, kid!"

Keech dared to lift his head again. The man was reloading, but worse, the other two bandits reappeared with their revolvers drawn. The fellow wearing the bandoliers yelled, "Yer done if you run, boy! Alfy's a crack shot with that musket."

The bowlegged bandit added, "That's a grand stallion you got! Once yer worm food, I'm gonna take him for my own."

A new level of rage flooded Keech's veins, but the pain in his forearm was too distracting for him to form a solid plan. He tried to remember Pa's training, but tears blurred his vision and his lungs rattled for breath.

An approaching noise touched his ears. A muffled rumble rolled across the plain, a steady thunder that refused to fade. He risked another peek at the approaching men. They had stopped moving and were peering to the east.

The bandolier-clad bandit asked his partner, "Are they headed this way?"

There was a quick silence, then the man shouted, "They sure is! Run!"

All three desperadoes turned on their heels and beat a retreat into the junipers.

Keech glanced back at what was creating the roar.

The entire buffalo herd was headed in his direction—thousands of heavy hooves pounding the wet ground, dashing up snow and mud, sending a constant vibration through the earth. The raw power of the charge seemed to chomp up the land. Anything caught in the stampede would find itself as flat as one of Granny Nell's flapjacks.

Keech struggled up to his boots. Bitter fear pulsed through his blood, momentarily dulling the pain in his forearm, as he tramped through the snow. The details of the stampede surged into view—the shaggy brown coats, the snorting nostrils, the upturned horns. Calves ran alongside their mothers, and hulking bulls stomped over stones and bushes. Within seconds, he would be overtaken.

Then suddenly Hector was trotting beside him. Keech gripped the saddle horn with one hand. Swinging himself up onto the horse's back, he shouted, "Hiyahh!" but Hector was already moving at a serious gallop.

Not too far ahead, the bandits burst out of the juniper trees on their frightened horses. They rode back toward the high ridge, away from the wagons, hoping to clear the path of the onrushing buffalo.

The ferocious rumble behind Keech grew to a near-deafening roar. In his panic, he tugged at Hector's reins to veer left toward the hill, but Hector refused the command. Instead, the stallion matched the direction of the raging assembly.

The congregation of snorting, rumbling brutes flowed past Keech on each side. Bristly hides brushed his legs, and the power of each passing animal left him feeling like a paper doll in the hands of an irate toddler. Both thrilled and terrified, he discovered he was screaming with glee along with the terrible thunder surrounding him.

The bandits had reached the grade and were racing uphill, away from the stampede. Standing at the top was the bearded man, Ian, and he was firing his revolver down at Keech. The distance was too far for accuracy, but his stray slugs were hitting the buffalo.

Keech's laughter jammed in his throat as anger surged through him again. "Not the buffalo!" Surely he could do something to defend the poor bison.

Doyle's journal sprang back to mind—the Black Verse once taught by the Reverend. Duck would scold him for even considering the words, but he had to try to help the animals.

"Let's see how *you* like it," Keech grumbled at the roughneck, and pointed at one of the angry bulls galloping at the head of the herd. Once again he muttered a dark phrase—the Invocation to Distort Natural Creations, the spell that had turned a normal cottonmouth snake into an abomination in 1833. He shouted, *"Ahthro' don-'u-Ruyon!"* The noise was terrible in his ears, and the uncanny garble focused his anger down his arm, through his finger, and toward the big leader of the herd.

The bull tumbled and rolled, tossing up a spray of slush as the members of his herd leaped over him. An unearthly wail poured from the critter, a sound of sorrow and pain. Keech felt a pinch of fear as the beast climbed back onto his hooves and shook froth from his black mouth. The bull had grown to nearly twice his original size, all in the span of a few seconds. The monstrous thing snorted and huffed, then started moving away from the herd. The towering beast rushed up the slope, chasing after the bandits.

The rest of the bison veered from their corrupted sibling. The animals stumbled past juniper trees and headed up into the canyon, leaving behind a swath of upturned ground and trampled brush. Hector kept pace with the herd till the panicked beasts eased off their mad charge.

Keech's fear vanished, replaced by a sense of strength. "Take that!" he called to the outlaws, though he knew they couldn't hear.

Keech steered Hector back toward the valley, the tangled mass of nervous buffalo allowing him to pass unprovoked. As he rode, sharp twinges of pain cascaded through his forearm. He glanced down to examine the wound and noticed tendrils of gray smoke rising from his fingertips.

He knew he should leave the Black Verse alone—the words were ugly and distorted and made his flesh crawl—but sometimes serving the greater good required thrusting your hands into the muck. As Pa Abner had once said, *Even the gentlest critter in the woods will bite to protect her young.*

Back to the east, Quinn and Duck were coming his way. He waved his good arm, and the pair waved back. Once they had ridden closer, Quinn pulled Lightnin' to a slow trot. "Sorry about that stampede, Keech. When we saw you was under attack, we had to do something. So I rode down behind the herd and kicked up a ruckus."

"*You* stirred them up?"

Quinn simply shrugged.

"I told him it was risky, but boys are stubborn," Duck said.

Just then a solitary figure sprinted over the slope where the bandits had retreated, running with wild abandon, screaming in terror. Keech recognized the figure as Ian, the bearded man. The fellow stumbled down the slope and fell to his knees. "Help!" He waved at them, then scrambled back to his boots.

A massive cloud of snow exploded on the ridge, and from the eruption burst the behemoth buffalo. The bull charged after Ian, releasing a roar that echoed across the valley. The scampering bandit made a hopeless attempt to dodge the buffalo's path, but the monster's swinging horns smashed into his back, sending Ian flying like a rag doll.

"What is that thing?" Duck asked.

The bull lifted his head and bellowed, a harrowing mixture of pain and confusion, then burst forward, snorting as he bounded down the hill.

"It's coming right for us!" Quinn cried.

"It has to be Rose's work." Duck yanked Irving's reins, hauling him around. "Burn the breeze, fellas!"

As they fled the oncoming monster, Keech couldn't help flinching at Duck's words. He may have felt desperate and angry while unleashing Doyle's phrase, but his intentions had been far from evil. Sam had told him *everything* depended on saving the wagons, and Keech had simply employed the most effective weapon in his arsenal.

"I gotta turn it back to normal," Keech murmured to himself.

"What?" said Duck.

"You two ride for the caravan. I got a plan."

To the northwest, the five wagons continued to struggle through the snow. If Duck and Quinn hid safely behind the train, he was sure he could draw the monster's attention, then use the proper words of the Black Verse to shrink the bull back to regular size.

"Dang it, Keech, what are you up to now?" Duck shouted.

"Go! Take cover!"

As soon as they peeled away to join the caravan, Keech turned his attention back to the bull. Twisting around in Hector's saddle, he flapped his one good arm. "This way! Follow me!"

But the charging buffalo ignored his taunts, heading straight for Duck and Quinn.

Keech's stomach clenched with fright. The behemoth was going to crash through the wagons and trample his trailmates. The drivers were abandoning their seats, hopping down into the snow and scattering. And it was all his fault.

He aimed his finger at the bull.

The moment Duck and Quinn galloped past the last wagon, Keech hollered the spell that Rose had cast upon the cottonmouth to reverse its terrible size: "*Ahthro' don-'il-Yon!*" The words took instant effect, swelling Keech's throat with nausea and making the inside of his skull creep with spidery dread.

As the behemoth buffalo shrank, the creature lost his balance. The bull's momentum carried him forward, skidding through mud and slush, till he slammed full force into the back of the final wagon.

Fiery waves ruptured the evening as the crushed wagon exploded.

Flames leaped into the sky, painting the winter clouds the color of hot coals. The incineration tossed the dwindling buffalo several feet over the ground. The bull crashed into a snow mound, tried to regain his legs, and tumbled back down. Whooshing out a heavy breath, the creature completed his transformation back to normal, then flopped onto his hooves. Rattling cinders and snow off his shaggy coat, he trotted back toward his herd as if nothing had happened.

A second blast tore through the wagon, splintering the sideboards into hundreds of pieces. The wagon's dray horses broke free of the shattering load and bolted away. Thick smoke billowed into the dusky heavens.

On the far side of the blaze, Keech spotted Duck and Quinn, looking dazed. He galloped across the field to reach them. The fire's heat poured over his skin, shoving back the cold. The wagon attendants regrouped and huddled together.

"What in blazes happened?" Quinn asked. "Why'd the wagon blow up?"

Keech scrutinized the remaining wagons. "No idea."

"They don't seem none too happy," Duck said, gesturing at the travelers. Then something over her features darkened. "What did you do to the buffalo?"

Keech's fingers were smoldering again; he tucked his hands down where Duck couldn't see. "They must've been hauling some sort of explosive," he said, hoping to divert her question.

"We should head over and tell the wagon drivers they're safe," Quinn said.

The wagoners were stomping toward them, all but one of them boasting the same oddly bronzed faces like Ian's gang. The only fellow without a deep tan walked ahead of the others—the captain of the crew, Keech reckoned. The man's face beamed a phantasmal white. He wore a floppy dark hat over thick eyebrows and heavy black muttonchop sideburns. When he spoke, his words carried the musical accent of a Frenchman. "*Bonsoir*, kids! Pleasant day."

The captain gripped a Colt Revolving Navy Pistol in his chubby hand. At Hook's Fort, the bandits had claimed the wagon train was unarmed, yet this fellow was packing some mean artillery. Surveying the fellow's men, Keech saw weapons belted to each of their hips. "Something ain't right," he muttered to Duck and Quinn.

Smiling, the Frenchman lifted his Colt. "Off those 'orses."

"Now hold on, mister." Quinn raised his hands. "We're on your side!"

The captain looked amused. "Is that so?"

A too-familiar squawk reverberated across the evening.

A massive black crow descended from the sky and landed on the shoulder of the pistol-toting captain. The other wagoners drew their revolvers and surrounded the Lost Causes. One man's coat fluttered open in the wind, and Keech spotted a brown paste smudged across his shirt. The man's golden neck appeared to be dappled with pale white splotches, and Keech realized the pasty flesh was the fellow's *real* skin, concealed under a thick layer of tan paint.

"You're *thralls*," he groaned, feeling his stomach twist.

The Frenchman spoke to the crow perched on his shoulder. "The trap worked like a charm, Reverend. We 'ave them."

This morning a heavy fog rolled across the territory, so smoky and thick it temporarily halted the progress of our company. We stopped to build a short-lived camp near a grove of frozen plum trees, and as we waited for the fog to lift, the Reverend taught from Stanza LXI in the <u>Book of the Black Verse</u>.

The primary incantation is thus spoken:

N'ghaf-l'-yon'

Translated to mean "Darkness upon you." The Reverend cautions that we must speak the verse quickly, as though uttering a single word.

The incantation renders the opponent blind, though I do not know the length of the spell or duration of the blindness. The Reverend maintains our force of will and state of heart and mind provide much of the outcome.

—R.J.

CHAPTER 9
LA SOMBRA

Nightfall descended on the foothills, casting deep purple hues over the pearly white landscape. A few of the drivers struck up lanterns, creating a ring of muted light around the gathering.

The wagon master with the bushy sideburns continued to train his Colt revolver on the Lost Causes as he directed the painted thralls to search their gear. The horses kicked up a fearful commotion as the thralls approached with lanterns and lariats.

"Just 'old them still," scolded the captain.

After the dead men pushed the horses into submission, they hunted through the Lost Causes' possessions, ransacking the dry goods purchased at the fort. The giant crow bounded off the captain's shoulder and flapped over to the poke bonnet covering of a wagon. Though the creature watched in silence, Keech could practically hear the Reverend's voice whisper, *Your days are numbered like a shadow that passeth away . . .*

"You're one of Rose's dead men," Duck said to the captain in disgust.

The mutton-chopped fellow rocked back on his bootheels and laughed. "A thrall! *Non*, I'm far too pretty to be a dead man."

"So you're a Thrall Master, like Bad Whiskey Nelson," Keech said.

"Wrong again." The captain gestured to the bronze-faced creatures pillaging the young riders' gear. "These wretches belong to a *bonhomme* named *Ignatio*."

Hearing that name—the one Doyle had whispered in Wisdom—Keech felt a disorienting tangle of shame and stubborn hope that all this might still be some terrible mix-up. But it wasn't. The Lost Causes had been bushwhacked.

Keech looked at Quinn and Duck and felt his face burn with remorse.

The captain sidled closer with his revolver. "All it took was a bit of prodding, and you tumbled right into our 'ands."

"Nobody prodded us," said Duck. "We ride of our own accord."

"But of course!" The captain pointed toward the dark ridge where Keech's mammoth buffalo had descended to attack Ian. "Why do you think those four bandits showed up in 'ook's Fort to begin with? They were *thralls* supplied by Ignatio. They pushed you to be'ave exactly as the Reverend wished, which was to ride out 'ere and put up a grand fuss."

"Mister, who are you?" asked Quinn.

The Frenchman's grin boasted a mouthful of white teeth, except for two needlepoint fangs where his two front teeth would sit. They weren't as prominent as John Wesley's Chamelia fangs, but they seemed vicious enough.

"Sorry. *Je me présente*. My name is Charles Gascon, but folks in these parts call me 'Black Charlie,' on account of my 'andsome black whiskers." The fanged man smoothed a hand over his thick sideburns. "You must be Oscar Revels, the runaway from Wisdom, *non*? I have 'eard tales about you. That you can sing yourself invisible and fight like a puma."

Quinn's cheeks shuddered with a fury Keech hadn't seen in months. "That ain't my name. Speak it again, and you'll lose those ugly fangs."

Black Charlie sneered, his pointed chompers jutting over his bottom lip. He leaned closer. "That so . . . *Oscar*?"

Darting forward, Quinn smacked his fist against Black Charlie's mouth. The fellow tumbled onto his rump, his throat barking surprise. One of his fangs flew into the snow.

"My tooth!" Black Charlie yelled, clasping his mouth.

Quinn hovered over the man. "I *spit* on the name 'Oscar,' shackled on me by terrible, slaving men. My name is *Quinn*, and I'm the son of George and Hettie Revels, who died in the cornfields of Tennessee. I got a free body. I got a free soul. And I won't ever wear chains again. Anybody tries to lock me up, I'll kill them dead or die fighting."

"We shall see about that," Black Charlie spat, scrambling back to his boots. As he wiped a trickle of blood from his lips, the Frenchman's eyes turned as black as oil—unnatural eyes, the peepers of a monster. Black Charlie yelped at his men. "Tie them up!"

The main clutch of thralls held their pistols on the Lost Causes as two dead men shoved them to their knees and bound their hands behind their backs with strands of prickly rope. Keech strained at the bindings, testing them, and found the knots secure.

Black Charlie probed his bloody mouth with a finger, then lifted his Colt. "That was my favorite tooth! You will pay for that."

"Try me, you dog. You'll lose the other one," Quinn answered.

Black Charlie thumbed back the Colt's hammer. "*L'orgueil précède la chute.* Do you know what that means? 'Pride precedes the fall.'"

The wicked fowl roosting on the nearby wagon screeched, "*Not yet, you fool.*"

At the sound of the unearthly voice, all the thralls surrounding dropped to their knees in terrified reverence.

The crow tilted its head. "*Find out what they know.*"

Black Charlie barked a command for the thralls to resume their saddlebag search. As the dead men scattered Duck's belongings across the snow, the Frenchman asked, "Anything, Rufus?" The fresh gap in his teeth made the words come out in a dry whistle.

"Nothin'," grumbled a thin man with a pointy chin.

The rabble was searching for the relics. The Reverend apparently thought the Lost Causes still had the Fang of Barachiel, perhaps even the amulet shards. Rose didn't know yet that Doyle had stolen everything.

The crow's heartless eyes gleamed blacker than a pair of beetles. A swirling redness blossomed within them, and Keech felt a stabbing sensation nip the edges of his mind. Images of Gail Travis's barn at Hook's Fort appeared in his memories. He saw Achilles barking at their feet, McCarty gazing at the kids with concern.

Fear overtook Keech's soul, and he cried out. Thus far, Rose's power had manifested as external attacks, occasionally darting from the skies in the form of a crow or invading the body of an outlaw, such as Bad Whiskey. But now he felt the Reverend clawing his way into his mind. He clamped down on his memories, fighting to hide his most recent thoughts of McCarty and Cutter and the mysterious Key they were supposed to track down.

The mental wall served no effect; the Reverend's crow cackled in triumph. "*You found O'Brien. I never suspected she was so close. She's managed to stay hidden near the Key of Enoch, guarding it like a stubborn watchdog.*"

The complete name of the relic—*the Key of Enoch*—sent a jolt through Keech, and he remembered his brother Sam reading from Pa's old Bible. "*This verse says, 'Enoch walked with God: and he was not; for God took him.' You know what that means? It means the prophet Enoch went right up to heaven without ever dying.*" Keech had waved away Sam's tale at the time, but now he wondered if he should have paid closer attention.

One thing seemed certain: He should have never listened to his dream at the cabin. The Key was nowhere near this caravan, and never had been. Whatever his vision of Sam had been trying to tell him, Keech had mistaken the message.

Based on the information Rose himself had offered, they were on the right trail, a couple of steps behind Coward and Cutter and the Char Stone, and within reach of the Key. They only had to secure the relics for themselves, and the Lost Causes could seal Rose's doom. Exactly how, Keech wasn't sure, but he had a hunch this Key of Enoch was the solution.

They would never achieve victory, though, if they were held captive. Keech had to do something to get them out of this mess.

Duck growled at the crow, "We never met any O'Brien."

The beetle-like eyes flicked toward Duck, giving Keech a momentary reprieve from Rose's sickening mental intrusion. *"You lie, child. But O'Brien will be dead before the next sunset. I'll find Jeffreys, too, since I now see that he has the Fang and two of the amulet shards."*

"I don't know what you're talking about," Duck spat.

"Should I kill them now?" asked Black Charlie.

The messenger crow hesitated. *"They could serve as bait for the Enforcer. O'Brien will never let children perish, no matter how forsaken she's become."*

"When we find O'Brien, can I kill 'er at least?" asked Black Charlie. "She must be the reason I had to go 'unting for all this extra munition." He pointed at the four remaining wagons in the train. "Her meddling cost me two months of work. Ignatio is not pleased. I'm needed back among the Weavers, too. I cannot run wagons forever."

The crow's head bobbed. *"Patience, Gascon. You will have your chance to spill blood."*

"That's why your wagon went up in smoke!" Keech said to the Frenchman. "You're hauling explosives to Ignatio. He's digging around for this Key of Enoch, using the people of Wisdom to do his dirty work, and you're running gunpowder to help him. Guess you didn't count on a giant buffalo taking down your stash."

"Foolish boy, gunpowder had nothing to do with the explosion," Black Charlie scoffed.

Standing at the rear of the fourth wagon, the thrall Rufus guffawed. "Apparently, you brats ain't never heard of *nitro-gliss-reen.*" Reaching one hand inside the wagon's covering, he pulled a large glass jar of clear fluid out of a crate.

Black Charlie waved his hands. "Put that down! You will blow us all to kingdom come!"

Embarrassed, Rufus set the jar of explosive at the edge of the wagon bed.

"There is one problem with nitro," Black Charlie continued, keeping a nervous eye on Rufus. "Even in those infernal crates packed with straw, it takes a mighty brave 'eart to carry them through the mountains, because even the smallest rattle could make it go *boom*."

"When I knock out your other fang, you'll feel a rattle," Quinn said.

Black Charlie sneered at the comment, then fired his pistol into the sky. The detonation echoed like Zeus's thunder in the canyon. Somewhere to the east, the rumbling rolled on, and Keech realized he wasn't hearing the Colt's reverberation, but the renewed running of the buffalo herd, panicked by the gun's report. The ground under Black Charlie's wagons trembled.

The jar Rufus had rested on the wagon shuddered, drawing Keech's attention. It would take only a little nudge to shake the jar loose and cause an explosion. A phrase from Doyle's journal would probably do the trick. At the very least, he could buy them a few seconds to run, though not enough time to get under cover.

There had to be another way.

Lowering his pistol, Black Charlie chuckled at Quinn. "Scorn all you want, *mon ami*. O'Brien will not stop us. Ignatio is 'ard at work in the mountains."

Still perched atop the wagon, the Reverend's crow flapped its black wings in irritation. "*Stop talking, Weaver,*" the creature hissed. "*You have no more to say here.*"

Black Charlie dropped his head at once. "*Désolé*, Reverend. I meant no 'arm."

A careful expression crossed Duck's face, a look Keech recognized as deep scheming. She said to the crow, "Reverend, I know you want us as bait for this O'Brien, but I'd wager it won't work. We tried to get her help, but she turned her back. She ain't interested in saving us." Mischief flickered in her eyes. "But I got a better deal for you."

The crow tilted its devilish head. "*Go on*."

"We promised our pard Quinn here we'd reunite him with his aunt. Take us into the mountains where Ignatio took his aunt, and let the two of them go. If you do that, we'll tell you where Jeffreys is holed up."

The crow's cackle was so shrill it echoed like Black Charlie's pistol shot. "*Take you to the mountains*," the creature repeated. "*You wish to meet Ignatio?*"

"Yes. Then you get the Enforcer."

Keech hadn't thought the February night could grow any colder, but suddenly the air was filled with a petrifying chill, as if the wind itself had turned to solid ice. The breeze swirled around their boots, dusting up the powder on the basin floor, and Keech caught sight of a shadow shaped like a man, creeping along the edge of the lantern light cast by the penitent thralls.

When the gathered thralls saw the shadow, they gasped in unison. "*La Sombra!*" they muttered, and dropped to their knees again.

"What's that mean?" Duck asked.

Black Charlie answered. "'The Shadow.' Your doom approaches."

The terrible shade stepped into the lamp glow, but instead of dissipating in light as a shadow ought to, the specter took on weight, as though the darkness that composed it was as physical as flesh and blood.

The apparition slithered past Black Charlie, then stopped to stand in front of Duck. The girl whimpered at the sight of it, but stood tall.

"*Buenas noches, niña,*" *La Sombra* said with a voice both smooth and temperate. "You wish to meet Ignatio in the mountains, *¿no?* No need to travel, child. I am here."

This evening, as a comfortable twilight fell upon the territory, the Reverend bid our company to reflect on the primary element of our being. Some of us suggested that the <u>heart</u> is the principal component, for without the heart we cannot feel, while others argued it is the <u>mind</u>, for without it we cannot reason.

"None of these are true," the Reverend replied. "The most essential portion of our being is the <u>soul</u>, for the essence of a soul fuels the energies of both the world we see and the one we cannot."

The Reverend then expounded upon one of the ancient artifacts we seek, a treasure known in legend as the Char Stone. This relic is vital to the Reverend's quest. He explains that the Stone is a "vessel" for the energies of a soul, though I cannot claim to fathom his meaning of such things. He spoke of an immaterial realm, a place where souls live in their own geographical plane, like smoke captured behind glass. The Reverend taught that only the most powerful of Prime users dare touch the Char Stone to glimpse the immaterial realm, as contact with the object would kill any who are unprepared.

I find myself intrigued by the Reverend's metaphysical lessons. Perhaps if we find this fabled Char Stone, we will uncover the greatest truths of our existence. Perhaps we will discover true knowledge and power.

—R.J.

CHAPTER 10

A FAMILIAR FACE

The night air vibrated with a fathomless rhythm that felt like the buffalo stampede. Keech tried to shuffle backward on his knees, hoping to gain distance from the spirit, but his limbs refused to move. In Wisdom, Edgar Doyle had warned the Lost Causes that Ignatio could mold shadows and manipulate darkness. Now here was a living shade calling itself *La Sombra*.

Waves of icy gloom poured from the shadow as it spoke. "Where is Red Jeffreys?"

"You won't get a syllable from me," Duck said, squirming. "Not till you free Quinn and his aunt."

La Sombra lifted a finger, a slender shimmer of pitch, and pointed at Quinn. "This one means naught to me. Tell me what I want to know, child, *o lo mato*. I will kill him." Vaporous tendrils rose off the shadow body and snaked up into the sky.

"Don't tell him anything!" Quinn said. "I'd rather die than help these worms."

A sickening wriggle invaded Keech's mind. The Reverend was prying into his head again, peeling back his thoughts. He tried to imagine a blank pool, an empty room, a barren field, anything to clear his mind, but Rose's fingers delved ever deeper.

"*Coal's daughter is bluffing.*" The voice from the crow dripped with disdain. "*They know nothing of Jeffreys's location.*"

Duck cried out, "That ain't true! We *do* know how to find him!"

"*You waste time with lies.*" The crow tilted its head toward the shadow and added, "*Leave one child alive to draw out O'Brien. The sooner we find her, the sooner we find Jeffreys.*"

"*Sí,* Master, as you command." *La Sombra* turned to face his thralls. "On your feet, my friends. We have work to attend to." The dead wagoners stood, gripping their pistols.

Keech strained at his bonds, his wounded arm screaming, but the ropes remained tight. There seemed only one move left. He would have to use the Black Verse, even if the words bought them only a few seconds.

"Which child do we spare?" Black Charlie asked.

Ignatio's shadow, *La Sombra,* returned his intangible gaze to the Lost Causes, then leaned toward Duck. "This one I like. I sense her father's strength." He turned his empty face toward Keech next. "On the other hand, Isaiah Raines protected this one. Em O'Brien rode with Raines. The two shared a close bond, like *familia.* Perhaps she would reveal herself to save him."

Keech clenched his teeth. "Get away from me."

The toothless gap in Black Charlie's mouth made him look like a petulant child. "So we keep the boy alive, finish the other two?"

"Do it," *La Sombra* hissed.

Not wasting any time, the Frenchman swiveled his Colt toward Quinn, who lifted his chin higher at the sight of the barrel.

"I don't fear no death," Quinn said. He peered off to the west, as though reaching for his aunt across the distance. "I'm sorry, Auntie Ruth. I tried to find ya, but I didn't make it."

"*Au revoir, mon garçon,*" Black Charlie said to Quinn.

Suddenly a slender brown object whizzed into the midst of Black Charlie's company. It stuck with a dull twang into the wood of the nearest wagon. The projectile quivered in the board, mere inches from the jar of nitro Rufus had lifted from one of the crates. Keech saw a fletching of turkey feathers at the stick's opposite end.

One of Ignatio's thralls pointed at the stick. "Hey, take a gander at *that*," the dead man muttered, his head tilting with curiosity. "It's an arrow!"

Before Black Charlie or *La Sombra* could react, a second arrow swished in through the crowd, thudding into the wagon's rear again, missing the jar by a dog's hair. Keech felt his breath freeze in his throat. He spun toward Duck and Quinn and bellowed, "*Lost Causes, get down!*"

Duck and Quinn dropped to the snow as a third arrow zipped in, this time achieving its target and shattering the jar of nitro on the wagon board.

The explosion was louder and more violent than the one before. A terrible flash of orange flared up, a blossoming cloud of heat and force. Fire shredded the wagon's fabric top, and wood shards sliced through the air. Huge chunks of embers rained down on the neighboring wagon, and flames capered across the bonnet.

"*Non! Non! Non!*" Black Charlie hollered, shielding his face with his arms.

Their hands still bound behind them, Quinn and Duck rolled away from the detonation as a whoosh of black smoke poured out of the next carriage. A cacophony of amber sparks sprayed out into the snow. From where he lay stretched on the ground, Keech lifted his head. Giant columns of fire spouted out of the next three wagon beds in the caravan. He felt his blood run cold when he realized the rest of the explosive crates were catching fire.

"Little brats brought a friend!" the thrall Rufus screamed.

"'*Oo is out there?*" Black Charlie growled at Keech. He slammed a boot down on Keech's back, pinning him to the snow.

Though Keech had no idea, he answered the Frenchman with a mean laugh. "You didn't think we'd come out here without backup, did ya?"

The Reverend's crow took to the air with a furious squawk as the burning wagons exploded in a chain of violent fireballs. Splinters ripped like bullets through the night air, riding a tide of heat that washed over Keech like a fiery tornado. Black Charlie's boot fell away from Keech's back as the eruption of the nitro crates sent the Frenchman tumbling. Thunder punched at Keech's ears, a terrible drumroll that left him feeling as if his skull had been stuffed with cotton. The sensation reminded him of their fateful night in Wisdom, when the whistle bomb destroyed the Big Snake Saloon—and Nat Embry along with it.

Though the explosions had pulverized many of their number, Ignatio's remaining thralls dashed about in the chaos, revolvers aimed at the surrounding hills. A few of them squeezed off, throwing lead at the shadows.

Keech tugged at his bindings, but the strain made his wounded arm sing with agony. He tried to rise but slipped in the snow. Duck appeared by his side, her face covered in mud and grime. Her hands were free. "You're loose!" he gasped. "How?"

Duck started laboring at his knots. "I dunno. I just yanked." She tugged at Keech's bindings, and he felt the ropes drop away. "There. I'm gonna go help Quinn."

Hopping to his feet, Keech searched for the unseen archer who had shot the nitro jar. Amid the bedlam, he heard the running of a horse in the dark, but he couldn't see the animal or its rider. He probed the landscape for *La Sombra*, but the apparition must have retreated back into the night.

Black Charlie bellowed for the bumbling thralls to douse the crates before the final wagon could ignite, but the dead men were too distracted to focus on the carriage. The wagon exploded, shredding a pair of thralls tottering away from the fire. Another wall of heat pressed against Keech, but he kept his feet.

Nearby, Duck had freed Quinn of his bindings. Black Charlie waved his Colt at them. "Stop right there! *Arrêtez!*"

Hollering with rage, Quinn rushed forward and slammed into Black Charlie. The snarling captain toppled, and his Colt fired. The lead scattered powder between their boots. Quinn threw his elbow, smashing the brute's face. Black Charlie wiggled his head and growled—a deep, inhuman noise that momentarily froze Quinn's face with shock. Then the Frenchman tossed Quinn away with a grunt.

Black Charlie stood, shaking dirt and snow out of his matted hair. "Now I 'ave you," he muttered.

But Quinn kicked out, his bootheel connecting with the outlaw's knee. Black Charlie stumbled backward in the snow, tripped over a divot of ground, and tumbled into the wreckage of a burning wagon. A wretched howl rose from inside the flames.

Just then, a decomposing thrall appeared beside Keech and

reached for his neck with ragged fingernails. "You'll pay for this!"

A buzzing arrow buried itself into the thing's shoulder, knocking the dead man back into the snow. Keech spun around, searching for the source of the shot.

Bursting out of the night, a brown pony galloped past him. Keech caught a glimpse of a buffalo robe and a longbow. "It's one of the Protectors!" he yelled. Then the rider turned, revealing a young face, somber and determined. "*Strong Heart!*"

The Osage girl who had fought beside them at Bonfire Crossing raised a triumphant fist as she steered her mount toward him. "Keech Blackwood!" she bellowed. "You found trouble again, I see!"

Before he could respond, a sudden crash pulled his attention.

Black Charlie rose from the fiery rubble, bellowing curses. The fellow no longer resembled the mutton-chopped desperado who'd captured them, but rather something out of a nightmare. The single fang that jutted from the captain's lips had grown, and his face had been charred black. Dusting red-hot cinders off his shoulders, he opened his mouth in a vicious snarl. "*Time to die!*" he roared.

"Get to the horses!" Keech shouted to his team, but Duck and Quinn were already dashing toward Irving and Lightnin'.

Black Charlie snatched up a blazing piece of wood and launched it at Keech's head.

Riding in close, Strong Heart whacked the timber out of the air with her war club. Then, in a swift motion, she hooked the club's curved head around her saddle horn and lifted her longbow again. Her other hand pulled a fresh arrow.

Black Charlie reared back to lob another fiery section of wagon. Strong Heart released her arrow and the shaft struck the monster in his chest, and he dropped back into the fire.

Duck and Quinn rode up on their ponies, gathering around the Protector. "I don't know where you came from, but thank you!" Duck said to the girl.

"Thank me later," Strong Heart said. "Many of the thralls are standing back up."

Sure enough, a handful of the ragged men were rising, scrambling for their pistols, the thirsty look of revenge on their dead faces.

Keech swung up onto Hector and gripped the reins. "Let's get out of here!"

"Follow me," Strong Heart told the trio, and with a click of her tongue, her pony snapped back into a gallop.

Frozen winds blew down from the canyon, colliding with the fierce heat that radiated from Black Charlie's incinerated wagons. As the Lost Causes cleared the vibrant ring of light, reckless gunshots rang out behind them. Keech worried the leftover thralls had salvaged a few long rifles, but the goons were firing pistols, and their slugs flew wide. Among the booms and echoes, Keech thought he heard the bellowing, cursing voice of Black Charlie Gascon—the monster whom the Reverend called a *Weaver*.

The young riders galloped into the twilight. The darkness felt alive around them, the great lungs of the night breathing frost and death. Only the burning wagons offered a faint light across the land.

After a few moments of hard riding, Quinn said, "We need to slow our pace. I don't want the horses to break a leg."

"Soon," Strong Heart answered. "For now, we need to gain distance."

Ack! Ack!

The terrible screeching drew Keech's attention. One of the Reverend's crows was pacing them, tracking their retreat. The glow from the flaming wagons lit the creature's warped shape in the sullen sky.

Revulsion coursed through Keech's veins. He held his breath, once again hoping to find his focus. But when the warm power refused to stir within, he knew what he had to do.

Keech pointed at the crow and yelled the Black Verse from Doyle's journal: "*No-ge-phal ul'-shogg!*" The dreaded phrase tasted like ash on his tongue, and yet the words carried a mad intensity that couldn't be denied.

Above them, the crow ruptured in a feathery flash.

Even as Duck and Quinn looked on with trepidation, a victorious red swarmed across Keech's vision. "Return to earth, you filthy beast," he spat. Pearly smoke poured from his fingertips, and he laughed. Keech sensed the feeling was wrong, but for the moment, he couldn't help relishing the glorious sensation of power.

The Black Verse came not from Man.

CHAPTER 11
THE VISION IN THE CAVE

The Lost Causes journeyed deeper into the canyon as the din of gunshots faded. The rugged terrain grew stonier as they traveled. Quinn hummed his *Odyssey* tune to obscure their passage into the gorge. The clouds broke, and dull moonlight suffused the frosty ground with ghostly silver. The troop slowed the horses to a careful walk, watching for deadfalls.

"I sure hope those thralls ain't tracking us," Duck said.

Except for the incessant wind, their back trail was quiet and still. "They will, eventually," Keech guessed. "The crow spotted us, but I destroyed it." When Duck said nothing in reply, he dropped his smile. "We'll be all right. We just have to find somewhere to hole up."

They rode awhile longer in silence, listening to Quinn's enchanted tune, till he strolled Lightnin' up to Strong Heart's pony and paused his singing. "I don't remember the Osage words for 'much obliged,' but I sure would say it if I could. You saved our bacon back there."

"*Weh-wee-nah*," Strong Heart instructed. "'I thank you.'"

"*Weh-wee-nah*," Quinn echoed.

"We'd be goners if it weren't for you," Duck said. "But how did you ever find us? We've been on the Santa Fe Trail for weeks."

Strong Heart said, "I've been following your group for a long time now."

"Why?" asked Quinn.

"After the attack on Bonfire Crossing, the Protectors parted ways for a time. Some journeyed home to bury our brother, *Mah-shoh^n Shkah*. Others rode east to join the winter buffalo hunt. *Wah-hu Sah-kee* and I remained with the elders, and I began the mourning ritual for my brother, *Mee-kah-k'-eh Moi^n*."

"Wandering Star," Duck said.

"Yes. While I mourned, *Wah-hu Sah-kee* and the elders spoke of many ways the Osage could help rid the world of Rose. But they were concerned that placing more trust in Red Jeffreys wouldn't be wise. Our people had given so much to Jeffreys and the Enforcers; the elders wanted no more part in their strife. But I needed to continue, for my brother and my parents. I asked the elders for their guidance. They listened to my pleas and spoke to my uncle. They held many discussions."

"Then what happened?" asked Quinn.

"The elders instructed me to find *you*, so that I could help ensure the safety of the Fang."

Keech shuddered at the girl's mention of the Fang of Barachiel. Strong Heart wouldn't be pleased to hear they had lost the dagger because of Doyle's betrayal. Hoping to shift the topic away from their failure, he said, "You should know that Rose is gathering an army. In Wisdom, we saw a stockpile of uniforms and military supplies."

Concerned, Strong Heart said, "If he succeeds in his plans, the world will die."

"'The land will lose the sun,'" Duck said, quoting the dire words of the elder Buffalo Woman.

"Since you've been following us on the trail all this time, why didn't you show yourself?" Quinn asked. "We could've ridden together."

Strong Heart pointed at the sky. "I didn't show myself because Rose was watching for you. I thought I could do more to help if I remained hidden. But when you were captured, I knew I must act."

"We're sure happy you did," Duck said. Then her breath hitched as she seemed to catch hold of a memory. "Strong Heart, how is Nat's horse?" After the battle of Bonfire Crossing, Duck had given Sally to the girl, sending the Fox Trotter to live with the Osage in southern Kansas.

"She's well," Strong Heart said, smiling. "My uncle took her to his favorite field, and she's fed well. She'll never have to know another battle."

"Good," Duck said softly.

Strong Heart turned to Keech. "Now, I need to see the Fang. I need to see it's safe."

Keech stiffened on his saddle. He wanted to tell her the truth, but he didn't know how the Protector would react. They could use her help to reach O'Brien and the Key of Enoch, but if she learned the Fang was gone, she might light out to hunt Edgar Doyle. "Later," he said, struggling to ignore the guilt weaving a tight web around his heart. "There's another blizzard on the way. We shouldn't linger, especially so close to Black Charlie. I don't suspect he's dead."

Quinn grimaced. "Me and Auntie Ruth knew men like Black Charlie in Tennessee. They're a sickness. Cruel and relentless. I've seen a lot of evil the past few months, but ain't nothing worse than a slaver."

Duck shook her head, as though she didn't know how to respond, then simply said, "I'm all for pushing on, but where to? We don't have a clear direction. The trail is gone, and I don't know how we'll ever find the Suffering Bluffs. They could be anywhere."

Quinn raised a finger toward the canyon. "Maybe *he* knows the way."

He was pointing at Achilles, sitting in a snowy basin a few yards up the gorge. A wedge of moonlight framed the dog's body, perched on a rock. The hound barked once as if to offer a greeting, then he trotted up the hill, weaving between frost-laden thickets of aspen and birch.

"I don't believe it!" Duck laughed. "That mutt stuck around."

Keech kicked at Hector's sides. "We best not lose him again."

Achilles led the Lost Causes on a gradual ascent through the canyon, corkscrewing around gulches and snow-packed pitfalls. Along the way, Quinn told Strong Heart the story of Cutter's kidnapping and their chancing upon the trapper McCarty. She listened intently, keeping her face and ears tucked into the folds of her buffalo robe, and to Keech's relief, she did not ask again about the Fang of Barachiel.

McCarty's dog kept several steps ahead of the group, holding to the sparse moonlight, pausing occasionally to ensure they were still following. Keech's mind drifted with thoughts of Doyle, the elders, the great bonfire on the Oregon Coast. He realized he was feeling dizzy.

"Look! He stopped," said Quinn.

Several yards ahead, their canine chaperon had paused near a large stone overhang. The rock wall curved inward, creating a shallow barrier from the wind, but the most noticeable feature was the deep oval of black that yawned from the wall.

"It's a cave," Keech said, feeling blurry. He blinked to clear his vision, but his thoughts rippled like ocean waves. "I think he wants us to camp inside."

Strong Heart and Quinn seemed eager to escape the dreadful cold, but Duck hesitated. "I don't know if I fancy going in another cave. The last one we visited wasn't all that agreeable." She covered her mouth as if she'd said something horrifying. "I'm so sorry, Strong Heart. I shouldn't have said that."

When Strong Heart nodded quietly, Keech understood. In Missouri, they had discovered the body of her brother, Wandering Star, in the Floodwood cave. He had fallen to an enormous bear while accompanying Doyle through the cave's cursed loops.

Thankfully, this particular cave wasn't anywhere near as menacing as the one in Floodwood.

The young riders studied the cave's egg-shaped mouth. They watched as Achilles entered the dark funnel, turned around, and barked. "Looks like the coast is clear," Quinn said.

Achilles waited deep in the cave as they approached. Thankfully, the cavity's entrance was tall enough to accommodate the horses, so the gang directed the animals into the shadowy oval, then the kids dismounted, careful not to bang their heads on the stone ceiling. The gale outside shrieked all the harder at their deliverance, throwing shards of sinister whistles against the jagged walls.

"This cave," Keech said, feeling uneasy. "It feels *familiar*."

"How do you reckon?" asked Duck.

Keech searched for the answer, but the shadows grew darker and the world swooned. He dropped to the cave floor. His chest smacked against a rock, but he felt no pain.

Deep in the fog in his ears, he heard his name called. When Keech turned his head, he saw Duck crouched by his side, holding his face out of the dirt. "What happened?"

"You fainted!"

Keech tried to laugh off his wound, but a wave of ragged coughs overcame him. He closed his eyes.

When he reopened them, Keech found himself wrapped in blankets next to a dwindling campfire. He was lying on his back in the cave, and needle-like pangs poked at his arm. He rolled back the blankets to inspect the damage from the gunshot and blinked in surprise to find several ribbons of cloth tied around his forearm. One of the young riders had dressed his wound while he was unconscious.

Outside, heavy clouds had engulfed the moon. Duck and Quinn were fast asleep, huddled under their pelts and blankets. Grateful to be out of the cold, the four horses stood lined up against the stone walls, two on each side of the fire.

Farther into the cave, Achilles lay flat on his side on the soft earth. The light of the dying fire painted the hound's fur a warm cinnamon color. Strong Heart rested beside the dog, wrapped up in her buffalo robe, her palm resting on the critter's side. The cave was comfortable and secure. Keech imagined that over the centuries, many travelers had stopped here for sanctuary.

"I *know* this place," he muttered. Just as he'd known the village of Snow in Missouri, the ghost town that Pa Abner had used as their hideout before heading to Bone Ridge with Keech's parents and the Char Stone.

"*Hey, brother,*" a thin voice whispered.

A surge of fear bolted through Keech, and he shook himself alert. The voice had come from the mouth of the cave, beyond the soft light of the campfire. He searched the dark landscape of the world outside. "Who's there?"

"*Who else? It's me.*" The voice was shallow, weak.

"Sam? Am I dreaming again?"

"*I'm watching you,*" Sam said. "*I'm close.*"

"Come into the cave," Keech said. "I can't see you."

"*Don't worry.*" Sam's voice was almost lost in the whistling winds. "*I can see you.*"

A flicker of movement at the cave's entrance caught Keech's attention. A few muttered words tumbled away in the night, then the whisper from the darkness said, "*You were too slow, Keech. You lost the Key. They took it up into the mountains before you could get to the wagons.*"

Keech shook his head. "They never *had* the Key, Sam. It was all a bushwhack. Why would you send me into a trap?"

"*How could you think I would do such a thing, Wolf? That sounds like Duck Embry's talk. Don't let her deceive ya. The Key's within reach; you just have to keep going a little farther.*"

"We're gonna find O'Brien. She's the next step."

"*But Black Charlie's after ya. He's as mad as a hornet and aims to kill you all. Or turn you over to Ignatio. How do you hope to stop him?*"

"I'll figure something out."

Sam's whisper fell silent for a moment, then returned stronger, closer. "*There is a way to defeat that monster. You know what I speak of.*"

He was talking about the curious phrases sprinkled throughout Edgar Doyle's journal. "The Black Verse," Keech said.

When Sam spoke again, he sounded as if he were grinning. "*That's right. When you use the words, they wake me up. I can help when I'm awake.*"

The idea that he could wake his brother stunned the breath out of him. At the Home for Lost Causes, Keech had chosen to escape and let Sam perish in the flames. But here he was, the Rabbit himself, conjured by the Black Verse. Keech felt a hope he hadn't felt in a long time.

"*Keep using the words, Keech. They're the secret way to defeat the Reverend.*"

Keech shivered under his blankets. As much as he wanted to use the words, a strange sort of shame tugged at his heart, despite his newfound hope. "I don't think I should. There's something wrong with them."

"*They're only wrong if you don't know how to control them. But you have the strength to bridle the Verse, right?*"

Keech thought back to all the moments on the trail when he'd used the writings. Each time, he had achieved his goal—destroying Rose's crows, transforming the buffalo. "Maybe. I don't know," he said. Then he glanced at his fingers and smiled at the memory of smoke rising from their tips. "Yes, I do. I *am* strong enough. But that doesn't take the bad off the words. I don't like how I feel when I use them." He paused, shook his head again. "Or maybe I like the way I feel too much. It's all powerful confusing."

"*You just need to practice.*"

"Maybe you're right. But what should I practice on?"

"*Somethin' small. You could build your campfire back up. Your trail-mates will thank ya.*"

The campfire flames had smoldered down to a smattering of paltry coals. Keech remembered seeing a fire incantation in Doyle's journal—an entry dated *22 August 1832*, the Enforcers' first encounter with the Reverend Rose.

Checking the others to make sure they weren't awake, Keech pulled the journal out of his coat. Reading by the dim coals, he turned to the passage in question. His finger moved down to the Reverend's words, and he mouthed the Black Verse to practice the phrase.

"*Speak them out loud. Watch what happens,*" Sam murmured.

Feeling his stomach tighten, Keech lowered Doyle's book to his lap, raised his index finger to the dead campfire, and spoke the incantation from the entry. "*Fm'latghor U'aahn.*"

As before, Keech's mouth filled up with the taste of charcoal dust.

The orange embers of the fire popped and sputtered anew. Bright sparks crackled in the circle of stones, steeping the cave walls in light, then a magnificent crown of tall flames leaped up from the cinders as if Keech had tossed on a handful of dry kindling.

Laughing, Keech held up his hand and watched as gray smoke poured from his fingertips. His mind released all the old vexations and fear he'd been carrying on the Santa Fe, and he felt the beautiful stirring of renewed hope. "I can control it."

"*That's right, Wolf. You can. You're strong enough.*"

"It won't control me."

"*Never. Now go rest up, big brother. And when you wake, find O'Brien. Persuade her to help you find the Key.*" Perhaps Sam said more, but his whispers were carried away by the angry howling that poured down through the canyon.

Keech felt dizzy. His strength was fading again, and the light at the edge of his vision was dimming. He covered back up with his blanket, feeling cold despite the newly stoked flames and homesick beyond measure.

He curled up by the fire and allowed sleep to swallow him.

THE TWO HORSEMEN

Heavy winds blustered like sullen voices as the two men stopped their horses on the Santa Fe Trail and dismounted. The first rider pointed through the white drift. "There. That's the cabin I spotted."

"You sure got a good eye," said the second rider.

"Decades of practice. Let's have a peek."

The shack was, indeed, barely noticeable, surrounded by a coppice of cottonwood trees. A perfect hideaway off the trail.

The two riders walked to the forgotten hut, watchful for any sudden movements or surge in the evening blizzard. They had been traveling for months together, riding from town to town and clue to clue, and by now they knew the exact motions of each other's boots on the ground and the practiced, precise way they approached a telltale clue. They had learned to think like the boy they were chasing, Keech Blackwood.

The younger of the pair eased back to let the older take the lead through the shack's entrance, a decrepit door riddled with moldy splits and crevices.

"Somebody's been here, all right," said the older horseman. "Take a gander at this." He retrieved a long, flat piece of pine bark lying in the snow by the door. "Someone carved words into this."

"*Amicus fidelis protectio fortis*,'" the younger rider read. "I don't know that language. What does it mean?"

"Don't know, either, but the carving looks fresh. A day or so."

Slipping the bark into his overcoat, the older rider moved inside and walked to the shack's old fireplace. He smoothed his glove over a discarded collection of cottonwood buds, mashed flat as if someone had used them for a medicine.

Bending, the younger horseman picked a small piece of paper off the floor. It was a playing card—a jack of diamonds, dirty and split at the corners. "Somebody must've lost this from a deck."

The older horseman took the card and held it up to the dusky light. "Think it's his?"

"Not sure. But my gut tells me we're awful close."

Slipping the jack of diamonds into his coat pocket, the older horseman peered out the cabin door, where the Santa Fe Trail slipped onward into snowy shadows. "Blackwood won't slip out of our reach this time. Let's get on to Hook's Fort. Someone there might know something."

"On to the fort," the other agreed, and the two walked back to their horses.

PART TWO

THE HIDEOUT

MIGUEL IN THE PASS

Miguel! Time to go," Bishop mutters in the dark. "Rattle your hocks, hermano." A vigorous hand shakes his shoulder.

Miguel turns over with a grumble. "Few more minutes, Bish."

"C'mon, we got work to do. The rancher's gonna be up at dawn. We'll lose our chance if we don't snag them Trotters now."

Even on the cooler side of morning, the oppressive Missouri heat smothers Miguel's skin when he gazes bleary-eyed around their hidden riverbank camp. The previous evening's fire smolders low, but the sky's vivid moonlight shows that Bishop is already dressed, boots and all, and sipping coffee from a tin cup. For a boy of fifteen, Frank Bishop is the most dedicated horse thief this side of the Mississippi. The first to rise, the first to cook breakfast, the first to plan their next job. Miguel has ridden with Bish for two years now, and the boy has never let him down. There is no better trailmate, no truer amigo. Bish even knows the best places to sell the rustled horses to get top dollar.

After saddling their ponies, Miguel follows Bishop through the forest to the edge of the ranch they've been scouting. It's a sizable piece of property, stretching over three hundred acres. A few days ago they spotted a pair of Fox Trotters in the pasture, a handsome combo that Bish guaranteed would fetch a substantial sum down in Arkansas. The big ranch also boasts a proper head of Texas longhorns, but Bishop never wants to go for the cattle. "The real dinero is in the bangtails," he says. Miguel has heard that other cattlemen are racking up pesos running longhorns over to West Texas, but he keeps his ideas on the business to himself.

The boys approach the property's long perimeter, stepping out of a dense patch of pin oaks. The morning moonlight falls bright on the ranch's back forty, a shimmering silver pasture that reminds Miguel of his family's small piece of land in New Mexico. Suddenly he hears footsteps approaching.

"It's the rancher!" Bishop whispers. "He's out too early."

The boys scramble to hide their horses in the pin oaks as a tall man in dark clothes rambles on foot through the back field, clambers over the fence, and trudges past. He's heading west, toward the river, walking at a hectic pace. Though Miguel can't make out his features, the moonlight reveals that the man is holding a long musket.

"What do we do?" Miguel asks.

"Wait here, keep a lookout. I'm gonna follow him. He's up to somethin'."

Before Miguel can protest, Bishop scurries off, holding to the pin oaks for cover. Miguel soon feels alone, abandoned. He spends a few minutes keeping his attention on the ranch, but after a while, his eyelids begin to weigh heavy. He props his head against a stump to rest, intending to steal a few minutes of shut-eye.

But then Bishop is shaking him awake. "Git up! We gotta skedaddle."

Miguel sits upright. The morning sun has broken over the horizon. He feels embarrassed that he catnapped while he was supposed to be on lookout. "Lo siento, Bish. I didn't mean to nap, but I got bored waiting."

Bishop waves away the excuse. "I gotta show ya somethin'. C'mon."

They ride back to their riverside camp, Miguel struggling to keep up. Along the way, he begs to know why Bishop is so excited, but his partner won't say.

As soon as they reach the camp, Bishop draws a red cloth out of his coat pocket. Something long and flat is wrapped inside.

"What's that?"

Bishop unwraps the cloth and reveals a huge knife, a blade almost as long as Miguel's forearm, its bone handle carved with intricate symbols. It looks like a cursed relic from some ancient fairy tale. Bish beams. "This here is a special knife."

"Special how?" But even as Miguel asks, he wonders if he wants to know.

Bishop squats by the embers of their fire, settling in to tell a story. "I followed the rancher to a strange hut out in the woods. Creepiest shack I ever saw. You won't believe it when I say it, but a witch lives there."

Miguel shudders. "A witch, like a bruja?" He hadn't heard that word in a long time, not since leaving Culpa to travel with Bishop.

"Somethin' like that, yeah. The rancher went inside for a spell. I got curious, so I crept over and listened by the front door."

"You could've been caught!"

"I'm too lucky to get caught. Anyway, they said a few peculiar things, so I crept over to a window and snuck a peek. That's when I saw the witch."

"What'd she look like?" Miguel asks.

"Not a she. He was an old man with wild gray hair down to his shoulders. But he called himself a witch. Said his name was Artemas Ward. The rancher tossed him a bag of coins, and the witch held up this knife." Bishop appears even more excited as he raises the blade. "He said this chopper was magical and would someday kill the Eye." The steel in Bish's hand catches glints of the early sun and sparks like a giant diamond.

None of what Bishop is saying makes any sense. "Eye?" To make sure he understands, Miguel points to his own eye.

"Well, no, not just any eye, but like a name. As in El Ojo."

Miguel's skin grows cold. "What happened then?"

Bishop hesitates, perhaps considering what to share. "I found a hidin' spot where I could wait. The rancher finally left, telling the witch he'd be back for the knife a day later. After he was gone, I peeked inside the hut again. The knife was on the table, right there beggin' to be snatched up. The witch-man spotted me and threatened a hex, but I reached in and grabbed it."

Hearing the story makes Miguel's heart beat faster. A brujo named Artemus Ward. A spellbound knife. It all sounded so dream-like, but Miguel had never known Bishop to make up tall tales. "Then you ran?"

"You bet I did. Straight back to ya." A conniving smile stretches across Bishop's face. "Here's the new plan. We hide this knife under a tree, then we head back to that ranch and liberate us a pair of bangtails. Once we've sold 'em, we come back here, dig it up, then see what kinda mischief we can get up to with this here magical blade. If it don't work, we'll sell it, too. I imagine it'll fetch a price as fine as cream gravy."

They bury the blade beneath a pin oak, marking the location so they can find the treasure upon returning. Miguel never thinks of the blade as his own. Bishop stole it from the brujo, and as far as Miguel is concerned, his partner can keep it. He wants nothing to do with cursed things. He'd leave it buried. If they came back for it, perhaps old Artemas Ward would come searching for it. Perhaps the brujo would stalk them wherever they rode, and Miguel would awaken one lonely night to see an ancient, wrinkled face staring down at him from the darkness.

Miguel sat up with a jolt, a terrified scream on the cusp of letting loose. He'd been dreaming about Bishop again. His first true friend, now deceased for months. Killed by a man named Bad Whiskey Nelson, *El Ojo*, after the one-eyed scoundrel had broken Coward out of the Arkansas prison.

It wasn't unusual for Miguel to dream about Bish. He often dreamed about their old days on the open range, just as he would dream about John Wesley. Dreams of his *amigos*, Miguel could handle, but he hated the memories of the prison. He tried to settle back to sleep and dream of nicer days before Barrenpoint prison and Coward and *El Ojo*.

Sleep refused to come, so Miguel sat by the campfire, huddled under his blanket, and watched the small man who had brought death into his life. Seeking comfort, Miguel let his hand venture into his coat and graze the straw of John Wesley's hat. John's voice whispered in his head. *Don't you fret. I'll find ya. Till then, ride tall.*

"I wish I could stop him, but I can't," Miguel muttered to himself.

Why not? John's voice argued. *He's asleep and you're not.*

Curled up beneath his furs, Coward snored. He slept in the quiet comfort of knowing that when he wanted Miguel to do something, all the small man had to do was tap the charred brand on his own palm, and the angry, spiral-like mark on Miguel's forehead would flare, sending shocks of pain through his entire body. The pain seemed to sear his soul and blunt his mind, so that pools of blackness overtook him, and when his senses recovered, Miguel would find himself miles away, unaware of where he'd been and what he'd been doing. After a few such incidents, Miguel had decided it was better if he simply obeyed Coward's requests rather than risk his body being controlled like a puppet.

Coward continued to snore.

This was the moment Miguel had been biding. He had no chance when the man was awake and could activate the Devil's mark, but if he hustled, he could attack Coward and free himself. The thought sent fear coursing through his veins, but an opportunity like this might never present itself again.

Miguel reached down to his belt and wrapped his fingers around the bone hilt of his prized blade. After recovering the knife, he had taken on the name Cutter. He'd never used the blade to kill anyone, but Miguel was determined to show the world he was a dangerous man who would remove anyone who stood in his way.

Drawing the blade out of its sheath, Miguel rose to his feet.

The lump of the little man's body beneath his fur lifted with each ragged snore. He was so close, so unaware. An easy lunge with the blade, a quick thrust, and Miguel could be free.

Beneath his fur, Coward snorted, his steady breathing interrupted. He was waking.

There was no choice now but to act. Miguel lunged, stabbing the needle-sharp blade into the fur blanket.

Coward sat up, panic twisting his face. A ribbon-thin cut across his shoulder glistened with fresh blood. "Get back! Get back!"

Miguel pulled back, freeing the knife. He shifted his stance, ready to stab again. He had only a second to attack again. *El diablito* wasn't thinking straight, but when he recovered his senses, he would touch his brand and render Miguel helpless.

Screaming, Miguel charged.

Coward rolled to his side, flailing. He spun around and lifted a small, square object in front of him out of blind protection. The silver chest that contained the Char Stone.

Miguel's knife pierced the metal lid.

A nightmarish cacophony drove into his ears like the sound of a thousand screeching bats. A pulse of lightning coursed through the knife. Miguel's hand went numb. He dropped the blade and staggered back, feeling as if he'd been pelted by heavy stones, his muscles frozen in place.

Coward dropped his hand to the brand on his opposite palm, ready to trigger the Devil's mark. "What were you thinking, Miguel? You could've killed me!" he shrieked—then Coward's gaze fell upon the bone-handled blade lying on the ground. The steel visibly trembled from its contact with the Char Stone. Coward's mouth tumbled open.

Dropping to his hands and knees, Coward hovered his nose over the knife and sniffed deeply. Miguel watched with confusion, his body rumbling with pain. Whatever happened to the blade, the Char Stone seemed to be the cause.

"This can't be," Coward said, the tiniest smirk parting his lips. The fear on Coward's face evaporated as he lifted the knife gently from the snow. He sniffed it again, turning the steel over and over as though sampling a fine cut of meat.

"Miguel, the prophecy is *real*," Coward said, holding the blade up to the campfire light. "I always doubted, but now I know. I *know*." He gazed at Miguel with clear exhilaration. "Pack up camp. We have a peak to reach. Ignatio is waiting."

Many months I have spent exploring the great Upper Peninsula, and nary a soul have I encountered. This territory is a wondrous beauty to behold, but the isolation of its forests and dales can be inhospitable.

This morning my solitude broke when I encountered a lone traveler riding a roan-colored Tennessee Pacer. The man looked as strong as two oxen, and no pair of eyes I have ever beheld were as deeply blue. He carried a well-polished Hawken rifle and a pair of snowshoes purchased from a Chippewa trader.

The fellow explained he was on his way to Lake Superior to meet two trappers and procure a supply of beaver pelts for trade down in Illinois. He said he could use a "young hand" like me to help with the load.

Promise of good pay and companionship felt tantalizing, so I told the horseman I was interested. He asked for my name.

I responded that I am Beauregard Jeffreys, but I answer to Red. "And what, pray tell, is your name?" I asked.

"Rowdy," the man replied, a nickname I find most humorous due to his serious demeanor. I inquired his proper name, and he said, "Bennett Coal."

Tomorrow I shall ride with Rowdy Bennett to Lake Superior to meet the two trappers. I think I shall fancy Rowdy's company. Perhaps time will tell otherwise, but I feel as if I can trust the fellow. In fact, I feel as if I have known Rowdy Bennett Coal my entire life.

—R.J.

CHAPTER 12
STRONG HEART'S PATH

The woeful sounds of a coyote whining in the dark hills yanked Keech out of sleep. He bolted upright, his heart galloping. He'd been dreaming of Edgar Doyle sitting on the bank of a muddy river and scribbling a solitary note—*The skeleton holds the key*—into his journal. In his dream, Keech had approached the man to inquire about the note's meaning. *The world is cruel and full of death*, the Ranger replied. *I have discovered the way to eternal life.* Then Keech awoke, almost screaming.

Cramming on his bowler hat, he pulled his pelt tight and walked to the mouth of the cave, his wounded arm aching. Everyone else was still asleep—except for Achilles and the horses, who watched him closely. Keech patted his thigh to call the mutt over, but the animal only tilted his head. A jingle sounded below the dog's throat, and Keech realized he was hearing the contents of the flat leather pouch tied around Achilles's neck. Earlier, Keech had wondered if the dog might be carrying treats in that little bag. Now he wasn't so sure.

Keech rubbed a hand over his swollen eyes. He hadn't only

dreamed about Doyle; his sleep had also been fitful with visions of Sam again, tiptoeing up to the cave, compelling him to keep using the Black Verse, an unnatural fire surging to life before him.

Now the campfire was only a few smoldering cinders. Perhaps he'd only imagined using the spell to stoke the fire, but he could still feel the dream's potency in his fingertips. The Lost Causes would be safer if Keech used the words. He could control the power. He could.

"It's time, Keech Blackwood," said a voice.

Wheeling around, he saw Strong Heart standing between the horses and the burned-out campfire, swaddled in her buffalo robe. Her long hair lay over her shoulders, and her fingers were absently twisting the dark strands.

"*Hah-weh*, Strong Heart. Time for what?"

"To show me the Fang."

Keech turned away and stepped out into the snow. "Not now. It's almost morning, and we need to get back on the trail."

Strong Heart called after him. "Keech Blackwood, stop! Tell me the truth."

"About what?"

"The Fang of Barachiel. You don't have it, do you?"

He thought about pressing the lie, but there would simply be no use fibbing. Shame flooded his cheeks as he turned back. "It was Doyle. He betrayed us. He stole the Fang and the amulet shards."

Silence overtook the girl. Then she murmured, "The elders spent *ten years* watching over the Fang. They left their homes, their families. The Protectors guarded the doorway without fail. Now you say the dagger has been stolen."

"We trusted Doyle when we shouldn't have," Keech said. "Even after we learned he wants to resurrect his daughter, we trusted him to stand with us." He realized his arm was throbbing to the pulse of his anger. "I reckon you think we're all a bunch of fools. After Doyle led your brother to his death, I bet you'd have never trusted him. You hate him as much as we do."

Strong Heart's forehead scrunched into a heavy scowl. "No, Keech. I *pity* him. For the family Red Jeffreys lost and for the feeling that he must betray others to gain back what he's lost." She paused for a moment. "But the Fang was entrusted to *you*. You told the elders you were ready."

"I *was* ready."

Strong Heart gave a loud scolding noise. "*Eh-sheh!* You should have known."

"What's going on?"

Keech turned to see Quinn standing near the campfire. Duck was also awake and listening intently as she rolled up her blanket. All around Quinn's feet were stick soldiers drawn in the cave dirt—evidence of Quinn's midnight battle scheming. He slid a boot over his handiwork, rubbing out the conflict with a single sweep.

Keech marched back into the cave to fetch his belongings. "Strong Heart thinks we all lost the Fang on *purpose*."

Strong Heart stomped after him. "*Hah"-kah-zhee!* I did not say that!"

But Keech didn't want to listen. If he continued arguing, he didn't know if he could keep his temper.

Quinn glanced up from where he was packing his things. "Does this mean you won't join us?" he asked Strong Heart.

Still frowning at Keech, Strong Heart said, "Nothing has changed, Quinn Revels. I've made a promise to join you and I intend to fulfill it. There is far too much at stake." She rubbed a hand over her face, then added, "Whatever my path, it is full of stones."

"What do you mean?" Quinn asked.

Strong Heart didn't answer at first. Instead, she stepped over to Flower Hunter and examined the eagle feather tied into the pony's mane. She closed her eyes, as though collecting her next thought. She kept them closed as she explained. "When I was young, my brother took me to a meadow near the Neosho River. He said, '*Wihtezi*, I want to show you something,' and he showed me a trail of red ants on the ground. We followed the ants for many steps—until their path split into two lines. The path on the left continued across the meadow, but the path on the right stopped at a large pebble. The ants surrounded the stone and began to push it.

"'Why are they pushing the rock?' I asked. 'Why would they not take the other path with their family?'"

Strong Heart opened her eyes. "My brother said to me, 'The path where the stone sits is their *true* path, the one that leads to their home, but the stone has tumbled in the way, so the strong ones stay behind to remove it.' He said, 'Sometimes, *Wah-kah^n-dah* will place you on a path full of stones. And you must face them to protect your family and your people.'"

A tear rolled down Strong Heart's face. She wiped her cheek and continued, this time addressing all three of them. "At first, my path led me to *you* to ensure the safety of the Fang. But now the Fang is no longer safe, so I must find Red Jeffreys and take it back." She turned wearily to Quinn. "Whatever my path, it is full of stones."

Quinn pulled off his forage cap. "Then I'll help you move them."

"So will I," added Duck. She looked at Keech, but he didn't know what to say. He felt out of place, like what Granny Nell might have called a "stick in the mud." He didn't know what to do with such isolation, so he tucked it down and forgot he was even feeling it.

After saddling up the horses, the Lost Causes huddled for a small breakfast of dried fruit and deer jerky—part of the scant rations that remained after Black Charlie's raid. Strong Heart placed some of the jerky in her parfleche, the small buffalo-hide container tied to the back of Flower Hunter.

Once they were done, Quinn stood outside in the morning's feeble light. "Black Charlie's gang is still out there," he said. "I'd be surprised if they ain't tracking us. We need to get up into the hills." He gestured to Achilles. "What do you think, boy? Will you show us the way?"

Barking twice, the hound scurried between Quinn's feet, dashed out of the cave, and plummeted full speed into the heavy snow of the canyon. Before Keech knew it, the dog was headed north, leaving his canine trail in the snow for the gang to pursue.

"That means we best go," Duck said, so the young riders followed.

CHAPTER 13
THE SUFFERING BLUFFS

They traveled at a steady pace the entire morning, picking up speed at noon, when the persistent snowfall relented a bit. Keeping several yards ahead, Achilles seemed willing to wait for them, halting occasionally on craggy lookouts to mark their progress. As Keech glanced back across the expanse, searching for signs of Black Charlie on their back trail, he spotted a large bird circling high above and worried it might be one of the Reverend's spies. His fingers twitched to use the Black Verse again, but Duck pulled out her spyglass and clarified they were being scrutinized by a bald eagle.

Keech tracked the eagle's flight across the sky and caught sight of a colossal mountain farther north. The peak's pointed summit lay covered in alabaster clouds. The eagle disappeared on the western side of the mountain's tip, diving into the pearly fog as if it were fishing in the mist. Gazing with wonder at the peak, he felt the familiar crawl of déjà vu, but he pushed away the sensation.

Jumping onto a high rock, Achilles barked at the tall summit. Quinn said, "I think he wants to go up that mountain."

They followed Achilles through a heavy patch of snow-coated spruce and soon found themselves back in the open, facing a long, narrow ravine. The gorge snaked between two towering cliffs, a pair of bluffs that hunched over the pass like old cowhands with crooked backs. One cliff stood to the east, the other to the west, and they perfectly framed the enormous mountain that Achilles had barked at. When Keech gazed straight through the ravine, he could see the hazy foot of the mountain rising not too far away. They could probably reach that mountain in an hour, maybe less if they rode hard.

"Those two cliffs must be the Suffering Bluffs," Duck said. "If that fella Hamilton was right, we'll reach O'Brien's place in no time."

Farther up the slender gorge, Keech spotted what appeared to be the carcasses of monstrous animals, their gangly bones and twisted spines half-buried under mounds of snow and shadow. As the young riders drew closer, he realized he was looking not at bones, but at the tumbledown remnants of *buildings*, long forgotten and left to rot. The structures were only mangled heaps of wood blocking the path.

Lumbering cloud banks rolled across the winter sky, casting a terrible shadow over the Suffering Bluffs. As they approached the dregs of the fallen town, Strong Heart gestured to a weatherworn sign leaning like a wraith against one of the cliffs.

YOU AR ENT RING

TRANQU LITY OVERLOOK

GATEW Y TO TH ROCKIES

Steering Irving past the sign, Duck said, "Mighty unlucky name for a town that dropped off a cliff."

Keech tried to piece together where the buildings of Tranquility Overlook had once stood—a general store here, a livery stable there—but none of the old wreckage made sense. "Let's just pass on through. This place gives me the willies."

"I couldn't agree more," Quinn said.

"*Lost Causes!*"

Black Charlie's voice bellowed at them from the south, echoing through the Suffering Bluffs like the shriek of a hawk.

"*Say your prayers, mes amis, because I will find you!*"

Duck peered nervously at the forest behind them. "How far back, y'all think?"

Strong Heart said, "He sounds close. Less than a mile."

"We're easy pickin's in this gorge. We have to move," Quinn said.

Keech took a moment to examine the ravine. Beyond the last skeletal ruin of Tranquility Overlook, a jagged trail cut to the right and ventured straight up and around the east-facing bluff. "I see a switchback we can take. We'll have to ride slow, but at least we won't be sitting ducks."

As soon as they all agreed, Keech prodded Hector toward the sawtooth trail.

Back in the forest, Black Charlie's voice beckoned. "*I am coming, Lost Causes! Weavers never relent!*"

After they reached the switchback, Keech goaded Hector up a few steps, testing the terrain for deadfall. When the incline seemed passable, he called down to the others. "We can take this straight up, but we'll have to be careful."

Quinn pointed down at all their hoofprints cluttering up the snow. "Black Charlie's gonna spot our trail. He'll see every step."

"Can you hide them?" Duck asked.

"I can try, but my throat's awful sore. Been hurting ever since I woke up. I ain't sure how long the tune'll work."

"Just do what you can," Duck said.

Starting up his *Odyssey* chant, Quinn followed after Keech up the switchback, clutching Lightnin's saddle horn with both hands. Keech felt the familiar tingles of warmth as Quinn's magic turned them invisible on the cliff. Seconds later the girls clucked to their own ponies and began the climb. Achilles brought up the rear.

Moments later Quinn coughed fiercely, and Keech felt the buzz of the incantation flicker away, leaving their figures and the horses' hoofprints visible once again.

"Sorry, but I can't!" Quinn said, his words breaking.

"Don't fret," Keech said. "You did your best."

For the next twenty minutes they climbed up the angled face of the bluff. Snow-sprinkled sagebrush lined the trail till the brush gave way to jagged rock. Knuckles of sandstone peeked out from the snow. They appeared ready to tumble at the slightest whisper of wind.

By the time they reached the top, Keech's ears were popping painfully and Hector was heaving for breath. The young riders dismounted. The clifftop ridge was flat for a short pace before the hill rose steeply to form a high wall of snow. They were standing on a checkerboard of stone foundations, a grid of flat rock that appeared man-made. "Hey, take a look at this." He pointed at the ground. "This must be where Tranquility Overlook once stood."

"I wonder what knocked it off the cliff," Duck said.

Keech surveyed the ridge but saw no more feasible trails. They had trapped themselves. If Black Charlie wanted to climb to get them, they would have no good means to escape. They would have to make their stand right here.

"Reckon we better take a peek, see how many we're facing," Quinn said.

Keech and Quinn stepped to the edge of the cliff. They had ascended at least thirty yards—enough to make Keech swoon.

Duck said, "Fellas, it probably ain't a good idea to stand there in the open."

No sooner did she speak the words than Keech spotted movement in the gorge. He dropped to his hands and knees. "Everybody down!" he said.

Tiny figures were trailing through the white ravine of the Suffering Bluffs like a line of black ants, scuttling around the wreckage of Tranquility Overlook. Quinn grimaced. "Sure enough, he's got a pack of thralls with him."

Duck pulled out her telescope. "Five, by my count. Black Charlie makes six."

Strong Heart asked Duck if she could borrow the spyglass. After surveying the Frenchman's steady advance, she lowered the scope and said, "When I first approached the wagons, I heard the voice of a Spanish man talking to you. *La Sombra.* The Shadow. But now I see only thralls and the monster I shot with the arrow."

Keech kept his eye on Black Charlie's crew. "Doesn't mean he ain't out there somewhere, biding his time. We can't lead him to O'Brien. Maybe I could tip a few boulders from the cliff. Roll them down on top of the thralls, stop them for good."

Strong Heart tilted her head. "How?"

"I've been working on my focus." Though even as the words fell, he knew the group would most likely recognize his lie. Keech's focus would never be enough to topple boulders. If he wanted to dispatch *real* energy, he would have to use the Black Verse.

Duck shook her head firmly. "Forget it. No power."

Feeling anger tightening his throat, Keech said, "Quinn's been using his focus this whole time, and you're fine with that."

"That's different, and you know it," Duck snapped. "Let's just push on. Maybe the fresh snow will cover our trail."

Strong Heart raised a hand to silence them. "Does anyone hear that?"

A peculiar wailing touched Keech's ears, like a large animal howling in rage. The noise gradually increased, building into a boisterous roar.

"What *is* that?" Duck asked.

"Sounds like the Chamelia," Quinn said. "Remember how that thing sounded when it was angry?"

Strong Heart said, "That noise is no beast. We're hearing *wind*."

Keech scanned the upper reaches of the foothills, noticed movement, and felt his stomach drop. A small army of twirling white tornadoes danced along the jagged ridge above their heads. For a moment, they appeared to surge in perfect formation, as though held together by unseen hands, then they branched out and churned up the slope in all directions. Behind the gusts, a steady thunder grumbled over the Suffering Bluffs. A vibration hummed through Keech's boots, coursed up his legs and into his knuckles.

Duck held out her hands to brace herself. "Earthquake?"

"No." Keech pointed up the hillside. "*Avalanche!*"

CHAPTER 14
THE COLLAPSING MOUNTAIN

A black fissure split the top of the snowy wall. Ceaseless thunder crackled across the canyon as the entire surface of the snow slid free. The land echoed with booming destruction as the sudden rush of snow began crashing down, a wave of unrelenting frost and stone.

"The whole hill's coming down!" Duck yelled.

Keech could see that the majority of the tumble would miss them and smash into the valley between the Suffering Bluffs, likely burying Black Charlie and the pursuing thralls. But a massive portion of the slide was sweeping toward *them*.

Straining to be heard, Strong Heart shouted, "There!" She pointed to a giant outcropping of stone that stood against the gray sky. Beneath this rocky overhang was a shallow recess, a space where they could hide from the toppling ice and debris.

Bounding back into their saddles, the Lost Causes raced toward the overhang. Hector shot ahead of the group, kicking up snow, zigzagging between tangles of dead sagebrush. The rumbling intensified.

Duck and Strong Heart were two steps behind him, but Quinn and Lightnin' had come to a dead stop. The pony was in a panic, rearing up on his hind legs. Quinn spilled out of the saddle and landed in the snow. Keech pulled back on his reins. Despite Hector's own terror, the horse turned back.

Duck and Strong Heart raced past them as Keech hollered at Quinn. "Get up!"

Quinn tried to grab Lightnin's reins, but the pony refused.

Thick frost whipped the air, obscuring Keech's vision. He pushed Hector closer and tried to reach for Lightnin's loose reins, to arrest the animal's tantrum, but his fingers fell out of reach. "Leave me!" Quinn yelled.

"Not a chance!" Keech swiped at the reins again. His fingers seized the leather, and he yanked down, stopping Lightnin's next outburst. "Here!" he called, showing Quinn the reins.

Quinn stumbled through the snow and grabbed the straps. He jumped back onto Lightnin' and shouted for them to hurry.

"Ride!" Keech said. "I'm right behind you."

The second Quinn started forward, Hector shot after him. All around, the world became a collision of tumbling stone and ice, exploding with terrible power as the avalanche annihilated the mountainside. An entire hill of husky evergreens snapped like twigs, and sprays of stinging snow harried the front of the wave.

Duck and Strong Heart had reached the recess, the outcropping rising above them like a barricade against the wave. The girls huddled close to the protective wall. Achilles had made it to safety with them, cowering near the hooves of Flower Hunter and Irving.

With the speed of a cannonball, a chunk of granite landed just ahead of Quinn, puffing up bursts of snow. "That was close!" he shouted as they skirted the stone. Glancing up, Keech saw a terrible white cloud bearing down on them, a deluge that would bury them in seconds.

They weren't going to make it.

There was only one way to survive. Keech raised his hand and shouted a Black Verse from the Ranger's journal. He tasted something rancid, like sulfur, then a surge of energy pulsed through his body. The curious power of the Prime coursed down his arm and launched out of his fingertips.

The raging whitecap crashed against an invisible barrier, leaving them untouched.

"What happened?" Quinn shouted.

"Just keep going!"

They rode the final few yards to the recess and squeezed in next to Duck and Strong Heart, who simply shook their heads in disbelief.

The Lost Causes waited next to their exhausted horses as the avalanche crashed around them. The mountain air was a frenzy of frost and thunder. They cupped their hands over their ears in a vain attempt to dampen the drumming.

After several more minutes of chaos, the terrible collapse quieted.

"I reckon now we know what knocked the town off the cliff," Duck said.

As the white mist thinned, the gang began chipping away at the snow that had formed a waist-high wall around the alcove. Achilles pitched in, using his front paws to dig a dog-sized hole through the snowpack. When they were done, they turned their attention back toward the switchback they had just fled. Gone were the trail and the stone foundations where Tranquility Overlook once sat; a smooth white slope replaced them, as if the gorge had never been there at all.

"Black Charlie and those thralls are done. Nothing could've survived that," Quinn said.

Duck peered around suspiciously. "That avalanche came along at the perfect time. Too perfect. I don't believe in that sort of luck."

"Neither do I," Strong Heart said. "Strange whirlwinds appeared across the ridge."

Keech had seen the whirlwinds, too—a perfect line of them before they scattered and tore up the hillside. "Whatever happened, we shouldn't be too sure Black Charlie's finished," he said, hoping to shift the subject away from the avalanche. He didn't want the others to find out he had used the Black Verse again, even if it was to save Quinn and himself. "We should get moving."

Achilles barked as if in agreement, then scurried off over the snow, heading toward the massive peak that towered in the distance.

For five days now, Rowdy Bennett and I have traveled together, and I find his company invigorating. His family roots are held in eastern Missouri, and he comes from a line of English cattlemen. After making his riches trading fur, he plans to return to the business of cattling and begin a family. He is an avid reader of Latin, and when I tested him yesterday on the depth of his knowledge, he replied, "Scio me nihil scire," which he claims to mean, "I know that I know nothing."

Today, upon the southern banks of Lake Superior, we waited at camp to meet the two men for the pelt supply and watched with much levity as they traveled down the channel in a birchbark canoe, their vessel nearly sinking under the weight of the beaver pelts they carried. They are jovial men, and I am certain the entire territory could hear their laughter as they paddled onto shore.

The older of the trappers is a Native man, a fellow from the great Osage tribe of the southern region. He goes by a name that means "Black Wood." Rowdy Bennett was thrilled to hear of another soul from his neck of the woods, and the two men spoke of Missouri's hills and rivers at great length.

For a man of twenty-five years, Black Wood seems astute in the ways of exploration. He left his home two years ago, leaving his friends and family in sadness. When we asked of his plans to travel back to his home, Black Wood replied that he would return only with great knowledge and a provision of wealth that could benefit his people.

Black Wood's business partner is a striking fellow with well-groomed hair and a thin mustache. I do not understand how the man can stay so perfectly combed in the wilderness. He goes by Milos Horner, and he desires nothing more than to goad his friend Black Wood with tomfoolery and horseplay. I find the way they banter quite humorous, and I see clearly that both trappers possess kind hearts.

Milos Horner has expressed a desire to meet with two other free trappers farther south, a pair of rugged hunters who carry a supply of muskrat furs. A consolidation of wares could benefit all parties, so Rowdy and I have agreed to continue.

—R.J.

CHAPTER 15

AMONG THE SAPLINGS

For the rest of the evening the Lost Causes rode through the winter chill, wandering along the path that Achilles cut through the snow. They made their way through a labyrinth of thick firs, always tending toward the north. With each passing hour the massive summit in the distance seemed to grow, swallowing the horizon inch by inch.

Quinn craned his head back to regard the peak. "How can anything be that tall?"

Duck said, "Night's approaching. We'll need to set camp soon."

Just then Achilles unleashed a series of excited yips and danced back and forth in the tall snow. He took off running around a short bend in the trail.

"What was that all about?" Quinn asked.

"I hope it means we're close," Strong Heart said.

The young riders trotted after the barking hound. As they rounded a foothill, the heavy clusters of fir opened into a clearing, a sweeping meadow filled with rows of tiny green saplings. Snow dusted the pyramid tops of the infant trees. On the far end of the clearing, an icy river burbled down the twisting canyon, infiltrating one corner of the field.

Duck gazed across the white-and-green meadow. "What a lonesome place."

"Lonesome, sure, but something is odd with these evergreens." Quinn pointed to the saplings. "The rows are straight. Somebody made them that way."

"They were planted not long ago," Strong Heart said.

"I bet the trapper planted them," Duck responded. "But why place a bunch of trees in the middle of nowhere?"

Studying the saplings, Keech didn't like the way the mountain breeze ruffled them, making the trees writhe the way a critter might squirm if held down by strong hands. "Something doesn't seem right. Those baby trees have a strange way about them."

A volley of emphatic barks interrupted him as Achilles weaved through the saplings, occasionally peering back to beckon them on. The dog dodged every limb as though he didn't want to graze them.

"This may sound strange, but I don't think we should touch those trees," Keech said.

As their horses stepped into the meadow, the thunderous crack of a rifle rattled the countryside. The lead ball pinged off a sandstone boulder. The animals jolted back, and the young riders ducked low.

Keech dared a quick look around. "I can't see where the shooter's hiding."

They waited stock-still at the edge of the clearing. Quinn grumbled, "Maybe it was just a hunter off his mark." He prodded Lightnin' forward.

A second rumble of gunfire filled the meadow, and Quinn shuffled back.

Duck pulled out her spyglass and studied the field. She locked the glass on a particular point, frowned, then handed the contraption to Keech. "Take a look."

Through the foggy lens, he spotted the trapper McCarty. Or rather, the Enforcer O'Brien. She was poised on a pine tree stump, reloading an old Kentucky long rifle, Achilles by her side. Her batwing chaps flapped against her thighs, and the wind blew heavily against the black hat she wore.

"It's her," Keech said. He handed the spyglass back to Duck. "She's about two hundred yards out. She could hit us if she wanted."

Quinn frowned. "She means to scare us off."

"If this woman was an Enforcer, then she'll be protective of her secrets," Strong Heart said.

True. If O'Brien was guarding her knowledge, she might be willing to blast them off their saddles before they could make it through the meadow.

Duck said, "We're gonna have to chance it. This woman is vital to our mission. We have to persuade her."

"I'll go," Strong Heart said. "I don't believe she will harm us." Without waiting for the others, she spoke an Osage command to her pony, and Flower Hunter stepped into the meadow. After a mere three paces, another deafening gunshot split the air—but neither the Protector nor her pony flinched. They trotted into the rows of wriggling baby evergreens and weaved an eastern path toward the woman. At one point Strong Heart's face wrinkled with distress, as if she smelled something foul.

"What's wrong?" asked Duck.

"Keech was right. Something is strange here. The air inside the meadow feels wrong, sour and thick. Follow me carefully."

A terrible smell assaulted Keech's nostrils as the group trailed Strong Heart. A bitter fragrance hung over the meadow as if the evergreen saplings were emanating poisonous fumes, curdling the mountain air.

"I don't like this place," murmured Duck.

"Just keep riding." Keech shifted his attention to the saplings. They seemed to move of their own volition. They were not wind-blown, but writhing, as if reaching for his legs.

He surveyed the meadow more closely, and another sense of déjà vu surfaced on the heels of this terrible dread, just as had happened at the cave.

Step by step they crossed the sapling field, till a fourth rifle shot boomed—a wide shot, intentionally off target.

The Enforcer bellowed at them: "Go away!"

"No!" Strong Heart shouted.

The voice called again: "I'll kill ya! Don't think I won't!"

"Well, stop your threatening, and get on with it!" yelled Quinn.

O'Brien set to reloading her rifle.

Keech considered using a phrase from Doyle's journal to stop O'Brien from shooting at them. The Ranger's writing had spoken of a special means to render armed opponents harmless. *The Black Verse indicates a way to disarm without bloodshed*, Doyle had written. *Use the phrase:* M'gah-ge-hye'thn, *translated to mean, "Stop your attack."*

Visualizing the dark words, Keech opened his mouth to turn them loose.

Before he could speak, O'Brien fired again. A lead ball

skimmed the cantle of Keech's saddle, a mere inch from his rear end. Hector stumbled back a step, and with a squeal, the stallion reared up on his hind legs.

Unprepared for the sudden lurch, Keech tugged at the reins, forcing Hector to career sideways. The horse's movement pitched Keech right off the saddle. He tumbled onto one of the squirming evergreen saplings. The impact was painful, but worse was the pernicious fumes boiling up from the ground. The sick stench infiltrated his nose.

A tornado of emotions—hatred, fear, regret, and most of all fury—engulfed Keech. All the emotions that Pa Abner had taught him never to allow inside his heart now choked him. Desperate fury surged through his mind. Without understanding why, he wanted to destroy everything in his path, leaving nothing untouched. His entire world drowned in a sea of rage.

CHAPTER 16
THE HOMESTEAD

Keech awoke to the smell of a pungent oil under his nose. The odor cascaded into his nostrils and worked its way up through his skull. When he opened his eyes, he saw that he was inside a cozy cabin, stretched out on the floor beside a stone hearth. The abode's fireplace crackled with glorious heat. In front of the fire lay a sodden pair of gloves and a flimsy black hat, sprinkles of snow melting off the brim. A Kentucky long rifle stood against the hearth. Across the cabin's walls hung dozens of hand-drawn maps, yellowed and ripped by the nails driven into their corners. A few stacks of flat wooden crates sat against the walls beneath the maps, their lids tacked down and brown packing straw sticking out from the cracks.

"Keech, you're awake!" The voice belonged to Quinn. He sat next to the fire, soaking in the heat. His lower lip appeared raw and sore.

Duck and Strong Heart stood nearby, their faces distressed.

"Sure glad you're okay," Quinn continued. "We thought you was a goner."

"A goner?" Keech struggled to sit up, but a firm hand pushed him back down. His boots had been taken off. For that matter, he was missing his coat and pelt and bowler hat. "What happened? Where am I? Where are the horses?"

"Yer in my home, tadpole. Keep breathin' the orchid. The horses are in the barn."

Keech turned his head and saw the red-haired trapper, McCarty—O'Brien—squatting beside him. She held a small tin cup near his face. He caught a whiff of sour vinegar and pulled back. "What is that stuff?" he asked. "Smells awful."

O'Brien said, "You took a nasty fall. I'm just helpin' ya along so you and yer l'il partners can leave and get back on the trail."

Beside the woman sat the shaggy dog, Achilles, warming himself by the fire. The dog lifted his head long enough to gnaw on a back paw for a moment before flopping over to expose his belly to the fire.

Duck said to O'Brien, "That was no fall, and you know it. Your reckless shot spooked his horse and threw him. And one of those weird trees grabbed him and *changed* him."

"There's a sickness to this place," added Strong Heart, glaring at O'Brien. "You've done something bad here."

Disorientation seized Keech's brain. He tried to shake himself clear, but nothing made sense. "What do you mean I *changed*?"

Quinn licked his wounded lip. "You should've seen yourself, Keech. Your eyes went as black as coal, and you started screaming somethin' awful. I tried to help and got this split lip for my trouble."

"Strong Heart smacked the back of your head with her club," Duck added. "We carried you over here."

"I only struck you hard enough to make you sleep," Strong Heart interjected.

"But I don't understand," Keech said, and rubbed the back of his head; a tender knot had blossomed across his skull. "Why would I start screaming and punching Quinn?"

"O'Brien, you owe us a dandy explanation," Duck said to the trapper.

The Enforcer tossed up her hands. "I reckon I shouldn't be surprised y'all know my true name. I knew you tadpoles wouldn't leave me alone. I shoulda kept a closer watch on Achilles. For weeks he's been rattlin' on about his old master, tellin' me Milos had sent help. Sure enough, you showed up at Hook's Fort."

Keech shook his head again—O'Brien spoke of Achilles as though the mutt could talk like a person—but his thoughts were still muddy, so he'd probably heard wrong. "O'Brien, we're in a cabin. But I never *saw* any cabin, only the meadow and the mountain."

O'Brien shoved the cup of steaming liquid under his nose again. She had seemed tipsy at Hook's Fort, but now she was as steady as an oak. "You never saw it because it's under my protection. No one's seen this place for years."

"You can hide this cabin?" Quinn asked. "Just like my singing?"

Duck glanced at Keech and Quinn. "I'd wager that's why we couldn't find her trail outside Hook's Fort. She cast a concealment spell on her tracks."

Pushing up onto wobbly knees, his wounded arm heavy and sore, Keech faced O'Brien. "I think it's high time you tell us what you're doing up here. Start with the stuff in that cup."

The Enforcer eyed the contents of the tin cup. "Most folks call it Adam and Eve root. It's a kind of orchid, but it don't grow here in the Rockies. Not to *my* knowledge, at least. I brought a few plants down from the north a long time ago, and over the years I've had to keep 'em in special containers and whatnot. It's been a challenge, but I've managed to keep 'em alive. I made a tea from the root and gave ya some after yer tumble."

"But what did breathing that stuff do to me?" Keech asked.

"It quieted the rage." Straightening, O'Brien stepped closer to the fireplace. Achilles climbed to his feet, stretched his back legs, and trundled over to Quinn, who scratched between the dog's ears. Keech heard the little *tink-tink* sound come from the dog's neck pouch again. O'Brien set her cup on the fireplace mantel. "The little trees you saw ain't normal, as you prob'ly made out. I call 'em my *leech trees*."

"Leech trees," Strong Heart repeated. "You planted a defense to keep people away?"

"That ain't their purpose." O'Brien put her hands to her temples. "You won't understand the leech trees if ya don't know other things first. Things that happened here a long time ago."

Once again, Keech remembered the strange sensation he'd felt when they first approached the meadow. "O'Brien, what is this place? I think I know it."

O'Brien gave him a grave look. "You know it 'cause you've been here before, Mr. Blackwood."

"So you know me?"

"You may have learned somethin' about me, but I've learned a lot about you in the past few hours," she answered. Then her wary frown broke into a meager smile. "Yer connected to this place."

"I don't understand," Keech said. "What do you mean?"

O'Brien shrugged. "I mean, you were *born* here, tadpole."

With shock and disbelief, Keech gazed around the log cabin. He took in the stone hearth, the walls covered in homemade maps. The outer property seemed familiar, but nothing about the cabin rang true to his memory.

The evening's harsh winds screamed around O'Brien's cottage, driving against the logs like an army of trolls trying to batter their way inside. The trapper pointed to the creaking rafters. "I reckon you tadpoles know this weather ain't natural. The Peak is known to send down a heavy snowfall or two, but nothin' so fierce as what we're seein' now. These hard blows have been conjured by those yer huntin'." A bitter growl coated her words. "By *Ignatio*."

"*La Sombra*," Quinn moaned.

O'Brien's head turned sideways at the dreaded name, as though it numbed her blood to hear it. "That is the power you kids are facin'. More than you can hope to defeat."

"We don't accept that answer," Duck said. "We ain't about to back down, so you can either help us or you can get out of our way."

O'Brien's defiant features sagged, like a snare-trapped animal who has lost its fighting spirit. Keech felt a dash of sympathy for her, but Milos Horner had sent them to the woman as their last source of hope. They were not about to back down.

"*This* cabin didn't exist when you was born," O'Brien said to Keech, "but you know the area nonetheless." She stepped back as she spoke, and her boots came to rest on a large woven rug that was frayed along the edges. She dropped to one knee beside it. "You've seen the mountain we sit beneath, and you've played in the meadow where the leech trees now grow. You won't recollect particulars—you was only three years old when you left—but it was yer home for those first few years of life. Here. Better to show ya."

Seizing the woven rug by one corner, O'Brien snatched it back, revealing a trapdoor. She pulled up the latch. There was no dark staircase leading to a cellar, only a narrow crawl space. The patch of ground Keech could see was strangled with tall stalks of grass and lime-green weeds. The long, thick leaves of the weeds were shiny, as if glazed with a clear sap, and a strong fruity odor wafted up from them. The sweet smell reminded Keech of the crates down in the basement of Mercy Mission in Kansas. Horner's whistle bombs had given off the same aroma.

Strong Heart tiptoed closer to the opening. "What is down there?"

O'Brien reached and grazed one of the weeds with her palm. As her fingers touched the shiny leaves, Keech thought he heard a sound emanate from the plant, a tiny whistling noise, like a breath of wind rushing through a narrow space. O'Brien smiled. "This is a very special plot of land, the only piece of ground around this mountain that can grow the plants I need. This is ground that survived the battle of 1845."

When Keech heard the date, more puzzle pieces suddenly fell into place. "That was the year Pa Abner took me in! Are you saying *this place* is where my parents were killed?"

O'Brien withdrew her hand and the strange weed stopped whistling. "Yes, Mr. Blackwood. The Reverend Rose had sent his henchmen, the Big Snake, across the territories to hunt a collection of special artifacts."

"We know this already, Miss O'Brien," Quinn said. "The Char Stone, the Fang of Barachiel, and something called the Key of Enoch."

O'Brien offered a slight nod. "Rose needed the relics to finish the ceremony that would grant him eternal life. We thought we had covered our trail, but they found us gathered here."

"But why *here*?" Keech asked. "What's so special about this place?"

O'Brien said, "The Big Snake was causin' a world of trouble all through the West, from Missouri to California, even down to Mexico, in their hunt for the relics. Yer father, Bill Blackwood, called for the Enforcers to meet so we could discuss a way to be rid of the relics. He wanted to hide 'em so they'd never be found again."

"So you stashed them away in Bone Ridge and Bonfire Crossing," Duck said. "And inside the House of the Rabbit, whatever that is."

Again, O'Brien seemed surprised, if not cautious. "Yes. But before that, we gathered here, upon this ground, to discuss where to hide the relics. That was just over ten years ago, in late April. I remember ridin' up and seein' little Keech in the meadow outside, chasin' squirrels and spring butterflies. We had brought two of the relics with us and was discussin' where to best hide 'em when the Big Snake ambushed us."

"They caught your scent," Quinn said.

O'Brien grunted. "That's why they'd been kickin' up such a ruckus in the other territories. It was all a ruse. They needed us to bring the relics together. We fell into their trap."

Keech asked, "What happened that day, O'Brien? How did my parents die?"

Looking mournful, O'Brien slammed the trapdoor back over the crawl space, concealing the smelly weeds and grass again, and tossed the woven rug back over the door. "I could tell y'all how the ground outside was cursed and what happened, but I suspect you'll better comprehend that day if you see for yerself."

"See?" Quinn mused. "You mean a vision?"

"Yer a perceptive lad." Walking over to the fireplace, O'Brien stooped near the hearth and paused to ponder the flames for a moment. Then she reached into her pocket and drew out a small leather bag that fit in the center of her hand. Loosening the twine around the pouch, she opened it to reveal a mound of slate-gray powder. Vivid sparkles winked inside the grains like minuscule diamonds.

"What is that stuff?" asked Duck.

"Oh, just my own special concoction of rosemary and sage. With a little extra *kick* thrown in from the magic planes. I call it the Cerridwen Herb." The Enforcer's strange word sounded like "carried wind." Keech had never heard of or seen such an herb.

O'Brien leaned into the hearth and blew the twinkling substance off her palm and into the open fire. All four young riders flinched back when the flames sputtered and popped—but their curiosity returned when the fire's glow transformed into a brilliant flare of sapphire.

Stepping back, O'Brien waved them toward to the fire transfigured by the Cerridwen Herb. "Gather 'round, tadpoles. Stare deep into the flame. Let it reveal what y'all came to see."

"We're just supposed to look at it?" asked Quinn.

"Like the concoction I gave Keech earlier, the firelight will open a place in yer minds. You'll be stumped at first—nothin' will look the same, and you'll feel lost as a goose—but don't be scared. Just accept what ya see."

Do not fear the fire, Keech thought, remembering the words of the elders at Bonfire Crossing. Perhaps O'Brien's little pouch of sparkly powder contained some of the same magic that once fashioned the containment fire on the western beach.

He followed his companions to the hearth. Understanding that his parents had been murdered here was difficult enough, but he feared that seeing the event itself might overwhelm his heart. Still, he was tired of puzzling over incomplete tidbits. It was time to learn the truth of what had happened on that fateful day.

Keech leaned close to the flames, gazed deeply into the sapphire glow, and braced for the unknown.

25 July 1832–Lake Superior–Ouisconsin Territory

Today our fine company—consisting of Rowdy Bennett Coal, Milos Horner, Black Wood, and I—encountered three ruffians on the Huron River. The bandits held us at gunpoint and demanded we turn over all possessions, including our canoes, pelts, and horses. We refused.

The situation seemed dire—till pistol shots sounded from the forest and two individuals stepped out, attired in deerskins. The pair drew down on the bandits and chased them along the Huron's bank. Numerous more shots echoed across the wilderness, then a terrible silence followed.

Rowdy worried that all the parties had perished in the gunfight. But our deer-clad saviors reappeared. The pair introduced themselves as Isaiah Raines and Em O'Brien, the trappers that Milos and Black Wood had previously spoken of.

From the look of their partnership, the two are very close. We exchanged greetings and thanked them for their intervention with the bandits. Then our parties negotiated a consolidation of our wares.

There is a fortitude and wisdom to these five strangers that I admire—and though such a sentiment may sound exaggerated, I feel as if we six were destined to find one another. I do not know what lies ahead with our business venture in Illinois, but I do hope to learn more about my new companions. In the wilds of the uncertain wilderness, numbers give strength.

—R.J.

CHAPTER 17
THE BATTLE OF '45

Deep in the beautiful azure flames, Keech sees O'Brien's cabin reflected back, as if captured within the prisms of an otherworldly mirror. Except the cabin inside the fire looks different. He glances away from the hearth, expecting to see O'Brien and the other young riders sitting around him. Instead the place is empty of people. A table and chairs stand in one corner of the room near a squat iron stove. A bed piled high with furs and blankets sits against the back wall. The space is comfortable, lived-in, boasting simple decorations of bellflowers and forget-me-nots, a modest bookcase with leatherbound volumes stacked on the shelves. This cabin is a home.

A heavy rug sits on the floor—a rug different from O'Brien's. Keech knows that a trapdoor still sits beneath it, but under this door lies a small hollow dug into the ground. Inside the hole rest two ancient artifacts reclaimed from a powerful being. They should not be here, these relics; their very presence corrupts this peaceful mountain with danger.

The sound of talking outside draws Keech to the cabin's front door. When he opens it, he sees a slender gunman clad in black standing on the front porch. The man is tall and delicate-looking, with a dark, pencil-thin *mustache lining his upper lip, but he commands a powerful demeanor as he gazes beyond the southern meadow.*

"Hello?" says Keech, but the gunman doesn't seem to hear. "Mister?" he says, but again, no answer.

Then Keech realizes the man is not really there. Neither is he. Keech knows he is still staring into the sapphire flames that O'Brien created with the Cerridwen Herb, watching a specific memory take shape before him. And within this peculiar space and time, he sees and hears and understands more than he ever could in the real world.

A second man, a gruff bruiser, stands next to the tall gunman. "Milos, what do you sense?" this new man inquires, and Keech smiles when he realizes who he's looking at. The fellow is bald, just as he was at the Home for Lost Causes, but his thick beard is missing in favor of a woolly mustache that hangs over his lips. Someday soon the bruiser will rename himself Abner Carson, but for now he is known as Isaiah Raines, sometimes called Ragin' Raines by his companions.

"Nothing. Everything's quiet," says Milos Horner, his eyes squinting past the sunny field. "But it always makes me nervous when it's too quiet. Let's make this meeting quick."

Across the porch, their partner Red Jeffreys sits in a cedar chair, gently rocking. "I couldn't agree more, gentlemen. I've had a bad feeling since I woke up." Jeffreys is dressed in his usual deerskin apparel, but Keech notices one different detail about the man in this particular time and place: the tin star on his chest. Since he joined the Texas Rangers, Jeffreys has been calling himself Edgar Doyle, but for this reunion, the Enforcers again refer to him as Red. He pulls a brown wool cloth from his coat pocket and polishes his wooden pipe. After packing the pipe with fresh tobacco, Red places it between his teeth.

"Then let's get down to it," barks a deep voice, calling the other

Enforcers on the porch to order. The voice belongs to a barrel-chested cow-puncher, a bearded ox of a man who has been calling himself Noah Embry for the past decade, but here and now he is Bennett Coal, or Rowdy Bennett. He is eager to resolve their business so he can travel back to his ranch in Missouri, where he left his son, Nathaniel, and pregnant wife, Sarah. *"The topic on the table is what to do with the relics inside this cabin. No one leaves this place till we find the solution. And after we leave, we never speak of these things again, not even to our loved ones. Understood?"*

The other men agree at once.

"O'Brien?" says Rowdy. *"Do you understand the terms?"*

Standing behind Red Jeffreys, a stocky woman with wild copper hair stares at the men with dark, unsettling eyes. *"I only understand that we was foolish to keep the relics together in the first place. Those cursed things oughta be a thousand miles apart, not hid together under a danged mattress."*

"The Fang of Barachiel is far from cursed," says Rowdy.

"If the Reverend wants to spill blood for it, it's cursed," O'Brien says.

Milos Horner turns to face his fellow Enforcers. *"Even still, O'Brien's right. Keeping the two artifacts together begs for trouble. They must go to different locations. If just one were discovered, it wouldn't be enough to release Rose."* As soon as he's done speaking, Milos swivels back to the edge of the porch to study the hills.

O'Brien cackles. *"This is only what I've been sayin' for years, boys. When we first ran from the Reverend, I suggested we hide the relics in separate locations, but you all insisted I was bein' overly cautious."*

"Come on, Em," Isaiah says. *"At the time, it made more sense to keep the relics on the move, together and accounted for. Far easier to carry a bundle than grapple for loose leaves in the wind. But now we're all settlin' down."*

"Exactly so," Red Jeffreys adds. "Things have changed since we broke rank. I'm tired of dealing with this mess. I got a family now. And a proper occupation." He taps the tin star on his chest. "I want to get on with my life."

"So we're decided, then," O'Brien says. "We split up the Fang and the Stone, as we should have a decade ago. Put 'em where they stay lost forever."

Milos points out across the meadow. "Perhaps Bill can talk to his people, fetch us some help in hiding them."

A few yards from the cabin, a man and woman stand in the knee-high grass and watch a dark-haired child race about in the field, chasing a butterfly. The man—known among the Enforcers as Bill, but whose real name is Black Wood—is handsome and tall and wears dark trousers and a beaded vest. With arms that look as strong as trees, he scoops up the toddler and swings him, to the boy's delight.

"Go to your gathering. I'll watch him." The woman, Erin, takes the boy with a tender embrace, but something in her expression speaks anger. This reunion is dangerous. Erin wants Black Wood to finish this business and send away his old team so they can return to their life hidden in the Rocky Mountains.

Black Wood leans into his wife. "This will be done before nightfall. Once we have this decided, you will never see these people again."

Erin kisses her husband's cheek. "Do what's right, then come back to me." They share a moment where they see only each other, then Black Wood turns and walks to join the other Enforcers on the porch. Erin urges her young son toward the barn. "Come, Keech, my little pumpkin. Let's go pet the ponies."

At the cabin, the Enforcers discuss the idea of Black Wood's appealing to the Osage in Missouri for help hiding the artifacts. "Perhaps the elders can help us," Black Wood confesses, "but this would be asking much."

Isaiah scrubs a hand over his trail-worn face. "I don't see any other way, old friend. The Char Stone must stay isolated. We'll need another means to hide it. Something separate from the Prime. Something Rose could never pry into."

"Everyone, hold." Milos Horner raises a hand to silence them. His ever-vigilant eyes—those of a Diviner, a mystic seer—fix on the forested hills beyond the meadow. "Something ain't right."

The Enforcers grow alert. Stowing his pipe, Red Jeffreys abandons his chair to stand at attention. His Ranger star gleams in the pale sunlight.

"What do you sense?" Isaiah asks.

For a moment, Milos says nothing. Each Enforcer waits with fear and anticipation as the Diviner's deep gaze penetrates the mountain territory. He shivers as he gives his grim report. "I see Coward. About thirty thralls armed with muskets. And Ignatio."

"Coward sniffed us out," Rowdy Bennett growls.

Milos closes his eyes. "I see Big Ben, as well as Bad Whiskey."

"What about Lost Tucker?" asks O'Brien.

"No, but I do sense Weavers, a good dozen of 'em, maybe more," says Milos. "I'm afraid they've got the drop on us. It's too late to flee."

"Dandy," O'Brien snarls.

Without delay, the Enforcers prepare their particular forms of magic. They draw upon their focus, marshal the energies of the unseen world. They are wizards of the West, a force not to be trifled with.

Except one of them is distracted.

Black Wood.

"My wife and son need me," he murmurs. Dipping into the cabin, Black Wood locates his longbow and quiver, then reappears on the porch. "You never should have come here," he tells his old partners, then dashes toward the barn.

"We'll take care of this!" Isaiah calls after him.

One second later, the world explodes as musket fire rains down on the meadow from the nearby hills. The Reverend's thralls charge out from the tree line, scuttling behind Coward and the vicious, red-bearded brute Big Ben Loving.

"Better say your prayers, you double-dealin' backstabbers!" roars Big Ben. He yanks a pouch out of his long leather coat and dips his fingers inside.

Coward's voice bellows out from beside the Harvester, "The Reverend seeks blood for your betrayal! Time to pay!"

The Enforcers stand shoulder to shoulder at the edge of the cabin. Rowdy Bennett gazes after Black Wood, who is racing to join his wife and son. He addresses the team. "Whatever happens to us or the relics, protect that child. We may have brought death to this place, but we will not allow death to touch the boy."

Isaiah is the first to sprint toward Rose's horde, hollering a battle cry as he goes. Musket lead zings past, missing him by inches, but he doesn't stop. He reaches into his shirt and pulls out a fragment of glowing silver. "You want blood, Coward! Come and get it!"

The other Enforcers leap to join the fray. Enemy bullets bounce off Rowdy's skin as he picks up a barrel-sized stone and hurls it across the meadow, where it tumbles through the front line of charging thralls. With frenzied fingers, Red Jeffreys summons a behemoth whirlwind that rumbles toward Big Ben. O'Brien throws a spray of emerald powder into the air, and invisible walls of protection form around the group.

The Enforcers function together with the nimble expertise that comes from years of training and riding as an outfit. Their coordinated defense makes them nigh unstoppable.

Isaiah smacks the glowing silver on his palm to the forehead of a gibbering thrall. The reanimated fiend collapses at his feet, shuddering and *jerking as a pollution of black smoke pours from its mouth. In seconds, Isaiah stills two more of the dead, spitting shouts and curses at Coward as he works. The remaining thrall army begins to fall back.*

Big Ben Loving swivels around to shout at the retreaters. "Stand your ground, you pathetic curs!"

Approaching the barn, Black Wood yells for his wife and son, but no voices return from inside. He prepares to enter when a dark voice calls out from behind the structure.

"Where do ya think yer *goin', pilgrim?"*

Bad Whiskey Nelson steps around the corner, standing in Black Wood's path. His black overcoat ripples in the breeze. The needlepoint quill of his goatee is slick and groomed. And, of course, this younger Whiskey has both of his eyes. With terrible speed, he draws a Colt six-shooter from a holster on his hip and cracks off three angry shots in succession. Black Wood leaps behind a broad hay bale, barely evading the gunfire.

"Aces move, Bill!" says Bad Whiskey, cackling. "But you know I'm faster in the end!"

Taking a deep breath, Black Wood readies his longbow as Whiskey's Colt bellows a fourth round at the bundle of hay.

"No sense in hidin', Bill! Yer mine!" the scoundrel hisses. "You don't stand a chance against—"

Before the outlaw can finish, Black Wood nocks an arrow, leans around the hay bale, and releases the shaft.

The obsidian arrowhead strikes Whiskey in his left eye—a perfect shot. The villainous man topples without another sound, landing in the charred grass with a heavy thud.

Black Wood hurries into the barn, searching for Erin and young Keech.

Back in the clearing, the battle rages in a blur of motion and gunsmoke. Rotted thralls fire their muskets, and someone has set a blaze to the cabin. The fire grows rapidly, spitting embers into the meadow.

A company of fanged men and women dashes out of the flames as though born of them. These are the Weavers, merciless creatures corrupted by the Prime, a nightmarish lot with skin as pale as curdled milk. They attack with ferocity, but the Enforcers counter every move they make, guarding one another's backs, pushing the monsters back into the fire.

There is but one misstep, one weakness in the Enforcers' armor. Isaiah has rushed too far ahead, stepping outside O'Brien's protective walls.

Coward shrieks, "We see you! Time to meet your maker, Raines!"

A monstrous ripple of energy flows across the meadow as Ignatio, the Reverend's lieutenant, emerges from the trees. Multitudes of hideous tattoos cover the sorcerer's skin, blanketing his chest and back, his face and neck. He shows Isaiah something black in his grasp, a squirming thing reminiscent of a leech. Ignatio murmurs, "Hasta siempre, Raines."

Before Isaiah can step behind O'Brien's shield, the tattooed man drops to one knee and slams the dark thing he holds into the ground. A pool of thick black liquid, slick and viscous, springs from the soil and forms tendrils. One snaps forward and grips Isaiah's boot. He tries to pull away, but the inky goo snakes up his leg, reaches for his hand, touches his skin.

Screaming, Isaiah drops to his knees as the darkness pushes into his flesh, rides his veins, grips his heart, infects his mind. His eyes glaze over with night, a pair of pitch-black coals.

While this happens, Rowdy Bennett knocks Big Ben Loving unconscious. Red Jeffreys's whirlwinds toss the Weaver army back into the flames engulfing the meadow. The other Enforcers are holding their positions.

But they are too late to help Isaiah.

He has been corrupted, tainted by Ignatio's curse. He snarls like a rabid dog, and pure fury engulfs his mind. "Bill!" Isaiah bellows. "You're mine!" He charges for the barn.

The walls of the structure don't slow Isaiah in the least. The cursed man crashes through the timber, snapping the wood as easily as crunching brittle twigs.

Inside the barn, the ponies shriek with terror. Isaiah barrels forward, Ignatio's curse aiming him straight at Black Wood.

Stepping in front of his wife and child, Black Wood mutters, "Isaiah, what are you doing?"

"Look at his eyes!" Erin shouts. "He ain't himself!"

Black Wood begs for his friend to regain his senses, but his words fall on deafened ears. Roaring with fury, Isaiah leaps at the man, leaving a trail of terrible murk in his wake. Black Wood stands firm, a solid wall in the way of Isaiah's rampage, and the two men crash together. An explosive crack thunders between them as their knuckles meet.

The toddler Keech starts to wail. Erin tries to comfort the boy, but her husband's battle drowns out her voice.

Black Wood and Isaiah grapple, two unstoppable forces searching for the slightest hints of weakness in each other. Amid the struggle, Black Wood screams, "Please, Isaiah, stop!"

Isaiah hears nothing; he can feel only the red storm of Ignatio's curse.

Black Wood hears Keech screaming and shakes with sorrow and fear. If he must kill his friend to save the boy, then so be it. He focuses all his power into his fist and drives his knuckles into Isaiah's chest. The cursed Isaiah flies backward, crashing into a post. The log shatters, causing a ripple effect that destroys the barn's roof. Long splinters explode throughout the structure. The horses shriek in their stalls.

Isaiah staggers back to his feet.

Black Wood realizes he has only a moment to rescue his wife and child. He turns to scoop them up and run. He is not ready for what he sees.

Erin staggers and drops to her knees, a spear of wood buried in the middle of her back. Keech tumbles from her arms and weeps. The light in Erin's eyes dims as she pitches forward, landing facedown in moldy hay.

Black Wood screams: "Mah-shchee^n-kah!" *Anguish paralyzes him—till Isaiah suddenly rises before him.*

"You killed her!" Black Wood shouts—but if he means to speak more, the words are cut off as the mindless, enraged Isaiah grips Black Wood's neck.

With cursed hands, Isaiah Raines crushes the life out of his friend.

CHAPTER 18
WATCHER OF THE PRIME

Wrenching out of the vision, Keech staggered to his feet, his eyes burning with tears. He stumbled backward, away from O'Brien's bewitched fire. His companions continued to sit unconscious, staring fixedly at the sapphire flames, making no move to stir from their own visions.

Sitting on her stool, O'Brien frowned. "You came out too early." She had been cleaning the barrel of her Kentucky rifle and now propped the gun back against the wall. "I feared the shock of seein' how your folks died might push you out."

"*Pa Abner*. Pa killed my parents! *With his own hands*." Keech tried to take a breath but couldn't. He panted for air. Wheeling about in circles, he clutched at his throat as if he, too, were being strangled by Pa's terrible hands. Finally the air came, but horrid memories of Bone Ridge tumbled in with it. Pa Abner's furious fists lashing out at Keech, walloping his face, following the commands of a cackling Bad Whiskey. That had been the *second time* Rose and his Big Snake had gotten their fangs into Pa Abner.

O'Brien shook a stern finger at Keech. "Make no mistake,

tadpole. The fault belongs to Ignatio. You saw it yerself. The *sorcerer* drove Isaiah to do what he did."

Remarkably, Keech's next thought of Pa was not one of betrayal or death, but a memory of the man's tenderness. Keech had been sitting on the bank of the Third Fork River one day, clutching his bowler hat and sobbing over a terrible dream he'd had the night before. Pa heard the whimpering and walked over. *My boy, what's wrong?*

Keech slumped into Pa's embrace, breathing in the comforting smells of pine wood and sawdust on his foster father's clothes. *It was the dream again, Pa.*

The one about the dust whirlwinds and the heat?

Yessir. And my real folks were dead, but you saved my life, and your silver charm was cold on my cheek, and we were running.

Pa Abner pulled Keech's hat from his grip and placed it back on his head. Pa's rugged hands, usually so confident, so calm, trembled. *Hush now, Keech, there's nothing to fear and no need to run. You're safe with Pa Abner. You're safe.*

This memory used to fill Keech with tranquility, but now he knew the truth. Everything he ever believed had been built upon a lie. Pa's unflappable wisdom, his promises of safety and peace, the training in the woods, a decade's worth of instruction—all had been burned to ash by O'Brien's flame.

Keech stood breathing into his hands, staring at the blue fire and his three mesmerized companions.

"The others'll wake soon," O'Brien said. "The vision lasts a smidge longer. It's like readin' a book. There's a beginnin' and end, and the watcher has to read all the way through to get the full story."

Keech's head teetered with confusion. "How do you remember what happened? Didn't you take the Oath of Memory that hid the information?"

O'Brien shuffled over to the fireplace, the enchanted flames painting her red hair a lustrous amber. Fetching a hooked metal rod, she fished up a small black kettle from the hearth and hung the pot over the flames. "The others took it, but not me. I took *another* task upon me."

"What task?" Keech said.

"Why don't we wait for yer trailmates? Then we'll talk."

The others soon rose out of their separate visions, disorientation awash on their faces. O'Brien retrieved her black kettle from the flames. Holding its handle with a thick mitt, she poured steaming liquid into four brass mugs and invited the young riders to sit at the table and drink her sour tea.

Quinn's face scrunched. "After what I saw, I don't know if I can stomach that."

"Go ahead. It'll settle yer guts," O'Brien said.

Strong Heart sniffed her tea, tilted her head away from the odor, then drained her cup in a single gulp. "Tastes terrible," she muttered.

Small sobs hitching in her throat, Duck stared at her tea. She said, "I saw my father. And Keech's folks." She looked at Keech and shook her head. "And I saw what your pa did."

Keech pushed his cup away. "Sorry, I don't think I want mine." He stared at the table, fearing that if he met eyes with his trailmates, there would be no stopping his tears.

O'Brien spoke again. "The patch of ground under the trapdoor is a special place unsullied by Ignatio's curse. But the rest of the meadow is deeply tainted. I've spent the last decade of my life workin' to keep the curse contained. I planted the leech trees to hold the darkness at bay. They pull the rage out of the ground, keep it from spreadin'."

O'Brien said more, but Keech barely heard. She explained the parts of the fire vision he had missed—that the other Enforcers had driven Ignatio away using their magic, and that Red Jeffreys had used the Fang of Barachiel to free poor Isaiah from the rage curse. "After Red freed him, Isaiah felt *burdened*." She paused to draw in a deep breath. "He swore to raise ya, Keech. He left in Milos Horner's wagon, loaded with . . ." Her voice trailed off.

"My folks," Keech finished.

"He buried 'em along with the Char Stone and took the Oath of Memory to hide their restin' place," O'Brien said. "After that, the two of us lost track. Isaiah had been my closest friend for years, but I lost him to his guilt."

Keech rubbed a shaky hand across his face, wanting so badly to unsee what he'd witnessed in the vision. He turned to his trailmates. "What else did you all see?"

Strong Heart said, "I saw the Enforcers work with the elders to create Floodwood, the place where my brother died."

"And I saw Ranger Doyle help create the fire at Bonfire Crossing," Quinn said.

"Seems like the fire gave us all the same vision," Duck said. "But there's one thing missing. We saw the other Enforcers hide the Char Stone and the Fang, but we never saw what happened to the Key. Or for that matter, where to find the House of the Rabbit."

Quinn's eyes widened. "She's right. It's like the vision skipped right over that part. Like it didn't want us to see the Key or something."

"O'Brien, what are we missing?" Duck asked.

A ferocious gust of wind rattled the tiny cabin, putting everyone on edge. O'Brien said, "The vision don't show the Key of Enoch because I told it not to."

"You can do that?" Quinn took a sip of tea.

The woman chuckled. "I can do lots of things, tadpole. I'm what's known as a Harvester. Red Jeffreys can manipulate the wind. Milos was a Diviner, so he could sense things from great distances. I can take plants and herbs from nature and make 'em do what I ask."

"Like the herb you scattered on the fire," Strong Heart said.

O'Brien nodded.

"Big Ben Loving could do that," Keech noted.

O'Brien glowered at the name. "Yes, he was a powerful Harvester, but he concocted most of his brews usin' the Prime, the terrible power that fuels the Underworld. My magics come from the *positive* forces found in nature."

"We've heard of the Prime," Duck said. "Edgar Doyle told us about it. He wanted to use the Prime to resurrect his daughter."

Keech had figured the news would surprise O'Brien, but it didn't seem to rattle her. "I know. I've looked into the Prime and seen his deeds."

Strong Heart's head tilted in curiosity. "You *saw* him?"

"Seein' is what I do, tadpole. It's one of the reasons I stay here in the mountains. Ten years ago, Ignatio cursed this ground with a mighty wallop of Prime. I can peek into the dark energy that lingers here, see what's happenin' in other places." O'Brien pointed to the fireplace. "I use the fire as you just did. Except I don't use the Cerridwen Herb."

"How do you look, then?" asked Duck.

O'Brien gestured toward the clearing outside her cabin. "The leech trees. When I burn a branch from one of the cursed trees, I can see all sorts of terrible things. It's how I saw that Red Jeffreys had tapped the Prime to break his Oath of Memory. It's also how I've tracked the movements of the Big Snake."

"That's why you rode down to Hook's Fort," Quinn said. "The leech trees gave you a glimpse of Rose's gang hauling explosives, and you went down to stop them."

O'Brien smiled. "I certainly didn't make no friends out of his wagon drivers. But when y'all met me at the fort, I wasn't there to sabotage Rose's latest wagon train. I was there 'cause Milos *told* me to be at the fort. He said friends were headed my way."

"How could Mr. Horner have told you about us?" asked Duck. "He died in November in the streets of Wisdom. He pointed us to you—or your fake name, McCarty—an hour before his death. How could he have warned you about us?"

O'Brien pointed to Achilles, who sat by the front door, fast asleep with his head tucked into his front paws. "Because Milos sent me a message through *Achilles*," she said. "He could communicate with animals."

Keech had forgotten the critter was still in the cabin—the hound never made a sound, except when he was barking his head off or jangling his leather-pouch necklace.

"Does the dog speak?" Strong Heart asked, her tone more curious than skeptical.

"Not with words. But Achilles made it clear enough I was to go to Hook's Fort. When I saw you tadpoles, I told that old hound there was no way I'd work with kids. I rode off, but he refused to head back with me. I reckon he wanted to lead y'all up to my cabin." She chortled, the laughter ringed with tinges of sadness. "He's always been loyal to Milos."

"This still don't explain why Mr. Horner sent us to find you," Quinn said. "He didn't send us marching down the Santa Fe Trail just to stare at a magic fire."

"Maybe he figured y'all might be capable of stoppin' the Big Snake. Maybe y'all ain't just innocent little tadpoles. After all, you've been touched by the Prime."

"What?" Duck frowned. "That's ridiculous."

"Don't bother to deny it. I can feel Prime power nestin' inside ya. You've been near the Char Stone. Three of ya, leastways." One by one, O'Brien pointed at Keech, then Duck, then Quinn. When her finger settled on Strong Heart, she said, "You haven't."

Keech pondered their travels the last couple of months. "We *were* near the Char Stone when we rode along with Doyle all the way from the Kansas River to Wisdom. We never knew he was carrying the Stone at the time, but it was in Doyle's knapsack till Coward stole it."

Realization dawned on Duck's face. "You're saying that being near the Char Stone *changed* us."

"Yes, tadpole. That's exactly what I'm sayin'."

This afternoon a man approached me and my new companions on the bank of the Great Lake. He greeted our party and invited us onto shore for coffee. Rowdy Bennett drew his musket for caution, but the man assured us he meant no harm. We retired to his camp, where he proceeded to offer us provisions.

The fellow hails from a mountainous region in Spain, a place he describes as beautiful but very harsh to travelers. Despite his rugged origins, the man speaks mildly and packs no firearm—though he does carry a peculiar dagger made of bone. His body is heavily marked with tattoos.

O'Brien inquired about the fellow's name. He addressed himself as Ignatio.

We asked about his tattoos, but he seemed intent on exhibiting an archaic scroll rolled inside a covering of dried brown leather. He explained that the scroll is quite valuable, a "treasure map" of sorts, written in an ancient tongue. When Isaiah pressed the man on what sort of treasure could be discovered, the Spaniard held up his bone dagger for all to see.

"There are many secrets hidden in the world," Ignatio said. "This cuchillo, for instance. Within this blade lies a kind of salvation. I can take you to more objects like it, if you so desire. The scroll can show us the way."

The Spaniard spoke of a traveling partner nearby, one he referred to only as "the Reverend." This partner is searching for a team and may wish to offer the six of us a proposition. "The Reverend is a great man," Ignatio explained. "He has shown me many splendid things, and if you heed his teachings, you will learn secrets undreamed."

—R.J.

CHAPTER 19
THE MAP

The young riders sat in silence for a moment, considering the dark magic of the Char Stone and what it meant to them. Outside the wind kicked up, and a strange roll of thunder shook the night as if the mountain were screaming for them to leave.

"O'Brien, does this mean we're tainted?" asked Quinn.

O'Brien considered the question. "Yes and no, Mr. Revels. The Char Stone opened you up to a whole heap of mystical energies. Yer closeness to the Stone broke down the natural barriers between this world and others, allowin' the Prime to seep through."

Strong Heart frowned. "Seep through?"

Another ferocious gust of wind surged against the cabin walls. "Wind's kickin' up," O'Brien said. "There is a membrane between this world and . . . other worlds. The barrier is thin near the Char Stone—once you've been exposed to the Stone, somethin' inside you is altered, makin' you more sensitive to the mystical forces in our world and others." The Enforcer paused to think, then resumed. "Think about it this way. Imagine a maple leaf, freshly fallen from the tree after a storm. The rain that soaks the leaf turns the surface thin, so fragile that, given time, the leaf will become one with the soil. In yer case, tadpoles, the Char Stone is the rain and you are the leaf."

"This explains a bunch, now, don't it?" Duck said to Keech. "*That's* why you can shoot Rose's birds out of the sky." She turned to Quinn next. "And I bet it's why your humming and songs can hide us on the trail."

Quinn asked, "What about you, though? You were just as close to the Stone as we were. Why ain't you got any sort of power?"

"I don't know." Duck pondered for a moment. "I don't think I want any."

"I'm guessin' when Milos met you tadpoles, he sensed you'd been opened." O'Brien shook her head, but another smile curled her lips.

Keech scowled at O'Brien. "Mr. Horner never told us a thing about the Stone seeping powers into us. He only told us to travel to Hook's Fort and find *you*."

"Perhaps he hoped that while you traveled out here, you'd learn to harness yer own focus enough to slow down Ignatio. Maybe even Rose himself," O'Brien said. "Milos tended to see the best in folks. But not me. I don't think you stand a chance."

"You don't have to believe in us," Duck said. "Just tell us where to find the Key of Enoch. We'll figure out how to finish things on our own."

O'Brien shook her head. "If I did, I'd be sendin' you to yer doom."

Quinn said, "You can keep hiding, tending your saplings, and ignoring the rest of the world. But my auntie Ruth is a prisoner out there. She was free, but they took her. Ain't no way I can just give up on her."

When O'Brien's features remained firm, Keech sought another way to reach her. He thought back to Doyle's journal again, the entry dated *25 July 1832*: *The pair introduced themselves as Isaiah Raines and Em O'Brien... From the look of their partnership, the two are very close*. If Keech had learned one thing about the Enforcers, it was that they valued their partnerships. *A faithful friend is a sturdy shelter*, as they liked to say in Latin.

Keech said, "If Pa Abner were still alive, he'd go hunting for this Key himself." When O'Brien still didn't respond, he added: "Partners stick together. Pa would want you to help us."

O'Brien propped her hand against the door, appearing bone-weary from years of solitude. "You tadpoles are determined to get yerselves killed. Fine. I can send y'all up the quickest route to the mining camp under Skeleton Peak." She pointed up to the cabin's ceiling.

For a moment, Keech was confused by the gesture, but realization struck him. She wasn't pointing at the ceiling, but at the massive peak outside. His heart leaped in his chest, and the words from Doyle's journal resurfaced in his mind. *The skeleton holds the key*. "The mountain standing over us is called *Skeleton Peak*?"

"Indeed," O'Brien said. "So named for the cliff ledges on the east face of the mountain. When approachin', the crags resemble—"

"Lemme guess. A big skeleton," Quinn said.

"More like a skull. Ain't a pretty sight, the Peak. Can be down-right unsettlin'."

In Hook's Fort, Keech had asked the trapper if she knew the

meaning of Doyle's cryptic phrase about the skeleton, and she had denied any knowledge of it. But now he saw she knew plenty. Hoping to get her to say more, he pulled out the Ranger's leatherbound book and laid it flat on his palm. "Do you recognize this?"

The Enforcer gave the journal a pondering look. "I may have seen him scribble in it once or twice."

"Doyle left it after betraying us," Keech said. He took a deep breath to try to calm his nerves. "I've spent weeks combing through his writings, but the only mention I've found about the Key is an entry dated September 1833. But I think you know more."

O'Brien sighed, a heavy exhalation. "There is a minin' camp at the base of the skull," she said. "That's where Ignatio is based. But it ain't no gold mine. Ain't no *gold* in Skeleton Peak, but there is treasure."

"The Key of Enoch," Quinn said.

O'Brien stepped to one of the cabin walls covered in scrawled maps. Scribbled arrows bisected one of the papers, and angry *X*s dotted the sketch, but O'Brien pointed at the bottom of the map. "The entire mountain's riddled through with tunnels and caves. Decades ago, miners blasted down into the Peak, built an underground camp, and pulled all sorts of ore out of the mountain. But those workers never learned about the place that sat *under* all that stone. You see, one of them deep shafts leads down to a secret cavern." She turned to face the Lost Causes. "I'm talkin' about the House of the Rabbit."

Tremors of excitement rippled down Keech's spine. He recalled how Pa Abner had prepared him with the nickname *Wolf* for the day he would need to use the word to enter Bonfire Crossing. Perhaps Pa had given Sam the nickname *Rabbit* for the same reason, as a way into the House.

"You know the way down to the Key," Quinn said. "Will you show us?"

O'Brien surprised them all by ripping the map of the Peak down from the wall. "Truth is, I've explored every tunnel under Skeleton Peak myself, but I've never been able to find the path into the House. Only one person ever found the way."

"Who?" Duck asked.

O'Brien peered at Keech. "*Your father*, boy. In thirty-three, the Reverend Rose brought us to the Peak to fetch the Key. He'd been followin' an ancient scroll—a document he claimed had been written by Enoch himself, God's right-hand man."

Keech said, "I've read about this scroll in Doyle's journal."

O'Brien didn't look too happy to share the memories of those days. "The scroll led us to Skeleton Peak. Once there, we tried to find a way in. Each of us took a different tunnel. We wandered but found only dead ends. Except for yer father, Black Wood. He disappeared for a time, then emerged with the Key. He returned a different man. A *haunted* man."

Quinn asked, "What did he see down there?"

"I don't rightly know," O'Brien said. "He called the place 'the House of the Rabbit.' Spoke of shiftin' walls and terrible rips in the earth, perils that threatened death at every turn. Nobody else has ever come close to gettin' in, but ol' Black Wood did it. After we six Enforcers broke away from Rose, he returned the Key to the House."

"You mean he went back in?" Duck asked. "He went through all that *twice*?"

Strong Heart said to Keech, "Many stories have been told of *Zha^n Sah-peh* and his deeds, but I never knew these things."

Keech's vision of the battle now made much more sense. The Enforcers of 1845 had brought only two artifacts to the meeting because his father had already stowed the Key back inside its original hiding place. Keech's mind reeled as he tried to imagine what dangers and wickedness his father had seen as he traveled down to the House of the Rabbit. He recalled what Travis the farrier had told him at Hook's Fort. "Back at Hook's Fort, I learned a few things from your farrier friend. She said you talked in your sleep about monsters and a *Dead Rift*."

Terrible unease stiffened O'Brien's face. "Travis ought not speak on things she don't understand."

"Does it have to do with the House of the Rabbit?" Keech pressed.

"Yes. A good part of it," O'Brien said. "The Dead Rift was an *event*. Happened long ago, durin' a time they call the First Age of Man."

Duck's eyes seemed to darken with fear. "What was it?"

"The Dead Rift happened when people first tampered with magic. Their meddlin' tore holes in the fabric of the world, opened gaps to the Underworld itself. The House of the Rabbit is one of those gaps."

"And the Scorpion's Nest, the Palace of the Thunders, is another?" Strong Heart asked.

"Yes again," O'Brien said. "I saw the terrible rift in the Palace with my own eyes. But before that, Black Wood told us he caught a glimpse of a Dead Rift hole right here in the midst of the Rocky Mountains."

Keech pondered the information. "The Key's hiding spot. Sounds like a good place to put a magical object, all right. Down in a place where few men could fetch it."

"*Nobody* can find it," O'Brien corrected. "Black Wood's death meant the path to the House was lost. I can point y'all to the south minin' entrance, not far from here, but after that, you tadpoles are on yer own." She turned the map around so everyone could see the scribbles. "These are the tunnels I've explored, but they're all dead ends."

Keech's heart dropped when he peered at the dozens of *X*s scrawled across the page. How many weeks and months had O'Brien spent exploring the channels of Skeleton Peak, stumbling down blind alleys? From the sound of things, traversing the mountain would make the Floodwood cave seem like a pleasant autumn stroll.

"Take this," O'Brien said, and she rolled up the map and handed it to Duck. She pointed to one of her walls of maps. "As y'all can see, I've made dozens, but no map I ever draw helps me find the House. This one, at least, will show where *not* to go."

"Much obliged." Duck tucked the curled paper into her coat.

"There's something else." Pivoting, O'Brien walked toward the hearth and gripped a stone. She tugged, and the rock came loose, revealing a hole. She reached inside and pulled out a few sheets of paper, old as fossils and full of scribbles. Keech felt his stomach tighten when he realized the pages were the same size and appearance as the leaves in Doyle's journal.

O'Brien held the papers out to Keech. "I didn't tell ya everything

I could've. In thirty-three, Red Jeffreys tore out a few of his journal pages—mostly ones about the Key and Skeleton Peak—and asked me to hold on to 'em. By that time, the events of July and August had left a sour taste in his mouth."

"What events?" Keech asked.

O'Brien thrust the journal pages into Keech's hands. "Read 'em on yer own time, and judge for yerself. These ain't mine to hold no more." As Keech crammed the loose pages into his coat pocket, O'Brien turned her attention to the others. "To speed up yer pace to the Peak, I can have Achilles lead y'all to the south entrance." She glanced at the shaggy hound. "You hear that, dog? I want you to take these tadpoles to the *south adit*."

To Keech's surprise, Achilles jumped up, spun a couple of times, and barked.

"What's an adit?" asked Quinn.

O'Brien gestured to one of her drawings of Skeleton Peak. "Think of them as open doors into a mountain. Miners would tunnel in sideways to drain water and pull out minerals. Be careful when ya go in. The older the adit, the more dangerous to—"

But she was cut off when the howling wind outside intensified. The cabin's front door shuddered and burst open, causing the fire in the hearth to cough red sparks. A tremendous rattle shook the roof as ceiling boards tore free and flew away. The air in the room hummed with a dull pressure.

"What's happening?" Quinn shouted.

Duck narrowly avoided a plank falling onto her. "We're being attacked!"

Keech dashed to the doorway, peered out into the frosty night, and saw a tall man in buckskin garments treading on foot across the meadow. Haggard moonlight illuminated the figure, and swirls of snow surrounded him like loose twines of spider silk. The fellow weaved in and out of the sapling rows, careful not to brush against O'Brien's leech trees. Keech could just make out the shape of a horse, following the man.

"Keech, get back!" O'Brien yanked him by his coat collar and took his place in the doorway. Holding her Kentucky rifle, she aimed the barrel at the figure and squeezed off. A booming shot rent the air, scattering powder at the approaching man's feet. "That's far enough!" O'Brien shouted, but the figure didn't stop.

The evening's twisting flurries howled even louder, and a burst of glacial air pulsed straight at the cabin. The current slammed into O'Brien like cannon fire, shoving her backward into Keech, and they both dropped with heavy grunts. The rifle skidded from the woman's grip. A lone flurry plucked the weapon off the floor and sent it spinning out of the cabin. The firearm landed in the attacker's outreached hand. Without breaking his stride, the fellow shattered the rifle against his leg.

Keech struggled to get out from underneath O'Brien, but the trapper seemed dazed and didn't move off him. The snow-shrouded figure was nearly upon them. Five more steps and he would take the porch.

O'Brien spoke, her voice filled with defeat. "I knew you'd come."

A hush settled across the cabin. The churning white powder sprinkled the porch boards, unveiling the figure. A bearded, wild-eyed man climbed onto the porch, filling the doorway with his wide stance.

"No," Keech muttered when he saw the man's face. "It can't be."

The fellow regarded Keech and the other young riders, then turned his grizzled gaze back to O'Brien. He dusted snow off his shoulders and adjusted his hat.

"Hello, Em. Been a long time," said Edgar Doyle. "I see you've met the Lost Causes."

CHAPTER 20
OLD FRIENDS

Duck shifted to flank the Ranger, while Strong Heart unsheathed a knife. Scrambling to his feet, Keech assumed a fighter's stance, clenched his hands into fists, and prepared to spring.

Quinn was the only one still and calm. "Everyone, stand down. We can handle this peaceful." He turned his attention to the man at the door. "Hello, Ranger Doyle."

"Mr. Revels." Doyle tipped his hat. "Happy to see you, my friend."

Climbing to her boots, O'Brien rubbed her backside. "You bruised my rump, Red."

"Sorry, Em. I didn't fancy you popping off at me with that rifle." Doyle shifted his gaze to take in the entire cabin. "I didn't come to hurt anyone, but I won't abide you kids' getting frisky. Listen to Mr. Revels, and keep your heads. Let me inside, and we can talk."

"After you abandoned the mission?" Duck snarled. "And stole the Fang of Barachiel?"

The Ranger made a small huffing sound, as if he found Duck's words amusing. "I never abandoned *my* mission, kid. My daughter is the reason I'm out here."

"You don't care about anybody but yourself," Duck shot back.

Doyle's lips pressed into a rigid line. "Have you seen my boy on the trail? Has John Wesley shown himself?"

"Not a sign," Keech said. "John's long gone. Not that you'd care."

"I see." Doyle shook his head, and shimmery tears formed in his eyes. The Ranger lowered his gaze, as though wanting to hide his grief, then took a long breath. When he glanced back up, his eyes were clear again. "How 'bout we all have a sit-down, and you can tell me what you're up to."

In his ever-calming voice, Quinn explained, "O'Brien here was just giving us a history lesson. She showed us a vision of everything that happened back in forty-five."

Doyle frowned at his old Enforcer partner. "What did you show them?"

"What they needed to see," O'Brien said.

"They *need* schoolbooks and daily chores."

Brushing grit off her trousers, O'Brien said, "They need to know the truth."

Keech's fists tightened so hard he heard a knuckle pop. "Why are you here? Why ain't you chasing after Coward and the Char Stone?"

Doyle scratched at his long beard, which had grown all the way to his Adam's apple. "Tracking that devil's no easy feat. He's clever at disguising his trail. After I parted ways with your gang, I rode back toward Wisdom to pick up his direction. I got close enough to spot him one day. Your friend Cutter was with him. Did y'all know?"

"Of course we knew," Duck said.

"How long did you follow them?" Strong Heart asked.

"Half a day. I'm an expert tracker, but Coward can confound his trail like no other. I suspect he sniffed me out. They vanished from sight, and his trail went cold."

"That fella sure gives me the creeps," Quinn said.

"Eventually I fell in behind *you* four," Doyle continued. "Caught sight of you just outside the Suffering Bluffs. Saw you were being hunted."

Understanding washed over Duck's face. "It was *you* back down in the pass, running those twisters across the ridge. You started the avalanche."

Doyle smiled. "Those snows didn't just happen to tumble at the perfect time. I *saved* you. If it weren't for me, Black Charlie would be laughing over your bones." On this he peered at O'Brien. "Did you tell them about the Weavers? About Lost Tucker?"

"In the vision O'Brien showed us, I *saw* Weavers," Keech said. "But I never saw a Lost Tucker. Who is that?"

"Black Charlie's boss, who commands Rose's largest army," Doyle answered, then gave O'Brien a concerned look. "They're still oblivious to the dangers waiting out there."

"I tried to tell 'em. They won't listen to sense," O'Brien said.

"Enough!" Strong Heart snarled. She gripped her knife as though ready to throw it at the slightest twitch from the Ranger. "I am sorry your daughter died, Red Jeffreys, but you betrayed our trust. Return the Fang. The elders entrusted it to the Lost Causes to carry, not you."

"Hand over the amulet shards while you're at it," Duck said. "They belong to us."

The Ranger's trail-worn face wrenched into a scowl. "Wrong, kid. One of those belonged to *me*. I took Rowdy Bennett's, true enough, but Mr. Blackwood here stole the one I'd been carrying for years. And the Fang never belonged to the elders." He turned to Strong Heart. "The elders are good people, but the Enforcers protected the Fang first. *We* built the bonfire, and *we* hid the relic there."

"You used the Osage to bury your sins," Strong Heart railed.

"Everybody, stay calm," Quinn pleaded. "No need to set off no tempers."

Strong Heart advanced toward Doyle with her blade. "Give me the Fang."

Lifting a gloved finger, Doyle made a rapid circling gesture. "Not today. I'm in no mood to scuffle." A thrumming pocket of wind swooped around the cabin. The wind spun around Strong Heart, driving her blade down and holding her in place.

Doyle returned his attention to O'Brien. "Em, I need you to lead me to the Key."

"Sorry to disappoint," O'Brien growled, "but I never found a way in."

Still blocking the doorway, Doyle peered at the maps on the walls, as if taking in all of O'Brien's failed attempts. "I will find it, Em. I *will* save my daughter."

Through the open front door, movement outside the cabin caught Keech's eye. Saint Peter, the Kelpie, strolled up toward the porch. The black stallion made no sound, and his hooves made no impressions in the snow. After Big Ben's attack on Bonfire

Crossing, the Kelpie had saved Keech's life, taking on a human form and hauling him out of the ocean. The wondrous sight of the shape-shifter distracted Keech—till he spotted the knapsack that held the bones of Eliza, Doyle's dead daughter.

"Return her bones to the earth," O'Brien said, sadness cracking her voice. She held out a hand, an offer of peace. "I'm sorry about Eliza, but what you seek is damnation. We saw what the Char Stone did to Rose. Yer daughter can't be saved, but *you* still can."

Doyle shook his head. "I'm sorry you refuse to help. I reckon I should leave," the Ranger said. "But first I need to collect the two shards you and Milos carried. Hand 'em over. Now."

No sooner did the Ranger speak the words than Achilles growled, stepping back and baring his fangs. A jangle sounded from the pouch tied to his neck.

Realization dawned on Keech again.

Pa Abner had said there were five broken shards of the amulet. Keech had lost his piece to Coward, and Doyle had stolen Duck's. The Ranger also carried his own, but that meant two other silver pieces were unaccounted for. *Find the shards, Keech, and unite them*, Pa had said before dying. The fragments had been scattered, but it stood to reason they could be gathered back together and used to stop the Reverend.

Locking eyes with Duck, Keech pointed at Achilles. *The dog.* He knew he could trust Duck to recognize what he wanted. The girl didn't disappoint.

She sprinted toward the growling mutt and reached for the small pouch around his neck.

Doyle flicked his finger. "Stop right there!"

The heavy gust restraining Strong Heart shifted across the

room, scooping Duck right off her feet. The girl tumbled side-ways and crashed into the wall, a grunt escaping her lips.

"Duck!" Quinn shouted.

Strong Heart lunged, her knife flashing in the cabin's flame-light, but with a jerk of Doyle's hand, the knife spun out of her grip. The girl flew with it. She landed beside Duck, bellowing in pain.

Keech's anger flashed like a wildfire, and his vision dimmed at the edges. All he could see now was Doyle blocking the doorway. Nothing else. A particular phrase from the journal returned to Keech's mind: the invocation to stop attacks without bloodshed. Doyle's own warning came with it—*I fear the slightest misspoken sound could prove fatal to my target.*

Pointing at Doyle's chest, Keech muttered, "*M'gah-ge-hye'thn!*" The syllables raked over his tongue and scalded his throat like boiling water. A pulse of terrible force erupted from Keech's fin-gertips, leaving his skin feeling charred.

Raw power ripped apart the threshold and shredded the cabin's walls, filling the air with timber shards. The hammerblow sent Doyle tumbling across the porch, end over end, and dumped him into the snowy meadow. A terrible shriek accompanied the blast, and Keech saw that the energy had thrown O'Brien to the ground. Across the cabin, his trailmates appeared rattled.

Shaking the stupor out of his head, Keech hurried outside, hopping over demolished logs to get to Doyle.

The Ranger lolled on his back, disoriented. Moans escaped his bloodied lips, and one of his wrists lay bent at an awkward angle. He was still alive, but he'd taken the brunt of the Black Verse. Fear that he'd gone a step too far flooded Keech's heart. He tried to shake off the uncertainty and called out to the man, "You brought this on yourself!"

Doyle simply groaned on the ground.

His fingertips smoldering, Keech stooped and opened the man's coat. The two amulet shards Doyle had taken were tied on separate cords around his neck. Keech yanked them loose. After stuffing the charms into his pocket, he patted down the stunned Ranger. Sheathed on Doyle's belt was the mystical bone dagger, the Fang of Barachiel. Keech pulled the blade free.

Doyle tried to sit up. "No, Keech. I *need* them."

Keech pushed the Ranger back into the snow. "Stay down."

Dark movement startled Keech's vision, and as he turned, he saw Saint Peter stomping toward him. Keech stumbled back in surprise. "Saint Peter, it's me!" he shouted, but the Kelpie pounded forward. A powerful hoof hammered down, but Keech rolled sideways in the snow, then pivoted to gain his feet. "I'm Keech, your friend! You saved my life, remember?"

No sign of anger burned in the creature's emerald eyes. Saint Peter wasn't trying to hurt him; he was trying to *scare* him. The Kelpie was protecting Doyle.

"I won't hurt him again," Keech said, backing away. "You have my word." As he hurried back to the devastated cabin, he slid the Fang into his belt.

Inside, Quinn and Strong Heart were kneeling beside O'Brien, who lay on her back, her hands clutched over her stomach. Blood stained her shirt a dark purple. When she noticed Keech, she muttered, "You little fool."

Duck gazed around at the ruined cabin, half-stunned. "Keech, what did you do?"

Keech had never expected the Black Verse to explode the entire wall. He only wanted to stop Doyle, not hurt anyone else. O'Brien had just been too close. He didn't know how to explain everything he was feeling, so he said, "It wasn't my fault."

"Those words you spoke," Quinn murmured. "They sounded sick."

"You're meddling with things you should leave alone," Strong Heart scolded.

Keech stood his ground. "I did what I had to do. And it worked. I got the relic back."

O'Brien sat up, grimacing in pain. "You tapped the Prime, you fool! You've called the Reverend down upon us!"

Keech frowned. "What are you talking about?"

"Don't you realize? The dark magic acts like a beacon. I've managed to keep this place hid for a decade, but now we're wide open. They'll be comin'! You ain't got a lot of time. Get to yer horses and ride."

CHAPTER 21
OLD ENEMIES

Dismal winds sputtered down from the Peak, blowing a terrible chill into the devastated cabin. Achilles barked, as if warning the Lost Causes of danger.

Strong Heart put a hand on Quinn's shoulder. "We will saddle the horses." Then to Duck, "You and Keech help the Enforcer, then join us outside." Together with Quinn, Strong Heart darted out of the cabin, pausing to look down at the moaning, weakened Ranger. Her gaze brimmed with equal parts pity and disgust. She shook her head, then turned and sprinted to the barn.

Keech and Duck helped O'Brien to her feet. Still clutching her wounded gut, the woman said, "Take me to the trapdoor." They helped her stagger over to the hidden hole. After inspecting the lime-green weeds and grasses that grew inside, she threw the trapdoor back down. "The plants are still hearty. That's good. I'll need 'em soon."

She stepped back, wobbling on her own. "Go. Help with the horses. You tadpoles need to make haste and ride out of here."

"We ain't leaving you," Duck said.

When O'Brien saw that Keech and Duck weren't moving, she waved them toward the barn. "Just go! Find the House of the Rabbit. And whatever ya do, don't let Rose's monsters get the Key."

Keech turned, then stopped. "You haven't told us what it does."

O'Brien winced in pain. "Enoch's Key is the way into the Palace. It's the only way the Reverend's men can get inside to free him."

"Sounds like we'd be better off leaving it lost," Duck said.

"No. That won't put an end to Rose," O'Brien said. "If ya find the Key, you have to travel to the Palace. You have to use the artifacts to finish him."

"But *how?*" Duck asked.

O'Brien glanced around in desperation, as though searching for a last-minute answer. "I don't know, tadpole. The Reverend only allowed a handful of Enforcers to witness the ritual. I suspect you'll find the answers once ya get inside."

"We'll find a way," Duck said.

"I surely hope so. Just make sure ya put all five pieces of the amulet together. Without the amulet restored, y'all can say farewell to hope."

"We understand," Keech said, again remembering Pa Abner's final message: *Find the shards, Keech, and unite them.*

O'Brien put a hand on Duck's arm. "One last thing. Somethin' was *triggered* when Black Wood picked up the Key. A charge of energy opened up a door on the Peak's summit, a door that grants passage between the places of power. Rose led us through it in thirty-three, and we stepped out into Thunder Pass, the canyon that hides the Palace."

"Magic doorway, Thunder Pass. Got it," Keech said. "Once we have the Key, how do we get to the summit to find the door?"

"Take a path known as Old Beggar's Trail. You'll find it on the map I gave ya. But yer team will need to make haste; if memory serves, the door won't stay open for long."

The hairs on Keech's arms prickled. But it wasn't the woman's words that made him shudder; the air inside the cabin was *humming*. The noise was low at first, reminding Keech of the dull buzzing in Floodwood forest, and then it surged with fury. Achilles faced the hearth and bared his fangs with a low grumble.

Inside the fireplace, something slithered behind the rising gray smoke.

"There's something *moving* in there!" Duck said.

A wave of sick intensity poured out of the hearth. Keech recognized it and backed away. "*La Sombra*. He's here."

Shimmering darkness flowed out of the fire. The malignant pitch twisted into the smoky shape of a man standing upon the hearthstones.

"*Buenas noches*, O'Brien," *La Sombra* said.

Achilles released a barrage of barks and snarls that could have rivaled the fiercest wolf. Thick fur bristled along the dog's spine as he padded backward to stand beneath the table.

The dark thing tilted its head toward the dog, then back up to the Enforcer. "I knew you were close, Em. Clever to hide yourself on cursed ground. We would never think to search here."

"You kids get movin' *now*," O'Brien commanded.

The bedeviled shadow watched Keech and Duck. "Good to see you again, *niños*. There is no need to run. I mean you no harm." The semblance of a smile cracked the smoky face.

Duck took a step away, but Keech held up his hand, stopping her. Perhaps they didn't need to run, not yet. In November, Doyle had said Ignatio could *manipulate shadows* and *mold darkness*, but the Ranger had never said anything about Ignatio's being able to kill with his shadows.

Keech said to the apparition, "You can't hurt us, can you? You can drown our senses, but I think you're just a bunch of smoke. The *real* Ignatio is somewhere around the Peak, searching to find the Key. But *you* can't touch us, can you, *La Sombra*?"

The shape stepped off the hearthstone and drifted closer. The sulfurous fog moved with the creature, reaching into every corner of O'Brien's cabin. Dreary laughter crept from the empty face. "True. I cannot touch you myself. But I can send out a call." A smoldering finger pointed behind Keech.

Keech wheeled around to see a stooped figure standing in the rubble where O'Brien's door used to be. He recognized the floppy hat and the black muttonchop sideburns.

It was Black Charlie, the wagon train captain.

"'Ello, *mes amis*," the dark-eyed man said.

In the depleted light of O'Brien's fire, Keech could see the Frenchman's single fang jutting from his mouth. Except it looked different now. The fang had grown longer and thicker. Extending from each of his thumbs, the fellow had grown a pair of scythe-like claws, barbed and deadly.

La Sombra stepped back into the dwindling flames of the hearth. "I have delivered them into your arms, Weaver. *¡Mátalos!*"

Before Keech or Duck could react, O'Brien was on the move, dashing toward Black Charlie, one hand still pressed against her wounded belly. She smashed her fist into Black Charlie's face.

The captain snarled as he took the hit, but he didn't fall as he had when Quinn struck him at the wagons. He had transformed into something worse, had become more powerful.

"Let's help her!" Keech yelled to Duck.

"No!" Still raining blows down on Black Charlie, O'Brien turned her hectic eyes toward Keech. "Go with yer team! I'll hold back the Weaver." She pulled her hand out of a pocket—Keech hadn't even noticed her reaching into her coat—and flung a handful of dust into Black Charlie's dark eyes. As the powder touched his skin, the grains glowed red and popped with searing heat. He screamed in pain and clutched at his face.

"Go now!" O'Brien ordered.

Duck darted out of the cabin, hurdling over the debris. The Weaver screamed as the red-hot pepper danced across his face.

O'Brien called to Achilles. "Go, mutt! Lead 'em to the Peak!"

The dog barked twice, then hurried out after Duck.

Keech hesitated, hating to leave the Enforcer to fight alone. "We'll come back for you!"

Black Charlie raised one of his claws, but O'Brien seized his wrist and shoved the arm down. "No! Go to yer friends!" She thrust her other hand into another pocket.

Keech bounded out of the cabin. He emerged to stand under the silver moon, unfettered by the clouds. The light illuminated the frosted meadow, the squirming leech trees, the mammoth outline of Skeleton Peak above the lea.

The place in the snow where Doyle had landed was empty. The Ranger's moccasin prints scrambled off into the nearby forest, and there was no sign of Saint Peter. They would have to worry about Doyle later.

Back inside the cabin, Black Charlie squealed, "You will die for that, Enforcer!"

Keech scampered toward O'Brien's barn. Achilles and Duck were just a few paces ahead, sprinting toward it. Strong Heart and Quinn had opened the doors wide, and lantern light spilled out. They emerged with the gang's four horses, harnessed up and ready to ride. The Protector was already astride Flower Hunter, one hand gripping a lantern.

Quinn beckoned to Duck and Keech. "Run faster!"

Keech rushed to Hector's side and mounted up, just as Ignatio's billowing black cloud poured out of the wrecked front wall. The obsidian belt of smoke rolled toward the Lost Causes, sidewinding like a rattler over the snow. "It's *La Sombra*. He's coming!" Keech said.

Achilles barked shrilly, drawing their attention. He was standing a few yards ahead, waiting at the fringe of the mountain evergreens.

"Everyone, follow Achilles!" Quinn said, then shouted a command at Lightnin'. The gelding jumped into action, kicking up a scatter of wet hay and dirt.

As the riders galloped into the forest, Keech dared a look back. Under the silver light of the moon, he could still make out O'Brien's barn and the ravaged cabin. Two figures stood in the snow between the buildings—O'Brien and Black Charlie—ripping and tearing at each other. "Don't y'all stop!" Keech heard the woman cry out. "Whatever ya do, keep ridin'!"

The Lost Causes chased Achilles up the mountain. They followed the snowy path to a steep rise, the golden light of Strong Heart's lantern guiding their way, and soon reached a rocky ledge, peering down at O'Brien's meadow far below. The narrow trail continued to curl upward, ascending Skeleton Peak like a swirl of smoke from a candlestick. As they rode, occasional roars cracked across the night.

"What is that?" Duck asked.

"Sounds like thunder," Strong Heart said.

"Not thunder—*explosives*," Quinn replied. "Distant, though."

The jagged terrain of Skeleton Peak made Hector move with a steady bump, sparking fresh fire in Keech's arm with every step. He winced at the pain till he remembered that he'd taken the Fang of Barachiel from Doyle. Letting the others trail ahead, he pulled the Fang out of his belt and gazed at the bone dagger in the moonlight.

If the account of the desperado Big Ben Loving was true, Keech was holding the dagger that Abraham had taken to slay his son Isaac. But the angel Barachiel had seized the knife before Abraham could fulfill the sacrifice, blessing the dagger so that it could never spill blood.

Peeling off one glove, Keech held the Fang's edge over his naked palm, took a deep breath, and dragged the razor-sharp bone across his skin. Instead of slicing his flesh, the ancient blade sent a torrent of healing warmth through his body. Within seconds, the pain he'd been enduring on the long trail—the ache from the bandit's bullet wound, the cuts on his neck and face and ear from the Reverend's attacking crows—disappeared as if they had never happened.

Strong Heart's lantern light pointed back at him. "Keech, don't linger!"

Keech returned the Fang to his belt. "Be right there!" he answered, and goaded Hector to catch up.

High above their heads, the snow-covered point of Skeleton Peak resembled a white fist thrust at the moon. The group trudged on, growing colder and wearier by the second. Not far ahead, Achilles slipped around a small hook in the trail and disappeared. When the horses finally rounded the bend, Duck said, "Look!"

Achilles had stopped at the foot of a gaping hole. The cavity loomed in the side of the mountain, and it resembled an open mouth with a heavy crossbeam timber for the top row of teeth. Two other long, rectangular timbers stood vertically on the left and right of the hole, forming an upside-down U in the mountain.

"It's the mining entrance," Keech said. "Achilles led us right to it."

"*Shoh"-geh thali!*" Strong Heart said with a laugh, then apparently realized she needed to translate. "Good dog!"

Quinn patted Lightnin's neck. "The ponies won't be too keen about going in there."

"We'll have to lead them on foot," Strong Heart said, then held up the lantern. "We should have enough light to continue."

Keech sized up the dark entrance. "We need a plan before heading in. Let's check the map and see if we can figure out where the tunnel leads."

Dismounting, the Lost Causes huddled in a tight circle, putting their backs to the frigid wind that surged up the path. Duck fished O'Brien's map out of her coat.

Before she could unroll the paper, a long, unearthly growl rattled up the mountainside. Keech expected to see the tops of moonlit trees covered in snow, but instead he saw a brume of cascading darkness on the ridge.

"*La Sombra*," Quinn groaned. "Don't these monsters ever stop?"

Working quickly, Duck unfurled the map, and they studied the labyrinth of arrows and lines, all indicating tunnels that O'Brien had once traveled inside the Peak. "I think this is the adit," Duck said, pointing to a dark square scribbled toward the bottom of the map—a location that seemed to indicate the south approach into Skeleton Peak. She ran her finger up the paper. "The channel forks to the east and west inside the mountain."

An eerie howl cracked across the night.

Keech stared deep into the depths of the dark entrance, then shrugged. "Looks like the tunnel it is."

But when they led the horses toward the mine, a stooped figure stepped between the group and the yawning adit. He stood a few feet away, his right arm tied up in a sling, and his wild eyes reflecting the yellow glow of Strong Heart's lantern. The black shape of a tall stallion waited behind the figure, as silent as a breeze.

"You kids ain't going anywhere," Doyle said. "Not till you return my relics."

Despite the icy winds blowing down from the summit, Keech felt his neck burn hot at the sight of the embattled Ranger. "Out of our way, Doyle. We don't have time for your madness."

A bitter gust kicked up before the Enforcer as he held out his unwounded hand. "The relics. *Now*."

Strong Heart stepped in front of Keech. "Walk away, Red Jeffreys. The Lost Causes were charged to guard the Fang, not you." Keech hadn't noticed the girl retrieve a weapon—or place her lantern on the ground, for that matter—but she suddenly raised her longbow. A sleek arrow waited on the string.

Doyle's resentful expression softened as he faced her. "My quarrel is not with you, Strong Heart. Nor is it with the Osage. I don't desire more conflict. Only peace. Please step aside."

"*Hah*ⁿ*-kah-zhee*," the Protector said, not moving.

"I've caused you and your family enough suffering. I don't want to harm you." Another surge of wind played around the Enforcer's boots.

Duck and Quinn appeared like sentries on each side of Strong Heart. Cracking his knuckles, Quinn said, "Sorry, Ranger Doyle, but if you aim to hurt her, you're gonna have to go through us."

Doyle's face drooped in disappointment. "Very well, then."

Keech prepared for the impending scuffle. But then a gruff voice called out, "I have a solution for you all."

Black Charlie Gascon stood on the path behind them, his face ravaged with deep cuts. The battle with O'Brien had shredded the Frenchman's coat into strands that rippled in the night wind. A perverse grin stretched his fanged mouth.

"'Ow 'bout I solve this little *problème* and take the relics for myself?"

This morning our company awoke to the presence of a slender man in Ignatio's camp. He was clad in a heavy overcoat and black boots, and his knees were bowed from years on horseback. He lacked three fingers on his left hand, but despite these blemishes, no one could deny the grandeur of his features. His countenance boasted a graceful nose and a strong jaw. Beneath his thick brown mustache, the man's smile invited friendship and trust. I liked him at once.

The handsome stranger said nothing for a time, only watched as we arose. We felt uneasy, but Ignatio calmed us with words of assurance. The man who had infiltrated the camp was the one called Rose. The Reverend.

After all our party had stirred, our fair visitor stretched his intact hand over the fireless pit and proceeded to utter a strange and terrible series of words—I have heard no language in my travels like the phrase he spoke.

"Fm'latghor U'aahn," the man said.

I stake my honor and reputation upon this next statement:

FLAMES IGNITED UPON THE DEAD CINDERS.

The six of us attempted to ascertain the fellow's method for restoring the campfire, but we could not. The Reverend invited us to gather around the emboldened flames, and as we formed a circle around the heat, he spoke.

"Take heart, my friends," the Reverend said to us with a voice that soothed our very souls. "Though the world is cruel and full of death, I have discovered the way to eternal life. Come with me, and we shall seek salvation together."

—R.J.

CHAPTER 22
THE WEAVER'S CHILDREN

Strong Heart shifted her longbow and pointed the waiting arrow at Black Charlie. "Go back to the shadows!" she snapped.

Seeing the Frenchman before them, Keech felt a stab of guilt. Black Charlie's presence on the mountain surely meant that O'Brien had perished at the cabin. Keech had accidentally wounded her when he used the Black Verse. If she'd been commanding her full strength, she would have destroyed the monster with ease. Her death rested on Keech's shoulders.

Black Charlie dragged one heavy boot through the snow, clearly suffering wounds of his own. "Weavers are mighty difficult to kill, *comme vous le savez*," he said.

Strong Heart took a step closer, the tip of her arrow never wavering. She surprised everyone by speaking French to the Weaver. "*On vous arrêtera de toute façon.*"

Black Charlie's arrogant smirk faltered. "Such big talk for a child."

Stepping away from the adit, Doyle joined the Lost Causes on the path. "You should have scampered back to Lost Tucker, Charlie. Coming here will be your end."

Though he never took his eyes off Strong Heart, Black Charlie said to Doyle, "Maybe you 'ave what it takes, *ami*, maybe you don't."

"I feel good about my chances," Doyle said. Then to Keech: "We ain't done here, Mr. Blackwood. For now, get your team back."

"Ranger, we can take him," Quinn said, glaring at Black Charlie. "That pond scum ain't so tough."

The Weaver loosed a taunting laugh. "Don't be fooled by your lucky strike before, *Oscar*. I was not fully awake then." Lifting a hand, he wiggled the black barb on his thumb.

Quinn's face quivered with fury. "I told you never to call me that again."

Keech realized he could incapacitate the Frenchman without harming any of his trailmates. At O'Brien's cabin, he'd lashed out at Doyle without proper aim. But here in the open, Keech could attack Black Charlie without danger of a rebound.

Stepping ahead of Strong Heart, Keech pointed at Black Charlie.

The frigid world went blank in his mind as he thought back to an entry in Doyle's journal, a lesson dated *22 January 1833*. Behind him, Duck shouted, "No, Keech! Don't!" but he blocked out her warning. He visualized the incantation, then called back, "Quinn, riddle me this. The more you have of me, the less you see. What am I?"

"Keech, this ain't no time for riddles," Quinn said.

"*Darkness*," Keech answered, then he bellowed the curse of blindness from the Ranger's journal: "*N'ghaf-l'-yon'!*"

Once again the words tasted as bitter as ash on his tongue.

Then a staggering force exploded from Keech's fingers. Black Charlie tumbled back as if a lightning bolt had struck the center of his chest. He thrashed in the snow and swiped at his face. "My eyes!"

A feeling of fiery vengeance burst forth, and Keech cackled at the blinded Weaver.

Duck grabbed at Keech's arm. "Stop using the words!"

Keech yanked away from her hand only to feel Strong Heart seize his other wrist. The Protector wrenched his arm back, causing his boots to slip in the snow. He tumbled off his feet and landed painfully on his side. But even as he fell, he couldn't stop feeling an exalted kind of victory over Black Charlie, over the Reverend Rose, over everything that stood in his path. Sam had told him the Lost Causes wouldn't believe, and even now they doubted his newfound power. But the Black Verse could save them all!

He struggled back up to his feet, preparing to proclaim that he would finish Black Charlie for good—when he noticed something in Strong Heart's hand.

The Protector was gripping a bone dagger, a determined scowl on her face.

Keech patted his waist. The Fang of Barachiel was no longer tucked in his belt. Strong Heart had taken the blade while pulling his arm.

Feeling a nearly unbearable swell of rage, Keech labored to calm his mind and body. He brushed snow off his side and adjusted his bowler hat, taking large breaths to ebb the flow of his anger. "Strong Heart, there's no need to fret," he said. "If you give the Fang back, I'll prove to you I'm worthy." He held out his hand, palm up. "See? Steady as a rock. Just give me the Fang."

Strong Heart flinched away from his palm. "You have lost yourself, Keech. You have let the darkness take hold."

"She's right; you don't even recognize what's true anymore!" Duck shouted.

Quinn's voice joined the storm of castigations. "You have to stand down, Keech. You've gone too far this time. Tell him, Ranger Doyle. Tell him!"

Doyle said nothing, only stared at Keech with a stupor that suggested dismay. Holding his injured wrist, he stepped closer, examining Keech as a hunter might approach a trapped cougar.

Before Keech could speak again, Black Charlie cried out once more. "*Blackwood!*" The Frenchman's cursed eyes probed the trail, passing over Doyle, then the young riders, but never seeing them. "You will pay for what you've done! I don't need to see to destroy you all."

Staggering to one knee, Black Charlie stabbed his long black thumb-claw into the snow and dragged a gash across the snowy ground. To Keech's surprise, the motion left a foot-long stretch of darkness carved into the ground before him.

Quinn looked horrified. "Ranger, what's he doing?"

His eyes frenzied, Doyle shouted, "You kids need to get outta here!"

"What in blazes?" said Duck, pointing at the impossible gash in the ground.

Leaning closer to the curious gap, Black Charlie murmured, "Come out, *mes enfants*. Time to play!" His mouth continued to move, but the whipping gusts blowing down from Skeleton Peak snatched away the rest of his words. Whatever the fiend was chanting, the vile exhilaration on his face warned that danger was imminent.

Something moved inside the gaping slash in the snow.

"Back, kids!" Doyle shouted. "They're coming!"

A black substance erupted out of the small rift.

At first, Keech thought he saw coal smoke billow out, but then the dark seepage spilled onto the snow and skittered across the ground. Under the moon's pearly light and the glow of the lantern, the writhing mass crawled and twitched, and Keech saw a swarming clutter of black legs and hard-shell backs.

Spiders.

But not ordinary spiders. These critters were the size of healthy rats, and they scurried toward the group in a chattering, chomping frenzy.

"The Weaver's released his horde! Get back!" Doyle shrieked. He began spinning his good hand in quick circles. Wailing winds crashed into the oncoming swarm, plucked dozens of the spider-things from the ground, and hurled them into the night, but the majority of the mass kept scuttling out of the impossible gash. "I have no way to close the rip," Doyle said through gritted teeth. "I'll hold 'em off, but I don't know for how long. They'll just keep pouring through."

Snatching up the lantern, Quinn pulled at Lightnin's reins and shouted at the young riders. "Lost Causes, we best go!" He stamped through the snow toward the yawning adit.

"We can still help," Keech insisted.

Duck gritted her teeth. "I think you've done enough. Come on!"

Biting back an angry retort, Keech followed. "Fine."

Doyle continued to spin his hand, weaving magic, chanting under his breath. He guided the winds to create a barrier between the Lost Causes and the spider horde. But his cyclone sputtered over the ground, and many of the creatures wriggled past.

"They are coming for you, Jeffreys! They will eat you right up!" Black Charlie yelled, his blank stare turned to the sky.

Strong Heart stepped toward the mine, then hesitated. She studied the Fang of Barachiel in her hand.

His face rigid with concentration, Doyle ignored the Weaver's taunts. "I can't hold them back much longer," he muttered to Strong Heart. "You need to run."

Instead of fleeing, Strong Heart stabbed the Fang into Doyle's wounded arm. He cried out in surprise, but when she withdrew the magical dagger, his injured wrist locked back into place, as healthy as it had been before Keech's Black Verse attack.

Stepping back with the Fang, Strong Heart said, "Now you can stop the Weaver."

Doyle slipped his hand out of the sling and wiggled it with delight. He seemed at a loss for words, so he simply nodded his appreciation.

Opening her buffalo robe, Strong Heart tucked the Fang into a cinch around her buckskin dress. "Don't betray us again," she said. Then she grabbed Flower Hunter's reins and led the pony into the mine after Duck, Quinn, and Achilles.

Pulling Hector by the bridle, Keech quickened his pace to the adit. He didn't get two steps before he heard Doyle cry out.

Dozens of black spiders had skittered past the Ranger's whirlwinds and were swarming around the man's boots. A sea of black creatures washed over him, drowning him in twitching legs and chomping fangs. He fell back onto the snowy ground, buried beneath the horrible tide. The protective twisters swirling around the trail died. Without the winds to hold back the spiders, the creatures surged onward.

Holding his hands out in front of him, Black Charlie laughed with terrible glee. He strolled toward the mine shaft, his chin lifted high and his blind eyes pointed at the moon. His swarm of spidery creatures poured toward the young riders.

Doyle pushed himself up, somehow still alive. Joggling spiders from his arms, he cried out, "No!" then pointed at the mountain. He bellowed a string of dark words, uncanny tones like those held in the Black Verse, but a spell unlike any Keech had ever seen in the journal. The Ranger was aiming at a space just above Skeleton Peak's entrance.

Waves of power surged from Doyle's fingers. The spell's invisible force smashed into the snow-covered mountainside. The granite above the shaft ruptured.

The last thing Keech saw was Doyle lunge with a fierce grimace and lock his hands around Black Charlie's head. There was a loud snapping sound, and the blind Weaver tumbled to the ground, limp. All around them, the scrambling spiders melted into black goo in the snow.

Then a curtain of rock poured over the shaft's opening, cutting off any further glimpse of Doyle or the mountain trail, and leaving Keech in dismal darkness.

THE TWO HORSEMEN

The two horsemen reached a narrow gorge and reined their horses to a halt. Heavy snow fell upon the land, turning the ravine into a snaking band of solid white. Standing tall over the riders were two giant overhangs, a pair of leaning cliffs that rose against the gray sky. Clustered across the canyon floor were great, heaping piles of discarded timbers, the scraps of a devastated village, buried in tons of snow and stone.

The younger horseman squinted up at the lonely cliffs. "I reckon these are the Suffering Bluffs."

The older horseman dismounted, planting his boots in snow that reached almost up to his knees. "Seems a danged avalanche took out much of the foothill. Someone made it out, though." He pointed to a trail of boot prints leading out of the tumble toward the distant peak.

"I reckon we can follow those tracks to pass through. But we shouldn't dally."

In Hook's Fort, where the horsemen had stopped to make a few inquiries, a Texan named Hamilton had told them that a trio of children had set out for the Suffering Bluffs. *They got a decent head start on ya*, the fellow had cautioned.

"How close do you reckon we are?"

The older horseman shrugged. "Hard to say. You know Mr. Blackwood. He's a slippery little squirt. They could be fifty miles away by now."

The man's young companion lowered his head to the wind. "Hey, do you see that? There's a person up yonder at the bend of the gorge!"

Sure enough, the older rider spotted a person waiting at a shallow curve in the canyon—a tall figure standing in the flurries, watching them.

"Do you think he's the one that made them tracks?"

"Maybe."

The older horseman returned to his saddle and thumbed away the strap over his Colt revolver. Perhaps the Suffering Bluffs were playing tricks on them, but he would be ready nonetheless. "Be careful. I reckon a traveler wandering out here without a horse might be trouble."

As they approached through the frantic snow, the figure's appearance sharpened, and the older rider gasped because the figure resembled *Hamilton*, the Texan they had interrogated at Hook's Fort. "That ain't possible," he grunted.

The snowfall blurred the figure out of sight, and when the person reappeared, the horseman realized he'd been fooled, because he was looking at a much older man, just with a similar mustache and a mess of shaggy white hair.

"Old-timer?" The younger rider stepped his pony closer.

The traveler waved. "Why, hello there!"

"What are you doing out here without a horse?"

The fellow chortled. "Don't you worry about a codger like me. Just worry about your mission."

The younger rider jolted with surprise. "What do you know about our mission?"

The old man grinned. "I know yer huntin' for a team of kids, and one kid in particular. Keech Blackwood. Am I right?"

The two horsemen traded a baffled glance. The older rider said, "Mister, who are you? I *know* you from somewhere, don't I?"

The old man waved away the question. "I said don't concern yerself with me. If you want to find the boy, you'll do as I say right now. Time is of the essence." Frozen flurries thickened as the white-haired man lifted a frail hand and pointed up the gorge. "There's trouble at Skeleton Peak, and Keech Blackwood has found the darkness. Find the trail that leads to the pinnacle and meet him at the door. But hurry. The darkness grows."

"Mister, that don't make a lick of sense," the older horseman said.

The blizzard gusted again, scalding their eyes. When the curtain of white dissipated, the figure was gone. Not even a boot print remained.

The two horsemen sat on their horses in stunned silence.

"Where'd he go?" the younger asked.

"No idea, son." The image of the stranger's face drifted through the older rider's memory. Something about that fellow seemed so familiar. "Let's get a move on. From the sound of things, we have a peak to find, and we need to do it fast."

Clucking at their horses, the two horsemen forged on into the mountains and continued their pursuit of Keech Blackwood.

PART THREE

THE HOUSE OF THE RABBIT

MIGUEL AT THE PEAK

After nearly three grueling months in the saddle, Miguel and Coward at last emerged from a clutch of evergreens to find themselves staring at the mining camp. Miguel would have been happier to be done with such a miserable journey—Coward had promised they would rest here and find hot meals—were it not for the distressing vision that rose before them.

Coward reined in his pony. "Quite a sight, eh?"

Standing starkly before them, the snow-laden cliffs of their destination seemed to form a giant skull that peered over the Rockies and the landscape beyond. Lofty ridges along the mountain face formed the skull's brow, and massive black caves seemed to indicate eyes, a nose, and a cavernous mouth that led deep into the mountain.

"*¡Dios mío!*" Miguel murmured.

Coward opened his arms wide. "Welcome to Skeleton Peak."

"I ain't never seen anything like that," Miguel said.

A heavy morning mist crowned the stony Peak, casting long shadows across the ragged formations. At the mountain's base lay the camp, a modest village of canvas tents and log cabins. The headquarters was on the verge of being swallowed by the great skeleton's maw. A small cavalry of uniformed soldiers patrolled the camp's perimeter, some mounted on dark horses, some standing guard in hastily constructed watchtowers.

"Your boss, Ignatio," Miguel said. "He's there?"

Scorn seared Coward's face. "Nobody is my *boss*. However, Ignatio *is* the Reverend's lieutenant. I want you to deliver the Char Stone into his hands."

Miguel snarled. "I don't want nothing to do with that thing." Before he could speak his next sentence, a painful charge flashed across his forehead. Coward had touched the charred circle on his palm, activating the Devil's mark on Miguel's forehead. "I wasn't misbehavin'!"

Coward smirked. "Before you meet Ignatio, I need you in the right mind-set. I also need to return something to you." Reaching into his coat pocket, he withdrew Miguel's bone-handled knife, still tucked in its leather sheath. Coward cradled the blade in his palm. "This belongs to you. Take it."

Miguel reached for the blade but hesitated. "This is a trick."

Coward chuckled. "The Devil's mark forces you to obey. I have no reason to trick you, boy. Take the knife."

"I don't understand," Miguel said.

"All will become clear when the time is right. Now take it."

Miguel accepted the weapon. A gentle vibration caused the blade to tremor in his palm. He looked up, frowning, and saw that Coward's finger hovered over the mark on his palm.

Coward rasped, "When you meet Ignatio, behave with respect

and obedience. Mention nothing about the knife. Keep it tucked in your belt, and the blade should go unnoticed."

Miguel peered into Coward's eyes, but he could read no hint of the man's plan. *The prophecy is real, el diablito* had said, but he had spoken no more about the knife after the Char Stone incident a few nights ago. "Coward, what are you up to?"

Instead of answering, Coward touched the blackened brand on his palm again.

More shattering pain exploded through Miguel's mind. He felt his thoughts twist under the strain of invisible vises. He wanted to resist, but there was nothing he could do. Miguel's free will melted beneath the heat of the Devil's mark. "*Sí.* I'll do what you want."

"Good boy." Coward flicked his reins, and his pony started forward. "Now, let's go meet Ignatio."

One of the guards that patrolled the mining camp approached, musket raised. The soldier's tattered getup and pasty features told Miguel he was a thrall. A glance around the camp revealed that all the armed troops were also members of the raised dead. The musket-bearing thrall poked the tip of his weapon closer. "State yer purpose."

"Where is Ignatio?" Coward said. "He's expecting me."

Mention of the sorcerer's name made the creature drop his jaw. "You're the fella we've been awaitin'. The tiny man."

Coward glared at the creature. "What did you just call me?"

The soldier took a step back. "I didn't mean no disrespect! Master's in his headquarters, top of the rise." He pointed a bony finger up a dirt path lined with ragged tents.

"Stand aside," Coward commanded.

Dozens of imprisoned workers moved about the camp. Some pushed wheelbarrows full of rocks; others carried pickaxes. Many wore shackles and chains, and all of them were covered in grime and misery. A small outfit of cowhands heaved a pair of logs across the path, while a cluster of women wearing ratty dresses piled stones into a long wall. Even children had been put to work.

Miguel felt his stomach twist with horror. When he and the Lost Causes had investigated the town of Wisdom in eastern Kansas, they had discovered that Ignatio had loaded the town's entire population into wagons and sent them out west. The reason now stood before him. The townsfolk had been forced to labor inside Skeleton Peak. Coward had called the site a *mining camp*, meaning the gaping holes that made up the skull must lead to tunnels inside the mountain. From all appearances, nothing of worth seemed to be coming out of the shafts. Not one deposit of silver, not a single nugget of gold. Only the sounds of labor and despair.

An old man burdened with a bundle of heavy planks stumbled past. His boot slipped in the snow and he collapsed, scattering boards in every direction. Nearby, a tall woman threw down the burlap sack she'd been carrying and hurried over to the man. Her leather shoes were split, her trousers threadbare. Heavy dirt caked her dark skin, and streaks of sweat cut trails down her forehead and cheeks.

One of the thrall soldiers cracked a whip. "Back to work!"

"This man needs water," the woman hissed.

Before the creature's whip came down again, Coward shouted, "Hold, you worm. She's right. The workers need to drink."

The woman turned toward them, fury burning in her gaze as

she took in first Coward, then Miguel. Her ferocity almost made Miguel wilt.

"Fetch a water bucket," Coward told the thrall. "We didn't haul this entire town six hundred miles into the mountains just to watch them die of thirst. We need them to *dig*."

The thrall barked orders to a pair of children. The kids scurried to the buckets and set to work dipping wooden ladles. The woman offered the old man the first sip, then let the children with the ladles take their drinks before she accepted her own. She returned her gaze to Coward. "Thank you," she said, but anger continued to boil in her eyes.

Miguel followed Coward through the camp to the base of the skull-faced cliffside. A modest log cabin and a few attending shacks sat in the clearing, surrounded by tall brown boulders and clusters of blue spruce. Winds descended from the high crags, delivering a bitter bite with the morning freeze. Around the Peak, a murder of the Reverend's crows circled in the gloom. Scrappy yard dogs stalked around the clearing, growling as Coward and Miguel approached on their horses. A sentry of musket-bearing thralls stood around the perimeter of the cabin. When Coward approached, one of the dead men knocked on the front door.

With a vicious creak, the door opened. Out stepped a tall Spanish man with a hooked nose like a hawk. Dark tattoos covered nearly every inch of his skin, including his face and ears. He wore buckskin trousers, short brown boots, and a fur coat that partially revealed a tattooed bare chest. Shiny metal bracelets jangled on his arms, and a revolver hung low on his left hip.

Something about the *villano* seemed unnatural. When the answer dawned on Miguel, trepidation crept over his bones.

The fellow cast no shadow.

"Hello, Ignatio," said Coward.

Miguel shivered. This was the *bandido* who had cast the curse of darkness over Wisdom.

Ignatio grimaced at Coward, revealing a bright gold tooth. "*Hola*, Coward. You're late." The fellow's smooth Spanish accent would have been pleasing, even reminiscent of Miguel's own *padre*, were he not one of Rose's disciples. Ignatio's eyes shifted over to Miguel. "I see that you've brought a new member to our pack and that you have marked him."

Coward hopped off his mount. "He prefers to be called Cutter. He's got a miserable attitude, but the brand keeps him in step."

His voice gentle, Ignatio said, "Typical of you, Coward, to bring me a *dolor de cabeza* instead of a proper *discípulo*. Why must your every move be so incompetent?"

The castigation seemed to scald Coward like hot water.

Ignatio turned his attention back to Miguel. He lifted a hand to show his palm, which also carried Rose's charred magical brand. "As you can see, *mi amigo*, I, too, wear the Reverend's mark. You work for *me* now."

Ignatio turned back to Coward, raised one of his arms, and gestured to one of the dreadful tattoos on his wrist. The inky patterns on the man's flesh *shivered*, as if the swirls and lines were alive. "Our workers have been clearing the way inside the Peak, but the Reverend fears more interruptions. If this boy causes trouble, Coward, I will make you both pay." He smirked, as if pleased by the notion of their suffering. "Now, the Char Stone. Show me."

Coward reached into his saddlebag and removed the silver containment box.

Ignatio's gold tooth gleamed. "Bring it to me."

Coward held the vessel out to Miguel. "You heard the man."

Accepting the box, Miguel dismounted Chantico and stumbled through the snow. Ignatio accepted the container and lifted the lid, revealing the cursed relic.

The poisonous throbbing of the Char Stone seeped into the air. Miguel turned away at once, recalling how the Stone had *screeched* when the tip of his knife had stabbed into the vessel.

Ignatio snapped the box shut. His gaze fell on the silver lid. "What's this?" He slipped a tattooed thumb over the gash where Miguel's blade had landed.

"Nothing at all," Coward murmured. "The boy tripped on the trail, and the box struck a sharp rock. It's of no concern. The containment will still work till we reach the Reverend."

His thumb still rubbing over the puncture, Ignatio peered devilishly at Miguel. "You should be careful where you walk, *joven.*" He turned to address one of his thrall soldiers. "Place twenty armed men to guard the cabin. No one is to enter, save for myself or Coward."

"Yessir, Master." The rotting thrall saluted, then shambled off to gather more guards.

Ignatio faced Coward. "Now hand me the amulet shard Big Ben took from Black Wood's boy."

Coward yanked at the cord around his neck. The crescent moon of silver—the fragment that had belonged to Keech Blackwood's foster father, Abner Carson—winked in the shallow morning light. Miguel watched as Coward passed the silver to Ignatio. The sorcerer turned and slipped back into the cabin with the relics. A moment later, he returned empty-handed.

A thunderous explosion rumbled inside the Peak's mine shaft. To Miguel, it sounded as if a dragon had just roared with fury.

Ignatio's terrible, tattooed face brightened. "Each blast moves us closer to the House. Soon I will bring the relics to the Reverend, and we will finish what we started so long ago."

Coward sniffed the foggy air of the Peak. "You talk large, Ignatio, but while I've brought you the Char Stone, you still haven't found the Key *or* the Fang."

Ignatio leaned toward the small man's face. "The only reason you are here, Coward—the only reason the Reverend allows your presence in our sacred circle—is because your gifts have served a purpose. If they ever *stop* serving the Master, *te mato*. I will kill you. Now, silence!"

Coward grimaced, his jowls shaking, but said no more.

Lifting his chin high, Ignatio moved his lips in a whispered chant. Miguel thought he heard the words *La Sombra*, the Shadow, in the strange man's mutterings.

Across the camp, a low wind kicked up, and a charcoal cloud spilled out of the trees to the south. The darkness roiled across the ground like a snake, slithering toward Ignatio. A pack of thralls stopped what they were doing and bowed their heads in fear and submission as the shape glided over the ground between their boots. The cloud pooled around the sorcerer's ankles, and with a strange noise that reminded Miguel of a hissing cat, the chalky substance attached itself to the tattooed man's feet.

Ignatio's shadow had returned.

The sorcerer muttered to his dark form a moment longer, nodding with interest as if the newly returned shade had just spoken. Finally, he fixed on Coward. "*La Sombra* tells me Jeffreys and

O'Brien have been in league with the children. The Weaver Black Charlie is dead. Now the *mocosos* are on the move inside Skeleton Peak."

More indistinct words fell from Ignatio's clenched teeth, then he wrenched open his fur coat, exposing his tattooed chest to the morning chill. Again, Miguel looked on in horror as the *villano* dug his finger into the flesh of his own stomach. His ragged fingernail hooked under a murky tattoo, a smudge of ink in the shape of a person. Miguel saw other designs—a storm cloud, a tornado, a star-shaped spot that resembled a mangled snowflake.

Ignatio peeled the inky black symbol off his stomach. It made a snapping sound, as if a piece of black tar had been torn apart. He held the patch of ink before him, regarding it with something like pride, then tossed the shape into the snow.

The tattoo writhed where it had fallen. A hazy mist rose from the black tangle like smoke. The form billowed, rising up into the morning air. Miguel felt dizzy with fear as he watched the shadow assume the shape of a short figure, a goblin formed of pitch.

The newly formed wraith stretched and stood ready before its master. Ignatio gestured toward the cave opening that served as the mouth of Skeleton Peak. "The *mocosos* have entered the mountain from the south. Find them, but do not reveal yourself. Simply show me where they are."

Without further instruction, the shadow goblin hurried away, floating off into the mine.

Ignatio grimaced at Coward. "Sic your new *compañero* on the children. I would prefer them alive, but if he must kill them, so be it."

Miguel looked at Coward, silently pleading. But *el diablito* had his own schemes—something involving Miguel's Prime-infused blade—and he didn't seem to care about Miguel's suffering.

Coward opened his palm, revealing the Reverend's charred brand.

"No. Please," Miguel begged. "Don't make me hurt them."

Coward pressed down on the brand.

The pain that enveloped Miguel cascaded through every corner of his mind. He dropped to the snow before Ignatio's feet. The Devil's mark shot tendrils of power through his limbs, and he felt himself rise. Words tumbled from his dry lips. "*Sí*, Master. I'll do what you want."

"Good boy," Coward said. "Now get moving."

Miguel stalked into the shadows of Skeleton Peak to find the Lost Causes.

Pages ripped from the journal of Red Jeffreys, dated 17 July 1833:

This morning dawned harsh, with storms upon the plains. We continued our push on to the Rocky Mountains, our destination. We skirted Fort Calhoun, deciding on a northwestern direction toward the Platte River, at which point the winds turned exceedingly cruel. A large tornado formed to the west, and the Reverend commanded that we go to ground at the nearest settlement.

Whiskey Nelson returned from scouting with news of a large homestead nestled inside a nearby valley. We descended upon the ranch house to find it occupied by one person—a woman, no older than eighteen years of age. Having buried her kin a few weeks prior, she lives alone in the wilderness, tending seven head of cattle, three horses, and numerous acres.

The Reverend ordered that we seize the house. The young woman put up a furious fight, but Sagebrush and The Gambler subdued her and we took shelter in the homestead. Black Wood expressed trepidation that we should be so cruel to a mourning woman, but the Reverend commanded the woman be bound and one of her cows slaughtered for ration.

I find my soul dismayed over our actions but lack the courage to speak. The only one among us to offer kindness to our captive is Black Wood, who offered her food. He spoke his Osage name.

I overheard the whisper of her own name. Erin Hart.

Tomorrow we continue our journey to the Rockies, where the Enforcers will explore the mountain known as Skeleton Peak. I go in fear.

—R.J.

CHAPTER 23
THE UNDERGROUND CAMP

Torrents of thick dust billowed through the mine shaft, coating the young riders and their horses in grit. Strong Heart's pony snorted in displeasure, and Duck's horse, Irving, loosed a powerful sneeze. Mercifully, the stone ceiling had fractured only near the adit's collapsed entrance, and nowhere else along the passageway.

"Everybody all right?" asked Quinn. The heavy fog of dirt threatened to blow out Strong Heart's lantern, but the flame hung on, offering a dim light.

"I'm okay." Keech brushed a hand across his cheek and found a layer of sludge on the tips of his fingers.

"I am, too," Duck said, hacking out a dust-filled cough. "I think."

"I should have stayed with my uncle," Strong Heart moaned, smearing grime off her pony's face. Flower Hunter nudged her hand, clearly appreciative.

The tunnel walls that stretched ahead of them were smooth and straight, but every few yards, hulking timber beams had been set in place to support the stone ceiling. Keech marveled at the fact that teams of miners had dug such tunnels with nothing but pickaxes.

Duck yanked out O'Brien's hand-drawn picture of Skeleton Peak and examined the honeycomb of shafts intersecting and crossing, dropping straight down into pits and opening into vast chambers. After a moment, she tapped her finger on a dark line that traveled east and west. "This is the end of the shaft. It branches off at a T."

Without waiting for them, Achilles started down the path. His barks and yaps filled the tunnel with thunderous echoes.

"I reckon that means we follow again," Quinn said.

The Lost Causes proceeded up the tunnel in single file, with Keech and Hector bringing up the rear. A few yards ahead, Achilles moved in zigzagging steps, sometimes pausing to sniff around, sometimes stopping to lick the moist wall. The low ceiling of the tunnel made Keech feel trapped inside a cage. He worried that Hector might panic at the closed-in space because the stallion was so tall he had to dip his long neck just to walk under the crossbeams.

The gang led their horses in silence for a spell till Quinn peered back at Strong Heart. "You sure let that Weaver have a piece of your mind back there. You never told us you could speak French."

"My family worked with many French traders over the years," Strong Heart said. "I also speak Spanish. *Sólo un poco*, but enough to converse with travelers."

Quinn looked impressed. "That might come in handy if we face down *La Sombra* again." He then turned to Keech. "I reckon now would be a good time to chat about this House of the Rabbit. What we may have to face."

"We don't know enough to make a plan," Keech said.

"We know your father found it and fetched the Key. And we know he nicknamed it," Quinn went on. "There's gotta be a reason. Why 'the Rabbit'?"

"In Aesop's fables, the hare is fast," Duck offered. "I'd wager five dollars we'll have to move quick to get inside."

"Maybe so, but I ain't too sure," Quinn said. "On the trail out of Tennessee, Auntie Ruth used to tell me stories about animals. She used to say the rabbit was always stirrin' up trouble. I'd wager we'll need to solve some kind of puzzle to get in."

"Or maybe a riddle, like Oedipus and the Sphinx," Duck said.

"Eddy-who and the what?" Quinn asked.

Strong Heart peered back at Keech. "Black Wood would have understood that to many people, the rabbit is a trickster. Perhaps he named this place 'Rabbit' as a warning that we would face a problem that seems simple but contains many surprises."

Keech mulled over the clues that O'Brien had given them. The Enforcer had said that Black Wood had returned a *haunted man* from his first trip into the House in thirty-three. "I agree with Duck. I think we'll have to move fast. Pa Abner wanted me and Sam to remember the word *rabbit*, just like he wanted us to know the Osage word for *wolf*. And I'll tell you this, Sam was faster than lightning."

They continued through the tunnels, breaking for a short rest to drink from their waterskins. When the oil in their lantern threatened to run out and strand them in darkness, they pushed on, following Achilles till the hound halted and sat on his haunches. A dull glow flickered in the distance.

"Looks like torchlight," Quinn noted.

Duck peered ahead at the eerie glimmer. "I'd wager thralls are running patrols all up and down these shafts."

"We should send a scout ahead," Strong Heart said.

Eager to heal his wounded pride alone for a while, Keech held up the two amulet shards he'd lifted from Doyle. "I'll go. I'll take one of these in case I run into trouble." He handed the other fragment to Duck. "This belongs to you."

Duck's eyes flashed gratitude as she accepted her father's silver. "I thought I'd never see this again."

Securing the first shard to his palm, Keech hurried down the tunnel. Blurry yellow light kicked to life on his palm, and the magical silver grew cold. Thralls were nearby. He fisted his hand to hide the freezing light.

As Keech traveled deeper into the Peak, a strange rumbling grew louder. The sound reminded him of the summer fair at Big Timber, the clamor of chattering people and neighing livestock. He peeked around a corner. A narrow passage ran to the right and, to his surprise, one wall appeared to be missing, opening out into a vast chasm. A ramshackle railing had been erected along the open part of the passage. A thrall dressed in a soldier's uniform leaned against the balcony, peering over at the base of the cavern fifty feet below.

Shuffling closer, Keech slapped his palm against the back of the creature's neck. The soldier stiffened with a small cry and fell limp. The body pitched forward, but Keech grabbed the thrall's coat and hauled him backward, stretching the corpse on the ground. He considered hurrying back to report his attack, but curiosity gripped him. Keech sneaked back to peer over the railing.

The massive chamber that yawned before him was an imposing sight. It was a great cavern, roughly circular in shape and filled with cave formations. The walls of the cavern were pocked with tunnel openings that ran into the mountain. The area resembled a small city of tottering towers and clumsily erected scaffolding. Rope bridges had been strung between platforms and openings, some swaying dozens of yards above the stone floor. Smoke billowed from torches set into ugly iron sconces, sending fumes up through natural chimney openings along the ceiling. Skewers of roasting meat had been set over a few tall fires built around the chasm.

Grotesque thrall soldiers patrolled the camp with muskets and rusted army swords. At first, they appeared to be a pallid rabble, but a ferocious cruelty drove them to whip and curse their prisoners.

Hundreds of weary people worked at all levels of the cavern. They shuffled about with carts and pickaxes, hauling dirt or stone, and all of them appeared empty of morale and strength. These were the townsfolk who had been dragged from Wisdom. The poor souls had been put to work in the tunnels of Skeleton Peak to locate the House of the Rabbit.

As Keech watched, he saw two workers set a small wooden barrel inside a jagged stone crevasse. The workers placed four glass jars of clear liquid around the barrel—the same substance that Black Charlie had called nitro. Then the men poured a trail of black powder straight to a tall wooden barricade, where they tucked themselves low. A burly man bellowed, "Heads down! Heads down!"

As the man's gruff voice echoed through the cavern, every captive and guard stopped what they were doing and hunkered down, arms curled over their heads.

The burly man touched a torch to the end of the black powder. The fire flared at once, and the crackling spark raced forward, a serpent of flame running to the barrel. As soon as the spark kissed the wood, the jars of clear liquid ignited in a fierce explosion. The crash reverberated off the chamber walls, forcing Keech to throw his head down and cover his ears.

Dust and grime rained down on Keech's bowler hat. He spat a mouthful of grit and now understood. Ignatio was excavating the inside of Skeleton Peak, using explosives to crack the very mountain.

Keech examined the craggy dome of the chamber and wondered just how much blasting the cavern could handle before the weight of the Peak caved in and buried everything. He couldn't help recalling the face-off with Bad Whiskey in the Floodwood cave. A few gunshots and a ravaging giant bear had brought the entire ceiling down.

"Will you take a gander at that?" a voice whispered.

Keech wheeled around to find Quinn hunched beside him. A few steps farther back, Duck and Strong Heart stood with their ponies.

"What are y'all doing here?"

"When that explosion went off, the ceiling started rumbling," Quinn muttered. "Better we come to you instead of get buried alive."

Keech pointed down to the chamber. "Ignatio's got prisoners down there. I'm pretty sure they're the Wisdom captives."

"We have to help them," Quinn said.

Keech pointed across the gap to where a group of soldiers stood upon a high, dangling rope bridge. "We'll have a few obstacles, but Duck and I can dispatch them with the shards."

"They must have twenty muskets," Strong Heart said. "We would have to move silently, take them by surprise."

Duck frowned. "There'll be no surprises. Thralls sense the shards if we get too close."

Strong Heart pondered the information, then gestured back to their mounts. "The horses present a problem, too."

Keech grimaced at their situation. The shard proximity aside, they couldn't just stroll up and down the tunnels with four horses. "Someone'll need to stay behind and watch them." He offered Strong Heart a smile, hoping she might volunteer.

The girl returned Keech a gaze that suggested he jump in a lake. "Give me one of the amulets. I'll fight the dead men while *you* care for the horses."

"Hang on, those soldiers are on the move," Duck said. Still watching the rope bridge in the distance, she pulled out her spyglass again and peered through it. "Most of the thralls are heading away, but now I see a woman."

Keech peered across the gap again. He saw the woman as well, a dark-skinned figure with silver hair crossing the rickety bridge with careful steps. Behind her, a thrall soldier prodded her shoulders.

Looking alarmed, Quinn tapped Duck's shoulder. "Can I borrow that?" When she handed him the spyglass, he trained the scope on the rope bridge. No sooner did he peek through the lens than Quinn slapped a hand over his mouth, dropping the spyglass into the dirt. He slumped to his knees and a whimper escaped his trembling lips.

"Quinn, what is it?" asked Strong Heart.

"I can't believe it," Quinn said breathlessly. "I've found her. I've found my auntie Ruth!"

Pages ripped from the journal of Red Jeffreys, dated 16 August 1833—Skeleton Peak, Rocky Mountains:

Having penned no entries for nigh on four weeks, I return to this journal in secret, fearing the Reverend will see my lamentations, burn my pages, and have me beaten. Factions have formed in our party, and I suspect Whiskey Nelson, Ben Loving, and a few others are watching the rest of us.

Tomorrow marks one month since the Enforcers kidnapped Erin Hart from her home near the Platte. The Reverend teaches no compassion, only cruelty. For this reason, I cannot speak out about Miss Hart. I will lose everything if I speak—the wisdom of the Black Verse, the chance to claim eternal life. Many of my companions, particularly Black Wood and Em O'Brien, feel disheartened by her mistreatment. Miss Hart herself remains strong.

This evening, before the first signs of twilight fell upon the mountains, our company arrived at a ghastly summit known as Skeleton Peak. The cliffside resembles a great skull, a sight that made me shiver.

At dusk we approached the Peak's abandoned mining camp. I heard Black Wood whisper assurances to Miss Hart. I have witnessed something grow between the two. I have heard Black Wood swear an oath to Miss Hart that she would be freed before summer's end. But now that we have arrived at the place of power, I worry Black Wood will not be able to keep that promise.

Tomorrow at first light we will enter Skeleton Peak and search for the Key of Enoch. I fear for Miss Hart's safety and for the safety of my good companions.

—R.J.

CHAPTER 24
DESCENT TO THE FLOOR

They watched as Quinn's long-lost aunt stepped off the bridge and entered a tunnel across the distance, followed by the thrall guard. As Keech observed the woman, he couldn't help recalling the night Quinn had joined the Lost Causes, telling the young riders how he and Ruth had escaped from Tennessee. *Auntie Ruth is all I got*, he had said. *I've got to get her back, no matter what.* And now Ruth was here, within his reach.

"I need to go to her," Quinn said.

He hopped to his feet, but Keech held up his hands to stop him. "Hold on a second. We need to make a plan."

Quinn was already sidestepping around him. "Go ahead and make your plans. This time you'll do it without me."

Keech turned to appeal to Strong Heart and Duck. "You both know he shouldn't go alone," he muttered, but neither girl spoke up as Quinn rounded the nearest bend with Lightnin' in tow. "He's gonna get himself killed."

"No he won't," said Strong Heart. Swiveling, she started down the tunnel after Quinn, leading Flower Hunter behind her.

"Not you too!" Keech said, his stomach twisting.

Holding out O'Brien's map, Duck took off running after Strong Heart. "Wait! You need to know where to go!"

Keech followed Duck down the passage, leading Hector and Irving by their straps as he went. Strong Heart stopped momentarily in her own sprint to join Quinn.

"*O-nah-lee*," she said. "I don't want to lose him."

Duck spread O'Brien's map across the tunnel floor, and Strong Heart crouched to study it. "This big circle appears to be the open chamber." Duck pointed to a scatter of hectic lines radiating out from a thick ring. "Looks like Ruth is headed down this channel." She traced a penciled line that stopped at the right edge of the paper. "That path leads outside, likely to Ignatio's mining camp. If you headed down that passage, I'd wager you and Quinn will find her there."

Strong Heart peered closer at the map, then pointed to another line. "What does 'Old Beggar's Trail' mean?"

"That's the trail O'Brien told us to take after we fetch the Key," Duck answered. "Looks like the path Quinn's aunt is taking meets right up with Old Beggar's Trail."

"Once we've found Ruth, Quinn and I will take the horses to this trail. Meet us there." Seizing Irving's reins, Strong Heart prepared to scuttle off again, but Achilles suddenly pushed his furry nose into the center of their huddle and wagged his head. The pouch around his neck jangled.

Keech couldn't believe he'd forgotten. Milos Horner had left the Lost Causes two small tokens of his appreciation. "The last two shards!" Keech reached for the bag around Achilles's neck. The dog raised his head a little to give Keech room to open the purse.

Inside were two silver fragments.

They weren't crescent-shaped like Pa Abner's and Noah Embry's, and they didn't have a triangular shape like the one Doyle had used in Wisdom. These were more uneven, like two pieces of jagged flint, yet they both carried the same embellishments of arcane swirls and symbols. Leather cords had been threaded through holes in each silver piece.

Keech handed both shards to Strong Heart and she wrapped their cords around one hand, cinching the ancient metal to her palm. Before turning to leave, she drew the Fang of Barachiel from her robe and offered the dagger to Duck. "Red Jeffreys may still be out there, hunting for this. If so, he will come after me. The relic will be safer if you carry it."

"I'll take care of it," Duck said, and slid the Fang into her belt.

Keech tried to tuck down his humiliation, but he felt his face burn red anyway. He turned to pat Hector's muzzle. "I'll see you soon, Heck. Go with Strong Heart." He passed her the reins.

"Get the Key and find us," Strong Heart said.

"We'll see you soon," Duck said. "Now go help Quinn."

Strong Heart led their horses along the passage. Achilles trotted after them. Soon they disappeared into the darkness.

Keech and Duck scurried down a passage that sloped away from the vast cavern. As they made their way through a dark tunnel, Keech watched his amulet shard for signs of increasing light—the telltale sign of a thrall's presence—but both charms remained dormant.

Moments later the tunnel opened into a small, square room lit by suspended lanterns. Thick cedar planks reinforced the limestone walls, and dozens of crates were stacked to the ceiling, along with piles of horse bridles and ropes.

"A supply room," Duck murmured. Muddy pickaxes stood along the walls, many of their heads broken or bent from all the whittling at mountain stone. She examined one of the tools. "Ignatio sure is serious about digging out this mountain peak."

"They need the Key to free Rose as much as we do to stop him," Keech replied. He grabbed a coil of rope off the wall and hooked it over his shoulder. When Duck gave him a curious look, he said, "You never know when a rope might come in handy."

Suddenly a recognizable disquiet returned to Duck's eyes and she tossed away the tool she'd been studying. "I need to get something off my chest."

Keech felt his stomach twist. "My shard's starting to glow. Can it wait?"

"No it can't. You've been reckless, Keech. Your anger's been hurting folks."

"We don't have time for this."

"We're gonna *make* time. Ever since you took up reading Doyle's journal, you've been taking us down a dark path. It's time to end that. Give me the journal."

When she reached out, Keech swiveled away. "If you haven't noticed, we've been surviving. My magic's been keeping us alive."

"Your magic wounded O'Brien," Duck reminded him. "Likely got her killed. And you corrupted that poor buffalo in the hills. I know you used the Black Verse." She held her hand out again. "Give me the book, Keech. We'll burn it. Each time you've used it, you've brought Rose down upon our heads."

"The Black Verse only helped us. And it brought me Sam!"

"*Sam* led us into Black Charlie's trap. And when you used the Black Verse on Doyle, *La Sombra* found us right away."

Fiery tears bubbled up in Keech's eyes. He didn't know if they were tears of humiliation or anger. "My brother's *real*, Duck. He comes to me. He wants to help."

"Let's burn the journal right here." She pointed to a torch. "It's dangerous."

Keech scrambled backward. "No! The Black Verse is the only way I can call Sam!"

Duck lunged for Keech's coat, reaching for his pocket, but Keech jumped aside. As they stared each other down, he recalled the words he'd spoken to Duck after battling Big Ben in the bonfire. *I won't leave you alone. Not ever. We're partners.* But she wanted to take Sam, wanted to sever Keech's connection to his brother.

A sudden bolt of ice cascaded up Keech's arm as a pale soldier shambled into the room. The goon looked up in surprise.

"Who in tarnation are y'all?" the thrall asked. "Where's yer chains?"

Neither of them had the chance to answer; the dead man's face contorted in fear as the call of the amulet shards energized his flesh. "Yer those kids! The Lost Brawlers!"

The creature raised his musket, but Keech bounded across the room and slapped the thrall's cheek with the amulet shard. The resurrected man shrieked and collapsed as a swirling fog of black poured out of his nostrils.

Duck said, "Somebody heard that."

Keech pointed to the passage sloping away from the supply room. "Let's get back to work."

"This conversation ain't finished," Duck said.

They hurried down the passage and moments later stumbled upon a large hole in the floor. A rickety ladder stood inside the opening, and when Keech and Duck descended, they found them-selves in a narrow, torchlit shaft.

"We're near the main chamber," Duck whispered.

They pushed through the cramped shaft till the mammoth cavern leaped into view. The collective murmur of shouts and groans touched Keech's ears again. The heat from all the fires around the site boiled up into the honeycomb crevices. A narrow walkway appeared at the lip of the shaft, slanting down into the main chamber, like the gangplank of a ship.

"We have to go down *that*?" Duck asked.

"No choice, lest we want to find another way."

They slunk down the rickety platform. When they reached the bottom, Keech followed Duck onto the muddy chamber floor, and they took cover behind a rock pile. Throngs of workers and guards milled about the camp like a disturbed anthill, frantic with movement.

Duck said, "The entrance to the House has to be one of the tunnels around here."

Keech peeked around the rubble. "There's too much activ-ity, though. We'll get caught for sure if we poke around each tunnel."

"We could start there." Duck pointed to a deserted passage with an O-shaped mouth.

Before they could move, three figures emerged from the O-shaped tunnel. Keech felt the cold of the shard deepen on his palm. Two pistol-wielding thralls were marching on either side of a boy wearing dusty brown clothes. A blue bandana hung around the boy's neck, and a red sash girded his waist.

"It's Cut!" Keech said. Cutter was not only alive, he was also being escorted by a pair of armed guards. Their friend hadn't betrayed them after all.

Keech pulled back behind the rubble. "We'll have to move fast. Those thralls will feel the shards any second now. They'll probably kill Cutter to force us out. You take the closer guard; I'll finish the other. Then we'll collect Cut and scoot."

"How do you know we can trust him?" Duck asked.

"I know you've got your doubts, but Cutter's one of us."

Duck gripped her pulsing amulet shard. "I sure hope you're right."

Stepping out from the rock pile, Keech dashed toward the thralls. Their rotting faces flashed surprise. Tucking low, Keech slid past the first brute and slammed into the second, toppling the creature with a swift kick to the shinbone. He leaped on the dumbfounded soldier, slapping his shard against the thrall's forehead. The monster bellowed a final cursed breath, released a cloud of black smoke, and lay still. Beside him, Duck had finished off her target.

"Keech? Duck?" Cutter faced them in a kind of stupor, the shadows of the tunnel masking his features. "Where did *y'all* come from?"

"We've come to rescue you!" Duck said.

But Cutter's shocked expression was short-lived. He grabbed at his forehead with quivering hands and cried out. When he lowered his fingers, Keech saw the spiral-like brand of the Reverend Rose charred into the boy's flesh.

"*The Devil's mark*," Keech moaned.

Cutter pulled his bone-handled knife. "Dead or alive, Blackwood, you're comin' with me. Master's orders." He charged at Keech.

CHAPTER 25
LITTLE BROTHER

Cutter barreled into Keech, lifting him off his feet and tackling him to the rugged floor. The impact drove the air out of Keech's lungs, and the back of his head smacked against a rock, blurring his vision. Before he could shake his head clear, Cutter drove a fist into his jaw. The iron taste of blood filled Keech's mouth.

"Cutter, stop!" Duck screamed.

Keech tried to say something, anything, that would stop Cutter's attack, but more blows crashed down on his shoulders and chest, driving away any hope of connection.

Cutter pressed his blade to Keech's neck. "Don't you move." He turned and sneered at Duck, "And you stop right there!"

Duck slid to a halt. "Cut, it's *us*, your friends."

Cutter wagged his head in confusion and pain. "If you don't cooperate, you're dead meat, is what you are. Now drop the shard."

Reeling and dizzy, Keech reached for Cutter's wrist. Before he could wrench the blade away, the other boy drove a heavy fist into his jaw. The world went fuzzy again.

Charging up, Duck kicked out with a loud cry, and her boot walloped Cutter in the side. The boy tumbled back across the cavern floor.

In his dazed condition, Keech wasn't sure he'd seen things properly. Duck was half Cutter's size, yet she had booted him clear off Keech.

Duck held out her hand. "Come on." As she pulled Keech to his feet, she pointed to the coil of rope he'd taken from the supply room. "We'll tie him up and haul him out."

Cutter reached for his dropped blade. "Master said he prefers you alive, but if you fought back, he'd accept you dead. He can always raise you as thralls to get what he wants."

Shouts of alarm spread across the cavern. Uniformed thralls abandoned their posts to scurry over. Most of the approaching guards carried clubs and knives, but a few dead men tarried on the chamber platforms and leveled muskets at them. The captive townsfolk stopped swinging their pickaxes and dropped the stones they'd been hauling to stand in place and stare. For a split second, the underground work site in Skeleton Peak fell still and quiet.

Then a hefty soldier shouted from one of the towers, "Don't move!" He pulled the trigger on his musket, and a plume of smoke erupted from the barrel. But the thrall had aimed too high, and the lead ball smashed into the stone above Keech's head.

Pandemonium broke loose as thralls stampeded the chamber, scampering toward Keech and Duck. The people of Wisdom cried out in fear and scuttled for cover. Thralls screamed instructions to surrender as Cutter jumped to his feet, his blade flashing.

Duck yanked at Keech's sleeve. "We gotta go!" They pedaled

away from Cutter and the advancing thralls. A soldier vaulted at them, swinging a dull pickax. Duck sidestepped the attack and touched her shard to the man's bare hand. The thrall froze in surprise, muttered something unintelligible, then collapsed.

The thralls stopped dead in their tracks.

"What happened to 'im?" one soldier grunted.

"She kilt him! I mean, kilt him for real!"

A third bewildered voice muttered, "That shiny piece of metal done it!"

Keech's dizziness settled enough for his vision to clear. He hurtled toward a dumbstruck thrall and slapped the creature with his charm. Yelping in surprise, the soldier stiffened at the silver's touch and keeled over.

"Don't let them touch your skin!" Cutter shouted at the thralls. He dashed toward Keech again, his knife slashing at the air. "Just keep them penned in. I'll handle the rest."

Keech swiveled and shoved one of the advancing thralls, forcing the fiend into Cutter's path. The soldier flailed and gripped Cutter's shoulders, spoiling his attack.

A hail of musket fire filled the cavern as the soldiers perched on the towers and platforms squeezed off. Lead balls thumped around Keech's feet. Duck reached to still another thrall, but the brute flinched back, avoiding the graze of the silver. "Don't come any closer!" she yelled, waving her arm back and forth in front of her, the amulet shard beaming like electricity itself. The crowd of soldiers seemed to wilt away, clearing her a broad path.

Keech joined her. "We can lose them in the tunnels."

"Blackwood!" Cutter had pushed aside the bumbling soldier and was once again driving toward him. Witnessing such murderous fury in Cut's eyes tore at Keech's heart. Despite their occasional differences, they had been true partners. They had shared stories over campfire meals, had giggled together at John Wesley's dumb jokes, had taken down Bad Whiskey Nelson as a team in Bone Ridge Cemetery. That Cutter might be lost forever to the Reverend was too much to bear.

But Keech knew the solution.

The Fang of Barachiel.

Back in Bonfire Crossing, Keech had accidentally stabbed the Chamelia with the relic, only to discover that the dagger had the power to heal the Devil's mark. One poke from Abraham's dagger would release Cutter from his branded torment.

Keech whispered to Duck, "You've got the Fang. When I draw Cut in close, use it to free him." He raised his fists, waiting for Cutter.

"Got it," Duck said, still waving her shard back and forth at the soldiers.

Snarling, Cutter twirled his own blade through his fingers—the usual display of arrogance, but this time it filled Keech with dread. "You should have yielded, Lost Cause."

Keech didn't dare glance at Duck, for fear of giving away his plan. "C'mon, Cut. Let's do this." He set his feet wide in the soil.

Suddenly a voice called out, "*Stop fighting, Keech. It's time to surrender.*"

From the same O-shaped tunnel from which Cutter had emerged walked a small figure, his arms outstretched. As he cleared the shadows of the tunnel and entered the light of the cavern, Keech staggered back a step, bumping into Duck.

It was his little brother.

Stunned, Keech dropped his arms. "Sam?"

Duck's face screwed up in confusion as the figure shuffled closer. "Wait—*this* is Sam?"

Keech gasped. "You can see him?"

Duck pointed. "I can see *him*. But I thought he was just a vision."

Sam appeared exactly as he had on the Santa Fe Trail, on the night he came rapping at the door of the abandoned shack. His boots were still muddy, the knees of his pants still ripped, his skin still crusted with frost. Even the lacebark limb was still in his hand, the one he and Keech had used a lifetime ago for a game of Grab the Musket.

The figure strolled toward them, stabbing the lacebark limb into his path like a cane. "You must be Duck Embry. Boy howdy, you sure messed up Big Ben Loving at Bonfire Crossing. No one should *ever* raise your bristles." The boy reached to shake her hand, but she jerked away from the fingers as if they were covered in bees.

Keech remembered the first time he'd shaken Sam's hand. Pa Abner introduced the blond-headed kid on the front porch of the farmhouse, which hadn't even been named the Home for Lost Causes yet. Keech was six years old, and Sam was five. Pa said, *This is Sam, and he don't have any family. But now he's gonna be your little brother and live with us. Show him your bedroom, introduce him to Granny, then explain all the chores.* Pa Abner had then tousled little Sam's hair. *I think you're gonna like it here, little Rabbit.*

"Sam, I don't understand," Keech muttered. "What are you doing here?"

Before he could receive the answer, Cutter slammed into

Duck's side, knocking her down to the rock-strewn floor. He pressed a boot down on Duck's wrist, and her fingers opened, releasing the Fang.

Keech moved to help her, but a band of soldiers hurried over to seize him. Bellowing in defiance, he swung his fist, grazing his shard over one greasy fellow's cheek. The soldier shrieked, dropped to the ground, and tumbled back to his true death. The other goons shoved Keech over and subdued the hand wielding the charm. "Let me go!" he screeched, but the monsters held him fast.

Keech couldn't believe they had been taken prisoner again, but their predicament felt secondary to the colossal question darkening his mind. "Sam, why are you helping them?"

Sam clicked his tongue three times in a scolding manner. "Shame on ya, Big Bad Wolf. You haven't been true to your own whisper." When he spoke, a blackness deeper than the darkest midnight stained the whites of his eyes. A child-like laugh tumbled from his lips, permeating the hollows of Skeleton Peak like a grim lullaby. "Everything you touch turns to ash. Your friends, your family, your precious *Lost Causes*."

Keech's lips trembled. "I don't understand."

"I think you do," Sam said.

Behind the rabble of thralls, a low-pitched voice murmured a command to step aside, and the soldiers obeyed at once, opening their ranks as if a prince had just arrived.

A tall man stepped into the circle, garbed in a heavy fur coat and heavily tattooed—and Keech knew at once he was looking at Ignatio, the *real* Ignatio, not the nightmarish shadow version of him. The fellow was a decade older than the man Keech had seen in the vision of forty-five, but he was clearly the same wicked disciple of Rose. When the man smiled at Keech and Duck, a gold tooth flashed in his mouth.

Close on Ignatio's heels was a short fellow wearing a frock coat and a curved sword on his hip. The man fluttered a fiendish hand. "Hello, children. I had hoped never to see you again, but you Lost Causes are stubborn little squirts."

"Coward," Duck hissed.

Keech watched in lingering disbelief as Sam sauntered over to Ignatio. The boy tilted his head at Keech, and this time when he spoke, the words ushered forth in bizarre unison with the tattooed fiend. The two formed an unholy harmony, as if their lips and tongues were connected, a frightening layer of two voices. "Did you truly believe your dead brother had come back to offer you advice? Did you think his *fantasma* had returned to save you?"

Opening his fur coat, Ignatio held his arms out to Sam like a father greeting his child. The boy's body *vibrated*, shimmering into a blur. Sam's laughter faded into a dull hum, and hazy darkness poured out of him. His form collapsed into a ribbon of quivering blackness. Ignatio opened his mouth and inhaled. The dark energy flowed into his mouth and seeped into the inked pores of his skin, till every aspect of what had just been Sam was consumed like water absorbed by a sponge.

Though the black tattoos crowded Ignatio's body, Keech had noticed a vacant spot on the man's left chest muscle, a flesh-colored oval void. But after Ignatio swallowed the dark substance that had been Sam, a blemish like a bruise formed in the empty space, then solidified into a fresh tattoo, a mark that resembled a large eye. Small lines extended from the eye, like the rays of the sun.

As his vision blurred with fresh tears, Keech felt the betrayal stabbing at his center, but he couldn't figure out exactly who had been disloyal. After all, Sam had never lied, because Sam was gone, buried in the ashes of the Home for Lost Causes.

Keech realized who the true traitor was. Himself. *He* had opened the door to Ignatio. The powerful lure of the Black Verse had been too tempting, too exquisite. Duck and Quinn and Strong Heart had warned him, but he'd been unwilling to listen. He had fallen right into Ignatio's trap.

Tears boiling down his face, Keech turned to his defeated trailmate. "I'm so sorry, Duck. Please forgive me. For everything. I've just led us to our doom."

Pages ripped from the journal of Red Jeffreys, dated 17 August 1833—Skeleton Peak, Rocky Mountains:

At dawn we entered the Peak.

I was standing near Black Wood and Erin Hart when the Reverend ordered the woman be killed. A scuffle broke out between Black Wood and Whiskey Nelson, but Ignatio subdued the skirmish by reciting an invocation. The Reverend commanded Black Wood to prove his loyalty by eliminating Miss Hart. I was ordered to stay behind and ensure the task was done.

Guided by the ancient scroll, the Reverend commenced his search for the Key of Enoch. Though the Master speaks little about the Key and the bone dagger, there is no doubt that both artifacts are vital in our search for eternal life. We have heard hushed conversations between Ignatio and the Reverend pertaining to a third relic—an object known as the Char Stone—but apparently this object is impossible to retrieve without the Key.

After all the other members of our party had disappeared into the mountain, Black Wood beseeched me to carry on into the tunnels while he dispatched Miss Hart. But I knew he would not take her life. Before entering the passages, I glanced back and saw Black Wood cutting Miss Hart's bindings to free her.

And now tonight I lie in my tent beneath this terrible mountain, and my friend Black Wood has not yet returned from the tunnels. Most of us have come back, all empty-handed. Whiskey Nelson stumbled out at twilight to give news that Sagebrush and the Gambler did not survive the day's excursion. My fear is that Black Wood has suffered a similar fate.

I hope to see my friend walk out of this mountain—just as I hope that Erin Hart finds her way back home.

—R.J.

CHAPTER 26

BLACK WOOD'S CLUE

Decaying thralls gripped Keech from behind and yanked his arms back. They tied his hands with painful ropes. Their heavy clutches lingered on his shoulders, holding him in place.

Duck remained silent as the soldiers bound her. At first, Keech thought she might be in shock, given the way she seemed to be staring vacantly at Ignatio's chest, but then he realized she was studying the new tattoo, the one that had just appeared on Ignatio's flesh. The symbol that the Sam-thing had become.

"That tattoo," Duck said, using her chin to gesture at the mark. "I know it from my studies. It's the Eye of Horus."

Ignatio smiled as if impressed. "Not quite, though I do see the resemblance. This is the symbol of a memory demon that allows me to see deep inside a person so I can read certain *histories*." He pointed at Keech. "When Mr. Blackwood opened himself to the Prime, I read his deepest desire—the return of his orphan brother. After that, I had little trouble goading him."

Horror spread over Duck's face. "All those tattoos are *demons?*"

Delighted, Ignatio stared down at the charcoal ink on the tops of his hands. "Think of them as pets. Through the Prime, I keep them leashed. When I need them to act, I release them on the world. Darkness, weather, fury, inferno—whatever I command, they fulfill."

"Hogwash," Duck said. "You're no master, but a servant."

"Such beautiful fire in your soul!" Ignatio said. "But I have no time for you." He turned to Cutter. "Fetch the Reverend's Fang, Miguel. The dirt is no place for a holy relic."

Cutter bent toward the Fang, but Coward blocked him. "No. Let me. We don't want any accidents." He shuffled to the Fang and scooped it up with relish. After stowing the artifact in a pocket, Coward untied the cord that bound the glowing amulet shard to Duck's palm and snatched away the fragment.

Anger supplanted the despair in Keech's soul. "Mark my words, Coward, justice is coming for you. You'll pay for branding Cutter."

A nervous chortle escaped Coward's mouth as he stepped over to Keech. "Maybe, Mr. Blackwood. But not today." He removed Keech's amulet shard and turned to address Ignatio. "I'll return these to your cabin, place them with the Char Stone."

"Not till we've hunted down the other two interlopers," Ignatio replied. "Are they still hidden from that nose of yours?"

Coward sniffed the cavern air. "Their concealment spell is impressive. They're somewhere in the Peak, but I can't seem to lock on to them."

"Then you'll stay by my side," Ignatio said. "You faced the

children in Wisdom, and they overwhelmed you. I'd hate for you to lose my relics."

Coward's face crinkled with dark emotion. "Don't talk down to me like I'm some runt, Ignatio. I delivered the Char Stone. What have *you* done but blast away at a bunch of rock?"

The tattoos on Ignatio's chest seemed to pulsate and quiver. "Watch your tongue."

Coward appeared to be on the verge of exploding with rage.

Ignatio turned back to regard Keech and Duck. "Right now we need to decide what to do with these two." To his resurrected soldiers, he called out, "What do you think, *amigos*? Should we kill the children or let them live?"

A kind of rhapsody seemed to invigorate the horde. "*The Perils!*" they bellowed. Their unified voices rumbled like another detonation across the cavern. "*Feed the Perils!*"

"The Perils?" Ignatio looked surprised at the proposition, but Keech knew better. The sorcerer was toying with them as a bored tomcat might play with a field mouse. "Surely you don't want me to send these children into the deadly Perils." Jabbing a tattooed finger at Keech, he said, "Perhaps I'll send this one. After all, he has Black Wood's blood coursing through his veins. He might be able to bring me the Key."

"The Perils are impossible," Coward said. "You'll get the boy killed."

Swiveling on his bootheel, Ignatio seized Coward by the throat. Again, the symbols on his body squirmed, as if the demons captured in the man's flesh were begging to be released. "This *boy* destroyed a Thrall Master and the Reverend's most powerful Harvester. If anyone can defeat the Perils, *he* can." Coward wriggled under the sorcerer's grasp till Ignatio released his neck. "If he dies like all the others, we will send the girl. And if *she* dies, no loss. We'll just continue to dig."

Duck shoved against the thralls holding her. "We'll never help you find the Key!"

Ignoring her shouts, Ignatio turned to face the open cavern and yelled at the captives, "Back to work!"

Work in the underground camp resumed, bristling with commotion.

Coward led the march to the O-shaped tunnel from which Cutter had emerged. The grunting soldiers pushed Keech and Duck into the passage. They both searched left and right for any path to escape, any means to distract their captors, but no opportunity presented itself.

After a brief journey down the passage, the rabble entered a small, square chamber, a frigid pocket of the inner mountain. Sputtering torches had been jabbed into sconces on the chamber walls, and the flamelight cast eerie saffron hues on the limestone. On the opposite side of the chamber, another tunnel gaped open. Coward ordered the guards to untie Keech and Duck. The thralls set to work unknotting the ropes, then shoved them onto their knees in front of the second mysterious passage.

Rubbing his wrists, Keech peered at the cryptic shaft and shivered. He didn't like the look of the jagged opening. "What is this place?"

Before Coward could answer, Ignatio appeared at the mouth of the tunnel and said, "This chamber is the end of the trail. Skeleton Peak is a maze of channels and shafts. Some existed well before any miner started digging. But *this* tunnel is different from the rest. We call it 'the Perils' because nobody ever comes out alive."

"That's why you've been blasting," Duck guessed. "You've been trying to dig around this one passage. You think you can bypass it."

"You're a smart one, *niña*." Ignatio reached into his fur coat and drew out a tied-up roll of cracked brown leather, a cylinder a bit shorter than Keech's forearm. "This can help explain things." Loosening the twine around the leather, Ignatio unfurled the roll, revealing an archaic text—likely the ancient scroll mentioned in Doyle's writings. Yellowed pieces of the paper chipped away and drifted to the chamber floor as Ignatio spread out the parchment. He held it to the flamelight, showing the collection of symbols covering the cracked paper. "You see, a prophet named Enoch once kept a record of his travels. He described many things. Objects he had placed all over the Earth. Sacred things. *Cursed* things. This scroll is part of that record."

Duck said, "You don't believe that scroll belonged to *the* Enoch, do ya? The fella from the Bible who God spared from death?"

Ignatio peered at the ancient text with something like amusement. "Believe what you like about Enoch's fate. My concern is what he wrote about this place."

Fascinated, Keech asked, "Enoch came to Skeleton Peak?"

"Once upon a time, he traveled across the entire face of the Earth," Ignatio said. "Enoch described many places of power. Even a few in the Americas, including the Palace of the Thunders and *this* place, the mountain in which we stand."

"If the scroll is so old, how do you know what it says?" asked Duck.

The sorcerer sneered. "During our travels together, the Reverend learned many languages. He translated much of the scroll, and I assisted with the rest." He turned his gaze down to the ancient lines. "According to these writings, there is but *one* way to enter Enoch's chamber, but the way is not specific." He shrugged. "I do not know if the Perils lead to the place of power. No one saw the path that Black Wood took when he found the Key. All we know is that those who go down *this* tunnel never come back."

"Just because the tunnel is dangerous doesn't mean it's the right path," Keech said.

Ignatio chuckled. "But I am sending you down it nonetheless."

A tremendous boom echoed through the chamber—more explosive digging. Everyone in the room crouched as the ceiling vibrated, raining grime.

When the dust settled, Ignatio swiped the dirt off the ancient scroll. "That is why we continue to dig, to skirt the deadly passage. But if Black Wood's son"—he pointed at Keech—"can unlock the way for us today, even better."

Keech struggled against the guards. "I'll never help you. Not in a thousand years."

"I believe you will. Because if you don't, I will kill her," Ignatio said, and upon his last two words, all the thralls in the chamber drew their pistols.

Duck's small frame rattled with laughter.

Ignatio blinked. "You find this amusing?"

Duck's guffawing turned her face red. Finally, she composed herself enough to say, "It's just that we've been here before, haven't we, Keech?"

"We surely have." But Keech still felt confused. "Have we?"

Ignatio's thralls scuttled back in fear as Duck swiped a fresh tear from her cheek. "Bad Whiskey held us prisoner just like this in Bone Ridge. Even held his rotten Dragoon on me while he forced you to hunt down the Char Stone."

"What is your point?" Ignatio growled.

Duck laughed a second longer, then abruptly stopped. "My *point*, you mangy cur, is that our posse sent Bad Whiskey Nelson back to the dirt. And we're gonna do the same to you."

Ignatio stepped closer, seemingly undaunted, gently re-rolling Enoch's scroll into its brown covering as he moved. He tucked the parchment back into his coat. "I do love the spirit of a child." Dropping a hand to his stomach, the sorcerer scratched at the flesh beside his belly button. One of the tattoos—a symbol that resembled a muskrat—peeled away under his nail. Soon Ignatio was holding a wriggling smudge of black. He held the living tattoo inches from Duck's face. She tried to appear calm at the sight, but when the ghastly patch *squealed* at her, she wrenched her face away.

"Do you know what this is?" Ignatio asked.

"Your pet leech?"

"Let's just say this will never allow you to sleep without nightmares again."

A giggle chirped out of Duck's throat. "That don't scare me. I already *got* nightmares."

"Not like this." The horrible smudge nearly touched her cheek.

"Stop it!" Keech shouted.

"But you said you would never help. *Someone* has to suffer, ¿no? Maybe you prefer more curses upon Miguel." Ignatio swiveled and dangled the shrieking tattoo near Cutter, who didn't budge, didn't even blink, but nonetheless fear leaped onto the boy's face.

"No harm will come to your friends if you find the House," Ignatio said to Keech. "If not, the girl goes in next, then Miguel, then your two other *compañeros* running around the Peak."

Keech's mind staggered through various plans, but nothing save a complete miracle rescue by Quinn and Strong Heart could hope to deliver them from Ignatio.

To calm his mind and body, Keech closed his eyes. He could hear the hissing breaths of the resurrected thralls and the agitated inhalations of Duck. He knew that the place of power had been called the *House of the Rabbit* for a reason. There had to be some clue connected to the name of the place. Keech recalled O'Brien's vision, how the Enforcers had discussed their plans to move and conceal the Char Stone and the Fang of Barachiel. He saw his father and mother, and himself as a child, strolling through the mountain meadow, a glade that would soon fall prey to Ignatio's curse. He witnessed the great battle with Rose's killers, saw Ignatio's curse inflicted upon Isaiah Raines. He saw Pa Abner attack his mother and father in the barn.

Keech heard his father cry out a single word as his mother took her last breath. He had called her *Mah-shchee^n-kah*. A nickname that meant "rabbit."

The missing pages from Doyle's journal had spoken of the Reverend Rose's taking Erin prisoner and hauling her to Skeleton Peak. Keech's father had fallen in love with her and cut her free, so that she could return to her home on the Plains.

But Erin had *not* returned to her homestead. She had remained near Skeleton Peak and built their cabin while she waited for Black Wood's return.

Just as Sam had been Keech's best friend and partner, Erin had been Black Wood's teammate. They had been united in everything.

Work as two, succeed as one, Keech thought, recalling the words of Hamilton, the lanky Texan at Hook's Fort. The words had first come from Pa Abner, but strangely, the Texan had known them.

A furious grunt caught his attention, and Keech opened his eyes. Nearby, Duck was struggling against her captors, her face a grimace of rage. She would never give up, never stop resisting. He knew he would rather die than abandon her.

And suddenly Keech understood.

His father had not entered the place of power alone. Black Wood had called it the House of the Rabbit because he'd discovered the way inside *with his Rabbit*.

Work as two, succeed as one.

Erin had gone inside with him.

CHAPTER 27
INTO THE PERILS

Keech adjusted the rope still wrapped around his shoulder, then stepped toward the tunnel and peered inside, buying a little time to form some sort of strategy. Beyond the chamber's torchlight, he couldn't see anything but a perfect oval of darkness. Perhaps the shaft led to nothing but death, but deep in his gut he knew he was standing at the entrance to the House.

He figured his mother had played a crucial role alongside his father in obtaining the Key, which meant if he was going to survive the Perils, he would need a partner.

Plucking a torch from the wall, Keech turned back to the group. "What will I find when I start down this path?"

"A kind of chute," Ignatio said. "We've lowered men on ropes, thinking we could scout what is down there, but the line is always cut when we pull back up. We call this area 'the Perils,' but I think of it as 'the hopeless slide into an endless abyss.'" He chuckled.

Shrugging the guard's restraining hands off her shoulders, Duck rushed over to Keech and wrapped her arms around his waist. "Please don't go," she moaned.

"Get her!" Ignatio ordered, and a pair of thrall soldiers scuttled to retrieve her.

Keech held up an insistent hand. "Let me at least say goodbye. Then I'll go."

The thralls hesitated, awaiting instruction from their master. "You have ten seconds," Ignatio said. "After that, my thralls will shoot."

"Oh, Keech!" Duck cried, her anguish surprising even him. She pressed herself close to his ear and whispered, "You got a plan. I can see it in your eyes. What's the move?"

Keech returned the whisper. "If we split up, we die. We have to head into the Perils together. Work as two, succeed as one. Ready?"

Duck grabbed his hand and took a step back. "I trust you."

Keech peered around the room. At the wall of soldiers holding their weapons at the ready. At Ignatio sneering with pleasure. At Coward frowning at his side. Finally, at Cutter, who was looking down at his own boots, unable to return Keech's stern gaze.

Returning his eyes to Duck, Keech said, "*Run.*"

Together they dashed into the tunnel, Keech's torchlight defining their path.

Behind them, a ruckus of confusion kicked up. A guard shouted, "Hey, y'all ain't supposed to do that!"

"Follow them!" Ignatio commanded. "Make sure they both go down the chute!"

Keech and Duck ran as fast as they could, their footsteps echoing as they descended into the passage. Soon the tunnel narrowed, and Keech was forced to lead the way while Duck fell in behind him.

"It's getting pretty steep," Keech warned as the passage sloped downward and curved to the left. "Keep a grip on the walls!" Stretching his left arm out, he pressed his palm against the stone while his other hand gripped the torch. The sound of stomping boots echoed behind them.

"I don't like this none," Duck said.

"Me neither. I'm losing my footing." Keech lowered his rump onto the stone floor. "I think we have to slide." He gave himself a little shove and slipped forward.

He skidded down the rock chute. Duck followed close behind. The slope dipped, and they found themselves picking up speed. For one terrible moment, Keech wondered if the chute would toss them into a bottomless pit, but when the floor disappeared, he fell a short distance and crashed onto a hard floor. He landed on his haunches, rolled to the side, and saw that the tunnel had spat him from a hole in the ceiling into some kind of circular room.

A second later, Duck sailed through the opening and dropped onto her hands and knees beside him.

A sudden scraping sound grated above their heads. A streak of metal flashed inside the hole, like the swing of a broadsword. Keech pointed up. "A knife just slashed across the chute!"

Duck studied the opening. "Ignatio did say the ropes would get cut anytime they tried to lower someone."

"Which tells me we must be on the right path. You don't take the trouble to build a rope-cutting blade contraption into a rock tunnel for no reason. You set a fail-safe to make sure whoever comes down has to *stay* down."

"At least we don't have to worry about Ignatio's thralls catching up to us," Duck said.

Drawing a nervous breath, Keech pushed up to his feet and waved the torch around. A thick white dust covered the floor. Stick-like objects crackled under his boots. He cast the torch down to fetch a closer look and reeled back in horror. Heaps of human bones littered the entire surface. Skulls gazed up from the shadows, a ghastly audience of cheerless smiles and hollow expressions.

Like the den of the great bear in Floodwood, this place was a tomb.

"Why does there always have to be a room full of bones?" Duck asked.

"Let's not give up hope just yet," Keech said. The large gray stones that made up the chamber walls formed a perimeter so perfectly circular he might as well have been standing inside a well. In the exact center of the room stood a heavy granite column, a round pillar roughly a man's height with an assortment of carvings hewn into the stone. Keech moved closer. The torchlight made strange shadows dance over the markings. He saw the chiseled shapes of various animals: a turtle, a goose, a fish, countless others.

Behind him, Duck muttered, "I think we might be in trouble."

He swiveled back to her and found Duck examining thousands of holes that spotted the walls, a sea of dark dots covering every square foot of the enclosure. The notches looked like tiny peepholes. Duck peeled off a glove and poked a finger into one of the pockets. "I feel a sharp metal point. The walls are loaded with spikes, like spears."

"But there are *thousands* of them," Keech gasped.

"Watch your step and try not to trigger anything."

Keech moved the torch around, hoping for any sign of an

escape, but the room was sealed up, a dead end. He offered Duck a feeble grin. "We're trapped and probably gonna die. But at least we're together."

Duck's head tilted. "That was your plan, wasn't it? Enter this place together. But why?"

Keech lifted the torch so Duck could see his face. "I wanted you by my side 'cause I think I know how to find the House of the Rabbit."

Duck tilted her head. "How?"

"Teamwork. I have a hunch we're *supposed* to work together. That was how my father found the Key, and how he returned it later. Because my mother went in with him."

Duck's mouth dropped open. "Erin Blackwood went into the Perils?"

"*She* was the Rabbit. My father called her *Mah-shchee^n-kah*, like in the vision. It's a word that means 'rabbit.' And it was her nickname."

"How do you know she went in?"

Keech patted the place in his coat where the Ranger's journal lived. "Doyle wrote a good bit about the events of 1833, when the Reverend ordered all the Enforcers to head into the mountain. They had taken my mother prisoner, but according to Doyle's writings, my father set her free while the rest of the gang went off looking for the Key. Except I don't think she left him after he untied her. I think she went into the Perils with my father. They worked as two and succeeded as one."

"As a team, then," Duck said. "Let's fetch the Key."

As they examined the room, Keech found himself returning to the peculiar column filled with animal icons. He motioned for

Duck to join him. Together they walked the circumference of the mast. Holding his glove between his teeth, Keech let his fingers graze the stone carvings. Each mysterious image had been chiseled onto a granite square, and the squares covered the column from base to peak.

Duck leaned in closer to one of the carvings, a shape that resembled an eagle. "Hold the torch a bit closer?" she asked. "I reckon each image can be pressed down, like you might push a wooden peg into a hole."

"Maybe that's the secret. Maybe we push the right image, and a door opens." Keech placed his hand on the eagle icon, then hesitated. "Wait a second. Let's think about this." He peered nervously around the chamber walls. "What if we push the wrong one and the spears pop out and skewer us?"

"I don't know," Duck said, "but what choice do we have?"

After a moment's consideration, Keech cracked his knuckles. "Okay, here goes."

He pressed the eagle. The stone icon slid into the pillar a mere inch—and stopped. A metallic clink sounded within the column, and every pinhole in the chamber ejected a deadly rod. Crying out in unison, Keech and Duck grabbed each other's arms and braced for a terrible death. Luckily, the needlepoint shafts emerged only a few feet, leaving them a foot or two out of range. Keech peeked around, his heart hammering.

"What happened?" Duck asked.

A second click rang out, and the spikes retracted into their stone sheaths.

"They came out only halfway," Keech said. "I think that was a warning."

"Let's not mess up again." Duck kicked at the white powder and bones around her feet. "I'm guessing the folks who came here before pressed one too many wrong carvings."

"Then, which icon do we pick?" Keech spent the next several minutes crawling around the pillar, examining every symbol. Each icon was a recognizable image. Most of the glyphs were animals, but others represented aspects of nature, such as a mountain or the sun or a tree.

Duck found a canine-shaped carving. "I think this is supposed to be a *wolf*."

A twinge of excitement buzzed over Keech's skin. "Maybe that's the one." Keech reached for the icon—and hesitated. "But what if we're wrong?"

"There has to be a way to know for sure," Duck said.

Peering up and down at the dozens of icons on the mast, Keech asked, "Shouldn't the room offer us some kind of clue?"

From the opposite side of the pillar, Duck gasped. "Keech, I think I might've found it! It ain't the wolf."

Rushing to the other side, Keech found his friend on her knees in the white dust, her fingers tracing a stone icon near the base of the mast. He stooped with the torch. What he saw flooded him with relief. "Of course! What else could it be?"

They were looking at the granite carving of a rabbit. The critter had been chiseled to appear in a brisk run, its long ears nestled back like a pair of folded wings.

Duck said, "Low to the ground. Quick on its feet. Bolts at the first sign of trouble."

A wonderful but curious sensation of admiration replaced

Keech's shock. All at once he knew his parents had indeed once stood in this very chamber and struggled with the same decisions that he and Duck now faced. He knew that his mother had discovered the icon of the rabbit and that his father had nicknamed her *Mah-shchee^n-kah* as a tribute to her courage and intelligence. He knew that Erin Blackwood had saved both of their lives.

Duck placed her hand on the rabbit. "Should I?"

"Have at it."

Duck pushed on the icon. A raucous click echoed from within the pillar and the entire chamber shifted on some invisible axle, rotating widdershins a few rattling feet.

"It's working!"

A heavy scraping noise filled the space, and the floor of the room shuddered as the chamber grated to a halt. Waving the torch around, Keech examined the walls, but as far as he could tell, nothing had changed. There was no open doorway. The heart-swell of good feelings dropped away. "There's still no way out."

The chamber rotated again, this time clockwise, grinding back to the position where it had first rested.

Duck looked exhausted. "The danged thing reset."

Keech yanked off his bowler hat in frustration. "The answer couldn't be that easy, of course. If all we had to do was push the rabbit, then *anyone* could get through the Perils." A delightful thought occurred to him. "Wait just a second. Remember my father's clue?"

Duck seemed to pluck the thought right out of his head. "Teamwork. *That's* the answer! We have to press more than one icon. Maybe on opposite sides of the column. A person alone can't do it, but together we can make it work." Squatting beside the rabbit carving, Duck pointed. "You stand on the opposite side while I try the rabbit again. Tell me what you see."

"Ready when you are," he said.

Keech heard the metallic click as Duck pressed the rabbit. Once again the room rotated counterclockwise. As the chamber shifted, the image of a thundercloud on Keech's side of the pillar extended out an inch farther than all the others. "The *cloud* poked out!" he shouted, but then the icon snapped back into its regular position before he could touch it. Excitedly, Keech realized that if he hadn't been standing on the opposite side from Duck, he would've missed which icon had moved. "I think these images come in a sequence, and the cloud is next. Should I press it?"

Duck's voice called back, "Have at it!"

Keech pushed the cloud into the column. The room rotated counterclockwise again, traveling a few feet farther this time. "I think it's working!"

From the other side of the mast, Duck said, "The turtle icon just popped out, then back again."

"Push it!"

Together, they traded off pushing the indicated carvings. With each click, the room shifted a few feet more, till Keech said, "I don't see one to press."

"Keech!" Duck gestured to a slender opening in the wall. "I see a way! We best get out before the room resets!"

The two dashed for the opening and slipped into a narrow tunnel. A few seconds after they exited, the heavy grating noise returned, and the passage rattled back to its original position. The opening disappeared, leaving a thick wall of smooth stone.

Duck panted for breath. "Did we do it? Did we beat the Perils?"

"We got past one room, at least. Look." Keech pointed down the new tunnel. The torchlight penetrated a few feet down the shaft, revealing the edge of a sheer cliff. Beyond, there was only darkness. "The path disappears. There's nowhere to go."

CHAPTER 28

THE BOTTOMLESS PIT

A bitter wind screamed into the midnight abyss that yawned below them. Keech and Duck stood on the edge of the cliff and stared down into the nothingness.

"I wonder how deep it goes," Keech said.

Duck picked up a rock and tossed it. They listened for the landing, but no telltale plop or thud echoed up from the crevasse. "Mighty deep, I'd say."

"But we solved the puzzle! This *can't* be a dead end. We shouldn't have split off from Quinn and Strong Heart. We could've helped them find Ruth, but I was too dead set on finding the House of the Rabbit. And now we're stuck."

"No time for wishing things had gone different," Duck said. "Hand me the torch. Maybe we missed a clue."

With the flame in hand, she examined the limestone walls. "Do you reckon we're supposed to jump? Take a leap of faith like we did in the Floodwood cave?"

"Even if there's water at the bottom, we'd get smooshed. It's too far down."

"You could lower me with the rope," Duck suggested.

"The rope's only about fifty feet. You'd just be dangling off a cliff."

Duck bit her bottom lip. "You're always quoting some training lesson from your pa. What would *he* say about this situation?"

Pa Abner's lessons flooded Keech's mind. *When facing an impossible situation, take a breath. You can think better if your soul is centered.* While Pa's advice had once been welcome, the man's words now felt tainted by the hostile memory of O'Brien's vision. On top of manipulating his love for Sam, Ignatio had poisoned Keech's memories of his pa. Everything that mattered to him had been soured.

"I don't know if I want to think about him, after what he did to my folks," Keech said.

"That's a bunch of hogwash." Duck's words sounded mean, but she placed a tender hand on his arm. "He was under Ignatio's curse. He wasn't to blame and you know it."

"I know it in my *head*, but my *heart's* having trouble catching up."

Duck sighed. "Who do you blame for Sam's visits on the trail?"

"Ignatio, of course. He dug around in my memories and used Sam against us." After a moment's thought, Keech added, "I also blame myself."

"Well, blaming yourself ain't gonna help nobody." Duck pointed back toward the general direction of Ignatio's camp. "Lay the blame at the feet of that rotten sorcerer. Ignatio is Rose's first lieutenant. He was with the Reverend before our fathers were even pulled into all this mess. The blame rests on *his* shoulders, not on your pa's, and not on yours."

For perhaps the hundredth time, Keech found himself marveling at Duck's wisdom and strength. "You know something? If anybody can defeat the Reverend Rose, it's you. I'm as certain of that as I am the sun rises every morning."

Duck smiled. "Back to my original question. What would your pa say in this situation?"

Keech listened to his mind for a moment, allowing Pa's training to resonate. "He'd say, 'When you can't see the solution to a problem, change your point of view. Open your eyes to new angles.' We should adjust the way we're seeing the world."

"So instead of looking *out* or *back*, we should look in another direction." Duck lifted the torch toward the stone above them and scanned the cavern wall. A flat, shadowy line cut across the rock a few feet above the tunnel's mouth.

Keech could barely believe what he saw. "Another ledge!"

"But how are we gonna get up there? We'd never make that jump."

"Maybe you can lift me. If I can pull myself up, I'll lower the rope." Asking Duck for a boost was tricky because the girl was half his weight, but she seemed to have deep reserves of rancher strength running through her body.

"I'll try." Duck locked her fingers together, creating a stirrup for Keech's boot. She hunkered low and spread her feet. "Climb on up."

Keech set the torch down, then stepped into her hands. "Here we go. One . . . two . . ." He felt her fingers lift as he jumped on "three!" He stretched out for the ledge and reached it with ease. Twisting in surprise, Keech sat with his back against the wall. The ledge was a couple of feet wide, but the stone felt secure. He called down, "Dandy of a toss, Duck! Send up the torch."

Duck tied the rope to the torch handle, and Keech pulled the flame up, setting it beside him. The ledge stretched a few feet to the left before dropping off into nothingness; to the right, the path ran a straight line till darkness swallowed it.

"Looks like maybe there's a way out." He sent the rope back down and stood with the line secured around his waist. "Ready when you are."

When he first felt Duck's weight, he worried she would pull him right off the ledge, so he adjusted his footing and braced himself. She had to climb only a few feet, and soon he spied her fingers reaching over and gripping the edge.

He tugged her up, and they started along the narrow ledge, their right hands slipping into cracks in the craggy wall for support. Leading with the light, Keech took careful steps, pressing his weight down to ensure the path wouldn't crumble. They walked for several minutes, and as they moved, the ledge thinned down so much that the tips of Keech's boots hung over the edge. "I'm running out of room," he said.

"Can you keep going?" Duck asked.

"I think so," he answered. To prove his point, Keech slid a step along the ledge. He felt secure enough, but suddenly his bootheel skidded across loose dust and he found himself leaning over the abyss. Pulses of fear crashed through him, and he jerked back.

But there wasn't enough room to correct the loss of balance. Keech's back bounced off the stone, and he pitched forward. His feet came free of the ledge, and then he was falling.

He dropped a mere two feet—then his pelt hitched under his arms, as if he were dangling from a fishhook.

"Duck!" he shouted, hanging over the chasm. "Help!"

"I got you!" Duck called. "Don't drop the torch!"

Keech choked up on the torch handle, then stiffly glanced over his shoulder. Duck was holding on to the skirt of his pelt, her small face shaking with concentration.

"You got me? What's got *you*?"

"Hang on!" With a hefty tug, Duck hauled him back up to the ledge. He reached out and gripped a crack in the wall. The moment his boots settled on the rim, Duck released her hold. Keech could feel his heart thumping, and though a thousand questions crowded his mind, he asked just one: "How in blazes did you catch me?"

"I jammed my fingers into this crack so I didn't fall after ya," Duck said.

"That don't explain how you didn't drop me. I weigh twice what you do! I should've pulled you right over. And you didn't just catch me; you hauled me back up like I was a kitten!"

Duck fell silent for a moment. "You didn't seem to weigh nothin', though."

Understanding struck Keech at once. "Duck, I think you found your focus. You're as strong as a bull!"

"My focus?" Duck scratched her head. "But I didn't do anything."

"It makes perfect sense, though. Remember how you punched that crow in the field? And how you snapped the ropes when Black Charlie had us all tied up?" And even as he spoke, Keech recalled how Nat Embry had broken free of his chains in the Wisdom jail. "I reckon *strength* might be the way Embrys show their focus."

The tiniest laugh escaped Duck's lips. "Like my father in the vision! He tossed a boulder big enough to put Big Ben down."

"And don't forget the bonfire," Keech added. "You walloped Big Ben something good."

Duck nodded at the memory. "I guess it does make sense. The only thing I ever wanted was to be as strong as Nat and my pa. Everybody always told me girls could never be strong like that, but I always told my ma I'd prove them wrong. And she always said I would."

For a moment, Keech and Duck stared at each other and marveled at her newly discovered abilities. Then Keech's pulse calmed enough that he felt ready to continue. This time, he faced the wall and used the crevices in the stone to steady himself. They inched along the ledge, and after a few steps, the mantel widened again.

"Hang on," Keech said, holding out the torch. The ledge had become a series of stairs, descending as the wall continued to curve. "The path takes us down from here."

"Feels like we've reached the other side of the pit," Duck said.

At the bottom of the staircase, they found a wide outskirt of rock and a hole in the cavern wall, a tunnel leading deeper into the solid granite of Skeleton Peak. Duck accepted the torch from Keech and led the way into the new passage. Unlike the last path, this one traveled down at a steep angle. The tunnel lacked the uniform nature of the previous shafts, shifting instead from narrow to wide, the ceiling often out of reach and other times so low they had to crawl.

The torch was dying. Soon they would be in total darkness. There was only enough glow from the flickering flame to see a few feet ahead.

The passage opened up to reveal a long chamber with sharp

corners. Intricate etchings scored the walls, symbols and shapes carved into the stone to create grand images, murals depicting events from a distant history long buried by the rolling centuries. At the center of the rectangular chamber rested a stone block, as tall and wide as a supper table, with smooth sides.

Unlike the circular room, this floor lacked the white powder and bones, though a few skeleton mounds did molder in the corners. Keech said, "Seems like a few people survived this far but met their fate here. I don't know how they made it past the other rooms, but something sure stopped them. We best be careful."

They stepped into the room. "Let's scout the perimeter, see if we can find a way out. All I see in this room are walls, no exit," Duck said.

Taking another step, Keech felt the slate tile under his boot sink an inch. A terrible grating noise thundered behind them as a rock barrier slammed down, cutting off their path.

CHAPTER 29

THE SACRIFICE CHAMBER

As the final flickers of the torch died, the edges of the chamber dimmed. Keech watched the sputtering fire shrink till only Duck's frightened face remained. Then the fire winked out, and complete darkness overtook them. Tossing aside the torch, Keech held out his hand. When Duck took it, he said, "Don't let go, no matter what. We don't want to lose track of each other."

Duck's fingers gripped his. "How're we gonna get out of here? I'd wager the story carved on the wall would help, but now we can't even read it."

"Maybe we can feel the carvings, figure out what they say." Stepping through the dark, Keech led Duck to the nearest wall. Blindly, he ran his fingers over the etchings. They spent several moments tracing the engravings, till he dropped his hands in defeat. "I have no idea what I'm touching. Feels like a bunch of bumps and swirls." He huffed in frustration. "I sure hope Strong Heart and Quinn are doing better than we are."

"I'm sure they are, but let's not give up," Duck said. "We won't solve this thing without light. Let's follow your pa's advice, try to see things from a new angle."

"But we can't see anything at all!"

Duck tugged his sleeve. "C'mon. Let's go over to that big block. I need to sit down."

Keech followed the sound of her boots. Once they reached the slab, he hopped up beside her.

The now-familiar sound of scraping granite crashed through the chamber. The slab they had just sat on skidded down a few inches. As the block descended, another hunk of stone slid aside in the far corner of the room's ceiling. Sapphire light poured through the newly opened space, revealing a way out.

Before Keech could grow too excited, a heavy rumble echoed through the room, followed by a splashing noise like a waterfall. The blue light shining through the gap showed him that other holes in the ceiling had opened up. A torrent of water now poured into the room.

"We have to get up through that hole before this room fills up!" Keech shouted.

But the moment he slid off the stone table, the slab rose back up, and the ceiling panel slid shut again, returning the room to pitch darkness. Water continued to cascade into the room.

Screaming over the flood's roar, Duck said, "Get back on the block!" When they hopped back onto the stone, the slab once again sank under their weight. And once again, the doorway opened. The sapphire light revealed that a foot of water had filled the chamber. Keech also saw that numerous other spouts had opened.

"Keech, we can't both go," Duck said almost calmly.

"What do you mean?" But Keech realized the problem. Without enough weight to hold down the block, the doorway would shut.

Even as the answer came, the water splashed across their boots.

Keech knew what must be done. "There's no time. You have to get out."

"No!" Duck snapped. "You have to escape, too. I won't leave you!"

Glacial water had now reached Keech's knees. "Please, Duck. I promised Nat I'd take care of you. I can't let you stay here and drown while I go on. You have to escape."

"And I can't lose another brother," Duck said.

Her words pierced Keech's heart. He took her in his arms and squeezed. "It's all right. Go fetch that Key, then find Quinn and Strong Heart. Finish this, Duck. I believe in you."

When he released her, Duck stepped back with tear-soaked cheeks. "I *can't*!"

"Yes, you can. Do it for Nat. For my parents and yours. Please hurry!" Desperate, Keech grabbed her by the shoulders and turned her around.

Her pleas all spent, Duck jumped into the water and paddled toward the opening. Soon she was bobbing beneath the hole in the ceiling. She yelled something at Keech, her face twisted in grief, but the splashing deluge drowned out her words.

The water climbed to Keech's chest. Panic reached for his heart, but he forced it down, recognizing that what he was doing existed far beyond fear. Nothing else mattered but this one final action. He stretched upward to press his hands against the stone. His entire body shivered. The water lifted him off the block below the surface. Without his weight holding down the block, the corner door slid shut, cutting off Duck's way out.

Determined to give her enough time to climb out, Keech pushed himself down against the slab. He felt the block retract again, and the corner door reopened. *Work as two, succeed as one*, he thought, crying out with joy as Duck pulled herself up through the hole.

"I made it!" she yelled.

"Good! Keep going!"

Keech kept applying pressure on the block till he saw her boots clear into the space above. Once she was safe, he relaxed. The icy water bit into his flesh and made his joints ache, but he was happy to stop pushing against the heavy block. The ceiling door slid shut, and the room once again fell into darkness.

Keech lifted his face toward the ceiling, taking desperate breaths as he floated. Perhaps there was a way to stop the flow—both of his parents had run the Perils and survived, after all. But they had likely solved the puzzle of the murals and not been forced to make a sacrifice.

Nevertheless, Keech prayed for some kind of salvation. Gasping, he gulped for breath as water washed over his face and buried him.

CHAPTER 30
THE HOUSE OF THE RABBIT

A sapphire glow touched the corner of Keech's vision.

Spinning underwater, he looked toward the corner where Duck had escaped and saw that the stone door in the ceiling had opened again, allowing light into the chamber. Through the murky water, he made out a small arm dipped into the cold, waving back and forth.

Kicking with all his might, Keech swam toward the arm.

Just when he thought he would drown, Duck's fingers grazed his palm, then gripped his hand. With a heavy tug, she pulled him to the opening, and his head broke the surface.

Keech pulled in lungfuls of air, and after climbing out of the hole, he huddled on his side and shivered. A new tunnel yawned before him, leading off to an uncharted space filled with the blue light. Whipping the soaked hair out of his eyes, he peered up into Duck's teary, smiling face and muttered, "How?"

Duck reached back into the floor's opening, sunk her hand into the water, and yanked out Keech's bowler hat. She set it next to him. "After I climbed out of the room, I found a rabbit icon carved into the tunnel wall. I pushed it, but nothing happened till the room was full of water." She shook her head. "I reckon the room wanted a sacrifice before it'd let me try to save you."

They shivered together as frigid water dripped off their clothes. Duck said, "We need to get moving so we don't freeze."

They continued down the passageway toward the strange bluish glow till Duck stopped on the dirt path. Her breath hitched in her throat. "Keech . . ."

"Yeah?"

"I think we found it. The House of the Rabbit."

The passage opened into a wide cavern, a boundless chamber of enormous height drenched in an azure glow. Mighty stone monoliths filled the cavern, towering ancient columns that gave the effect of curious citadels and strongholds. Riding a warm breeze, a dank scent rolled out of the subterranean arena, a mixture of spoiled fish and pungent sulfur.

"Not too inviting," Keech said.

"But as big as a city," Duck replied. "I wish Quinn and Strong Heart could see this."

"Whatever we do, let's stay vigilant. We may not be done with the Perils."

Walking side by side, Keech and Duck entered the House of the Rabbit.

As they took in the ominous place of power, Keech wondered at the source of the blue illumination. The light seemed to shine from the cavern walls themselves, as if a cold fire burned within the granite. As he neared one of the monoliths, he saw that a series of carved glyphs decorated the stone. The images appeared to tell stories of past people living upon the sea and along shorelines, tales of long-lost kings and forgotten nations. Perhaps at one time this place of power had stood near an ocean, but the idea baffled Keech, because they were now beneath a mountain peak deep in the Rocky Mountains. "What *was* this place?"

"I'd wager we could search for weeks and never answer that," Duck said. "But for some reason, this is where Enoch hid the Key."

"I expected it to be more cheerful," Keech said. "The beach at Bonfire Crossing was nice, like a pleasant dream. *This* place is like a nightmare."

Duck's face filled with dread. "Like the nightmare we shared back at the Moss farm?"

Keech pondered the memory of their mutual dream of the light-filled cavern. He shook his head. "No, I don't think so. This place is something else. Murky. Or *sick*. Like the Withers has infected the rock."

Duck sniffed the cavern, then wrinkled her nose. "You're right."

"Maybe 'cause we're standing near a Dead Rift hole," Keech said. What were O'Brien's words? *The Dead Rift was an* event. *Happened long ago, durin' a time they call the First Age of Man.* No wonder the air reeked. Nothing that old would smell nice.

They wandered for a time, not speaking. The cavern felt oddly warm, the way cold October mornings in Missouri would heat up by noon. Soon they were sweating inside their damp clothes. As they opened their pelts and coats, Keech felt an itch scramble down the back of his neck—a tickle, as if he were being watched. He scrutinized the shadows as he looked down various passageways, searching for hints of movement, but saw nothing.

They proceeded through the cavern, Duck walking a few paces ahead, till she rounded the next corner and gasped. "Keech!"

A massive granite staircase stood before them. The flight ascended through the dark space to terminate at the foot of a platform, a colossal white slab upon which rested a stonework table of some sort, bathed in bluish light. Two intricately decorated posts stood on each side of the altar. Behind all this was another massive wall of solid stone.

A long, slender object dangled between the posts, but Keech couldn't tell what it was.

Advancing with caution, they climbed the tall stairs and reached the platform. Leaning against the altar's base was a human skeleton clad in musty rags, a long metal chain and shackle held in its delicate palms. The wretched form had wasted away to barren bone and dust, a body that had been resting in the dark cavern for centuries.

Duck dared to lean in closer. "Another victim of the Perils?"

Keech gazed around, searching for a mechanism that could have killed the person. "I sure hope not. I don't know if I fancy another puzzle."

Duck turned her attention to the altar. "What was this place, some kind of church?"

"More like a *shrine*." He studied the object that hung between the posts. It was a golden block roughly the size of a fist, secured with moldering ropes. An ancient-looking sigil had been carved into the face of the gold. Another rabbit icon.

Duck extended a hand toward the block. "Maybe the Key's inside this thing. Maybe you have to open the square."

"I wouldn't touch that."

Duck promptly withdrew her hand. Shuffling back a few steps, they inspected the altar. Like other places in the House, this pedestal had images carved into its stone top. When Keech leaned to fetch a closer look, he counted seven symbols arranged in a semicircle across the surface:

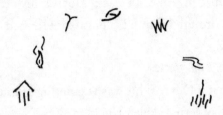

"What do you reckon *those* mean? Another test?" Duck asked.

Keech circled the altar, trying to decipher the markings engraved in the stone. "Maybe. They look awfully familiar, but I can't put my finger on why."

Duck took a moment to study the symbols, pausing at the shape that resembled a small flame. "Wait a danged second—" she began.

"What is it?"

Duck's eyes sparkled with recognition. "I've seen parts of these shapes on the amulet shards! They're spread out over the fragments!"

Keech scrutinized each symbol again, thinking back to the strange lines and loops that decorated Pa Abner's charm, but so far he didn't see the connection. "It's hard to be sure without having all the shards to compare."

"Seven symbols," Duck said pensively. "The Bible speaks a lot about the number seven, don't it?"

"Pa Abner once told Sam the number seven means *completion* in the Bible, a holy number that symbolizes perfection. The number crops up everywhere in the old stories. Seven days to create the world, seven seals in the book of Revelation, you name it."

"Whatever these symbols are, they must mean something important," Duck said.

Keech continued to circle the altar, this time stepping over the skeleton propped against its base. Doyle's mysterious journal entry echoed through his mind, a phrase Keech had contemplated for weeks now.

The skeleton holds the key.

"Duck, what if Doyle's clue wasn't pointing us toward Skeleton Peak? What if an actual skeleton held the Key?" Keech gestured at the shackle in the corpse's hands.

"Hmm. Mighty interesting." Duck studied the strand of rusted metal. "The skeleton ain't cuffed to the chain."

"Exactly. He's *holding* it. Prisoners don't hold their shackles." Keech felt his heart kick up a beat. "Duck, we might just be looking at *Enoch himself.*"

Looking unsure, Duck peered at the chain, then at the dead person resting at the altar's base. "You think that *chain* is the Key of Enoch? I was picturing, I dunno, a *key.* Something that could open a door."

Keech considered. "Think about the Fang of Barachiel. It looks like a regular old dagger, but it's a healing tool. Maybe none of the relics behave the way a person expects."

"Maybe so. But a chain? That don't make sense."

"I'm gonna pick it up." Keech stepped closer.

Duck grabbed his coat sleeve. "Wait! We don't know what it does. It might turn you into something nasty the second you touch it."

"It just might, but my gut's telling me to follow through on this hunch." Keech bent toward the chain—then stopped. "If this thing turns me into a toad, just step on me." Smiling feebly, he proceeded to lift the rusted metal from the skeleton's grasp.

As soon as the chain's weight shifted, the corpse's upper torso creaked forward, crumbling on the floor. The chain's links felt cold against his fingers, but otherwise mundane, just like any other iron shackle. He winced as the rings clanged loose and dangled from his hands. Nothing nasty happened. He was still Keech, and not a toad. "Doesn't feel like anything special."

"Maybe you're wrong, then. Maybe that danglin' gold block holds the Key after all."

Keech wrapped the archaic chain around his arm a few times. Again he waited for something terrible to flash out of the metal and into his body—perhaps the same kind of lightning bolts that had struck Big Ben Loving in the magical bonfire—but nothing happened.

A split second later, a torturous grinding noise made them jump. A large square chunk of the cavern wall had just slid aside behind the altar, revealing another dark passage.

"Why'd that door just open?" Duck asked.

Keech stared suspiciously at the corpse. "That poor soul must've been rigged so that when he falls over, the door opens. See?" He pointed to a thin, rotten rope attached to the skeleton's midsection, a braid running back to the pedestal.

"But if your father came through here, how did all this get reset?" Duck asked.

"Maybe he reset everything when he came back to return the Key," Keech replied. "He would've suspected, probably, that Rose would keep searching for it. He would've wanted to keep it hidden."

Suddenly a loud *clonk* sounded from the posts on either side of the altar. The golden block hanging between the pillars slid down as the ropes lowered the block onto the altar. The second the gold touched the stone, the top of the altar began to glow, and a dazzling ray of turquoise light erupted from the block where the rabbit was carved. The illumination rose straight up into the House, a pillar of sea-green light that radiated into the high shadows of the rocky dome. The column was bright enough to make Keech squint.

Shielding her eyes, Duck asked, "Is that good or bad?"

"Remember what O'Brien said? How lifting the Key would trigger a charge of energy? I think taking the chain from the skeleton started up something." He peered down gravely at the chain in his grip. "We've got our answer."

"That thing *is* the Key of Enoch."

Keech nodded with fascination. "When my father replaced the chain, he must've reset the energy for this place. And now we've just undone it again."

As if perfectly on cue, a horrible growl echoed through the chamber. It rippled like dark water over the expanse, and they looked at each other in stunned silence.

"What do you reckon *that* was?" Duck asked.

The guttural growl rumbled again, this time accompanied by a series of answering shrieks and hungry cries.

"Duck," Keech whispered. "I think we woke up something."

In the distance, a congregation of long-limbed creatures slithered over the floor, cutting off the path Keech and Duck had taken into the House. Something about them was like the spiders that Black Charlie had conjured out of the mountain, but these monsters were more serpentine, like miniature Chamelia without the spikes or fur. Whatever they were, they moved fast and looked ravenous.

"Dead Rift creatures," Keech said. O'Brien's words returned like the echo of a nightmare: *The Dead Rift happened when people first tampered with magic. Their meddlin' tore holes in the fabric of the world* . . .

"A gap into the Underworld," Duck finished. "And those things have come spilling out." Shoving her hat down tight, she scurried through the newly opened doorway behind the altar. "C'mon, Keech! We'd best skedaddle."

Before Keech could follow, a mammoth figure stepped out of the distant shadows to join the grotesque rabble. It was a creature unlike anything he'd ever seen. Its giant head looked like a knotted tree stump, and its rugged hide resembled the color of old driftwood, dappled and cracked. Keech could tell the behemoth was as tall as Pa Abner's barn.

Raising two heavily muscled arms above its head, the creature reared back and bellowed. The walls trembled, and chunks of clay shook loose. Keech turned toward the new corridor and sprinted after Duck, the mysterious chain still wrapped around his arm. The monstrosity dropped to all four limbs and lurched after them, followed by its legion of gangly smaller critters.

Keech and Duck entered a cramped tunnel, the ceiling low and packed with tiny stalactites. The cerulean glow that filled the House of the Rabbit poured into the shaft, turning the stone around them a greenish color.

Then the corridor ended—so unexpectedly that Duck smacked against it and tumbled backward.

"Duck!" Keech caught up to her and pulled her back up to her boots.

Shaking off the impact, Duck slapped her palms against the wall. "Did we miss a turn somewhere?"

"I didn't see a thing," Keech said. Though the tunnel was still empty, the sounds of the pursuing creatures grew in volume, a hideous chorus of gnashing teeth and wild grunts.

"Those things are gonna eat us alive." Desperation blackened Duck's words, but she didn't stop feeling along the wall. "Wait! I feel something! Another rabbit."

Keech squinted in the dim light. She had found another carving in the dead-end stone. He traced the rabbit symbol with his finger. "It must mean our way out is through here."

"Through solid rock?" Duck pushed, but the symbol didn't budge.

Keech's mind scrambled for a solution as the clamor of approaching madness howled behind them, but he couldn't think of a thing. In seconds, the creatures in the House would find them. Furious at their lack of options, he struck the rabbit icon on the wall with the arm wearing the chain.

His hand disappeared into the stone, then his forearm, as if the wall were nothing more than empty air.

The pure shock at seeing his arm buried up to the elbow in the wall almost made him scream, but instead, Keech yanked it back out and saw that his hand and forearm were still attached to his body. He stared at the chain. "What just happened?"

"Your arm just went through the wall."

"Are you sure there's a wall there?"

Duck slapped her hand against the solid rock. "Feels like one to me."

His mind reeling, Keech pushed his hand into the stone. He felt no resistance as his arm disappeared in the rock, as if he were a ghost. They both gaped as he drew it back out, as whole as before. "I know why this thing is called a Key." He reached out and grabbed Duck's hand. "Touch the wall now."

Duck swiped at the stone, and her hand passed into the rock. "How is this possible?"

"We'll have to figure that out later," Keech said. "We better get a move on." The smidgen of blue light pouring into the tunnel suddenly waned as writhing creatures clogged the passageway. Clutching the chain in one hand and Duck's fingers in the other, Keech reached for the wall again.

"Whatever you do, don't let go of me," he said.

"I won't."

Together they stepped into the wall.

CHAPTER 31
THE KEY OF ENOCH

After a few short steps through absolute darkness and the deepest silence Keech had ever known, they emerged from a solid wall into a torchlit mine shaft.

"Did we just walk through stone?" Duck asked, stunned.

Keech reached back, expecting his arm to disappear as before, but his hand slapped jagged rock. Confused, he said, "I don't understand. The wall's hard again." He peered at the mystical chain—the Key of Enoch.

Duck said, "We'll figure it out later. For now, let's get out of here. We need to find Quinn and Strong Heart."

Keech peered up and down the tunnel. "But which way do we go?"

Before they could decide, two thrall soldiers wandered into the shaft. The dead men skidded to a halt. "The greenhorns are back!" one shouted, reaching for his pistol.

Duck grabbed Keech's hand and yanked him in the opposite direction. They took off at a hard sprint as alarmed shouts rose up from the soldiers. The passageway soon widened, and another small group of thralls stepped in front of them, blocking their path. One of the scoundrels, a ghoulish man without ears or a nose, grumbled, "No way out, kittens. You'll have to go through us."

Keech tightened his grip on one end of the chain. "Watch your head, Duck. I'll clear us a path." Duck stooped as he started swinging the shackle around his head, the wrist fetter whistling through the air.

"Look out!" another soldier warned. "He's got a chain!"

Leaping, Keech swung at the monster who was missing his ears and nose. He worried the iron manacle might swoosh right through the soldier's skull, just as the metal had passed through the corridor wall, but instead it smashed into the creature's head with a sickening *thunk* and the soldier crumbled. "*Don't* call us kittens," Keech said.

"C'mon, Keech." Duck hopped over the fallen guard and dashed up the tunnel.

Yanking at the chain, Keech flung the shackle toward the other thralls. When the soldiers flinched away, he hurried after Duck. As they dashed up the tunnel, he looped the curious chain back around his forearm.

A moment later, they emerged into the main cavern of Skeleton Peak, where Ignatio had established his underground camp.

Duck stopped in her tracks.

At least a dozen rotten soldiers crowded before them, pointing muskets and bayonets. Standing at the front of the company, Ignatio crossed his tattooed arms in casual repose. Coward lurked behind the sorcerer like a child peeking out from behind his father's legs. Cutter waited a few steps behind them, the torchlight of the cavern painting his harrowed face a deep bronze.

Ignatio clapped his hands in delight. "I have spent months digging through Skeleton Peak in search of the Key, and in one hour you two accomplish what only one other could do!" He held out his hand. "Now, bring it to me. It must be a heavy burden."

Keech clutched the chain even tighter. "Nah, I think I'll keep it."

Coward shouted, "Give us the shackle, Keech! I want to leave this wretched place."

Before Keech could respond, Ignatio backhanded Coward. The man stumbled, squawking in surprise. "I didn't say nothing wrong!" Coward barked, but when the sorcerer raised his hand a second time, Coward recoiled with a pathetic whimper.

Shaking his head, Ignatio returned his attention to Keech and Duck. "You'll have to forgive my *compañero*. He lacks manners. Now bring me the Key, and I'll release you."

"You think we're gonna believe that?" Duck growled. "For all we know, you'll use this Key to chain up the whole world."

Ignatio chortled, his gold tooth flashing in the firelight. "The Key is not for binding, *niña*. It is for *liberación*." He took a gentle step closer to Keech. "What you hold, Mr. Blackwood, was first used to liberate three men from the flames of Nebuchadnezzar, the great king of Babylon."

"Wait a second, I *know* this story," Keech said. He recalled Sam's jubilant voice—the *real* Sam, the Sam of his fondest memories—reading him a story from the book of Daniel as they sat on the riverbank near the Home for Lost Causes. *This one's about standing true*, Sam had said, holding Pa's old Bible. *The Lord delivers the brave from the fires of evil.*

Ignoring Keech, Ignatio continued. "When Shadrach, Meshach, and Abednego would not bow to the king's golden image,

Nebuchadnezzar bound them and cast them into a fiery furnace. But inside the flames, an angel of God delivered them from death." The sorcerer paused to raise a thick eyebrow. "Surely you can guess the name of the angel."

Keech pondered for a second, then realized the answer was obvious. Before he could voice his reply, however, Duck beat him to it.

"*Barachiel*. The same angel who blessed Abraham's dagger. He also turned Nebuchadnezzar's chain magical."

Ignatio's shiny tooth flashed again. "Yes, Barachiel shielded the men from the fire. He turned the very shackle holding them into the instrument of their *liberación*. As long as Shadrach, Meshach, and Abednego held the chain, the fierce heat and burning fire could not harm them."

"And they walked through the walls," Duck added. "Which is why you want the Key."

"Betrayal trapped the Reverend inside the Palace of the Thunders," Ignatio said. "That chain shall finally set him free. But enough talk. Hand over the Key."

Thrall soldiers advanced up the tunnel behind them. Letting out some slack in the chain, Keech started swinging the shackle above his head. "Anybody comes close, I'll drop them."

The thralls slowed their approach.

A boisterous shout made Keech and Duck spin on their heels. Cutter was rushing them at full charge. His outstretched arms slammed into Keech and Duck, and they both went tumbling to the jagged floor.

Dazed, Keech tried to rise, but Cutter's fist clipped his jaw. The boy's knee pressed against his chest. "Stay down, Blackwood,"

Cutter said as he yanked the chain free. The Key in hand, he straightened, adjusted his red sash, and strolled back to Ignatio and Coward.

Duck rolled onto her side, her brow dark with blood. "Keech, are you all right?"

Keech blinked a few times. "I think."

"¡*Silencio!*" Ignatio called out. Turning to Cutter, he lifted the clump of chain from the grimacing boy's hands. "The Key of Enoch. At last, all the relics!" Shaking with joy, he offered Coward the chain. "Take the Key and the Fang back to my cabin. Wait for me there."

Coward accepted the coil, wrapping the metal around his waist and tying the loose end in a makeshift knot. "Finally, we can leave this wretched mountain. On to the Palace!"

"There is one more thing to be done," Ignatio said. He addressed one of his thralls, a bearded thug with a dough-pale face. "Clear this mountain. Start with the prisoners, then eliminate the *niños*. Spare no one."

CHAPTER 32

REVOLT

Ignatio's soldiers wailed with repugnant glee, a monstrous call to carnage. The captive villagers peered up from their pickaxes and shovels, a collective fear leaping onto their faces. Many of them tried to flee into the honeycomb tunnels, but thralls blocked their way.

"Keech, we have to do something!" Duck cried.

Keech struggled to rise, but Cutter shoved him back down with his boot. "Stop fighting. It's over."

Pushing the fog out of his vision, Keech rummaged through Pa Abner's rules of survival—*Hesitation means death; if trouble stirs, move away from immediate danger; win yourself distance, win time to think*—but none of Pa's lessons seemed to be helpful for the predicament.

There was, however, one effective way for Keech to foil Ignatio.

He could use the Black Verse, speak the Invocation to Disrupt Concentrated Energies. He could point his finger at Ignatio and speak one dark spell—*No-ge-phal-ul'-shogg*—and the sorcerer would perish under a full blast of Prime.

Keech lifted a shaking hand, aiming past Cutter and toward Ignatio. He opened his mouth to release the invocation.

But he hesitated.

To use the Black Verse was to touch the malicious energy of the truest darkness. Each time he'd gone down that path, depravity had corrupted his plans. Keech lowered his hand.

There had to be another way.

Ignatio's thralls shoved the prisoners into the center of the camp. The monsters gathered in a tight semicircle, standing shoulder to shoulder, fencing in the people of Wisdom. The sight of the captives huddled in a panic-stricken mass filled Keech with horror.

"Ready yer aim, men!" the bearded thrall yelled.

Moving with incredible speed, Duck hopped to her feet, stepped to a nearby rubble pile, and scooped up a boulder nearly twice her size. "All of you stop and back away, or I'll flatten every last one of you mangy curs!" To prove her point, she lifted the stone above her head.

The soldiers hesitated, their eyes widening at the sight of the boulder.

"You truly are the daughter of Bennett Coal," Ignatio said, smiling.

"You're danged right I am," Duck spat. "Now get up, Keech." When Cutter refused to let him up, she growled, "Back off, Cut, or I'll flatten you, too. Don't test me!"

With a disoriented sort of snarl, Cutter lifted his boot off Keech and stepped away.

"This is quite entertaining!" Ignatio sang. "Let's see how this plays out."

As Keech rose, he saw a curious thing. Two of the thralls at the far end of the rank dropped to the cavern floor as if their legs had been chopped out from beneath them. Then one after the next, their chattering neighbors started tumbling off their boots as well. Clouds of black smoke spouted from their mouths.

One confused thrall bawled, "What's happenin'?"

The entire brigade erupted in a chaos of movement.

The mirth on Ignatio's face disappeared. "Stand firm!" he shouted.

An ear-rattling bark echoed across the cavern, and Keech spotted a patch of gray fur charging low among the black smoke. A luminous yellow glow floated with the fur.

"*Achilles!*" Duck yelled.

The hound dashed through the legs of the resurrected men, an amulet shard clutched between his teeth. He bounded through the armed ranks and smacked the shard against the exposed flesh of a panicked thrall. The soldier dropped his musket and keeled over in the dirt. Thralls swiped the air with their weapons, but Achilles moved too swiftly. Before Keech could lock on the hound's movement, two more thralls went shuddering to the cavern floor.

"Stop that dog!" Ignatio bellowed as a maelstrom of movement filled the cavern.

Achilles wove in and out of the horde, stilling thralls as the people of Wisdom scampered to their freedom. A few of the thralls gave pursuit into the surrounding tunnels, but most of them appeared confused by the roving hound.

Keech glanced toward Ignatio in time to see the lightning-quick shaft of an arrow hiss down from high above. The projectile shattered against the sorcerer's skull upon impact, as if Ignatio's skin were made of marble. The fiend shouted, "*Who did that?*"

A second arrow whizzed down and struck Ignatio's chest, but rather than sinking into his flesh, the projectile shattered into splinters.

Keech searched the cavern's upper levels and spotted a figure on the scaffolding. Strong Heart peeked over the ledge and nocked a third arrow.

Ignatio pointed up at the girl. "*I see you!*"

Still clutching the boulder, Duck murmured at Keech, "Now's our chance! Strong Heart's distracted him!" With a vigorous grunt, she lobbed her cargo at the approaching thralls. The heavy slab bowled into the monsters, knocking them asunder.

"Time to take this fight to them."

A reverberating cry roared through the cavern as a new group of men and women emerged from the tunnels. Dozens of prisoners from the outside camp, freshly armed with muskets and shovels, charged at the dumbfounded thralls. Leading this company was the silver-haired woman they had spotted earlier—Quinn's aunt Ruth. She directed the rebellion, bellowing orders while swinging a hammer at ambushing thralls. The soldiers tried to raise their weapons as the townsfolk collided into them, but they couldn't withstand the wave of angry prisoners.

"Take 'em down, every last one!" a familiar voice shouted.

Keech hollered in delight as Quinn Revels leaped down from a scaffold, gripping the war ax he'd built on the Santa Fe Trail. Quinn crashed into an unsuspecting thrall, knocking the fiend backward. Then he put two fingers to his mouth and loosed a shrill whistle. Achilles loped to his side, still clenching the amulet shard in his mouth. "Good dog!" Quinn said, and took the radiant silver.

"Quinn had a plan after all!" Duck hollered at Keech.

A bedlam of gunfire boomed across the cavern as the outnumbered soldiers began targeting the captives. A soldier near Quinn dropped to one knee and fired upon a charging prisoner. The musket ball grazed the man's shoulder, but the brave fellow kept swinging his fists at attackers. Rushing over, Quinn slapped his silver against the soldier's neck. The thrall's face erupted in a spiderweb of black veins, and he perished with a feeble curse. Pressing a hand against his wounded shoulder, the prisoner said to Quinn, "Much obliged!"

"Get back to the surface," Quinn said to the fellow. "Help as many as you can."

The skirmish spilled into every corner of the cavern. A rotted monster approached Keech with a rusty sword. Keech crouched low and kicked, snapping the creature's knee. The thrall dropped onto his face and the sword skittered out of his hand. "Yer gonna pay for that," the dead man muttered.

"Heads up, partner," Keech said to the thrall.

Suddenly Duck appeared and dropped another boulder onto the thrall's back, pinning him to the ground. She laughed as the trapped creature squealed in rage. "We needed a miracle, and we got one. Quinn and Strong Heart started a revolt!"

Standing amid the carnage, Ignatio screamed in fury as another arrow snapped against him. "You waste your time!" he bellowed up at Strong Heart, still perched atop her scaffold. "I will end you!"

"*Mah-thee^n thi-eh!*" came the girl's reply.

Dodging another thrall's bayonet, Keech spotted a terrified Coward hunching pathetically near Ignatio's side.

"The prisoners are surrounding us!" Coward bleated, tugging at the sorcerer's coat. He was still wearing the Key of Enoch like a belt, and the Wisdom fighters had cut off his passage to the outside camp. He shoved Cutter in front of him. "Protect me, Miguel!"

Without a word of protest, Cutter elbowed an attacking prisoner. Another fellow slammed the flat head of a shovel against Cutter's back, knocking the boy to his knees. Bellowing in rage, Cutter launched himself at the man and whacked the shovel loose.

Keech grimaced at Duck. "We need to get Cut away from Coward. That monster's gonna get him killed."

"How, though? Cutter's got the Devil's mark."

"Follow me, but stay back a ways. If I get pinned down, I'll need your muscles."

Tightening down his hat, Keech rushed toward Cutter, keeping low to avoid Ignatio's watchful eye. Duck followed a few feet behind.

Suddenly Quinn's aunt Ruth appeared in front of him, swinging her hammer at a thrall's chomping mouth. When the dead man dropped, Keech lunged to still the monster with his shard, then glanced up at the woman with a grin.

"Hi, Miss Ruth. I'm Keech, a friend of your nephew's," he said.

"Pleasure to meet ya!" Spinning, Ruth swiped her weapon at another encroaching monster.

Before Keech could take another step, a muttering thrall jumped in front of him and tackled him to the ground. "Time to die, kid!" the thing screeched.

"I don't think so," Duck's voice called out. A heavy brown timber swung into view, and with a loud *thwock!* the creature went sailing. When Keech hopped back up, he saw that Duck was clutching a wooden beam twice her height. She had used the long post like a club.

"If Nat could see me now!" Duck sang.

They resumed their advance on Cutter, but they didn't get five paces before Coward turned and spotted them. The fiend tugged on Ignatio's coat, trying to get the sorcerer's attention. Swiveling, Ignatio swatted the man with the back of his hand. Releasing a pitiful wail, Coward crumbled to the floor. Animosity teemed in his tearstained eyes. Sputtering indiscernible words, he drove his thumb down upon the magical brand on his opposite palm.

Slapping his hands to his forehead, Cutter screamed.

Pressing the Devil's mark, Coward pointed sharply at Ignatio. "Now, Miguel! Do it *now*!"

Unsheathing his bone-handled blade, Cutter raised the steel to attack.

"Keech!" Duck shouted. "He's gonna—"

But Keech was already kicking off into a sprint. He bounded across the chamber, leaping over rock and debris, hoping to tackle the boy and wake him from his stupor. "Cut, don't do it!"

He was too late.

Cold surprise splashed across Ignatio's face as Cutter lunged. Though every other attack had bounced off the monster's stone-hard skin, Cutter's blade stabbed through the eye tattoo, sinking deep into the sorcerer's chest.

The world seemed to freeze as Ignatio fixed his stare on the bone handle sticking out of his body.

Releasing the knife, Cutter stepped back. His face twisted with shock.

A mangled series of expressions crossed Ignatio's face. First, confusion, as if he couldn't understand how the blade had pierced him, then surprise that he'd been mortally wounded. *"Imposible,"* he hissed, then turned his bewildered eyes toward Coward. "Traitor!"

Coward's lips pulled back into a sneer. *"Now the Reverend will see my strength!"*

Grimacing with a rage as dark as midnight, Ignatio dug at a tattoo on his stomach and peeled it free. "This demon is for *you*, Coward. A demon for your betrayal." Then, turning his agonized gaze toward Cutter, he said, "Destroy him, Miguel. Hold nothing back."

Shuddering, the sorcerer pitched backward in the dirt.

Within a heartbeat, every thrall in the cavern stiffened and screeched in fear. Cries of triumph rose from the people of Wisdom as the soldiers crumbled where they stood. Keech recalled the moment Bad Whiskey had perished in Bone Ridge, how the rejuvenated dead of the graveyard had tumbled back to their true deaths upon Whiskey's demise.

Keech hooted his own victorious cry—but stopped when Ignatio's fist fell open and a strange puddle of darkness poured off his palm. It was the tattoo Ignatio had peeled from his stomach in his final gesture of rebellion. The black liquid rippled along the ground, flowed over Cutter's boots, and climbed his leg with blinding speed.

Cutter dropped to his knees and shrieked as the substance seeped around his neck.

Keech recognized the spell. It was the curse of fury, the same curse that Ignatio had placed on Pa Abner in 1845. Though Ignatio was gone, his final affliction still lived.

With eyes drenched in terrible darkness, Cutter leaped to his boots and howled. He spun toward Coward, his tormentor. Panicked whimpers escaped Coward's throat, and he backpedaled on his hands and knees. "Stop, Miguel! I command you to stop!" Once again he shoved his finger into the brand on his palm, but this time to no avail.

Cutter surged forward, slamming into the man, and his fists crashed down like a storm. Coward's shouts and curses seemed incapable of penetrating the boy's fury. Opening his mouth, Coward released a vicious hacking noise, and Keech couldn't understand, at first, why the fellow would cough into Cut's face. Then he remembered how the man had knocked Quinn unconscious in Wisdom with a strange cough.

But Coward's magic didn't seem to work against Ignatio's curse. Cutter continued his frenzied assault. Frantic, Coward reached into his frock coat and pulled out a bone blade.

Abruptly, the blows stopped and Cutter jerked back, staggering away a few steps, hands clutching his stomach. Then he collapsed, unmoving.

CHAPTER 33
THE COUGH

Keech and Duck hurried to Cutter's side and dropped to their knees.

"Cut!" Duck yelled. "Talk to us!"

At first, Cutter didn't move or make a sound—but then he moaned.

Nearby, Coward struggled to his feet. In his hand, he gripped the Fang of Barachiel. A gathering of enraged townsfolk surrounded the dazed outlaw, pinning him against a far corner of the cavern. He looked subdued, with no more struggle left in him.

Stunned by their twist of luck, Keech turned back to Cutter. His friend's eyes were frightened and surprised—but clean of Ignatio's darkness. The Devil's mark on Cut's forehead was gone. Keech flung his arms around the boy's neck. "I'm so glad you're all right!"

Cutter rubbed his head weakly. "What happened?"

"Coward sliced you with the Fang. It was his only way to stop you from killing him, but it also freed you from his brand."

Cutter peered at the tear in his shirt where the healing dagger had penetrated, but there was no blood, not even the hint of a wound. He blinked up at them, stunned. "Duck?"

"Hey, Cut. Welcome back."

Disoriented, Cutter scrubbed a grimy palm over his face. "Where's John Wesley? He said he was comin' to find me." He glanced around the cavern.

Duck handed Cutter his dusty hat, which had fallen off his head during the skirmish. "He ain't here, Cut. John left months ago. He's a Chamelia now."

Cutter shook his head, bleary-eyed. "I've been trapped in a bad dream."

"But you're awake now," Keech said.

Cutter continued as if Keech hadn't spoken. "John was there, in the dream. He talked to me. Told me everything was gonna be okay." A deep gurgle rose in Cutter's throat, and he sobbed. Throwing his arms around his knees, he rocked back and forth in the dirt. "I did terrible things. I never wanted to, but I couldn't help it."

"Coward had you under his control. *He's* to blame for anything you did." Duck gestured across the cavern, where Coward was muttering curses at the townsfolk holding him prisoner.

"Let's go fetch the relics from Coward," Keech said—but was interrupted as a jubilant bark echoed across the cavern. Keech turned to see Achilles strolling proudly next to Quinn, who lifted his homemade ax high when he saw Keech and Duck. Walking behind him was Strong Heart, gripping her silver amulet shard and a jagged piece of her longbow, which had been broken in half. Her buckskin dress was torn in places, and the leggings around her calves had come untied. But she looked unharmed.

Keech and Duck greeted the pair with triumphant calls.

"*Hah-weh*, Keech," Strong Heart returned, her voice weary. She held out her palm to show a shard now dormant and dim. "The dead men are gone. Skeleton Peak is safe."

As if to prove her point, Quinn's aunt emerged from one of the tunnels, limping slightly and still holding the hammer she'd been wielding during the battle. The moment Ruth saw her nephew, she dropped the tool and quickened her pace to reach him. Crying joyfully, Ruth enfolded Quinn in her arms, and they embraced. Beside them, Achilles perched on his haunches and waited, his tongue batting the air.

"My dear Quinn! We did it! Just as you promised," Ruth said, rocking back and forth with Quinn in her arms. A small trickle of blood streamed down her cheek, but otherwise, she appeared unblemished. "We owe our lives to you and the Protector."

"You don't owe nobody, Auntie Ruth," Quinn said. "You fought your own battle to be free. I'm just so glad you're safe. I've missed you something terrible." Stepping back a bit, he examined the woman's face and wiped the blood off her cheek. "Do you have the strength to go a little farther? Most of the townsfolk are headed out to the main camp. Somebody needs to help them."

"I ain't leaving your side again," Ruth said.

Quinn grasped the woman's hand. "It's okay, Auntie. My friends and I are gonna mull over what to do next, then we'll meet you outside. Get out of this awful place."

Reluctantly, Ruth nodded. "Come fetch me as soon as you can."

As the woman limped out of the cavern, Keech gazed around Ignatio's devastated mining camp. "How on earth did y'all manage to stir up such a fight?"

Quinn shrugged. "When I found Auntie Ruth, she was itching to spring a revolt on the Big Snake. She'd already been scheming, so when we showed up, it didn't take much to get the camp organized." He paused to take a breath, then turned to Duck. "My eyes must've been fooling me earlier. I thought I saw you chuck a boulder the size of a cow."

Duck's cheeks reddened. "Thank the Char Stone for that."

"You never thought the Stone affected you, but I reckon it did," Quinn said, looking astonished; then he spotted Cutter and dropped to one knee beside him. "Cut, it's so good to see you again! We thought you was a goner."

Cutter said nothing in return. He simply rocked back and forth on the ground.

Kneeling, Strong Heart placed a hand under Cutter's chin and lifted his face so she could have a better look at him. He didn't seem to notice her touch. "What has happened to him?"

Keech explained the frenzied events leading up to Ignatio's death, including the rage curse the sorcerer had placed on Cutter to wield him like a weapon against Coward.

"He would've killed him if Coward hadn't used the Fang to stop the attack," Duck added. "The Fang released him from the curse, but it also freed Cut of the Devil's mark."

Keech went on to explain the rest of their story—their infiltration into the House of the Rabbit, the discovery of the Key of Enoch, and their forced surrender of the relic to Ignatio.

"And now Coward's got it," Duck said.

"He's got the Fang, too," Keech added.

"And don't forget the Char Stone," a quivering voice muttered.

Everyone turned to see Cutter struggling up from the ground.

Quinn helped the boy to his feet, and when Cut finally gained enough strength to stand, he said, "Ignatio ordered Coward to take the Stone to his cabin at the main camp."

"Then we'll need to go get it after we relieve Coward of the Key and the Fang," Keech said, turning again to Cutter: "Do you think you can ride?"

Cutter's face brightened. "You'll still ride with me? After everything that's happened?"

Keech said, "You belong beside us. Always have." Then Ignatio's body on the ground caught his attention. The bone handle of Cutter's blade still protruded from the sorcerer's chest. Keech moved to retrieve it, but Cutter stopped him.

"No, Blackwood. This is *my* burden. Let me."

Keech stepped back, letting the boy move closer.

Cutter peered down at the knife, which had pierced Ignatio's eye tattoo. He shook his head. "The prophecy came true after all. In Missouri, Bishop and I learned that the knife would someday kill 'the Eye,' but I'd always thought it meant Bad Whiskey. Now I know the knife's true purpose was to stop Ignatio."

"I can't believe that old thing was magic," Duck said.

"When we first met, it wasn't," Cutter said, then went on to explain his nighttime attack on Coward and how the blade had changed after striking the Char Stone. "The Stone must've filled it with enough power to stick Ignatio, and Coward knew it. Afterward, he let me keep the knife, told me I had a purpose. I think he wants to be Rose's lieutenant and was willing to kill anyone standing in his path."

Suddenly, a clamor echoed through the cavern—a booming sound, like the crack of a musket, only it sounded more like a human cough. The noise blasted over the Lost Causes with the force of a detonation, throwing all of them to the ground. Even Achilles tumbled off his paws, landing with a startled yelp on the rocky floor. Keech felt his head go fuzzy and dark, and a strange paralysis overtook his body. Against his will, his eyes fluttered shut.

When he could finally open them, Keech glanced around the camp, bewildered. "What in blazes happened?" he muttered.

Duck and Strong Heart were already back on their feet, gazing around with confused expressions.

"It was Coward!" Quinn shouted. "He knocked out the whole danged camp!"

Keech glanced across the cavern. Sure enough, the Wisdom prisoners who'd been holding Coward were scattered unconscious on the ground. Coward was gone. As were the Key and the Fang.

"No!" Keech exclaimed.

Duck's face clouded over with dread. "I'd wager he's headed to the summit."

"To catch the door," Quinn finished.

Strong Heart quoted the words from her elder, Buffalo Woman: "The land will lose the sun."

"Not if we can help it," Keech said. "It's a long way to the top, and Coward's tired and beaten. We can head him off."

"No time for standin' around, tadpoles!" shouted a voice.

Em O'Brien emerged from the mouth of a nearby tunnel. Her face was bruised from her scuffle with Black Charlie, the tangle that Keech had assumed was her last. But the fierce fire in the woman's eyes told him the Enforcer still had plenty of fight left. She shuffled toward them, clutching her stomach and favoring one leg. Blood spattered the bull hide of her batwing chaps, and the brim of her hat looked mangled. As she moved closer, O'Brien scrutinized each of their battle-worn faces.

"I'm afraid Coward put y'all down longer than ya think."

Keech felt the terrible wash of dread return to his heart. "How long, O'Brien?"

"I have peered into the Prime, and as we speak, Coward's almost to the mountaintop. Which means the relics are one step closer to the Palace of the Thunders." The Enforcer wiped a splash of blood off her cheek. "Collect yer horses and gather yer grit. We've got ourselves a door to catch."

15 March 1855

My dearest Eliza,

Thirteen days have passed since your mother and I lost you to the Erinyes River. Thirteen eternal days, but I still hear your bright laughter as if you were standing beside me. I feel your presence in the meadows and woods, the hollows where I build my camps. I speak to you in the stillness of the dark and wonder if you can hear the voice of your beloved father.

Dearest daughter, I have left our home to save you. I have abandoned my darling Gerty, and your brother, John, holding to the highest hope that the conjurings I chased in my youth can serve a happier, more hopeful purpose.

For the task I now undertake—for the terrible things I must surely do—I beg your forgiveness. I beg that you trust me as I take your body from the ground.

Trust your father, dear Eliza, as I go to find your soul. Trust me as I go to pull you from the dark of death. Trust me that I will bring you home.

I promise that you will see your life again. Even if I must perish, you will see it.

Love,

Father

CHAPTER 34
THE DOOR AT THE SUMMIT

O'Brien led the way up Old Beggar's Trail, keeping her horse's pace to a steady trot to avoid tiring the rest of the group. After emerging from the Peak, they had met back up with Ruth, who had insisted on accompanying Quinn up to the summit. As they all hastened up the mountain trail, the snow melted from the thickets. The ice that had clung to the bitterbrush steadily dripped into puddles, turning the dirt path into a slushy mess.

"Why are the snows thawing?" Strong Heart asked.

"Ignatio's death," O'Brien said. "When the Enforcers rode with him, the scoundrel bragged he could bridle Mother Nature herself. The demons he commanded could do many things, such as spread darkness over towns and woods, but his most insidious trick was twistin' the weather to his will. Ignatio could summon blizzards and thunderstorms so violent they could blot out the land for months."

"That explains the constant ice storms in Kansas," Duck said.

"And the never-ending blizzards we've been suffering here," said Ruth.

A few minutes later, the group proceeded through a nest of ponderosa pines and emerged on a sprawling crest, a summit so high that Keech thought he might be standing at the top of the world. Around them, the lesser mountains of the Rockies rolled across the land, gathering around Skeleton Peak like minions kneeling before their king.

"Look! There!" said Strong Heart.

Several yards away, tall white stones stood in a semicircle. In the center of this half ring, a brilliant blue column of energy pulsed. The shimmering gateway was similar to the golden doors of the Kansas bending trees that had allowed the Lost Causes passage to and from the western shore of Bonfire Crossing.

Near this glimmering pillar of light, a ferocious struggle ensued. Keech recognized the small form of Coward facing off against Edgar Doyle, who appeared to be down on one knee and holding up his hands in a defensive posture. Saint Peter reared up wildly behind Coward, as if trying to knock the outlaw away from the magic door. Furious winds swirled around the three, whipping dust and thawing snow into a violent twister.

"It ain't too late!" said Quinn. "The Ranger's stopping him!"

Keech wanted to feel the same hope, but a dismal realization occurred to him. "If Doyle gets his hands on the relics, it won't matter if he stops Coward. He'll take them to the Palace himself. We have to catch up!"

Galloping hard up the final stretch of Old Beggar's Trail, Keech watched the struggle in the distance unfold like a bad dream, as Coward sprang at his harried opponent.

"Ranger Doyle!" Quinn shouted, whipping Lightnin's reins back and forth. Behind him, Ruth held on to Quinn's waist for dear life.

Suddenly, Keech saw the Ranger pitch forward onto his hands and knees. At the same time, Coward leaned in as if whispering in Doyle's ear.

"He's putting him down with his cough!" Quinn shouted.

As soon as Quinn spoke the words, Doyle collapsed, tumbling onto his back. A second later, Coward leaped onto his chest.

Behind the outlaw, Saint Peter's form shifted into that of a man, his eyes a vibrant emerald, his hair the pitch-black of a raven. Keech had seen the Kelpie's human figure once before, under the ocean surface at Bonfire Crossing.

With long, muscled arms, Saint Peter reached for Coward.

Spinning, Coward thrust an open metal box at Saint Peter's naked chest. The moment the contents of the box touched the Kelpie's flesh, Saint Peter shrieked with an inhuman cry, floundered violently, and toppled onto his side.

"They're in trouble!" Keech yelled at the group.

Another terrible scream shattered the air as Doyle writhed beneath Coward. A heartbeat later, the outlaw shuffled to his feet. Shouting triumphantly, he seized Doyle's coat collar with one hand and snatched up the gear containing the relics with the other. Then with startling strength, Coward tugged the squirming Ranger through the glowing blue doorway. Keech heard Doyle bellow, "*Stop, Coward! I can't leave her! Stop!*" But a second later, the magical radiance surrounded the two men, and they blinked out of sight. Only Saint Peter remained, but his body appeared to fade from sight, as if the sunlight were dissolving him.

"We're too late!" Duck hollered.

At last, the group reached the site of the doorway and bounded off their horses. Keech hurried toward Saint Peter's body, hoping for a way to assist, but naught could be done. Like a block of melting ice, the Kelpie sank into the soil, inch by inch. A strange wheezing haunted the air as Saint Peter disappeared. Duck and Strong Heart gasped, while Achilles whined in sorrow.

"What happened?" Keech asked, running his hand over the place where Saint Peter had been lying.

O'Brien said, "The box Coward held contains the Char Stone. Even the slightest brush against the Stone is certain death."

"But where'd he go?"

O'Brien's voice trembled as she said, "Saint Peter was an *elemental* creature. Hard to say, but I believe he's passed back into the ground and the deep waters beneath."

Achilles sniffed at the place where Saint Peter's body had vanished, then backed away toward Quinn, yelping. "It's okay," Quinn said. "You're safe."

The Kelpie's transformation into a man had left Doyle's belongings on the ground, including the Ranger's saddle and all the tack he'd been riding with for months. Keech unlashed Doyle's knapsack from the fallen saddle and reached inside. His hand enclosed a hard, round object, and he pulled it out. It was the skull of Doyle's lost daughter, Eliza. Horrified, Keech placed the remains gently back into the bag. He stepped away from the knapsack, shaking his head in sorrow and disgust, till Duck said, "I reckon she can be buried now."

"Maybe," Keech said, "but then again, maybe not." He grabbed Doyle's knapsack and slung it over one shoulder, feeling the light heft of Eliza's bones inside. "Call it another hunch. We should take this along."

On the other side of the magical door, Strong Heart said to the group, "There was a fire pit here. The ashes are still warm. It burned recently."

Sure enough, the remnants of a small campfire smoldered near the stone floor of the semicircle. A few blood-soaked bandages lay scattered on the ground.

O'Brien squatted over the cinders. "Red must've known we'd eventually come up this way. I'd wager he waited for Coward to find the door."

Duck shook her head. "And now he's a hostage. We best get moving."

O'Brien said, "You tadpoles oughta know that even if ya do stop Coward, reclaimin' the relics won't be enough. As long as Rose stays hidden inside the Palace, he'll keep corruptin' the world. He has to be stopped *all the way*. We Enforcers thought we could hide the relics and bury the past, but it all caught up to us. If we go through that door, we have to face Rose and finish him."

Keech gazed at the glimmering door, dreading what lay beyond. He remembered O'Brien's words in her cabin: *Rose led us through it in thirty-three, and we stepped out into Thunder Pass, the canyon that hides the Palace.*

There was one last thing to do before they continued. "I almost forgot," he said, reaching into his coat pocket. Keech pulled out the Ranger's leatherbound book and the ripped-out pages O'Brien had given him. He held them up. "Not long ago, you told me we oughta burn this. You were right," he said to Duck. A small laugh escaped his lips. "You tend to be right most of the time."

Silence overtook the group as they regarded the old journal. So much of Doyle's knowledge filled the pages within—a world of insights that could, given time, open the Lost Causes to all the answers they would need to stop the Reverend Rose. Even more, the pages contained Doyle's heart. A thousand moments of lonesome trail writing, captured between these bindings.

But the pages also contained unfathomable darkness.

Letting out a deep breath, Keech tossed the Ranger's journal and the ripped pages onto the ashen pile of the campfire. As he did, he felt a stirring in his gut. Free of anger, he could once again hear the tune of the world. He could *focus*.

Keech pointed his finger at the smoldering cinders. A fervent energy rose from deep inside his center, and without speaking a word, he directed the power into a fingertip. New flames sputtered from the smoke, and the campfire burst to life. A moment later, Doyle's journal was no more.

"There, it's finished," Keech said.

The young riders shuffled to their horses, except for Quinn, who went to his aunt Ruth. Taking her hands, he said, "I finally found you, and I thought getting you back was all I needed. But I ain't done fighting yet, Auntie. My team needs my help. I've got to go away again, but I'll be back soon. I swear it."

O'Brien interjected. "Realize, Quinn, that this is a one-way trip through the door. If we succeed, we won't be comin' back soon. It'll take weeks, maybe months, to reach yer aunt again."

Quinn and Ruth shared pained expressions at the news, then the woman Quinn had been seeking for months kissed his cheek and embraced him. Tears tumbled from her eyes as she said, "Do what you have to do, son. I'll head back down to the camp, keep helping the folks of Wisdom pack for the journey home. When you're finished, find your way back to me, alive and well."

"Don't you worry," Quinn said. "I'll come back."

Leading their horses, the young riders hurried over to the shimmering doorway. Achilles ran beside then, yipping with excitement. O'Brien paused for a moment by the Ranger's campfire, glancing down at the flames.

"O'Brien, what are you doing?" asked Duck.

"Where we're goin', we'll need weapons. I got a bundle of tricks in my tack, but we'll need somethin' with a little more *oomph*." Cracking her knuckles, she opened a pouch on her filly's saddle and pulled out a handful of lime-green weeds, plants that whistled as she touched them. Keech recognized the strange brush at once. They were the special weeds from her cabin, the ones that grew in the untainted ground below her trapdoor.

"I grabbed a fistful of these after my scuffle with Black Charlie," O'Brien said, kneeling beside Doyle's fire. "Time to show you tadpoles what they can do." She then crafted the whistling stalks into a loose ball, a sphere the size of her palm, and rolled the green ball back and forth through the gray ash of the campfire. Before Keech's eyes, the soot-covered orb changed color, turning a shiny black, and appeared to stiffen like baked tar in the Enforcer's hand.

"*Dios mío*, it's a whistle bomb!" Cutter exclaimed.

O'Brien smiled shrewdly, then proceeded to make five more bombs out of the weeds and ash. When she was done, she carefully tucked the explosives into her saddlebag. "*Now* we can ride," she said.

"*Everyone halt there!*" a gruff voice bellowed.

Keech wheeled around in surprise. O'Brien dropped her hand to a pouch on her hip, and Achilles let out a short barrage of startled barks.

330

Two horsemen galloped up the final stretch of Old Beggar's Trail. One of the riders was a middle-aged man, broad-shouldered, with a heavy, untamed beard. The second rider was a blond-haired boy, no older than twelve or thirteen.

By the time the horsemen reached them, Keech's mind was already rejecting what his eyes were seeing. What he was seeing couldn't be.

"Thank the merciful heavens," the big man said to Keech, adjusting his tan hat. "I never thought we'd reach you."

The horseman who'd spoken looked the spitting image of Bose Turner, the sheriff of Big Timber, the lawman who had stood tall with the Lost Causes in Missouri.

But it was the sight of the *second* horseman—the young boy with the dandelion hair, sitting atop a pony that looked astoundingly like Minerva, Felix's old partner—that nearly stopped Keech's heart with disbelief.

"Keech!" the boy bellowed, dismounting his pony with a leap. His face was full of light, his voice full of astonishment, doubt, relief. "At long last, I've found ya! I've finally found ya, big brother! It's *me*. It's the Rabbit!"

CHAPTER 35
THE RABBIT AND THE WOLF

For one crystallized moment, Keech dared not blink or breathe as he took in this new vision of Sam. A thousand warring emotions blustered through his heart. He couldn't discern whether he was seeing the real Sam or another hallucination. Ignatio was dead and gone, which meant the boy standing before him couldn't be another shadow demon, but Rose's magic had deceived Keech so many times before. *This* Sam looked different in subtle ways—a few months older, his features weathered by months of traveling over frigid wilderness—and the changes made sense in a way the dream Sam never did. Keech's gut told him this *was* the real Sam, yet his heart pulled back from the idea, afraid to open up to the pain of being hoodwinked yet again.

Keech shuffled closer. "*Sam?* Are you a . . . *trick?*"

The blond-haired boy sprinted toward Keech, peeling off his riding gloves. He opened his arms wide for a hug, but Keech approached the kid with caution and reached out with one hand. Sam mirrored the motion, and their fingers touched, hesitated, then locked together.

Keech cried out in shock. The boy's skin felt warm and alive—nothing like the ice-cold phantom on the Sante Fe Trail. Sam grinned. "It's *me*, Keech. We've come a long way."

Still grasping Sam's living hand, Keech peered at the weather-worn form of Bose Turner. "*Sheriff?* Is that you, too?"

Sheriff Turner had grown a bulky beard to go with his mustache, and the shoulder that Bad Whiskey's thrall had wounded in the town of Whistler drooped a bit. He said, "In the flesh, Mr. Blackwood. It's good to see you again. We've been chasing your trail for over two months now. I was beginnin' to wonder if we'd ever catch up."

Keech peered skeptically at Sam again. "But *how?* I saw the flames overtake the Home!"

Sam unlocked his fingers and placed his hand on Keech's shoulder. "It was chaos that night when Bad Whiskey took Pa. It was hard to see anything true. I'm afraid you saw only a tiny scrap of what happened, Keech. Remember what Pa used to say in the training circle? 'When survival's at stake—'"

"'The mind can deceive,'" Keech finished, then seized the moment to hug Sam with all his might. "You're real! You're actually real."

Sam's laughter filled the summit. "Real as the rain, Keech. The sheriff told me how you figured we all had died in the fire. But it was all a big mix-up."

Keech said, "I don't understand, Sam. You were *in the flames.* You were signaling me to run 'cause you were a goner!"

Sam laughed again. "I was *telling* you to head back to Big Timber, where we could meet up. Pa Abner *knew*, Keech. He knew the Reverend's men would come after him someday. So he put precautions all over the Home. He built a secret tunnel out of the cellar, a shaft that ran all the way down to the southern woods. That's how we all survived. Granny Nell led everyone to safety. Later, I met up with the sheriff." Sam glanced at Bose Turner and smiled.

Sheriff Turner continued the story. "After I returned from Bone Ridge, I found your family alive and well in Big Timber. They caught me up on their side of things, and I told Sam here about your brave stand against Bad Whiskey. I realized I'd sent you Lost Causes to the town of Wisdom for a new lead, so we decided to hunt down your trail to bring you home. But your team had already ridden too far; your trail vanished for a long while in Kansas."

Quinn gazed around at the others, clearly marveling at the sudden turn of events. "I'd wager it vanished because we hopped all the way to Oregon Territory."

"To Bonfire Crossing," Strong Heart added with a curious grin.

Turner looked impressed. "So you found the Crossing after all."

Keech gripped his orphan brother's arm. Out of everything he was hearing, he still couldn't believe one impossible detail. "Sam, you're saying the whole family is *alive*? Patrick, Little Eugena, Robby? And Granny Nell, too?"

"For the smartest kid I know, you sure don't listen good," said Sam. "That's what I'm tellin' you, all right. They're all waitin' back in the Timber!"

Keech's knees gave up their strength, and he crumpled where he stood. But Sam caught his arms and tugged him back up. Indeed, the impossible had happened. Keech's family had returned to him.

Moving to Minerva, Keech laid his hand on the pony's neck. "Hello, sweet girl. I never thought I'd see you again."

As Minerva nuzzled Keech's arm, Sam said, "I see you got yourself a cremello stallion, Keech. Where's Felix?"

Shaking with emotions too profound to grasp, Keech said, "He passed on to the next meadow. I'll tell you the whole story someday." He patted Minerva's neck once more, then turned to his trailmates. "Everyone, this is my brother. His name is *Sam*."

Duck tipped her hat politely, but the tiniest tremor stole to her lip. After so many months on the trail, he could read her expressions as plainly as words on a page. The sight of Sam caused her pain, and Keech understood why. His orphan brother had come back to him, a walking miracle. But Duck's brother, Nat, was still gone, as were her folks.

Strong Heart held a similar ache in her eyes. As did Cutter and Quinn. Their families were gone, with only Quinn's aunt Ruth and Strong Heart's uncle, Strong Bones, remaining.

But they still had a mission. They still sought justice.

Which meant Keech did, too.

Working hard to calm his mind, to find some kind of rational thought inside this cloud of revelations, he said to Sam, "I can't ride back to Big Timber just yet. Right now, we have to stop what's on the other side of that door."

Sam peered at the glowing column. "Back home, I saw dead men get up and walk around the yard. I saw a crow whisper in Bad Whiskey's ear. But I never saw *anything* like this."

O'Brien cleared her throat. "I hate to interrupt yer reunion, Keech, but our clock is tickin'. Every second we pause, Coward gets closer to freein' Rose from the Palace."

Sam frowned bitterly at the name. "If the Reverend Rose intends to unleash more wickedness upon the Earth, then you best believe I'm riding through that door."

Keech's mouth dropped open. "You'll go with me?"

"I didn't come this far to let you slip away again."

Relieved, but understanding he needed to be fair to his team, Keech looked at the others. "Well, Lost Causes, what do you say? Sam might be smaller than a tick, but Pa Abner trained him like me, and he's quicker than a bullet. I vouch for him."

"Nathaniel always did put things up for a vote," Duck said. "I vote *yes*."

After Strong Heart, Cutter, and Quinn voted their affirmatives, Sam's face beamed. "Sheriff Turner, you're coming, too. You *have* to. Won't you?"

The sheriff smirked. "What's that? Stay on this muddy mountain and miss my chance to ride through a magic door? Whether you need me or not, you've got my pistol."

Mounting her filly, O'Brien said, "We're gonna need ya, all right. Now, we best get going. That door's about to disappear." Before heading into the glimmer, she swiveled around in her saddle and faced the posse one last time. "Watch one another's backs, and expect the fight of yer lives. It's time to stand tall."

Achilles barked wildly and sprang toward the light.

Grabbing Hector's reins, Keech followed his friends to the door. Giving final nods of assurance, O'Brien spurred her horse into the dazzling blue. Sheriff Turner followed with a loud "Hyahh!" then Duck and Cutter proceeded next, blinking away as easy as smoke, followed by Strong Heart and Quinn.

Keech and Sam were last to approach.

"The Rabbit and the Wolf, side by side again," Sam said.

"Just like it's supposed to be," Keech added. Then, seizing Hector's reins with purpose, he lifted his fist to the sky and bellowed his next words at the top of his lungs, words he recalled from Sam's readings of the Bible. *"Behold a pale horse, Reverend! And the rider that sits upon him is Death! We're coming for you! The Lost Causes are coming, and we're bringing the fire with us!"*

Snapping their reins in unison, Keech and Sam rode their horses into the light.

PART FOUR

THE PALACE OF THE THUNDERS

CHAPTER 36
LAND OF THE PURPLE SKY

Read the earth. Let it tell you its story.
—PA ABNER

At first, Keech couldn't see anything but flashes of light all around. Then the brilliant sparkles deepened into a strange glow the color of plum wine. He glanced back and caught his final glimpse of the summit of Skeleton Peak. The Rocky Mountains dissolved as the door's opening winked out and a new landscape unfurled around Keech like a giant patchwork quilt. Warmth cascaded over his face, and he wheezed as if he'd breathed in a lungful of campfire smoke. Even worse, a musty scent rode the acrid breeze, forcing him to wonder if the door had spirited them away to a domain of demons and Dead Rift creatures.

"Where are we?" asked Sam.

Gone were the ponderosa pines and the tall white stones, the stone ruin in which the Peak's door had stood. Neither was there any sign of snow on the ground. In fact, they were now standing on a cracked pavement of sorts, a solid floor of hundreds of bone-colored fieldstones. To their right, rolling hills stretched, the dry grasses that covered them sepia-toned, like old daguerreotype portraits. The land on their left dropped off a bluff into a deep gorge below.

The new sky burned a bizarre purple better suited to a wild dream, drowning any sense of day or night. Across this murky violet curtain, flashes of light erupted. Terrible thunder grumbled, but the relentless growl seemed to bear no connection to the lightning. Keech searched for any sign of sunlight so they could calculate the time, but he couldn't see the first hint of a sunray, nor any moon or stars.

"Wherever we are, I much don't care for it," Cutter said.

Duck said, "Me neither. I ain't even sure we're still standing on Earth."

"We are still in our world," Strong Heart assured them. She pointed to layers of prickly brown scrub enshrouding the stony land. "The ground here grows *mo^n-hi^n-pa*. Or as you would say, bitterweed. It would be strange for another world to grow *mo^n-hi^n-pa*, I think."

O'Brien climbed down from her filly and took an inventory of herb pouches in her saddlebag. She paused to glance at their surroundings. "We've come to the canyon known as Thunder Pass. Believe it or not, tadpoles, we're standin' over one thousand miles from Skeleton Peak. We're in Oregon Territory, hundreds of miles northeast of Bonfire Crossin'. And what's happenin' here, the awful darkness, is no natural occurrence or coincidence. It's the Prime. It's preparin' the way for the Reverend's liberation."

Dismounting, Cutter led Chantico toward the steep bluff. He whistled at the gorge. "*¡Dios mío!* Now ain't *that* a sight."

Hundreds of feet below, a tumbling river carved a channel through the deep ravine. A steady roar rumbled from the white waters, and sprays of foam exploded along the river. Under the swirling dark sky, the tributary looked like a highway of liquid copper burning a long furrow into the earth.

"That there," O'Brien said, "is the Rattlebrook River."

On the opposite side of the Rattlebrook, a tower of bone-white granite rose against the purple, a giant face of jagged outcroppings and sheer cliffs that stole Keech's breath away. Broken steeples of rock teetered along the heights like spires atop some ancient castle.

O'Brien's face turned dire as she took in the cliffs. "The Palace of the Thunders."

As if in response, the sky flashed with lightning, sparks of energy crisscrossing the sky.

A dusty path just wide enough for a horse led off to the side, switching back and forth and disappearing behind crooked pines and scabrous rocks. "That's the way down," O'Brien said. "It'll take a short while to navigate. I suspect Coward's on it as we speak."

"Looks like we'll have to ride single file," Sheriff Turner cautioned.

"I'll take the lead," O'Brien said. "Sheriff, you back me up. Keep your pistol drawn."

Strong Heart gestured down to the riverbank pines across the water. "There's movement behind the trees, near the base of the wall."

The relentless thunder echoed all around, making it hard for Keech to concentrate as he scanned the Rattlebrook's opposite bank. But sure enough, he spotted a lurking figure. At first, he thought it might be Coward, or perhaps Doyle, already down the bluff and across the rapids, but then more sinister movement caught Keech's eye. A battalion of shadowy footmen skulked behind the pines. Then a flood of soldiers infiltrated Thunder Pass from upriver, their boots chomping up the ground in lumbering lockstep. Hot winds kicked up from the canyon floor, and Keech smelled a sour tang in the air.

"That's a whole danged army!" Sam barked.

"We've been expecting this," Duck said. She yanked her amulet shard out of her coat. The silver was dormant. "We're too far away to tell if they're thralls, but my hunch is, those men are as dead as they smell."

O'Brien grunted. "They're thralls, all right. And over yonder"— she pointed to a strange desperado crawling up the Palace wall like a lizard—"that's the Weaver boss, Lost Tucker."

The gangly woman creeping up the limestone wore tattered garments and no boots. She splayed against the rock and surveyed the valley. Another figure scurried up to her, then slid into a gap in the wall, like a spider hiding in a crack. A third Weaver mounted a jagged pillar and issued a bloodcurdling scream.

"What is wrong with her?" Strong Heart asked.

O'Brien scowled. "She once rode with the Enforcers. When the Reverend brought us into the Palace, she dared to touch the Dead Rift inside. She reached out with just a finger, but it was plenty. Somethin' from the other side got into 'er. Tainted Tucker's soul. She *changed*. Became that thing. Whatever you tadpoles do, don't let her bite ya, else she'll turn ya into a Weaver, and you'll lust for blood and death till yer dyin' day."

Sheriff Turner turned his gaze toward the Palace wall. "There's at least three hundred down there. Maybe four hundred souls."

"Not souls, my friend. They ain't *got* souls," O'Brien said as she studied the troops. "Once Coward crosses the Rattlebrook, that horde will stand in our way, protectin' Coward as he uses the Key to enter the Palace. Once he's in, there won't be a way to follow. He'll begin the ritual that'll finally set Rose free."

"*I'll* stop him," Cutter growled, flashing his knife. "Make him regret the day he gave Miguel Herrera the Devil's mark."

O'Brien hopped up into her saddle. "I admire yer pluck, tadpole, but we'll need a better tactic than rushin' up. I got a few tricks up my sleeve, but first we need to get down there. It's a steep ride, so watch every step." Spurring her filly, the Enforcer started down the path.

CHAPTER 37
COWARD AND THE KEY

This world has many crows, and those crows can see far
and take what they see to dangerous places.
—PA ABNER

They were halfway down the switchback when the crows attacked.

The descent was frightening enough, given the steep drop. Keech worried most about Hector; the path was particularly narrow for such a large stallion. But despite Hector's unmistakable discomfort, he progressed steadily down the path, following the others with his head up and ears alert.

A deafening *Ack! Ack!* made Keech jump in his saddle.

A spray of black erupted from the top of the far granite cliff like a whale spouting ebony ink. Dozens of Rose's crows twisted together in the sky, forming a grotesque braid, then dived at the Lost Causes. Across the Rattlebrook River, a malicious cheer broke out.

"So much for the element of surprise," Sheriff Turner moaned.

The lead crow swooped down on Cutter as he brought up the rear of their line. At the last possible second, the crow veered to the side, aiming its razor-sharp beak at Chantico's hindquarters, and narrowly missed the horse's flesh. Cutter lunged at the crow with his blade. The knife slashed the creature's wing, and red flames engulfed it. The next crow tried to fly upward, but once more, Cutter's blade sent the bird to a fiery death.

The rest of the crows pulled back, screeching their frustration.

Keech glanced ahead to see Duck and Strong Heart holding their amulet shards at the ready, the charms now glowing a bright yellow across their palms. Sheriff Turner pulled his revolver and squeezed off a few rounds at the crows, but his shots missed their marks.

"Hurry to the bottom!" O'Brien called. "If they spook the horses, we could tumble!"

Keech glanced down the side of the bluff and felt his stomach clench at the long drop. Trusting Hector, he released his reins and twisted in the saddle to better track the crows. A few of the creatures broke formation, swinging wide of Cutter and his deadly blade.

A pair of crows flashed past Sam and Minerva, cutting into the pony's flank and slashing at the forearm Sam had thrown up to shield his head.

Keech realized he could best protect the troop by finding his focus. He lifted his hand, pointed at one of the crows, and felt a surge of energy flow from his core. "Bang!" he yelled.

The bird exploded.

Bellowing at the crows, O'Brien flung a handful of greenish dust over the drop. For an instant, the powder hung in the air like a lazy cloud of pollen. Then specks of green shot out of the mist. The grains flew like hornets at the crows. Though many missed their targets, dozens of the particles struck home, tearing into the flock.

Moments later, the group reached the bottom of the canyon.

They gathered behind a long boulder near the riverbank and dismounted. They were banged up, but Keech supposed things could have been worse.

The crows continued to circle overhead. O'Brien had greatly reduced their numbers, but a new swarm of birds emerged from the top of the Palace and joined the others.

"Those rotten things just keep coming," Sam said.

"As long as we have the amulet shards, we can keep them at bay," said Duck. "My concern is Coward. Where in blazes could he be?"

As if to answer to her, Coward sprang into view on the opposite bank of the river. He approached a squad of thrall soldiers and yelled at the men. Keech searched the rabble for Doyle, but the Ranger was nowhere to be seen.

Then Coward pointed across the river, aiming his finger at the boulder that sheltered the Lost Causes. Quinn muttered, "Uh-oh. We've been spotted!"

Saluting the outlaw, the rotting soldiers raised their muskets. Thunder Pass erupted with the volley of musket fire. Though the boulder offered some protection, the posse still dropped to their stomachs as lead balls pinged off the rocks around them.

"That weasel's almost to the Palace wall," O'Brien grumbled.

"I'd wager there's a place upriver where we could cross," said Turner, "but by the time we find it, we'd be too late."

Keech risked a peek around the boulder. Across the river, portions of the army had parted to allow Coward through. The outlaw had reached the stone wall of the Palace.

"I can't see nothing over there," said Sam. "Where's your Ranger friend?"

Keech squinted for a better glimpse across the Rattlebrook and thought he saw a patch of brown leather behind Coward. But then a lead ball zinged past his face, and Keech pulled back. When he looked again, Rose's horde had closed up the space around Coward, and any possible sign of Doyle was lost.

Turning momentarily from the wall, Coward shouted a quick speech to the undead mob. "My friends, today is the day!" His words boomed over Thunder Pass as if a giant were speaking. "The Reverend shall be made new!" Then Coward pulled the Key of Enoch from his saddlebag. Wrapping the shackle and chain around his arm, he shouted, "All who see the Master's face shall tremble!"

"We're too late!" Duck cried.

"We *must* cross the river," Strong Heart said.

A fresh salvo of musket fire cracked the humid air, pushing the Lost Causes back down to their stomachs. High above, the crows whirled frantically through the violet sky. When Keech heard a break in the gunfire, he again lifted his head and saw Doyle stumbling behind Coward. A crowd of jeering thralls surrounded them.

"I see the Ranger! Coward's dragging him in!" Keech yelled.

Time seemed to freeze as Coward stepped into the solid rock wall, hauling Doyle with him, and both men passed like phantoms into the Palace. Once they disappeared, Lost Tucker, her Weavers, and every thrall in Thunder Pass shouted waves of triumphant mirth that echoed up and down the canyon. The crows in the sky cawed with maniacal glee.

O'Brien dropped her head in defeat. "That's it, then. The end of it. We're done for."

"Now hold on," Quinn said. "Maybe there's still another way." He looked deep in thought as he turned his gaze upward.

"Well, spill the beans, Revels," Duck said. "We ain't getting any younger."

Adjusting his forage cap, Quinn gestured to the top of the great wall, where the crows were swarming. "Those birds are flying out of the Palace, right? So maybe there's something like a *chimney*. And maybe we can use it to sneak in."

"*Dios mío*, you gotta be kidding," Cutter mumbled.

Keech felt his insides bunch up like knotted ropes. "You're suggesting we cross this river, stroll past that army, and scale a wall. Then face all those crows, and climb down a chimney—assuming there even *is* a chimney—to get to Rose."

Quinn offered the group a feeble smile. "Yeah, I reckon that's what I'm saying."

Sam looked eager to weigh in. "While we were riding down, I studied the Palace wall. I think I spotted a way up. I could lead a team if we can get past Rose's army."

"Hiding us won't be a problem," Quinn said. "What I can't figure out is how we'll get across the Rattlebrook. The rapids are too heavy."

Keech wanted to suggest they use a series of ropes to ford the river. But before he could start, O'Brien pulled a small leather pouch out of her coat and held it up to the light.

"Leave that part to me," she said.

Quinn glanced at the pouch with interest, then said, "In that case, everybody listen up . . ."

CHAPTER 38
THE FROZEN RIVER

If you're ever in danger, be smart. Weigh every decision with care.
—PA ABNER

T he company huddled close as Quinn drew up their battle scheme, scratching a few lines in the sand with a fingertip. Achilles nestled under Quinn's arm, as if wanting the first peek at the strategy. Speaking quickly, Quinn laid out the plan, making sure to include Sam's approach to the Palace wall. Strong Heart expressed concern about leaving O'Brien and the sheriff to hold back the army, but the Enforcer assured the girl she had plenty more pouches and tricks.

"I'll buy you tadpoles the time ya need," O'Brien said.

Sheriff Turner patted the grip of his Colt revolver. "We won't let those goons get anywhere near you."

Achilles barked and hopped back and forth. Patting the dog's head, Quinn said, "You stay close to O'Brien and the sheriff, hear? They're gonna need backup."

Opening the pouch she'd taken from her coat, O'Brien drew out a bluish powder and placed the substance on her palm. Dozens of tiny, brilliant sparkles flashed in the grains.

"Everybody ready?" O'Brien asked.

When the Lost Causes gave their collective nod, the Enforcer pursed her lips and blew the soft blue grains toward the raging Rattlebrook. A cloud of sapphire puffed into the air, catching in the wind. Wisps of powder drifted over the water.

Muskets roared, and lead balls smashed into the boulder and dirt near the Lost Causes. Angry hissing filled the air as Lost Tucker and her Weaver spawn cried out.

O'Brien dodged back to her cover. "Now we give it a second to work."

"For *what* to work?" asked Cutter.

The Enforcer flashed her wild grin. "Wait for the signal."

A high-pitched voice echoed from across the channel. "I saw you, Em! My Weavers are champin' at the bit to shred your bones!"

"Lost Tucker," O'Brien muttered to the group, then hollered back to the woman, "If yer Weavers are so eager to tussle, send 'em across the Rattle to git me!"

A shrill cackle followed from Lost Tucker. "Just you wait, Em! You'll see what the Master has in store for you! For all of you!"

The purple sky flashed with a fresh explosion of lightning. The foulness in the bitter breeze seemed to sour further. The air was warm, something Keech had missed the last few months, but now the heat seemed oppressive.

Then he noticed something curious. The constant roar of the river had disappeared. A supernatural stillness washed over Thunder Pass.

"The Rattle's gone silent!" Duck said. "I reckon that's the signal."

Needing no further instructions, Quinn sang a passage from *The Odyssey*. His voice sounded scratchy and spent, but as he sang,

Keech felt the familiar cascade of energy concealing the group inside Quinn's magical bubble.

"We best hurry," Keech said, checking that Doyle's satchel was secure around his shoulder.

"The horses should be safe here," Strong Heart said.

Sam pulled a long coil of rope down from Minerva's saddle. "We'll need this, I reckon."

Cutter spun his magic-infused blade. "Don't forget this."

"I'll clear us a path to the wall," Duck said, wrapping her hands around a chunk of stone nearly as big as her own body. She glanced at Quinn. "Ready?"

Quinn gave a quick thumbs-up, his eyes roving and alert.

The Lost Causes stepped out from their cover to find the Rattlebrook River frozen solid, a twisting tumble of motionless ice, thanks to O'Brien's blue powder. The posse raced toward the petrified waters. As they reached the shoreline, Keech could see thralls hunched behind rocks and tree trunks, holding their muskets in firing position. They weren't shooting, Keech reckoned, because they couldn't see the Lost Causes approaching.

With a furious grunt, Duck hurled the stone she carried. The rock sailed like a cannonball across the paralyzed river and crashed with monstrous force onto the far bank. Pine trunks shattered, and thrall bodies flew in every direction. Rose's army bellowed, and muskets fired in unison. The volleys weren't aimed at the group, but a few shots whizzed close enough that Keech yelled to O'Brien, "We need cover!"

"Comin' right up," the Enforcer said. She tapped Sheriff Turner's shoulder and whistled to Achilles. "Let's go!" The three peeled off from the young riders, racing down the Rattlebrook's bank. In only a few steps, they left Quinn's protective bubble and were exposed.

A thrall in the distance pointed at O'Brien and the sheriff. More muskets were roused in clumsy succession. Turner cracked off a few shots from his Colt, kicking up dirt on the opposite shore. O'Brien flung another handful of green dust, and once again a swarm of mites shot out of the emerald cloud. The cluster buzzed like angry wasps toward Rose's army, giving O'Brien, Turner, and Achilles time to head for cover.

Following Duck and Strong Heart, Keech stepped out onto the frozen river. They likely had only a few more seconds before the spell on the water broke, so he moved urgently. He'd expected to slide across the surface, as if coasting over a sheet of ice, but the water was soft beneath his boots, like stepping through a patch of rotten pumpkins. In seconds, the Lost Causes reached the other side and gathered in a tight cluster.

Thralls lingered not ten feet away on the shore, staring across the river to where O'Brien, Turner, and Achilles were holed up. A hairy man in ragged clothes stalked past the thrall soldiers and hissed, "Hurry up, ya worthless fools! Load yer muskets and fire! You'll be rewarded for every runt ya kill, but if ya shy away from battle, I'll take yer heads!" As he spoke, Keech spotted rows of fanged teeth, like Black Charlie's. The brute was a Weaver, and he seemed to be one of the commanders leading the thrall army.

Sam gave a brisk signal—*This way*—using one of the hand motions he and Keech had long ago mastered. The Lost Causes shuffled past the dead horde toward the vast stone wall of the Palace, holding close to Quinn, who continued to gently sing.

Like a sudden burst of heavy rain, the Rattlebrook's violent roar resumed as O'Brien's spell on the water wore off. Keech spotted the Enforcer on the far side, scattering another handful of a new powder across the sand.

A swarm of small monstrosities erupted from the ground. From this distance it was hard to tell for certain, but the creatures looked like insects built out of sticks and twigs, each no larger than Achilles. The stick bugs sprang into the Rattlebrook and scuttled through the white water—on a course that would take them directly to Rose's army.

The young riders reached the Palace wall, the very spot where Coward and Doyle had entered mere minutes earlier. Keech pressed his palm against the stone, hoping the passage might still be open after Coward's use of the Key, but the rock was solid beneath his hand.

"Looks like it's time to climb," Sam said. He pointed to a jagged lip in the wall, a nearby split in the stone with enough gaps and crevices to let them scale it.

Gripping notches in the stone, Sam led the way up the rock face. Keech adjusted Doyle's satchel against his back and started climbing. Because the ascent was quite steep—at times almost straight up—they took care to set their boots and check their grips. When they reached nearly one hundred feet, they rounded a bend in the rock. Suddenly, Sam jerked back. He threw a sign at Keech. *Enemy near.*

Drawing his blade, Cutter skirted past the group. He peeked around the corner, raised the knife, and lunged. There was a startled gasp on the other side, a chomping noise like chattery teeth, then a rotting thrall tumbled into view. The skeletal thing pitched over the edge, sailed through the air, and smacked against the stones below, shattering into dozens of bony pieces. Where the dead thing landed, a group of pale-faced foot soldiers sprang back in surprise. They pointed up at the short ledge where the Lost Causes were standing, then started yelling for reinforcements.

"Well, they know we're here now," Duck said.

A general ruckus broke out as the thrall army scampered about, calling for help. One of Lost Tucker's Weavers followed the gestures of the thralls. With unnerving grace, he pattered up the Palace wall toward the young riders as though he were scurrying up a fence post.

Strong Heart glanced down at the approaching Weaver. "We should go. *Now*."

"I'll stay and take care of that *demonio*," Cutter said. "The rest of you keep climbing."

"Not a chance," Keech said. "That thing will tear you apart."

"You forget, Lost Cause. I have *this*." Cutter held up his knife. "It took down Ignatio. I suspect it can dispatch a Weaver just as easy. *Go!*"

Duck glanced nervously at Quinn, but Strong Heart prodded the group to hasten the decision. "*O-nah-lee!* We must hurry!" she shouted.

Keech hated to leave Cutter behind, but Cut was likely the best equipped to deal with the Weaver. As Pa Abner often taught, *When the clock's ticking, make a choice. Or else one will be made for you.* "Hey, Cut! Don't forget—a faithful friend . . ."

Cutter grinned. "Is a sturdy shelter, *amigo*."

The Lost Causes resumed their climb.

CHAPTER 39
CUTTER AND THE BEAST

Always make a backup plan. Never leave the first option the only one.
—PA ABNER

They lost sight of Cutter around the bend. Keech kept his ears open for sounds of a skirmish, but with the constant crack of musket fire, the roar of the Rattlebrook, and the war cries of the thrall army, there was no way to hear anything clearly. Each step was hard won as they continued their climb, but they shuffled along with confidence.

As the gang neared the top of Sam's makeshift trail, Keech glanced down at the riverside conflict. Because of their height and the encroaching stone spires, much of the battlefield lay hidden from sight. Keech could see a rabble of thralls firing muskets and revolvers across the channel, aiming at O'Brien's wood insects that swarmed the sandy banks. A few Weavers barked orders, and the nightmarish woman who led them, Lost Tucker, squatted atop a jagged pillar. One of the Reverend's crows rested on the desperado's shoulder and appeared to speak in her ear—likely the Reverend himself, tucked somewhere safe inside the Palace, issuing strategy.

Across the Rattlebrook, a brigade of thralls emerged from the waters and started a swift charge toward O'Brien's flank. The squad rushed forward, firing pistols. O'Brien dipped into her saddlebag and tossed something at the soldiers. A giant explosion rocked the canyon, decimating a third of the brigade, and Keech realized she'd thrown one of the whistle bombs she'd made at Skeleton Peak. A second later, O'Brien and Turner broke cover and dashed downriver for a new position. They appeared to be holding up, but Keech wondered for how much longer.

He turned his attention back to the climb. But as they crested the top of the wall, Quinn's voice gave out, and with it their protective spell. "I'm sorry!" he rasped. "I can't!" He held his hand to his throat and coughed.

A murderous flock of crows circled above the group. The Lost Causes were exposed.

Suddenly, a new column of crows burst from a small hole in the ground not twenty feet away, joining the rest of their flock in the air with malicious squawks and cackles.

Strong Heart pointed to the hole. "The Chimney!" she shouted.

The moment he saw it, Keech formed their next plan. "Sam, Quinn, get the rope ready to lower somebody. Find a place to tie it off. Me and the girls will keep these crows off your backs." He didn't wait for a response. They would get the job done. Dropping to one knee, Keech took a breath, allowing his focus energy to pool in his gut, then pointed his finger at a crow plummeting straight toward him. "*Bang!*" he yelled.

But this time nothing happened.

Keech dived away, but the crow's talons raked his shoulder, sending hot sparks of pain across his back. He tumbled onto his side as a second crow buzzed past a few inches away.

Nearby, Duck clutched a large rock the size of her head, but when she tried to lift it, the stone remained firmly in place. "My strength ain't working!" she cried.

"My focus isn't, either!" Keech returned. "Something's blocking our powers!"

Hoping to shield Sam from the flurry of talons and beaks, Keech pushed to his feet and ran toward his brother, but one of the skybound fiends smashed into Keech's back. The blow sent his bowler hat flying, and he careened into the dirt. He felt the beast descend upon him and begin shredding his coat, leaving long, shallow cuts down his spine. The weight of the bird held Keech facedown, and he screamed his pain and frustration.

"Get off him!" Sam screamed, kicking at the crow.

Then the weight fell away as the creature erupted into a slurry of mud, spraying viscous goo across Keech and the rocky ground.

Strong Heart appeared over him, holding out her hand. Her silver shard pulsed energy upon her palm. "The amulet pieces still work," she said, looking weary but determined. Before he could say thanks, the girl dashed onward, leaping at more crows.

As a new batch of crows erupted from the Chimney, Duck cried, "There's too many! We'll never get down the hole this way!" Keech's body felt on fire, as if his skin had been cut a thousand times. Glancing up, he saw a crow diving for his face, talons extended.

Cutter appeared out of nowhere and jumped in front of him, and with a fierce cry, slashed at the bird. The moment the Prime-infused blade grazed the thing's stomach, the creature burst into a ball of red flame.

A terrible gash ran across Cutter's face, a wound that appeared to have taken his left eye. "That Weaver got me good," Cutter said. "But I finally sent him over."

Keech's heart tumbled. "Your eye!"

Cutter shrugged. "Yeah, it's a goner." His knee buckled, and he stumbled forward. More crows flew overhead, squawking, but they pulled away, perhaps at the sight of Cutter's deadly blade.

"You're banged up something awful," moaned Duck.

"Don't matter. Finish the mission. Get inside and stop Rose."

Keech grabbed Cutter's left arm, supporting him. Together with Duck, they led him over to the others. Strong Heart examined Cutter's eye, then she dropped her gaze in sadness.

Cutter pulled out his blue bandana and covered the devastated eye, tying off the cloth behind his head. His face turning haggard and gray, he glanced down at a terrible gash running across his stomach. "That Weaver got me worse than I thought." He tumbled onto his side.

"He's bleeding!" Duck cried. Dropping to her knees, she pressed a hand to Cutter's wound, but nothing she could do stopped the flow. "We can heal him with the Fang, but it's inside the Palace with Coward."

"Then we have to fetch it," Keech said.

"No." Cutter's voice was difficult to hear beneath the rolling thunder, the cackling of the crows, and the din of gunfire. "Y'all know better than I do. I ain't gonna make it. I'm a goner."

Duck tore off her hat and threw it to the ground. "Stop that fool talk! You'll be fine!"

With a quivering hand, Cutter reached for the girl's hat and offered it back. "We both know that ain't true, *hermana*."

Tears welled up in Duck's eyes as she snatched the hat. "You *can't* leave us, Cut. We just got you back."

Cutter said, "I'm sorry, Duck. For everything."

"No need to be sorry for nothing. We know the Devil's mark bound you to Coward."

"You don't know the whole story," Cutter wheezed. "*I'm* the one. The one who got your folks killed."

Bewilderment cascaded over Duck's features. "Big Ben Loving killed them, Cut."

Through gritted teeth, Cutter said, "Me and my partner, Bishop, we used to run *caballos* out of Missouri. Rustled them off ranches and traded them down to Arkansas. Back in July, we snuck onto your ranch and stole your Fox Trotters."

Duck shook her head. "You're talking nonsense."

Another one of O'Brien's whistle bombs erupted below, echoing across Thunder Pass, as Cutter coughed with a grimace. "It was Bishop's idea, but I went along. We had just crossed the state line when lawdogs bushwhacked our trail. They returned the Trotters to your folks and sent me and Bish off to do time at a *cárcel* called Barrenpoint."

Keech placed his hand on the boy's shoulder. "Stop talking, Cut. You'll make the wound worse."

"No, Blackwood. I gotta say this while there's time." Cutter turned his attention back to Duck. "Coward was a prisoner there. He *smelled* your pa's scent on me and knew the trail right back to your ranch."

Duck cupped a hand over her mouth.

"The Big Snake showed up to bust Coward out of Barrenpoint. That's when Bad Whiskey—*El Ojo*—killed my friend. I managed to get away, and not long after, I dug up the knife that Bish took from a *brujo* named Artemas Ward. I thought my blade would kill *El Ojo*. I hoofed it back to Sainte Genevieve to warn your folks but . . ." He trailed off for a moment, as though choosing his words carefully. "Big Ben may have pulled the trigger, *amiga*, but I lit his path to your front door. I'm so sorry." Cutter covered his bleeding face in his coat sleeve.

Duck's hands trembled as she put her hat back on. "No, Cut. None of it was your fault. You never could've known about Coward's nose or Rose's dark ways. You got caught up in something too big for anyone. You're the same as the rest of us. You're a Lost Cause!" She rested a hand on his arm. "Now, hang on till we can find the Fang. We'll fix you right up."

Cutter opened his mouth to speak again, but more coughs overwhelmed him. When he quieted down, he fell still, and his right eye shut.

"No, Cut, no!" Duck murmured. "*Please* don't go!"

Monstrous cackles of triumph roared out of the crows above. When Keech glanced up, he saw that the birds were once again plummeting toward them. Anger and despair swept over Keech like a prairie fire. "Just leave us alone!" he shouted.

A dark voice—the *Reverend's* voice—bellowed out of the collective flock like an utterance from a wrathful, fallen god. "*Never!*"

Trembling with rage and fear, Keech reached for Cutter's blade, lying in the dirt near Cut's unmoving hand.

His fingers froze around the bone handle as inhuman growls tore across Thunder Pass. Except they sounded nearby, perhaps only a few steps down the curving path, and the Lost Causes spun to mark them.

"What in tarnation!" shouted Sam.

They quickly discovered the answer as two massive, wolf-like beasts erupted from the tree line. Keech recognized the creatures all too well.

Chamelia.

As the Shifters moved toward them, Keech searched for any sign of Devil's marks, but they appeared to be free of the cursed brand. Howling ferociously, both Chamelia hunkered low on their haunches.

"Lost Causes," Duck said, "*run!*"

But instead of attacking them, the Shifters bounded high into the air, soared over the young riders, and crashed midair into Rose's diving crows.

Their claws flashing with impossible speed, the monsters snatched the twisted birds out of their flight. As soon as they landed, the Chamelia tore into the fiends, decimating feathers and bones.

After roaring up at the sky, the Chamelia swiveled back to face the Lost Causes. Their fangs gnashed in their bloodstained jowls as they approached the young riders.

Strong Heart reached for Duck's hand. The two girls huddled closer.

"Keech," muttered Sam, "what do we do?"

Keech lifted Cutter's knife. "Get behind me." The hand clutching the magic blade trembled, so he took a deep breath to steady his grip.

But then the smaller of the Chamelia stepped in front of the other and held up its blood-soaked paws.

"*We won't hurt ya*," the beast grumbled, its voice deep and menacing. "*It's me! It's John Wesley.*"

CHAPTER 40
THE CHIMNEY

When facing an impossible situation, take a breath.
You can think better if your soul is centered.
—PA ABNER

The Lost Causes stood in shocked silence as the Chamelia shrank. The creature's long snout receded, its canine ears shortened, and the dark scales that covered its hide sank into pale skin. The Shifter rose back onto its hind legs, and the yellowish eyes met Keech's gaze.

"John?" said Duck, stepping up gingerly. "Is that you?"

When the Chamelia spoke again, its features dwindled at last from that of beast to big John Wesley, son of Edgar Doyle. "Good to see ya again, Duck. I feared we'd never cross paths again. But here we are." John gestured to his Chamelia companion, who continued to growl at the Lost Causes. Keech realized he was looking at the Shifter who had attacked them in Kansas, the same monster Big Ben Loving had once captured with the Devil's mark.

"We came up here to help you with the crows. The rest of our pack is . . ." John paused to grin, revealing rows of needle-point fangs. "Well, come see for yourselves."

The Lost Causes followed John Wesley to the drop-off and peered down into Thunder Pass. The ongoing battle raged like a wildfire. Dozens of muskets erupted, sending up clouds of gunsmoke. More whistle-bomb explosions rolled across the canyon, sending thralls and Weavers flying. Keech even spotted a flash of gray fur as Achilles pounced at a thrall and bowled the soldier off his feet. O'Brien and Turner were still fighting strong, but they appeared to have lost ground and looked to be in trouble.

Suddenly, a chorus of bloodcurdling howls echoed across the expanse, and a throng of wolf-like creatures exploded out of the trees upriver. The beasts were long and slender and moved with the grace of mountain lions. In a flash, they made the battlefield. At least two dozen Chamelia crashed into the thrall flank, ripping and biting at the dead men.

"Would ya look at that!" exclaimed Sam.

"My pack," John Wesley said proudly.

Down in the canyon, Lost Tucker's Weavers bounded from their perches and rushed the Chamelia. They crashed into the Shifters, exchanging blows. Some of them scored magical lines into the ground as Black Charlie had done, opening up gashes to another place. Swarms of black spiders crawled out of the gaps and scuttled toward the Chamelia.

"Don't worry, the pack will protect your friends," John Wesley said to the group.

"John, how did you find us?" Quinn asked.

"That's hard to explain, but after I changed, I followed the call of the Chamelia out here, in the West. The pack showed me how to live like this." He gestured to his body, mostly human, but still bearing beastly quills along his arms. "After I turned, I started hearin' voices. Those of my pack. Once I learned how to speak without talkin', I reached out to Cut. I knew he weren't a Chamelia, but I tried anyhow. I weren't sure if he could hear me, but I told him to hang on, that we'd find each other again soon. I persuaded the pack to follow Rose's foul scent, and we found *this* place. We was preparin' our attack when *you* all showed up out of nowhere."

Duck explained how they had passed through a door like the one to Bonfire Crossing, then she pointed to the Chimney. "We've come to finish off Rose ourselves, and we found the only way into this rotten place."

"John, Coward has taken your father into the Palace," added Strong Heart.

John Wesley's nose twitched at the information. "*Papa*," he said. "Keech, y'all need to find him. Y'all need to—" But before he could finish, he sniffed the wind, then he peered beyond them and locked his eyes on Cutter's body. He scampered past the Lost Causes and over to Cutter's side.

"Cut, get up!" John Wesley cried. "I came to find ya, like I promised. Get up!" He nudged Cutter's side, gently rocking the boy's body. When Cutter didn't stir, growls of sorrow erupted from John's throat.

Sam said, "I'm sorry, friend. He fought hard. Saved us all."

John Wesley seized the bone-handled knife on the ground. Trembling, he shifted back into his Chamelia form and offered Cutter's knife to Keech. "Take it. Use it against Rose. I'll stay up here with Cut, hold the crows back." He growled at the misshapen birds above, then said, "Finish this, Keech. Put an end to that devil."

"Don't you worry," Keech said as he placed the blade into Doyle's satchel. He noticed his bowler hat lying nearby and scooped it up.

The Lost Causes returned to the Chimney, stepping up to the

hole with caution. Keech peered down into the opening. Darkness pervaded the drop, but far down, a faint yellow glow appeared to illuminate the bottom.

Strong Heart shed her buffalo coat. "My uncle always says, 'Darkness only hurts if you let it.' I refuse to let it hurt me. I will go first."

Sam secured one end of the rope around a nearby stump, while Strong Heart tied the other end around her waist. After testing the line, she squeezed into the Chimney feetfirst. The others held the rope and watched Strong Heart squirm as she slid down.

"It's very close!" she called up, sliding deeper into the hole.

As they played out the rope, John Wesley prowled around them, protecting the area from crows. He had shifted further into his bestial form, and when a trio of crows tried to swoop in and harass the young riders, he swiped his deadly claws at the birds, which flapped away to a safe distance.

Leaning over the Chimney, Keech saw only a profound blackness. The gang checked their grips and secured their stances. Then a sudden weight tugged at the line as Strong Heart hung free inside the Palace.

"What do you see?" Quinn asked, his voice gritty with fatigue.

"I'm hanging as high as the mountain! I see a ledge in the wall. I may be able to reach it."

Working together, Sam and Quinn paid out the rest of the rope till only the tree stump held Strong Heart. A second later, the line shifted sideways at the lip of the hole.

Then the rope was still. "I'm safe!" called Strong Heart's voice.

"Do you see a way to the bottom?" Duck yelled.

"A spiraling path! I've untied myself. Pull the rope!"

As Sam and Quinn yanked up the line, Keech cracked his knuckles. "I'll go next."

Quinn sized up Keech's girth with the knapsack and shook his head. "You might get stuck," he rasped, then gestured to himself, Sam, and Duck. "Us first," he added.

Keech understood Quinn's meaning. He was the oldest, and therefore the biggest of them, and if he were to get wedged in the Chimney, he might plug up the hole like a cork in a bottle. Stepping aside, Keech spent the next few moments helping Quinn, then Sam, and finally Duck. He sent the Ranger's knapsack down with Duck, assuring her he would take it back once he joined them.

Before stepping to the lip, Keech turned back to John Wesley, who looked monstrous in his half-Chamelia form. "John, if I get stuck, you'll have to pull me up," Keech said. When the Chamelia huffed in response, Keech chuckled. "Maybe shift all the way into a person before you start tugging on the rope. I don't want you to accidentally cut the line with those claws of yours."

"I'll do my best," John Wesley growled, then raised one clawed hand and appeared to concentrate. The long black nails slipped back into his fingers.

Keech lowered himself into the Chimney. For the first few feet, he moved easily enough, sliding inch by inch through the jagged funnel. Then suddenly, he stopped. The weight of his body pulled, but he was hooked on something. Sweat dripped into his eyes, and Keech felt the Chimney's walls pushing in, as if the rocky formation were trying to squeeze him to death. He sensed he had only a few more feet to fall free, but no matter how he squirmed, he couldn't seem to come unstuck. "John Wesley! You up there?" he called, but there was no answer.

Panic snatched at the edges of Keech's mind, and the absurdity of it all struck him. The idea that he could come so far—face down the worst of the Big Snake, survive the battle of Bonfire Crossing and the dangers of the Perils, only to willfully wedge himself into a tiny rock funnel—was so ridiculous that he laughed.

You have to calm down, Keech.

The voice of Pa Abner came to him like a welcome breeze.

Your body is stuck because your mind is. Center yourself.

So Keech took a deep breath and focused on the problem. Looking up again, he realized that his left shoulder needed only to shift around a stubborn rock. He made the adjustment, and his body mercifully dropped another foot. A second later, Keech tumbled into open space. The rope snapped tight, squeezing his waist, and he dangled like a limp puppet on a string.

Sam shouted his name from a nearby ledge.

"I'm all right!" Keech declared. He peered around at the chamber and saw the otherworldly light glowing in the distant bowels of the Palace, illuminating the massive space beneath. A corkscrew path stuck a few feet out from the wall and ran down. It was outlined with a spectral honeycomb yellow. A loathsome stink hung in the air—a dark, moldy smell that seemed to drift up from the bottom, like a moth-eaten blanket left in a summer rain.

Once Keech had joined them, the Lost Causes descended the great spiral walkway in single file with Strong Heart in the lead. The path was only a couple of feet wide, and they had to walk sideways with their backs to the limestone walls. The sickly yellow glow in the place gave them enough light to navigate the ever-widening coil.

After a time, Strong Heart stopped. "I see images on the walls!"

The group took a moment to study the stone in front of their faces. The surfaces teemed with ancient-looking petroglyphs, graven images worn down by centuries to smooth furrows in the rock. Most of the carvings depicted wild animals, like the chiseled icons down in the Perils of Skeleton Peak, but others resembled malformed beasts with dozens of tentacles branching out in all directions. Duck pointed to a carving of a gruesome spider and said, "That looks like one of the critters that came out of the hole Black Charlie cut."

Keech said, "We're a thousand miles away from the Dead Rift under Skeleton Peak, but the walls here show the same monsters that chased us there."

The Lost Causes continued their descent, splaying their palms over the stone as they slipped down the spiral. Somewhere outside the Palace, the distant eruption of another whistle bomb agitated the limestone under their hands. Keech thought he saw a sudden wiggle on the surface in front of him, like a caterpillar with uncanny speed, but when he looked closer, he couldn't see anything but a small petroglyph of a serpent. He kept moving.

Though Keech couldn't be sure, it seemed the tainted energy within the Palace was disrupting his focus energy. Duck and Strong Heart had their amulet shards, but he wondered what *he* would do when they came face-to-face with Rose. Using the Black Verse was out of the question—never again would those insidious words cross his lips—but he wished they had *some* kind of powers to help them stop the fiend.

"Look!" Quinn called out, his voice raw. "The spiral ends."

They followed Quinn's gesture. Sure enough, the walkway dropped off into nothingness a few feet away. The luminous chamber opened up beyond the spiral, and Keech caught his first glimpse of the Palace floor, a surface that seemed to produce the vibrant illumination around them. Lines that glowed an other-worldly yellow crisscrossed the bottom in intricate patterns, all of them leading inward to the same end point, a broad circular basin set into the floor like a giant bowl. In the center of this bowl stood a long, slender table, a block of white stone that reminded Keech of an Egyptian sarcophagus. Movement at the room's edges caught Keech's eye—a gruesome black shape skittered along the floor. A second later, he saw another. "Things are crawling around down there!"

"They look like Black Charlie's spiders, only bigger," Quinn said.

Duck tapped Keech's shoulder. "Look up!" she said.

Pulling his gaze away from the terrible scuttling things, Keech glanced up, observing what they had descended. He felt his breath freeze in his lungs at what he saw.

The spiral shaft that loomed above their heads formed the very shape the Reverend's men used to brand their victims, the shape that bound unfortunate souls to Rose's will.

They were looking at the Devil's mark.

CHAPTER 41
THE SEVEN SYMBOLS

To understand your enemies, search for the method behind their actions.
—PA ABNER

T he Lost Causes gazed up in disbelief at the colossal cork-screw. The architecture of the hollowed-out ceiling was unmistakable. It was Rose's brand.

"The Reverend must've based his mark on that image," Keech said. "He must've stood in this very place and looked up, like we're doing now."

"He's been trapped here for so long, he likely grew obsessed with it," Quinn added.

Nearby, Strong Heart called out to them. She had slipped away from the group and now stood inside a small passage whose mouth began where their spiral walkway ended.

When Keech and the others joined her, they found her standing next to a series of petroglyphs arranged in a rough circle on the wall. "Look at these." She pointed at the shapes.

The young riders gathered around the alcove to study the images.

"What are these?" asked Sam.

Keech couldn't believe his own eyes. "These are the same symbols we saw in the House of the Rabbit!"

Duck's eyes flared with exhilaration. "Except here the Devil's mark stands in their center." She lightly traced each symbol in the air, careful not to touch them.

"You were right, Duck. These are the same seven images engraved on the shards; I'm sure of it," Keech said.

Duck pulled out her silver charm to have a look. The fragment showed part of a crooked *Y*, like the branching symbol on the wall. The other side of the shard revealed a portion of a slitted, sideways eye—again, the same image as the eye carved before them. "I knew it! If we assembled all five shards, we'd see each of these symbols."

Sam looked nervous. "The number seven's mighty important in the Bible."

Keech said, "That's what I said at first, too. Except I don't think we'd find these symbols in the Bible. I think they *do* tell a story, but one about the *Big Snake*."

"What do you mean?" asked Quinn.

"Seven symbols, seven rascals we've encountered." Keech held up his hands and counted fingers. "*One.* Bad Whiskey Nelson. *Two.* Big Ben Loving. *Three.* Coward. *Four.* Ignatio. That awful Weaver, Black Charlie, makes *five.* And Lost Tucker, the fiend Sheriff Turner and O'Brien are fighting outside—that makes *six.* And last but not least . . ."

"*Rose*," Duck answered.

Keech tapped the concentric shapes carved into the stone. "*Seven outlaws*, all gathering together inside the great spiral, the Palace of the Thunders. I don't know what the symbols are supposed to mean, but I'd wager Enoch prophesied about the coming of the Big Snake, and the taking of the relics. *That's* what we're seeing."

Sam's eyes bulged in surprise. "Did you say Enoch? As in the *Old Testament* Enoch?"

Keech slapped a hand against Sam's back. "Long story. I'll tell it on the ride home." He gave all his trailmates a serious look. "And we *will* ride home. All of us."

The Lost Causes started down the passage, their footsteps echoing along the walkway. As they moved, they noticed the walls were covered with more etchings of grotesque creatures. The unsettling images made Keech wonder about the ancient inhabitants who had created this secret place. Perhaps they had built the Palace to revere the Dead Rift, the cataclysmic result of destructive magic. Or, perhaps, they had built it to keep the Dead Rift and its monsters from spreading over the Earth.

After a short time, the corridor leveled out and the walls widened till the young riders emerged into a cavern, a mind-boggling chamber that glowed with a fierce yellow light. Rows of giant pillars supported the ceiling, each column stretching on for several yards.

"I ain't believing my eyes," muttered Quinn.

The illumination didn't look like any natural light Keech had ever seen. It seemed to fill the chamber, yet numerous shadows lurked in the edges and cracks of the cavern. There was something sickly about the light, as if it wanted desperately to be darkness but was cursed to glimmer instead.

"The Dead Rift has tainted this place," Strong Heart said.

Moldering heaps of gray muck were scattered across the cavern floor. Quinn stepped toward one, then reeled back. "It smells bad."

"Best not touch it," Duck said.

Keech lifted his eyes to survey the vast room. Despite the morbid light, the Palace walls and the columns jutting up to the ceiling were the deepest black. Engravings that depicted unnatural beasts and terrible monsters covered every inch. The etchings seemed to *move*, as if they were trying to rise from the very stone.

Keech whispered, "Duck, we know this place."

"*Our dream.*" Duck gripped his hand. "This is the place we dreamed about!"

A barrage of horrid images assaulted Keech's mind, images from the nightmare he and Duck had shared inside the Moss House in Kansas, where they'd first met Doyle and slept mere feet from the Char Stone. The dream had shown them horrible things. A great cavern filled with impossible light, black stone walls teeming with grotesque life, and shadow versions of their fathers, Bill Blackwood and Noah Embry, leading them toward the Reverend.

"In the dream, my father said the Reverend had woken in the Palace . . ."

"My pa said the same thing," Duck reminded him. "But why would the dream show us *this* place?"

"*Because you were always meant to come here.*"

The voice spoke from the reaches of the vast chamber. It was a baritone voice, calm and inviting, and it echoed off the walls. Keech recognized it immediately.

Edgar Doyle stepped out of a shadowy corner, limping as he approached.

"When the Reverend first brought us here, he called this room the *Antechamber*," the Ranger continued, waving his arms at the walls and ceiling. "Based on his readings of the Enoch scroll, he believed it to be some kind of courtyard, or great hall, where gatherings occurred. This room leads into the main temple, the source of the power."

Doyle's face remained hidden, but Keech could make out splotches of blood on his leather garb. The Ranger grinned, his whiskered mouth the only visible part of his features. He lifted his hand toward them, an open palm inviting them closer. When they didn't budge, he gently laughed. "Don't fret, my friends. I've taken care of everything. The Reverend won't pose a problem anymore."

"Ranger Doyle? Are you okay?" asked Quinn, frowning.

"Of course, Mr. Revels! I was mighty sick before, blind to the true consequences of my actions, but now I've been . . ." Doyle's voice faded to a mere whisper. "*Fixed.*" When the Lost Causes glanced at one another with concern, the man added, "Come with me and I'll show you."

"Not a chance, Doyle." Perhaps a few months ago, Keech would have granted the Ranger the benefit of the doubt, but he'd learned plenty of lessons on trust.

The Enforcer once known as Red Jeffreys stepped closer, moving out of the shadows so that Keech could see the rest of his face. Doyle's skin looked pasty and ill, his neck dripping with sweat, his dark eyes winking maniacal energy. The Ranger's forehead had been badly charred. The burn was not a simple wound, but a deliberate shape.

A spiral.

CHAPTER 42
THE SOURCE

Know your friend, know your enemy.
—PA ABNER

Strong Heart turned to the others. "He wears the Scorpion's brand. Unless we find a way to free him, we have to consider him the enemy."

Keech watched as Doyle's shadowy form walked down a corridor and slipped out of view. "We have to let him take us to Rose. Otherwise, we might wander these corridors till Rose finds *us*. We don't want to wage a battle inside a cramped tunnel. No high ground, and he'd likely use the layout of this place against us."

Sam's face was a confusion of excitement and dread. "So we're gonna fall for the trap on *purpose*?"

"Looks that way," said Keech.

Leaving the column-filled enclosure Doyle had called the Antechamber, they entered the tunnel the Ranger had taken. The path sloped downward again, leading the troop ever deeper into the Palace of the Thunders. As they descended, the incessant buzzing grew as loud as angry hornets. The air felt sticky and close, pushing in around them with coffin tightness. As the passage leveled out, more strange illumination brightened their way, and a moment later, the tunnel opened up into a colossal new chamber, a sanctuary as large as a hundred barns.

"This must be the main temple," Duck said with awe.

The Ranger's silhouette appeared at the tunnel's mouth. "Come on in," he murmured.

As they followed Doyle into the great room, Keech gazed around in chilled amazement. This was unlike any temple he'd ever seen in Pa's history books. The walls were curved, reminding him of the spear-loaded Peril full of bones under Skeleton Peak, and several other corridors led off to unknown places, perhaps to other gathering halls. Across most of the temple's floor, beams of amber light filled the spiderweb cracks in the stone, puffing otherworldly fumes and smoke, as if the unseen spaces below the fissures were teeming with flames. At the center of the temple stretched a giant crater that could have been the product of a devastating earthquake long ago.

A few yards to the right of this basin, the floor dropped away sharply, yielding to a coal-black abyss, a chasm that would have cut off access to the Palace's largest tunnel were it not for a narrow granite bridge that reached over the gulf. Straining to get his bearings, Keech suspected that if they were to cross that bridge, the big passageway beyond would lead out to the main wall where Coward and Doyle had slipped through with the Key.

It was then that Keech realized they were standing in the room they had seen while descending the spiral.

"Everyone, look up!" he said. "We've made it back to the center. We're standing under the Chimney as we speak."

The others gazed up at the shadowy spiral. "So strange!" exclaimed Duck. "It felt like we traveled *yards* away from this room."

"Appearances can deceive in the Palace," said Doyle, leading them farther into the temple. "In the realm of the Prime, space and time can often . . . *slip*."

"Ranger, where *are* we?" asked Quinn.

Doyle's face blazed with a disconcerting kind of reverence. "Welcome to the Source, my friends, the origin of the Prime. When the Dead Rift occurred in the First Age of Man, this is the place that first cracked open to reveal the other side. This is the heart of the Palace, where the Reverend brought us in thirty-three."

"The place where my father led the revolt," mused Keech.

"Yes," the Ranger said.

As they continued walking, the bothersome drone infecting the air stepped up in intensity. Sam and Strong Heart clapped their hands over their ears. "What's making that awful racket?" moaned Sam.

"I'd wager *that* is," said Keech, pointing toward the opposite side of the basin, where a black vertical opening yawned in the Palace wall. Beyond that portal was only darkness, and yet Keech sensed constant movement on the other side. Not something that could be *seen*, but a presence that could be *felt*.

"It's like the darkness is alive," said Duck, scowling at the doorway of gloom.

Keech recalled O'Brien's frightening words. *The Dead Rift happened when people first tampered with magic. Their meddlin' tore holes in the fabric of the world, opened gaps to the Underworld itself . . .*

Doyle spoke, grinning slightly. "Legend has it the Chamelia came from there. As well as other creatures unseen for millennia. If you've heard tall tales about shades and boogermen, chances are good they originated from *this place*."

"Whatever we do, let's not go near that," Duck admonished them. "We all heard what happened to Lost Tucker when she touched it."

The Ranger led them a few more steps across the temple. Keech followed with caution, keeping a close eye on Doyle's hands for any sudden movements. Doyle's satchel, filled with Eliza's bones, hung heavy on Keech's shoulders as he moved.

"My friends, prepare yourselves," Doyle said, stopping inches from the great concavity in the floor. "We've reached him."

Now, Keech could easily see down into the cracked crater. At the bottom was the sarcophagus he'd seen from high above. Covered with strange, grotesque glyphs, it stood on five thick stone legs.

A bearded man lay on the sarcophagus, wearing only a long robe. Perhaps the fabric had once been white, but the robe was rotted and holey, stained brown by decades of muck. Though the figure's eyes were closed, the eyelids fluttered, and a distressed moan emanated from his throat. The man's bare feet twitched. Something protruded from his chest—the bone handle of the Fang of Barachiel. The figure's skeletal arms spasmed, and one of his hands jerked up to snatch at empty air. Three fingers were missing from the hand.

Keech recalled another passage from Doyle's journal. *He lacked three fingers on his left hand, but despite these blemishes, no one could deny the grandeur of his features . . .*

"It's him," Keech said, nearly in a whisper. "It's the Reverend."

At the head of the sarcophagus sat a smooth, pitch-black stone, resting inside a small divot shaped out of dark clay. The Char Stone. Gossamer threads of black smoke appeared to waft off the cursed artifact, like fumes from a ghost fire.

"You're too late!" a frantic voice shouted.

Keech thought the voice had come from the very darkness of the Dead Rift itself. Then he noticed the brim of a hat and two small shoulders, nearly eclipsed by the edge of the sarcophagus. It was Coward, standing near the head of the table.

"The ritual has already resumed!" Coward proclaimed. "Soon the Reverend will rise in his full strength!"

CHAPTER 43
THE RANGER'S STAND

To learn a man's heart, watch his actions.
—PA ABNER

Keech harkened back to their descent down the Chimney, to the moment they had first seen the sarcophagus. Aside from the squirming, beetle-like creatures on the walls and floor, this section of the Palace had been empty. No Coward, no emaciated figure on the table.

Still poised on the far side of the crater, Coward seemed to pluck the thought straight out of Keech's mind. Stepping around the sarcophagus, he said with mocking delight, "You children don't know what you're seeing; you're confused and scared. Understandable. It took me much longer than expected to find the Master. When I reached the Source, he was gone, no longer lying on his table. Imagine my surprise!"

"Mister, you sure do got a leaky mouth," grumbled Sam.

Coward cackled at this—the laughter of a madman. "The Enforcers left the Master to lie on this cold slab, suffering like an animal, for more than *two decades*. And when he woke, he must have been so lonely. Doomed to walk the prison of his Palace, alone, covered in filth, creating his blessed crows from the blood of his own body."

Keech's mind staggered at Coward's words. The crows were not simple messengers or weapons for the Reverend. They were *Rose himself.*

Coward continued his lunatic speech. "Alone in this place for years, with only the creatures of the Dead Rift to keep him company. Forever trapped, forever wounded. Till our friend Red Jeffreys awakened him."

Quinn turned to face Doyle. "What's he talking about, Ranger?"

When Doyle simply hung his head, Coward cackled again. "He never told you, I see. That his contact with the Prime was the match that lit the bonfire. Poor Jeffreys!"

Keech felt a terrible chill run through his heart. Many months ago, while lying wounded on the trail to Bonfire Crossing, Doyle told the Lost Causes his sorrowful tale of grief. How his youngest child, Eliza, had drowned in the river near their home, and how the girl's loss had nearly destroyed the man. How he'd taken his daughter's body from the ground, intending to recover the Char Stone, bring Eliza to the Palace, and reenact Rose's ritual of eternal life. But to do that, the Ranger had used the Black Verse to break his Oath of Memory, the magical pledge that clouded all notions of the Stone from the Enforcers' minds.

But with dark magic, there was always a terrible trade. Doyle's contact with the Underworld had sent a ripple across the Prime, a groundswell of darkness that stirred the Reverend from his slumber.

Coward gestured to the fuming Char Stone resting inside its nook. "Soon the ritual will be complete. And when the Reverend rises in his glory, I alone will be his general! No longer will I cower behind the likes of Ignatio and Ben. *I* am the one who saved the Master!"

Duck said, "We're gonna relish bringing you to justice."

"How will you do that, you silly ragamuffin? The Fang is restoring the Master as we speak, and the Char Stone has reconnected him to the Source of the Prime, renewing his strength, pushing him toward immortality." As he spoke, Coward climbed partway up the slope of the basin. Keech spotted a rusty chain tied around the man's waist, an open shackle dangling at one end: the Key of Enoch.

"We *will* stop you," Strong Heart said.

Coward laughed. "Do you think I would've invited you here if there were the slightest chance of failure? I merely wanted you to join us for this glorious moment, but if you insist on being bad guests, I reckon I'll ask my old friend here to sweep you all into the pit." He pointed to the chasm behind them, then with a heavy sneer, he opened his hand and pressed the Devil's mark. "Get to work, Red."

A shock of pain cinched Doyle's features. His eyes filled with madness.

The Lost Causes looked at one another with dread, then Quinn yelled, "Split up!"

The group scattered as Doyle screamed a phrase of the Black Verse, an incantation Keech recognized all too well. "*No-ge-phal-ul'-shogg!*" It was Stanza XVII, the Invocation to Disrupt Concentrated Energies.

The segment of floor where they'd been standing shattered into a cloud of dust. Rock chunks flew in every direction, peppering the gang with sharp gravel.

Keech and Sam sprinted left, while Strong Heart and Duck headed for the bridge and Quinn hurried toward a nearby tunnel. A creature the size of a barn cat emerged from the shadows. It skittered forward on seven muscled legs, its body covered in white bristles too thick to be hair. The critter snapped at Keech with a fang-filled beak.

Sam skidded to a halt. "What in blazes?"

Walking toward them, Doyle bellowed another foul passage of Black Verse, one that Keech had used days earlier on a buffalo. "*Ahthro'don-'u-Ruyon!*"

The monster rolled up like an armadillo, and hideous wails escaped its maw. The legs distorted, joints popped, and the beak shattered. Throbbing ridges broke across the creature's rounded back, and its writhing body inflated like a frog's throat. The entire transformation took only seconds, but when it was done, the thing was as large as a mule.

Keech grabbed Sam's hand and yanked him out of the way as the creature leaped. Bone-white barbs tore at Sam's arm as it flew past. Grimacing, Sam slapped a protective hand over the wound. "We need a plan!"

"Hog-tie!" Keech said at once. In the months they'd been apart, he'd forgotten how smoothly he and Sam could communicate.

Seizing the coil of rope he carried on his shoulder, Sam gripped one end of the line and tossed the other end to Keech. When the distorted beast lunged again, Keech shifted his momentum and tumbled past, throwing a loop over the creature's torso. Sam whistled for the thing's attention. As the abomination scurried after him, Sam flipped another loop around its thorny neck and sprang out of the way. The second he regained his feet, Sam shouted, "*Pull!*"

Tugging from different ends, they yanked the rope. The loops tightened around the creature, bunching up its legs. The beast tipped over, shrieking, and smashed its open maw against the floor.

With Doyle's creature subdued, Keech turned and saw that the Ranger was tussling with Strong Heart and Duck. More Dead Rift creatures had been altered, but the girls were destroying the monsters with their amulet shards.

Keech saw apprehension tightening Coward's brow. *Good!* he thought. Coward had expected the Ranger to make short work of them, but even without their focus powers, the team had plenty of fight left. Perhaps if Doyle could have used his own focus, he could have swept them into the abyss with a whirlwind, but the Dead Rift forced the man to rely on the Black Verse.

Keech pointed at Coward. "*He's* our target, Sam. Let's take him down."

Leaping into the concavity, they sprinted toward the outlaw. With a terrified grimace, Coward opened his mouth and hacked a blaring cough at them. A sickening energy rippled from his throat.

But Keech slammed into the man's body in time to avoid the blast. With Sam stumbling behind him, they all pitched down the basin and rolled to the foot of the sarcophagus, where Rose's body rested. When they crashed to a stop, Sam's eyes were closed. "Sam!" he shouted, but the boy was senseless. He had taken the entire force of the cough.

Blood poured from Coward's bald head. His eyes burning hatred and fear, he bawled, "I've had enough of you!" He opened his mouth again.

Appearing out of nowhere, Quinn slammed a fist into Coward's head. The outlaw buckled and dropped like a stone to the floor of the basin.

Keech blinked up at Quinn. "Thanks!"

"You're welcome," Quinn said, helping Keech to his feet. "Now let's help your brother."

But when the boys turned, they found Sam sitting up against Rose's table and shaking his head, as if rousing from a hard night's sleep. Apparently, the outlaw's spell had been too rushed to be potent. In a slurred voice, Sam asked, "What in heck happened?"

Keech said, "Coward knocked you out, then Quinn saved us both. But there's no time to dally. Doyle's still on the attack."

As Quinn helped Sam to stand, Keech rifled through the unconscious Coward's pockets. He nearly cried out in victory when he saw two glowing amulet shards. He pulled the fragments free, then reached for the Key around the outlaw's waist.

A tremendous crash vibrated the Palace, followed by a high-pitched scream.

"That sounded like Duck!" Sam said.

Quinn turned to Keech. "Go help the girls. I'll fetch the Key."

Keech tossed one of the amulet pieces to Sam. "Tie this to your palm like so," he said, wrapping the leather straps of the second charm to his own hand.

As Sam tied the gleaming shard to his palm, he clenched his teeth. "The metal's freezin'!"

"You'll get used to it. It destroys anything made by the Prime. Ready?"

Side by side, Keech and Sam sprinted up the basin and emerged to find Doyle down on one knee. His hat lay crumpled on the floor, and blood matted his head. Keech spotted Strong Heart dashing along the edges of the temple, leaping over a fallen boulder. In one hand she gripped a jagged stone, and without slowing, she flung it at Doyle. The Ranger shifted to the side, narrowly avoiding the missile.

Nearby, Duck staggered to her feet. A pile of rubble had been torn out of the Palace wall, and Keech reckoned flying debris must have hit her. Her movement was uneasy and slow, and blood and bruises covered her disoriented face. He rushed across the chamber, calling out her name.

Duck held up a hand to stop him. "I'm okay! Help Strong Heart!"

Skidding to a halt, Keech spun around in time to see Strong Heart dive to the floor with a shout. A blink later, a massive chunk of rubble smashed the place where she'd been running. She tried to regain her feet, but her leg buckled and she tumbled back down to her hands and knees. She was facing off against Doyle and his Black Verse nearly single-handedly, but Keech could see she was on the verge of collapse.

Pointing at the Palace wall, Doyle muttered another incantation. Stones exploded above Strong Heart, showering the girl with dust and pebbles. Then a tremendous crack split the granite, and a slab the size of a house peeled loose from the chamber.

"*No!*" Quinn's terrified voice clapped across the Palace. He sprinted past Keech and dashed toward Strong Heart, but Keech could see that he wouldn't have enough time to drag her to safety. Instead, Quinn flung himself over Strong Heart.

The Ranger's boulder crashed down, slamming on top of them both. Like the deafening explosion of a whistle bomb, the crash clattered throughout the temple.

Duck and Sam screamed in horror. Keech wanted to scream, too, but the sight paralyzed him.

Then suddenly, Quinn and Strong Heart emerged from the rock, covered in gray dust. Like a pair of ghosts, they stepped out of the rubble, clutching each other's hands. Wrapped around Quinn's shoulder was the Key of Enoch. Thanks to the relic, they had passed right through the falling stone untouched.

"I wasn't sure that'd work!" Quinn muttered.

Before the Lost Causes could celebrate, Edgar Doyle trudged toward them again, his grizzled face a mask of rage. Keech glanced around and realized the Ranger was driving them all toward the chasm at the edge of the room.

Doyle raised his quivering hand. "I'll have your hides yet, you sniveling brats."

Keech searched desperately for some kind of weapon, but nothing fell in sight. Truth be told, nothing could stop the mighty Enforcer, nothing save the Black Verse itself, which Keech refused to use.

Then he saw something. A bundle lying near Doyle's feet. Keech's mouth dropped open when he realized they *did* have a weapon.

"Jab at the heart, put the beast on his knees," he murmured.

Lunging for the Ranger's satchel, Keech yanked open the bag.

With a loud cry, he drew out Eliza's skull and held it up. "Doyle, stop!"

Snarling, Doyle pointed his finger at Keech. With one dark phrase, the man could incinerate him.

"Remember who you are!" Keech shouted, standing his ground. "Remember who you've lost!"

The Ranger's finger dropped to his side. He appeared to focus on the skull, and when he did, he lurched backward as if he'd been slapped across the face.

"You don't want to do this! You don't want to hurt anyone!"

Scowling and shaking, Doyle peered deeply at the skull. He grumbled a single word, a groan that carried throughout the entire temple. "*Eliza.*"

"That's right, Ranger. The reason all this started." Keech stepped closer. "Your grief drove you to do awful things, but I know you remember who you were. Who you *are.*"

"Stop," Doyle said, his finger rising toward Keech again.

As the other Lost Causes waited silently, Keech took another careful step forward. "You're not a monster. You're our *friend.*"

Raising his hands, Doyle clawed at his forehead, as if hoping to tear the Devil's mark from his very flesh.

His heart pounding, Keech continued. "You're a father who loves his children. Both John and Eliza. That love can be enough to save you."

Again, Doyle staggered backward. This time his heels stopped inches from the chasm.

Vile cackling echoed in the Palace as Coward stepped over the lip of the basin, holding a hand over his wounded head. On unsteady legs he shuffled across the temple and toward Doyle.

"You petulant child," he said to Keech. "Nothing you say will overcome the Prime!" Stopping beside the Ranger, Coward raised up on his tiptoes and growled at the man's ear, "Finish them, Red."

But Doyle didn't obey. Instead, he dropped his gaze to the floor, as if fiercely concentrating on a single point.

Coward glared at the man. "The Master's mark is unbreakable! You have no choice!"

Sweat pouring from his pallid face, Doyle plucked the silver charm he carried out of his pocket. "True, Coward, the brand is strong. But not as strong as a father's love for his children," he said, then tossed the glowing fragment toward the young riders. Through gritted teeth, the Ranger addressed Keech and Duck. "Your fathers were good men. Some of the finest I ever met. I know they're proud of you today."

Confusion and rage twisted Coward's features as he glared at Doyle. "What are you doing, you fool!" He pressed the Devil's mark on his palm again.

A single tear streamed down the Ranger's face, cutting a path through the dust and blood caked on his cheek. With trembling lips, he said to Keech, "Tell my boy I love him. Tell him I never intended to leave him alone. You tell him that, Keech." Then turning toward the darkness, he murmured, "Papa's sorry, Eliza."

Then with a sudden, swift motion, Edgar Doyle scooped up Coward and tumbled sideways, pitching them both over the edge of the chasm. Coward's scream followed them down the pit and abruptly fell silent.

"Ranger Doyle!" Quinn dashed over to the edge, reaching out with one hand as if to try to save the man.

Except for the incessant murmuring from the Dead Rift, the

Palace fell quiet. Wiping away a stream of sudden tears, Keech opened the satchel and gently placed Eliza's skull back inside. He felt his mouth tremble as the weight of Doyle's sacrifice bore down on his heart.

Quinn sobbed as he peered down into the abyss. "I know he never meant to hurt anybody. He was a good man. He just got lost."

"Take your sorrow and turn it into anger," Strong Heart said. "We still have work to do."

Drying his eyes, Quinn stooped and picked up the shard. "Then let's get to it. We've got the charms now. *All* of them." He tied the fifth piece of silver to his palm.

The Lost Causes gathered in a huddle.

"We're almost home," Keech said. "We only need to stop the ritual."

Together, they shuffled toward the basin, most of them limping. But as soon as the sarcophagus came into view, they stopped in their tracks.

The Reverend Rose was sitting up on the slab.

CHAPTER 44
THE REVEREND

See your opponent clearly.

—Pa Abner

Tossing back the folds of his filthy robe, the Reverend slid off the sarcophagus and placed his bare feet on the limestone floor. He winced a little, seemingly at the touch of stone on his naked soles, then stretched, his ancient joints creaking. A slight smile grew on his lips.

"Seems the Fang still has work to do," Rose said, his voice grating but sharp, the sound of shattering glass. He touched the bone hilt of the Fang of Barachiel protruding from his chest, and a small chortle escaped him. "Decades of decay require more effort to mend than a mere cut."

"Reverend! We've come to stop you!" Keech yelled, hoping his voice carried enough courage to send a message of resolve. "We've defeated the Big Snake. Now it's your turn. It's your judgment day."

The Reverend stepped around the sarcophagus and faced the Lost Causes, who formed a semicircle at the top of the basin, around the gaunt sorcerer. With every step, Rose seemed to grow stronger.

Keech considered their options. As far as he could see, they had only one hope to stop the devil: the Prime-infused blade waiting in Doyle's satchel.

Pivoting so that his movement would be less noticeable, Keech slid his hand into the bag and wrapped his fingers around the blade's hilt. His palm felt a tiny thrum of electricity.

The Reverend scowled and shook his head, reminding Keech of a disappointed parent. "*Blackwood.* What do *you* know of judgment?"

"I know you're nothing more than a no-good thief who walks on others to find your way," Keech growled. "You plunder tribes and lands and call it strength. That's not strength. That's a *plague.* You're no better than the Withers, Rose."

The Reverend nodded, as if earnestly contemplating Keech's tirade. "I have endured more than you could possibly fathom, boy. These last two decades, trapped here in the Palace, have felt like a *curse.*" Rose tugged at his long beard with a slender hand. "But now I am whole, and nothing else can hurt me. Especially not the exhortations of a simple *orphan.*"

Feeling his body tremble with rage, Keech glanced back at his trailmates. "Bad Whiskey and Big Ben thought they were invincible, too, didn't they?"

"They sure did," said Duck.

"And old Ignatio thought he'd never see the Long Trail, either. Am I right?"

"Right as rain," answered Quinn.

Keech turned back to Rose, Cutter's blade in hand. "But we found a way to bring them low. And we're gonna do the same to you."

The Reverend's eyes ignited into brilliant green orbs as he fixed a deadly gaze on Keech. They could have been the eyes of a dragon, newly born and ravenous, and Keech realized he'd seen them before. In Bone Ridge Cemetery, when Rose had taken over Bad Whiskey's body.

"I promised you, Blackwood, that on the day we met, you would know true *fear*." The Reverend then stretched out his arms, lifted his face to the dark ceiling, and muttered words that Keech recognized as Black Verse.

A terrible thunder erupted all around and grew in volume. Suddenly, hundreds of misshapen crows burst from the adjacent tunnels, cawing furiously. They swept through the dark temple like a tornado, shrieking in unison and circling high into the upper shadows.

"Find cover!" Quinn screamed. Together with Duck, he helped Strong Heart limp toward a heaping pile of rocky debris.

Even armed with the amulet shards, there was no way they could survive such a rampage of crows. Their only hope was to stop Rose. And he held the only way to finish the job. Still clutching Cutter's blade, he turned to his brother. "Sam, remember your mad dash into Greely's?"

"How could I forget?" said Sam. The day Tommy Claymore attacked Frosty Potter's office in Big Timber, Sam had scurried into Greely's General Goods to cause a distraction for Keech on Main Street.

"On the count of three," Keech muttered.

But Sam didn't wait for the count. Shouting a curse at Rose, he leaped over the edge of the basin and slid toward Rose's left side. The Reverend's wicked gaze followed. Without hesitating, Keech dashed the opposite way with Cutter's knife held high.

Somersaulting over the sarcophagus, Sam landed on one foot

and kicked out at Rose's knee with the other. Though his boot glanced off without effect, the distraction seemed to work. The Reverend swiveled and reached for Sam with his good hand. He gripped the boy's shoulder and squeezed. The fingers tore into Sam's flesh, and even over the clamor of the crows, Keech heard Sam's howl of pain. The boy tumbled to the floor in a faint.

Keech leaped at Rose's back, the magic knife leading his attack.

But the Reverend spun around with lightning ease, quicker than any human could move. He caught Keech around the forearm, stopping the steel mere inches from his neck. "You shall *not* take vengeance," he murmured, and squeezed Keech's arm. Keech heard a dreadful *snap!* as his bones cracked.

The shock of pain that shuddered through his arm overwhelmed him, but even as darkness gathered at the edges of his vision, Keech bellowed defiantly in Rose's face. The sound that spilled from his throat was a mixture of fury, agony, and despair.

As Keech dangled, Rose used his free hand to peel Keech's fingers from the blade's bone hilt. He lifted the Prime-corrupted knife and smiled, as if admiring it. "This is the knife that killed Ignatio. I wonder if it could have hurt me?"

Keech tried to mutter something, but the pain was too great.

Then he saw the Fang of Barachiel lodged in the Reverend's chest.

"This blade is too dangerous for children." With a smooth flicking motion, Rose tossed Cutter's knife across the temple, where it tumbled into the chasm.

Keech felt himself lifted higher.

"And now for you, Blackwood."

Before the Reverend could toss him, Keech grabbed the bone

handle of the Fang. Rose released him with a surprised growl, and Keech tumbled over the sarcophagus. He crashed to the floor beside the unconscious Sam.

He was gripping the Fang.

From the opposite side of the sarcophagus, the Reverend Rose glanced down at his chest, clearly surprised by Keech's sleight of hand. He touched the slit in his filthy robe where the Fang had been planted. "Clever boy!" he sang. "But *keep* the Fang. I no longer need it."

Ignoring the Reverend's taunts, Keech plunged the dagger into his broken arm. He felt no pain at the insertion, only that strange healing warmth. As soon as he could move his hand again, he jabbed the Fang into Sam's bloody shoulder.

Sam shrieked, and his eyes flew open. He glanced down at the dagger sticking out of his body, and his eyes teemed with fear. "Keech, help me! I've been stuck!"

"Sam, don't worry! *Look*." Keech yanked the Fang free and held it up. There was no blood on the blade.

Sam opened his mouth, no doubt to mutter questions, but Keech stopped him. "No time to explain. We have to help the others."

Reinvigorated, they hurried up the slope of the basin. As soon as they stepped out onto the temple floor, a flurry of crows descended on them, blocking any sign of the Reverend on the other side of the bowl. They swatted at the birds with their amulet pieces. The few monsters that Keech's fragment touched exploded into a slurry of feathers and gore, but most of the creatures sailed past with bloodstained claws.

Quinn and Duck had taken cover behind a pile of broken stones, standing over a battered Strong Heart. Rose's relentless offspring flitted down from the ceiling and pecked at the trio, but their own amulet shards were staving off the assault.

As soon as Keech and Sam reached them, Duck flung her arms around Keech's neck. "We thought you two were goners!"

"We nearly were, but we fetched this instead." He showed her the Fang, then he turned his attention to Strong Heart, who was clutching her ribs and groaning. "Are you all right?"

Through a heavy grimace, the girl nodded.

On the far side of the temple, the Reverend Rose stopped next to the granite bridge, squatted, and seized the narrow slab on each side.

"What's he up to?" said Quinn.

With a monstrous grunt, Rose lifted the bridge away from the chasm and raised it above his head as if it weighed no more than a feed sack. Keech watched in disbelief as Rose hauled the slab across the temple, descended the basin, and shuffled toward the Dead Rift door. With nothing more than a grunt, he hurled the slab over the buzzing portal, blocking the other world from sight. Murmuring something indiscernible, he brushed grit off his fingers, then turned back to find the Lost Causes.

"Why on earth would he want to close off the Dead Rift?" asked Quinn.

Keech worked to discern the answer, but there was no time to think. The Reverend's eyes were flashing green again. The monster bellowed at his crows, "Pick their bones clean! Then bring me the Key! I'm ready to see the world again."

Shrieking, the horde of birds poured down on the Lost Causes, talons extended.

Working swiftly, Quinn untied his shard. "We've got one move left," he said, and held out the charm to Duck. "You best hurry."

Huddling, the Lost Causes handed their amulet pieces to Duck as the flurry of crows slashed and chomped mere inches away, their scythe-like beaks and talons held narrowly at bay by the rhythmic pulsing power of the shards. With the five pieces resting on her palm, Duck arranged the shards into a loose circle, setting each against the next like pieces of a puzzle.

"Go faster!" said Sam. "These things are breathin' down our necks!"

"Almost there!" Duck frantically searched for the correct pattern.

With a terrible screech, one of the creatures whittled its way closer and scored a deep gash across Strong Heart's cheek. Crying out, she slapped a hand across the cut, but before the wound could even bleed a drop, Keech used the Fang to heal her.

"I think I've got it!" Duck hollered.

Resting on the ground, the amulet shards were united into a single silver plate, a flat discus slightly larger than one of Granny Nell's teacup saucers. The etchings across the surface formed the seven symbols—the same ones inscribed on the altar in the House of the Rabbit, and again on the Palace wall.

Before Keech could ask what they should do next, a brilliant light flashed from the restored amulet. The Lost Causes tumbled back as a series of explosive claps sounded overhead. A cascade of sludge showered down on them and across the temple.

After wiping his eyes clear, Keech glanced up.

The crows were gone. Every bird had melted back into grayish goop.

Seizing the amulet with both hands, Duck lifted the plate high above her head. The large silver disc illuminated the entire chamber. She shouted defiantly at Rose, "Do you see? We'll keep on fighting you! We'll never give up!"

Rose's smile looked gentle, disappointed. "What can any of you do?" Bending, he scooped up a handful of muck from the Palace floor. "Whatever you destroy, I can make anew." With a fluid motion, he dragged a jagged fingernail across his own thumb. A bead of bright red blood formed along the cut, and Rose held the wounded thumb over the mud in his opposite hand. A tear-shaped drop fell.

As the blood mixed with the mud, the handful of clay pulsed with life. The Reverend murmured, "*Ah ya nw'glewiin*," and tossed the substance across the room. As soon as it left Rose's hand, the material sprouted a massive beak and long, crooked wings and flapped about with crimson, rage-filled eyes.

Keech clenched his teeth in frustration. Rose seemed to have no weakness they could exploit.

Then he recalled what Quinn said—*Why on earth would he want to close off the Dead Rift?*—and his mouth dropped open.

The Dead Rift was the answer.

"I think I know how to stop him," Keech muttered to the gang. "But I'm gonna have to do something, the only thing I think will surprise him."

"Keech Blackwood, what are you planning?" Duck asked, clearly alarmed.

"To throw him off balance. And here's how."

Without another word, Keech sprinted toward the basin, hopped over the edge, and slid down the slippery granite to the sarcophagus. Leaping onto the table, he reached for the Char Stone.

"What are you doing?" the Reverend shouted.

The moment Keech's fingers grazed the pulsing black rock, his knees buckled and he felt himself collapsing. Deep in his mind, he heard Pa Abner screaming his old warnings about the Stone—*Forget you ever heard of it!*—as well as Milos Horner shouting his own admonitions in Wisdom—*Avoid the lure of the Char Stone at all costs!* But the deed was done. The Palace of the Thunders snuffed out like a flame, and Keech's world capsized into darkness.

CHAPTER 45
THE CHAR STONE

When survival's at stake, the mind can deceive. Accept what is real.
Recognize the lies. Cast them aside.

—PA ABNER

A pleasant warmth bathed Keech's skin. He took a deep breath, and the familiar scents of pine needles, honeysuckle, and wild onions filled his lungs. He opened his eyes to find he was lying on a quiet riverbank drenched in sunlight. The soil beneath him was soft and dark. Confused, Keech sat up and looked around. He recognized the place. The river flowing before him had long been a beloved haunt for him and Sam.

He was sitting on the bank of the Third Fork River.

"What in blazes?" he muttered.

The obvious answer was that touching the Char Stone had returned him home to Missouri. Except, Keech couldn't bring himself to believe such a hopeful notion.

This vision had to have meaning. Perhaps a clue that could help him defeat the Reverend Rose. Determined to keep his eyes open, Keech examined the world around him. High-pitched birdsong trilled in the nearby forest. Above, the sky was blue, and a cool breeze brushed at his hair. The steady tumble of the river's lazy run reminded Keech of the morning he and Sam played Grab the Musket.

Somewhere along the riverbank, he heard a man's voice singing a low tune.

The sound was haunting, perhaps even dangerous. Straining
to better hear the song, Keech caught a flavor of weary melancholy that filled him with a curiosity he couldn't fight. He walked
downstream, heading toward the voice. His path wound back and
forth, following the movement of the Third Fork River.

"Not real," Keech told himself. "It's a vision. A dream." Yet
the world around him felt authentic. He *was* on the river. He was
back *home*.

Pushing through branches along the bank, Keech pressed on
toward the music. The fellow ahead had an agreeable singing
voice, baritone and wistful. His anthem rolled over the river like
an empty boat.

"How happy the soldier who lives on his pay,
And spends half a crown on six pence a day;
He fears neither justices, warrants, nor bums,
But pays all his debts with a roll of the drums . . ."

Keech stepped up his pace, slogging through ankle-high mud to
reach the singer. Rounding a small curve in the river, he raked back
a handful of branches and caught a glimpse of the man's back. The
fellow was hunched over on the bank, grasping his knees as he faced
the sun-kissed water. He wore a long black overcoat and black
boots, and his greasy black hair was drawn tightly into a ponytail.

"With a row de dow,
Row de dow, Row de dow,
And he pays all his debts with a roll of his drums."

Keech staggered backward, losing his bowler hat in the limbs
of a dogwood. "Bad Whiskey!" he cried.

Halting his song, the one-eyed desperado glanced over his shoulder. His one good eye squinted at Keech as if confused. "No one here," Bad Whiskey muttered. "Ain't no one here." He turned back to the river and resumed his phantom tune, rocking in the mud as he sang.

A mix of determination and anger erupted in Keech. He pushed forward. "What are you doing here, Bad? Rose's crows killed you dead in Bone Ridge."

The outlaw paused his song again. "I *live* here, little pilgrim. Have for many years." With a chortle, Bad Whiskey returned to his melody. He appeared to stare into the depths of the river at some kind of sparkling ring, a circle shining up from the bottom like a lost penny catching a sunray.

"What is that?" Keech asked.

"Don't know," mumbled Bad Whiskey. "It appeared not too long ago. Somethin' happened to the Stone, I reckon. I wonder what it is but don't dare go in the water. Souls get *lost* in the water."

Peeling his gaze away from the disk of light, Keech said, "This place ain't real, and you're not here." To prove it to himself, he reached out and touched the outlaw's shoulder.

Bad Whiskey swung around and seized Keech's wrist—an assault that felt real enough. Keech tried to pull back, but the desperado's grip was merciless.

"Yer *wrong*," Bad Whiskey snarled. "It's as real as can be, pilgrim. Two kinds of folk live here. The dead who rise, and the ones who touch the Stone. Look for yerself." The outlaw pointed across the Third Fork, where a field stretched toward the forested hills.

Keech knew the pasture well. Pa Abner had often taken the orphans there during autumn days to hunt quail. Only now the meadow stirred with a multitude of strange people—hundreds, maybe thousands of men and women stumbling about in confounded circles, like wanderers stranded in the wilderness.

A passage from Doyle's journal, something the Reverend Rose himself had said to the Enforcers, struck Keech's memory. *The most essential portion of our being is the soul, for the essence of a soul fuels the energies of both the world we see and the one we cannot.* "The immaterial realm," Keech murmured. "A place where souls live . . . like smoke captured behind glass." He stepped closer to the river's edge to fetch a better look at the wandering souls.

Among the rabble was the one-legged bandit, Tommy Claymore. He looked to be chattering at a gopher hole in the ground. Nearby stood another familiar man, a leather-coated fellow named Rance, and behind him both the skeletal outlaw, Scurvy, and the monstrous brute with the gold nose ring, Bull.

He turned back to Bad Whiskey. "Those are *your* men!"

The desperado rattled his head. "Not no more, pilgrim. Not in here."

All around the meadow, Keech spotted the faces of other outlaws who had once plagued the Lost Causes. He spotted a timid fellow named Cooper whom Pa Abner had shot on the front porch of the Home, as well as several goons Keech had seen in the town of Wisdom, killers raised by Ignatio and under the command of Big Ben Loving.

All of them had one thing in common.

"They were *thralls*," Keech said to Bad Whiskey. "Like you."

"Once upon a time, yes," the outlaw muttered. "We all got raised from the muck and the blood. Now we're jus' dead souls tucked away in the Stone."

Feeling fear creep into his heart again, Keech turned away from the river and marched up the muddy bank. His ears picked up a new sound—mirthful, child-like giggles off to the south. Keech left Bad Whiskey to swaying in the mud and singing. He hurried off through the woods, following the distant laughter.

A short time later, he peeled back a final branch and saw it.

The Home for Lost Causes.

The farmhouse stood on Pa Abner's property as it had for most of Keech's life—a sturdy rampart against the encroaching wilderness. The gabled rooftop pointed with fortitude up to the blue sky, and the windows glinted in the sun like sets of eyes winking deep secrets. The youthful giggles came from inside the house. Keech hurried across the front yard and past the rickety shakepole fence.

He tossed open the front door, feeling a fine breeze rustle over the threshold. "Granny! Everyone! I'm home!" he shouted. "I made it back!"

He couldn't decide if he believed his own words or not, but the truth no longer mattered, because he was standing in his long-lost home, touching Pa Abner's handmade furniture and inhaling the wonderful smells of pine and cedar and freshly baked bread.

Crying out for joy, Keech dashed to the kitchen, expecting to find Granny Nell by the cast-iron stove. Only, the kitchen was empty.

"Granny?"

There were place settings on the dining table—one for each orphan—but no one came in to join him.

The child-like laughter came again, this time rolling down the stairwell. Spinning on one bootheel, Keech scurried toward the stairs and bounded up the steps two at a time. "Patrick, I hear you!" he yelled.

Except that when Keech reached the bedroom that Patrick shared with Little Eugena, he found no laughing children inside. No one hiding under the bed, no one concealing themselves behind Granny's curtains.

Keech was alone. Yet the haunting laughter continued.

Time slipped from his grasp like a handful of sand. The sunlight in the windows faded to a dark evening. Frightened, Keech sank to his knees at the foot of the stairs and clutched the banister. "When the mind deceives, recognize the lies," he muttered.

Then from outside there came a pounding noise—the familiar *thwack* of a hammer striking wood. Keech couldn't hear the laughter anymore, only the hammering, the persistent music of carpentry.

"Pa Abner!"

Keech hurried out the back door and bolted to the woodshed, skidding to a stop when he saw a bearded, heavyset man with a shiny bald head. Pa hunched over his trusty worktable. He was tinkering with a wooden box, a container small enough to fit in the palm of his hand. Pa was securing a tiny lid with a metal latch.

"Pa, it's me! I've made it home!"

Pa Abner didn't speak at first. Only after he finished securing the lid did he turn around. "Hello, my boy," Pa said, his voice gentle and unsurprised, as if he might have been expecting Keech.

Unable to hold back, Keech hugged the big man with all his might. He tried to speak his fears, his hopes, his anger, but all that seemed to come out of his mouth was a garble of choked noises.

Pa Abner patted his back. "There, there, Keech. It's okay. It's okay."

Keech stepped back. "Pa, what *is* this place? And why are you here?"

"It is a cursed place, my boy, a snare for the deepest parts of our being. When Bad Whiskey used the Prime to raise me as a thrall, the Char Stone captured a part of me, my soul, and trapped it here."

Keech glanced around in fascination, seeing only his home, the place where he'd been raised after his parents died. To think it was all the ruse of a cursed relic was mind-boggling. "Is there a way to escape?"

Pa Abner didn't answer; he simply sat on his stool and fiddled with the little box he'd built. He chewed at the whiskers around his lips, then finally looked up. "Truth be told, I don't know how to get out. There may be no way. When I first came, I searched everywhere, but I finally had to give up." He then held out his wooden box to Keech. "Instead of trying to leave, I made *this*."

Keech took the box and scrutinized it. "What *is* this thing?"

"It's something I've dreamed about, night and day. I don't rightly understand it, but I believe it's a *cage*."

Keech blinked. "It could barely hold a penny!"

Pa Abner scratched at the stubble on his neck, then turned away, distracted, as if he'd heard something in the distance. "Time for supper. You best be on your way." He waved his hand, shooing Keech off.

Keech wanted to feel anger toward Pa's sudden dismissal, but instead he felt only a burdensome grief, a profound sorrow for all the happiness lost to the Reverend's malice. Wiping at fresh tears, he said to Pa, "I want you to know something. I saw what happened to my folks, and I don't blame you. You're a good man, Pa, and after Ignatio's curse took them, I know you did your best. So I just want to say . . ." Keech hesitated, searching for the words he should have said months ago in Bone Ridge Cemetery, when Pa Abner was slipping away. "Thank you for saving me. For the life you gave me, and for teaching me to stand tall."

Smiling, Pa Abner kissed his dusty palm and touched it to Keech's forehead. "My boy, you knew how to stand tall well before *I* came along. You are the son of Bill and Erin Blackwood, and you've made them proud from the first day you drew breath. Now"—Pa Abner glanced up at the sky, then back to Keech—"it's time for you to run along." And he pointed to the little box in Keech's hand.

Before stepping away, Keech said, "One last thing. They're *alive*, Pa. The entire family. Granny Nell and Patrick and Little Eugena and Robby. *Sam* told me. He's waiting on the other side of the Stone. You protected them all."

Upon hearing the news, Pa's eyes filled with a light that Keech had never seen on the man's face before. He said nothing, but Keech understood that Pa's heart was too full to let the response come.

A single word finally fell from the man's lips: "*Go.*"

With Pa's little box in hand, Keech turned and realized he was no longer standing in the shed, but was back in the woods. He now stood in a thicket of red buckeye trees, and the orphanage was no longer in sight. A strange sound touched Keech's ears. A nervous voice, muttering. He walked toward the noise, pushing back the buckeye branches.

A tall figure in a fancy suit stood alone inside a circle of field-stones. He held a tattered scroll of papyrus in his hands and was poring over the writings. Words spilled from his mouth in a running stream of gibberish.

Keech stepped into the circle. As his boots scraped over the stones, the man wheeled about, his eyes wide with surprise.

"Who are you? What are you doing here?" he snapped.

"I'm Keech. I think I'm lost."

"We're *all* lost." The figure waved his hands at the buckeye trees around them. "We are in the wilderness of nowhere, and we cannot go forth or back." The fellow rubbed his swollen eyes. "How are we supposed to learn the secrets of the scroll if we can't study them in proper peace?" He jabbed a finger at the papyrus. "How can I ever decipher the codes under these conditions?"

The man's left hand was missing three fingers. He was gaunt, his cheeks sunken and flat, but he was still quite handsome. His brown hair was raked back and long so that it touched his shoulders. Like Bad Whiskey's, his garments were black from head to toe, except for a white collar around his neck. A *priest's* collar.

"You're the Reverend!" Keech said.

The slender fellow blinked at him. "I don't recognize you, boy. How have you heard of me?"

Keech almost answered, but instead he asked, "What are you doing with the scroll?"

The Reverend grinned—a smile full of malice and cruelty. "I am learning the secrets of Enoch, the path to immortality. But I can't seem to see the words correctly." He squinted at the papyrus. "They dance away from me! The meaning refuses to stand still. If I can *just read the words*, I can get back in."

"Back in where?"

"My body, of course! I can finish the ritual. I can live *forever.*"

Fresh anger burned through Keech's veins. "Don't you real-ize? The ritual is finished, Rose. You've awoken in the Palace. You're fighting to get free."

The Reverend laughed. "Not *I*, foolish boy. The Char Stone pulled me out of my body, and something else entered from the other side. But once I decipher Enoch's words, I'll go back to claim the power that's rightfully mine. I'll be a god among men!"

Keech fisted his hands. "Even here, you're insane."

But the Reverend didn't seem to hear the insult. His eyes had fallen on the wooden box in Keech's hand. He tilted his head. "What do you have there?"

"My pa Abner made it for me."

"Your *pa*." The Reverend spoke the words as if they pained him, as if he suddenly remembered who Pa Abner was. "Give it to me."

Keech flinched away. "Not a chance."

"It *must* contain the secret, the answer to Enoch's cipher! Isaiah figured it out!" Without warning, Rose lunged like a rattlesnake and crashed into Keech. The sudden attack surprised him and he stumbled backward, his boots slipping on the fieldstones. The tiny coffer tumbled out of his hand and landed at Rose's feet. Keech reached for the box, but he was too slow.

Rose picked up the container and unlatched the top. Grinning madly, he opened the lid, reached a finger inside—

—and vanished.

The box dropped to the fieldstones.

Bewildered, Keech picked up the wooden case. The lid was shut, the hook latched. The vessel felt warm in his hand. He shook it, but it sounded empty. And yet Keech knew that Rose was trapped inside, caught within the box.

It's something I've dreamed about, night and day. I don't rightly understand it, but I believe it's a cage.

Keech's mind reeled as he realized the box's true purpose. "To hold the Reverend's soul," he muttered.

Once again, the lonely dirge of singing touched Keech's ears. With the box in his grasp, he turned and walked again toward the voice. A moment later, he pushed through more buckeye branches and found himself back on the muddy banks of the Third Fork River.

Squatting beside a feeble campfire, Bad Whiskey looked up. "Welcome back, little pilgrim. Come on over and we can sing a fine duet, right here on the bank." Closing his one good eye, the desperado crooned his old tune:

"With a row de dow,

Row de dow, Row de dow,

And he pays all his debts with a roll of his drums . . ."

As Bad Whiskey sang, Keech walked to the river's edge and peered again at the strange spark of light beneath the water's surface. He glanced at the box in his hand, then back at the submerged light, and he promptly realized what he must do.

"Sorry, Bad, I got somewhere to be." Keech took a broad step into the frigid waters of the Third Fork.

Bad Whiskey jumped to his feet. "Get back! There's only death in there!"

"I've made a bundle of mistakes," Keech replied, not looking back. "But if I've learned anything in my travels, Bad, I've learned that when a wretched outlaw tells you what to do, you do the opposite."

Ignoring Bad Whiskey's curses, he dived into the water.

For most of his life, Keech had played in the Third Fork and knew the river to be shallow. Yet the tributary was now a bottomless crater. Keech felt himself sinking into obscurity, and his stomach lurched. He searched for something to grasp, but the darkness reached in all directions. Even above him, the water seemed to take on endless depth, stretching upward for miles and miles. A past dream in which he was drowning under the ocean struck his memories, and Keech spun desperately in the cold.

A violent hand landed on his shoulder, clawing at his shirt.

Keech whirled around to see Bad Whiskey pulling at him, tugging him back toward the riverbank. The thrall's eye glared madly at Keech in the murky waters. A flurry of air bubbles poured out of Keech's mouth as he screamed. He kicked at the desperado, but Bad Whiskey refused to turn loose.

Suddenly, a human-shaped creature with emerald-green eyes swam up behind Bad Whiskey and seized the outlaw's arms. Bad Whiskey bellowed with rage as the spectral figure of Saint Peter yanked him away.

Keech suddenly recalled how Coward had touched the shapeshifter with the Char Stone at the top of Skeleton Peak. Saint Peter had collapsed and faded into the ground. Now Keech knew his soul had been captured by the Stone.

Because he was underwater, Keech couldn't offer proper thanks other than a nod, but Saint Peter saw the gesture and smiled. A curious but gentle voice murmured in Keech's mind— *Keep going*, it said, *you're nearly there*—and he realized he was hearing the Kelpie.

Kicking with all his might, Keech turned and stared down into the opaque waters.

A vibrant spark flashed through the darkness—the same glow Keech had seen from the riverbank. He swam toward it. Within seconds, he arrived at the bottom. Smooth pebbles littered the riverbed, and in the midst of Keech's field of vision, the circle of light beamed like the world's brightest lantern. He reached for it.

The moment his finger pierced the illumination, Keech tugged at the opening. There was no more breath in his lungs, but he slipped more fingers into the light and pulled.

The glowing disk widened.

With a howling, wind-like sound, the waters around him poured through the light. Keech tugged harder, and the light ripped open even farther, till the glowing space was the size of a barrelhead. The water continued to gush down into the hole, as if the cork had been removed from a washbasin, and Keech felt himself being pulled toward the opening.

Before he could slip through, Saint Peter swam past, his emerald hands still clutching a furious Bad Whiskey. Both figures plunged through the glowing hole and winked out of view.

No sooner had they vanished than others followed, coursing through the water and toward the glow like swarms of fireflies fluttering through the mouth of a jar. All the faces that glided past Keech belonged to thralls, the departed men and women whom Rose and his cursed ilk had raised over the years.

Then Pa Abner himself drifted past, a contented look on his face, and Keech understood.

He had pulled open a breach in the Stone, and the souls within were escaping.

Except for one.

The tiny lockbox Pa had given Keech remained in his hand.

Keech could no longer fight the persistent force of the water. He flowed into the glowing disk, following the deluge of souls, riding the fierce momentum as if he were swimming over a waterfall. He tumbled till energy and light and pure, unbridled joy surrounded his being. And he let himself go.

CHAPTER 46
THE AMULET

Let your team contribute to your strength.

—PA ABNER

K eech opened his eyes to discover he was lying in a heap beside the sarcophagus. His head pounded fiercely, most likely from knocking it against the table on the way down, and something steadily throbbed in his closed hand. When he opened his fingers, he realized what he was gripping and gasped. It wasn't Pa's lockbox. It was the Char Stone.

"To touch the Stone is death!" Rose shouted.

The Reverend was wrong, of course. Keech had found his way back out. And in the process, released the many souls the Reverend had captured. Now the Stone was empty of all souls save *one*.

And Keech intended to return that soul to its body.

Pushing up to his feet, he peered over the edge of the basin. Rose had wandered away from the bridge he'd used to seal the Dead Rift. A newly created crow sat on his shoulder, its crimson eyes glowing with terrible power. Taking casual steps on bare feet, the Reverend walked toward the others. "Your friend Blackwood was foolish. And now the Stone has claimed him. But do not fret, children! Blackwood will live on inside my veins as *Prime*."

Moving with the stealth he'd learned from Pa, Keech slunk out of the basin.

The Reverend continued his bothersome bravado. "Now, children, should I tear you to pieces? Or would it be a better revenge to toss you all into the chasm after Red and Coward?"

Quinn stepped away from the others, toward the chasm. The Key of Enoch dangled in his hand like a whip. He said, "Take another step, you foul devil, and I'll launch this Key into the abyss."

"You still think you have a card to play?" The Reverend laughed. "If you throw the Key over the edge, I'll send a crow down to retrieve it. The pit may seem bottomless, but it isn't. And I have closed off all means of escape." The Reverend's eyes flared green again and his lips peeled back, revealing a mouthful of sharp yellow teeth. "The game is over. There is naught for you to do but die."

Keech emerged from the basin to find himself mere feet behind the Reverend. He crept forward, hoping the monster wouldn't hear the scraping of his boots. Gripping the Char Stone, he reached out.

The Reverend spun with unearthly speed and grabbed Keech around the neck.

"Keech!" Sam shouted from across the chamber.

Pain cascaded through Keech's body as the Reverend's grip tightened. "No one escapes the Stone!" Rose rumbled.

"*I . . . found . . . you,*" Keech hissed.

"Don't you understand, Blackwood? I can see into your mind," Rose murmured as he squeezed Keech's neck. It was, Keech realized, the exact way that the rage-cursed Pa Abner had ended Bill Blackwood. "You tampered with the darkness. You invited me in with the Black Verse. Nothing you do will escape my infinite gaze.

419

'If thy hand or thy foot offend thee, cut them off, and cast them from thee.' I will cast you aside, boy. I will *destroy* you . . .'"

His vision fluttering, Keech listened for the voice of the man who had trained him to survive, who had loved Keech like his own son.

Don't hesitate, Keech. Hesitation means death.

Keech rammed his knee into the Reverend's stomach. The action did nothing to release Rose's fingers, but it did force the fiend's grip to slacken just enough to let Keech raise his arms. He lifted the Char Stone, and with a final mighty push, he shoved the cursed relic against Rose's face.

The effect was instantaneous. The Reverend released Keech's neck, and his hands flew up to seize the Stone. Screaming, he tore the relic out of Keech's grip and away from his face and hurled it across the temple as if it were fire itself.

Keech crumbled to the floor on numbed legs, his vision a sickening blur of tears. In the distance, he could hear voices hollering his name, and he tried to turn toward them, but he couldn't seem to move.

Then a curious warmth entered Keech's body. His throat opened with a stinging cough, and he drew in a blissful breath. When he opened his eyes, he rolled onto his back to find Duck and Sam hunched over him. Sam was holding the Fang of Barachiel.

The Reverend staggered around the temple, doubled over and gibbering to himself, "No! This body is *mine!*"

"What's happening to him?" Duck asked.

Keech pushed up to his feet, gripping his throat. "The Char Stone. When I was inside, I found Rose's soul. But Pa Abner was there, too."

"*Pa?*" muttered Sam.

"He gave me a way to bring Rose's soul back out."

Across the room, the Reverend stumbled to his knees and bellowed to no one, as if shrieking to someone inside his own head. "*No! You can't have it back!*"

Keech smiled when he realized his plan was working. When Rose first touched the Stone all those years ago, he opened his mind and body to a demon from the Dead Rift, a demon that clearly wanted solitary possession. But by giving Rose's soul *back* to his body, Keech had kicked the demon off balance.

Rose's crow took to the air and circled above, crying *Ack! Ack! Ack!*

The Reverend glared up at the young riders, his blazing green eyes wild with terror and rage. "Nothing has changed! You haven't won! I'll find a way out yet!"

Racing in close, Strong Heart kicked at the Reverend's leg. The demon stumbled back, but caught himself just before striking the floor. Whipping around, he lashed out with a blind swing to wallop Strong Heart, but the girl ducked beneath his knuckles and struck his other leg, this time with a fist.

The roar that emanated from the Reverend's lungs seemed to rattle the entire Palace. "*My wrath will fall upon your heads!*"

Strong Heart cried, "Quinn, the Key!"

Quinn tossed the chain. Keech heard the heavy *swoosh* of the ancient shackle as the Key flew through the air in crooked loops. It careened toward the drop-off, where the Reverend had thrown Cutter's knife, and for one terrifying second, Keech thought Strong Heart would miss it. But then she vaulted over the distance and caught the shackle with one hand before the chain could tumble over the edge.

As soon as she landed, Strong Heart sprinted toward the Reverend, swinging the shackle above her head like a lasso. Rose lifted his good hand as if preparing to summon a spell, but before he could unleash a dark enchantment, Strong Heart released her hold on the Key. The chain whipped around Rose's arms and waist in a tight coil. Tumbling in front of Rose's legs, Strong Heart snapped the dangling shackle around his wrist, then she faced the Reverend. "You are nothing but a stone in my path," she said.

With a loud cry, Strong Heart kicked Rose squarely in the chest, her foot slamming into him so hard he tumbled head over heels and smacked against the slab that blocked the Dead Rift. But the fiend didn't stop. Instead, the Key's magic sent Rose careening through the barrier like a phantom through a wall. As the Reverend plunged into the Dead Rift, he shrieked a death rattle of outrage and surprise.

A second later, the voice fell silent.

The crow overhead dived blindly at the Lost Causes, screeching murderous rage as it plummeted toward them. But its flight was short-lived. The creature disintegrated into a black cloud of dust that sprinkled across the Palace floor.

The Palace was still for a moment. Even the horrible buzzing that had permeated the temple was gone.

Quinn murmured, "Is it over?"

"I think it might be," said Sam.

But then the Palace floor trembled under their feet as a massive crack tore through the heavy slab that plugged the Dead Rift.

Strong Heart jumped back. "*Hah^n-kah-zhee!*" she cried.

The stone barrier split down the middle as if something on the other side had smashed its way upward. Behind the gap, the living darkness of the Dead Rift roiled.

The Reverend was climbing back to the surface.

"Duck, the amulet!" Keech bellowed.

Holding the silver metal disc before her, Duck raced toward the Dead Rift. As she neared the breaking slab, sapphire sparks of energy shot from the amulet like a miniature lightning storm. The gut-wrenching sounds of a wounded animal poured out of the Dead Rift. Duck dropped to her knees in front of the cracking stone and raised the amulet high.

A monstrous face appeared in the gap, the true face of the nameless demon that had consumed Rose's body and soul. Fangs gleamed from the thing's open maw.

"Time to break the crocodile's teeth!" Duck slammed the amulet against the hole.

A tremendous thunderclap rattled the Palace, and a sterling light flashed so bright that Keech threw his arms up to protect his eyes. When he blinked them open again, he saw that the slab was once again whole, a single block of stone. The silver disk lay fastened to the stone, sealed in place by the magic of the amulet.

The Lost Causes stood for a moment, waiting, expecting another terrible surprise, but all remained silent. Keech noticed the Char Stone resting near the chasm. With a swift kick, he sent the malignant relic over the edge, where it tumbled through the darkness and disappeared.

Sam asked, "Is it over *now?*"

Taking a deep breath, Keech closed his eyes. All the months

and days and hours spent on the trail, battling Rose's evil, fighting for justice, sloughed away from his tired bones.

"It's over," he said.

Duck wiped grit off her hands. "Dandy. Now how do we get out of here?"

CHAPTER 47
THE LAWMAN'S GIFT

Work as two, succeed as one.

—Pa Abner

Nursing their cuts and bruises, the Lost Causes hiked back through the tunnels and the Antechamber of the Palace and ascended the spiral path. Once they reached the opening, Keech called up to John Wesley, who lowered a rope. One by one, John lifted them through the Chimney.

By the time they returned to the outer wall, evening was upon the canyon. The sky's unnatural purple had faded to a fair crimson, and the incessant rumble of thunder was now nothing more than a dying murmur. At the sight of the young riders, Achilles dashed about in happy circles and covered Quinn with slobbery licks. The dog then led the team to O'Brien, who rested against a large rock, waiting in silence.

Thunder Pass was a turmoil of thrall corpses, fallen Weavers, and shattered stick creatures. With the help of John Wesley's Chamelia pack, O'Brien and Sheriff Turner had obliterated Rose's horde. Only one of the Chamelia had fallen during the battle, and it was from a deadly wound inflicted by Lost Tucker.

Strong Heart inquired about the Weaver boss's fate.

"She crumbled to dust the moment you sealed the Rift," O'Brien said. "The rest of her Weavers went with 'er. Darkness can't live when the light shines on it. And today, you tadpoles brought the light."

"We couldn't have done it without you," said Quinn.

Sam peered over the battleground, surveying the piles of thrall and Weaver bodies. "O'Brien, where's the sheriff? Where is Bose?" he asked.

O'Brien lowered her head. "Follow me," she said.

She led the Lost Causes down a rocky trail to the riverbank, several yards away from the battleground. Lying on a shaded, sandy spot near the Rattlebrook was Sheriff Turner.

The lawman's head rested on his faded horse blanket, and his eyes were closed, as if he were merely napping by the water. O'Brien had crossed his hands over his broad chest.

When Sam saw him, he dashed over to the sheriff's side and slumped to his knees in the sand. Keech and the others gathered behind him. Keech noticed a tiny hole in Sheriff Turner's leather vest—the place where a thrall's lead ball had apparently ended his life—and a hitching sob caught in his throat.

"I'm so sorry, tadpoles," O'Brien said, slipping off her hat. "He stood tall the whole time. I ain't never seen a man fight so valiantly."

Hunkered over the sheriff, Sam said, "On the trail to find you, Keech, I wanted to turn back so many times. I told myself it wouldn't be no use to keep looking for you. But Sheriff Turner wouldn't let me quit. He'd say, 'Let's ride another mile or two. Maybe we'll get lucky and find a horse track.' So we'd ride another mile, then another, then another. He never let me give up." Sam stopped to let a hitching sob run its course. "He was my friend."

Keech dropped to his knees beside Sam. "He stood tall with *all* of us."

Behind them, O'Brien murmured, "Before he passed, Turner said he wanted to give somethin' to yer group. He pointed to his saddlebag and said to tell ya, 'Now it's official.'"

Letting Sam tarry by Turner's side, Keech stepped over to the sheriff's horse. He opened the saddlebag, peered inside, and saw a few small objects waiting, winking up at Keech with a metallic gleam. Feeling a hard lump form in his throat, Keech brought them out.

He showed a handful of silver star-shaped badges to the Lost Causes. Imprinted on each star were the words DEPUTY SHERIFF. Keech felt tears steal into his eyes. "The sheriff deputized us back in Bone Ridge Cemetery, but he didn't have any stars to make it official."

"You know what that means, *amigos?* Means you're real lawdogs now."

The voice came from farther up the bank, and everyone spun around to meet it. To Keech's surprise, Cutter came limping up the bank of the Rattlebrook. Though he looked terribly battered and his bandana still covered his missing eye, he moved with a curious strength. John Wesley walked a few steps behind in his human form.

"Cutter!" Strong Heart exclaimed.

"How in blazes are you still alive? We saw you die!" said Quinn.

After reaching them, Cutter propped himself up on John Wesley's shoulder. "I near did. But then I remembered, I ain't no good at goodbyes. So I asked John here to help me out. He cut me with his claw and *aquí estoy.*"

"But you're infected now!" Duck said.

"That's right. I'm a Chamelia. But that means I can go with my *amigo*. We don't never have to be apart again." Then, grinning, Cutter added, "And now I can do *this*." He lifted his hands, concentrated for a second, and beamed with pride as his fingernails sprouted razor-sharp claws.

John Wesley placed a hand on Cutter's shoulder. "We should go. The pack's callin'."

Keech said, "Wait, John. I've got something to give you."

Like a curious dog, John Wesley's head tilted sideways.

Keech held up the satchel containing Eliza Doyle's remains. "Your father's been carrying this knapsack. It holds the bones of your sister. I figured you'd want to give her a proper burial."

Looking stunned, John Wesley accepted the satchel. After slipping the sack's long strap around his waist, he said, "I sure am sorry for all the trouble Papa stirred."

Keech said, "He was a good man, in the end. He turned back to the light just in time. His last words were for you and Eliza. He wanted you to know he was sorry for what he did. And that he loved you."

Tears burned in John Wesley's scarlet eyes. "Much obliged," he said, wiping his face. He turned as if to scurry away but stopped himself. "Keech?" he said.

"Yeah?"

"Thanks for standin' tall."

Keech felt a strange shiver run down his body, the kind of shiver that could be sorrow but could also be joy. "You too, Big John. You too."

As John Wesley waited near the woods, Cutter stepped up to

his palomino, Chantico, who peered at the boy with a kind of curiosity. Placing his forehead on the mare's neck, Cut whispered something to her, then offered her reins to O'Brien. "*Señora*, if you would, take care of Chantico for me. I can't take her where I'm going."

Accepting the reins, O'Brien said, "I'll make sure she finds her way."

"*Gracias*," Cutter said; then he turned to Keech. "Well, Lost Cause, I reckon this is it."

Keech didn't want to say goodbye, but there was nothing for it. "So long, Miguel. I hope our paths cross again."

Cutter's wide grin revealed rows of new fangs. "Don't you worry, *amigo*. We'll see each other again. If you ever find yourself in trouble, look to the woods. You've got friends."

"I'll remember that," Keech said, smiling.

After exchanging their final farewells, Cutter and John Wesley turned to leave. As they shuffled toward the tree line, both boys shifted. Black scales emerged across their hides, and long, prickly spines sprouted from their backs. Their faces stretched into toothy muzzles, and they hunched forward to scurry on all fours.

The Chamelia disappeared down the river, and soon after, two triumphant howls echoed across Thunder Pass.

CHAPTER 48
THE MAN BEYOND TIME

If you look hard enough, you might find two ways to look at a thing.
—PA ABNER

Later that evening, the Lost Causes and O'Brien buried Bose Turner in a quiet clearing, far away from the Palace wall. Sam spoke a few words and pocketed the sheriff's gold star.

After the burial, the company gathered around their campfire beside the Rattlebrook River. Quinn offered to ignite the flame using O'Brien's matches, but Keech said he wanted to try something first. Pointing at their mound of driftwood, he closed his eyes and concentrated on rousing a flame. A nudge of force surged through his veins and cascaded through his pointing finger, and the driftwood blazed to life.

"Looks like we've still got our powers," mused Quinn.

Strong Heart said, "No one would have suffered the Scorpion's evils if he had not tampered with magic he shouldn't have. It's better to leave such things alone."

"Maybe we should use them only if we have to," Duck said.

"I'd say that's a wise choice," said O'Brien.

So Keech, Duck, and Quinn—the ones affected by the Char

Stone's influence—vowed to keep their abilities hidden to the world, to be used only if needed. Even O'Brien joined the pact.

"Now, let's rest up," the Enforcer said. "We've got long days of travel ahead."

Exhausted, the troop leaned back on their saddle seats and listened as Strong Heart softly sang an Osage song. The Rattlebrook's incessant grumble resounded through the pines, and somewhere, a blue heron croaked across the water's reach. Before long, they were all fast asleep.

Except for Keech. He found himself pondering the home that still awaited, the family he'd thought dead, the life he'd presumed long gone now within reach.

A sudden twinkle of orange light appeared on the black water of the Rattlebrook. Keech rubbed at his eyes and leaned forward.

Not five yards away, the silhouette of a man sat cross-legged on the river's surface. Dark currents flowed past the figure, surging beneath him as if he were perched atop a giant, bobbing cork.

Strangely enough, Keech felt no sense of urgency to flee, no sense of danger. "Hello?" he murmured.

"Howdy, Mr. Blackwood," the fellow said, and Keech realized the orange light he'd seen was a smoking cigar between his lips. "I was hoping to have a chat." The man's voice was deep and friendly—perhaps even *familiar*.

"Who are you?"

The specter pushed up to his feet on the water, then walked closer—casual strides across the Rattlebrook. The dark of the evening shrouded the figure as he walked, but Keech could make out the profile of a wide-brimmed hat. As the man stepped onto the muddy bank and into the telling glow of the firelight, Keech recognized him as the big Texan who had helped the Lost Causes in Kansas Territory.

"I know you! We spoke at Hook's Fort. You're Hamilton!"

The fellow smiled. "Yes, that's my name. Sometimes. Over the years I've gone by many. Your friend Miguel knew me as Artemus Ward. *You* have known me by another."

The Texan peeled off his hat, and his features blurred as if a mist had rolled across his face. When the strange fog cleared, he was now an old man with a mess of shaggy white hair, wearing a pair of ragged bib overalls.

Keech staggered on the bank. "*Mr. Twiggs*. You're the old-timer we saved at Whistler! You said you were the mayor. You told us about Floodwood!"

The countenance of the old man went fuzzy as before, and this time his face became that of the dark-skinned deer hunter who had pointed the Lost Causes toward Hook's Fort. Before Keech could even react in surprise again, the smiling visage of Hamilton the Texan reappeared. "I've watched your group since the start."

After considering the fellow's words, Keech asked, "Who are you, really?"

The Texan smiled again. "You may call me *Enoch*."

This time Keech's legs felt as flimsy as toothpicks.

The man said, "I have walked the Earth for many years, Mr. Blackwood. I have sought to help folks overcome the forces of darkness. While I'm not allowed to personally engage in struggles with evil, on occasions when things are particularly dire, I try to nudge things back onto, let's say, a *better path*."

"Like when you told us how to find O'Brien."

"Right again. And I crafted a special blade and made sure it fell into the hands of your friend, Miguel—or as you call him, *Cutter*. I worried I had crossed the line with that action, but because Miguel wielded the blade, it worked out in the end." Enoch chuckled.

Keech still couldn't think straight. "You've been watching us? You watched when Pa Abner died and did nothing?"

Enoch dropped his head low, his hat brim nearly covering his face. "I am truly sorry about Abner. But as I said, I cannot interfere. When evil rears up, the darkness affects lives, families, villages, and I watch for the folks who will rise to the challenge. But there is a balance in the world, and the sad truth is that if I were to interfere, laws of symmetry would demand that even worse things happen."

"Laws of symmetry," Keech repeated, recalling now the deadly traps and challenges below Skeleton Peak, the snares that demanded teamwork. "Is that why you built the Perils? To test the balance of things?"

Enoch considered for a moment. "In a way, yes. But most of all to keep the wretched and cruel away from the dangerous things I was charged to protect."

Keech listened, fascinated. "You also made the amulet?"

"From the same metals I used to craft the Char Stone's confinement chest, a protective vessel I fashioned to bear the Stone before I discovered the Palace."

Keech thought of the tiny box Pa Abner had given him inside the Stone, the wooden case that trapped the Reverend's soul. Perhaps Pa had been inspired by Enoch's own contraption. "What about the skeleton in the House of the Rabbit, the one holding the Key? Who was he?"

"He never gave me his name," Enoch said with a grin. "To tell the truth, I suspect he was a simple treasure seeker, a misguided grave robber unlucky enough to discover a place of power. He was already long dead when I entered the mountain. After securing the Key, and building my safeguards, I used the poor fellow as a kind of..." Again, Enoch paused to consider his words. "*Discouragement*, if you will."

"You put him there to scare folks," Keech mused.

Enoch chortled. "And little good it did! When your parents came to the Peak, they saw through my old charade right away. But unlike all others, they *earned* the Key. Like you and your trail-mate, Duck."

"But why *us*?" Keech asked. "Why *me*?"

"When terrible things occur, the strong and capable are chosen to stand up for the weak," Enoch said. "You and your friends were exactly the ones needed to defeat the Reverend Rose. Remember the images you found in the mountain?"

Keech nodded. "The seven symbols. We figured they represented the Big Snake."

"I can see how you'd come to that. But I carved those symbols many years ago. I *dreamed* of this future, you see, and the darkness that Rose would threaten to unleash. My dream showed me seven who would fight against the evil, so I created the symbols to represent *you*."

The fellow then crouched and drew in the riverbank soil. Keech peered over his shoulder as he worked. Enoch re-created the entire collection of symbols, including the Devil's mark, only his version included words beneath the seven images:

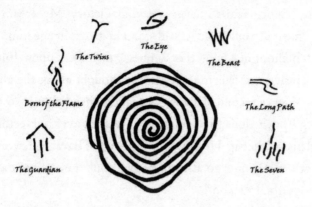

The Twins   The Eye   The Beast

Born of the Flame   The Long Path

The Guardian   The Seven

Enoch said, "In my dream so long ago, I saw 'The Guardian.' That's *you*, Mr. Blackwood, the guardian of your home, your orphan family. Then I dreamed of *Samuel*, 'The One Born of the Flame,'" the boy who survived the fire that you believed had killed him. 'The Twins' represented *Duck and Nathaniel Embry*, two branches of the same strong tree. 'The Eye' is *Miguel*, who would go on to vanquish the sorcerer, Ignatio. The one called *John*, who took on the form of a Chamelia to save his friends, I marked as 'The Beast.' I saw 'The Long Path' in my dream and came to realize this was the one called *Quinn*, who took years to escape to freedom with his beloved aunt. Finally, I saw 'The Seven,' the mighty Protectors of Bonfire Crossing, led by *Strong Heart*, who helped to save the world. Do you see, Mr. Blackwood? I dreamed of seven defenders to fight the Reverend Rose. Seven champions fated to come together and confront evil. I dreamed of the Lost Causes."

A giant question arose in Keech's mind. "If you saw us stop Rose, did that mean we were *fated* to defeat him?"

"No," Enoch said. "I never saw your victory. My dream only showed me that your band would stand up to challenge him."

Keech thought about the symbols, inscribed upon Enoch's magic amulet, and this in turn led to a thought about the ancient relics. "Wait a second. I have something that belongs to you." Leaving Enoch alone for a moment, he dashed over to Hector and opened his saddlebag. He drew out the Fang of Barachiel, wrapped in a cloth. Returning to Enoch, he held out the ancient dagger. "This is yours, I reckon."

Enoch pushed away the relic. "Strong Heart should keep the dagger. Give it to her when she awakens. She'll continue to protect it, as she was always meant to. Now, go back to your camp. You've earned your rest."

Keech peered once more at the symbols on the ground. "Where will you go now?"

But when he glanced up, Enoch was gone. He had left not even a footprint.

CHAPTER 49
FAREWELLS

Keep each other safe and never stop fighting.
—Nathaniel Embry

Led by Em O'Brien, the Lost Causes followed a long and wandering trail through the many valleys and rises of the Rocky Mountains. They rode for weeks, fishing and gathering roots and nuts, living off hardtack when other food was scarce. They told stories and laughed. At other times, they were silent and content to stare at the clouds and the peaceful sky. Along the way, they greeted scouts from various tribes and travelers who shared news of the world.

During the nights, Duck often had trouble sleeping. When she did finally doze off, her dreams sounded troubled, full of ghosts. Along their journey, Keech listened to her speak about Sainte Genevieve and her parents and more often about Nat. One afternoon while resting their horses near a lazy river, Keech mentioned her brother's courage in the town of Wisdom, and Duck began to sob. "Nathaniel wouldn't want me to cry, but I can't help it," she said.

Keech put his arm around the girl. "You cry as much as you want to. We're family now, Duck. All of us are connected, like the links of the Key. We support one another, and that won't ever change."

"Like the links of the Key," Duck echoed, wiping her eyes.

Two months passed. Quinn and Achilles formed a tight hunting partnership, often scouting ahead of the travelers in the morning and returning with freshly caught meat around suppertime. Over campfire meals, Quinn would regale the company with his dreams of taking his aunt Ruth to the Free State of Massachusetts. "After everything she's done for me, I'll get her there. Maybe Auntie can run that sewing shop I told y'all about, and I could go to school and study music." He rubbed absently at his throat. "A few weeks' rest has done my voice a ton of wonders. I'm ready to start singing again."

"You'll be the finest singer in all of Boston. Just be careful not to turn invisible in front of your audience," Keech joked.

For much of the journey, Strong Heart rode in silence. After Keech's discussion with Enoch, she had reclaimed the Fang of Barachiel and swore to keep the dagger safe again. Thoughts of her departed brother and her life as a Protector kept her somber, but Strong Heart's face brightened whenever she told stories of her home and her people in southern Kansas. One day she asked if Keech ever felt a kinship to the Osage, having grown up so differently, and Keech realized that after Bad Whiskey's attack, he had never been given time to sit and think about such matters. "I've missed a great deal of possibilities," he said. "But I gained others with the life Pa Abner gave me. I can't go back and change things, but I can make sure to respect where my true father came from."

Strong Heart nodded and said she understood.

Keech and Sam took to wearing their deputy stars on their

breast pockets. They persuaded Duck to wear hers as well. They told stories about Sheriff Turner, and Sam bragged about the lawman's keen judgment on the long trail to find Keech. When the conversation turned one evening to all the harrowing events in Kansas, Keech finally told Sam the full story of how he'd lost his old friend Felix to Big Ben and the Marsh Bane. After that tale, Keech never spoke of the Big Snake again.

When the company finally emerged from the Rockies into Nebraska Territory, O'Brien offered each of the Lost Causes a tender embrace. This was the place where they would part ways.

"Keep headin' southeast and you'll run into Kansas in no time," she said.

"Will you be taking Achilles?" Quinn asked.

O'Brien gave the old hound a scratch behind the ear, then gently pushed the animal toward Quinn. "No sir. He ain't my dog and never was. He traveled with Milos. But I suspect he fancies a *new* partner. Ain't that right, pup?"

Achilles yapped excitedly, licked the woman's face, then scurried closer to his new companion. Beaming with unmistakable joy, Quinn said, "Much obliged for your help, Miss O'Brien."

The trail-hardened toughness of O'Brien's face softened, and the woman's lips trembled. But then just as quickly, the Enforcer snarled and said, "I done told you tadpoles a thousand times. *I ain't no 'Miss.'*"

Then, tipping her hat, Em O'Brien rode away.

One bright morning a few weeks later, the Lost Causes crested a hill in Kansas Territory and spotted the town of Wisdom. Though much of the settlement had been destroyed, new buildings had been erected along Main Street. A new chapel was under construction, and the Big Snake's ramshackle log wall had been torn down.

The young riders galloped into town and asked for Ruth. They found her supervising a medical tent, where she cared for the sick and the wounded still recovering after their journey from Skeleton Peak. Quinn dashed to the woman, yelling her name, and they tumbled into each other's arms.

"I never worried one second," Ruth said as she covered Quinn with kisses. "Every night I prayed for your safety and fell asleep with a warm surety in my heart that you were alive."

"I'm alive because of *you*," Quinn told the woman.

That same afternoon, Quinn and his aunt prepared to leave Wisdom for good. They suspected their journey north would be nearly as perilous as their passage from Tennessee, so Quinn loaded Lightnin' and Ruth's horse with enough provisions to keep them on the move for several days. With Duck's help, they studied maps and planned the routes they hoped would take them on the safest path to Massachusetts.

"I will leave for my home today as well," Strong Heart said. "I miss my people, and I know my uncle, *Wah-hu Sah-kee*, is waiting for me."

Quinn reached for Strong Heart's hand, but instead of taking it, she embraced him for a full minute. "*Weh-wee-nah*, Quinn Revels. The world is cruel and cannot see the person I see. But I will never forget you. I will never look away."

Resting his forehead upon her shoulder, Quinn said, "I see you, too, Strong Heart. Thank you for saving my life. *Weh-wee-nah.*"

Smiling tenderly at her trailmates, Duck said, "Somewhere, Strong Heart, our brothers are watching. And they're proud."

Strong Heart pondered the girl's words. "I believe this, too, Duck Embry. When I face the eastern sun tomorrow, I will tell my brother what you've done. I will tell him you are *ee-koh-wah*. Our friend."

Keech looked deeply at each of his companions, taking in their faces, memorizing their smiles, their tears, their laughter. He said to them, "You should know that you're all my family. I used to love the heroes Pa told stories about—Daniel Boone, Davy Crockett—but now I know the *real* ones. And I'm proud to stand by you."

With all their goodbyes spoken, the Lost Causes parted ways.

Before riding out of Wisdom, Strong Heart shouted the same words she had spoken to the Lost Causes after departing Bonfire Crossing. "*Wah-Shka^n!*" she called with a strong voice.

Do your best, never quit, and be fearless.

Not long after, Keech, Sam, and Duck left Wisdom and started east.

EPILOGUE

On the twenty-sixth day of May 1856, Keech, Sam, and Duck rounded a curve on a quiet gravel road in northwestern Missouri.

A large, egg-shaped boulder sprang into view, and the trio halted their horses. A tremendous warmth permeated Keech's heart and soul as he took in the familiar landmark on Big Timber Road.

"Copperhead Rock," he said.

Duck peered up at the big stone. "I remember this place! This is where we first met. Me and Cutter and John Wesley bushwhacked you just over yonder in the woods." She winked at Sam. "Keech thought we were a gang of penny thieves."

"Y'all pinned me down, three to one!"

Sam chuckled. "C'mon. Let's head down to Pa's property."

Just beyond the Rock, they crested White Elm Peak, and Keech couldn't believe his eyes when he looked down on the little valley.

Construction was underway. Dozens of Big Timber townsfolk were carrying boards, driving nails, sawing wood, a chorus of work to rebuild the Home for Lost Causes. The house stood larger than before, with an extra wing of rooms extending off the east side and a covered porch that ran around the entire structure.

Keech glanced at Sam in delighted shock. "You never told me a word about this!"

Sam returned a boastful smirk. "Granny wanted more rooms so that we could take in more orphans. She said there's lots of children out there who need caring for."

"Duck, borrow the spyglass?" Keech asked.

When Duck handed over the telescope, Keech gazed around the property in awe. Then his eyes went cloudy with tears when he spotted a familiar boy perched on the peak of the new Home, pounding nails into the roof.

"*Robby*," Keech whispered, then shifted the spyglass a little to the north. There was Little Eugena, framed in perfect sunlight. She sat on the lowest limb of a pin oak tree, a yellow straw hat sitting askew on her head, and held her trusty bugle. When she glanced up and spotted Keech, a huge smile crossed her face. She hopped down from the oak and raised the trumpet. What followed was the most perfect melody Keech had ever heard. Each note was clear and dauntless, a heralding tune that spoke of victory and joy.

At the sound of the bugle, every worker on the property stopped what they were doing and turned to see the young riders at the top of the hill. A cheer broke out across the valley.

To the anthem of applause and Little Eugena's bugle, the trio rode down to the property. As they approached the shakepole fence that bordered the yard, Sam reached out and smacked the painted sign that hung above the gate.

CARSON'S HOME

FOR LOST CAUSES

PROTECT US, SAINT JUDE, FROM HARM

As the trio dismounted, the townsfolk gathered around Keech and Sam to welcome them home. A moment later, the front door of the new orphanage squeaked open, and Granny Nell stepped out. The second she saw them, she yelled, "*My boys!*" and hurried across the yard.

She grabbed Keech and Sam and hugged them so tightly that Keech thought he would burst like a grape. The past few months had not robbed an ounce of the woman's vigor. "I was so worried! So very worried! But here you both are, safe and sound!" Granny bawled.

"I missed you so much," Keech cried. Then from the corner of his eye, he noticed a bundle of blazing red hair on the front porch of the Home. The hair belonged to a tiny boy who bounded toward them with the speed of a young lion.

"Keech! Sam!" hollered Patrick, the youngest of the orphans. He seized Keech's leg and squeezed it in a bear hug. "I knew y'all would come back! I just knew it!"

Keech's eyes poured tears of joy as he grabbed Patrick under the arms and hauled him up. "Hey, flapjack. Look how you've grown!"

Pressing tightly against Keech's face, Patrick said, "Granny said y'all went on a grand adventure. She said y'all are legends in these parts!"

"Legends?" Keech turned to Granny Nell, and they shared a profound, understanding look, a glimpse that spoke of all the dark times that had befallen Pa Abner and the orphanage. But then, the somber moment broke, and Granny smiled. "Patty here's asked every day about your whereabouts, Keech. I told him—" She hesitated, her throat hitching with sobs. "I told him that you went off to seek justice for Pa and that you'd come back a hero. I wasn't wrong."

Still clinging to Keech, Patrick said, "Robby and the townsfolk have been busy. They built all our rooms bigger. Even added a few more!"

"That's mighty good to hear," Keech said. "Because we all have a new sister." He turned back to Duck, and she stepped forward with a small, nearly bashful grin.

"It's very nice to meet you," Duck said to the boy. "I've heard some tall tales about you, and I suspect every one of them is true."

"What's your name?" Patrick asked.

"Duck."

Patrick chewed on the name for a second. "That's the best name I ever heard."

Scratching his cheek, Keech glanced at Duck again. "You know, something just occurred to me. I never learned your *real* name."

Duck mulled over Keech's words, then grinned. "I think I'll keep it a secret a little while longer. Maybe after our next adventure, I'll spill the beans."

Keech laughed.

Later that day, after a long celebration with the family, Keech and Duck and Sam walked down to the Third Fork River and kicked off their boots. They rolled up their trouser legs, sat on the muddy bank, and talked about all their perilous travels. They swapped all the best stories about their friends Cutter and John Wesley and Quinn and Strong Heart.

After a time, Sam said to Duck, "Hey, wanna hear my favorite song? It's one me and Keech learned from Pa Abner."

Duck said, "I'd love to hear it."

So Sam taught the lyrics to Duck, and together they all sang as they watched the sun settle over the western horizon.

"Ol' Lonesome Joe, come ride next to me.

Let's roll, ol' Joe, to the Alamo Tree.

Lonesome in the heart, lonesome as can be . . ."

As they sang, Keech took in the hills and the trees, all the way to the limit of his sight. *Read the earth*, Pa Abner once taught. *Let it tell you its story.* So Keech took everything in and let the Earth speak its tale. This is what it told him, on that quiet, peaceful evening in 1856:

The Reverend Rose is no more, but the hatred and greed that created him still exist. The world is an ever-changing mold of clay, capable of terrible deformities, but also beautiful creations. You should not rest till the world is a place in which folks are free to live in peace, to raise their families in harmony with the good earth, and to love and be loved as desired. Do not simply wish for such a world. Strive for it to be.

Sitting on the riverbank beside his friends, Keech Blackwood knew he would continue to work for a better world, a place of companionship and support for all those in need. With this purpose in mind, he looked at both his brother Sam and his sister Duck. And they shared joyous laughter as they continued to sing.

"You won't be so lonesome at the Alamo Tree,

When you sit next to me, when you sit next to me."

AMICUS FIDELIS PROTECTIO FORTIS

A FAITHFUL FRIEND IS A STURDY SHELTER.

A NOTE FROM THE AUTHORS

The book you hold in your hands—as well as its predecessors, *Legends of the Lost Causes* and *The Fang of Bonfire Crossing*—is more than the solitary endeavor of two authors. Since 2015, we've been fortunate enough to work closely with the *Wah-Zha-Zhi* Cultural Center and Language Department—two organizations that help comprise the Osage Heritage Center in Pawhuska, Oklahoma.

When we started planning the Legends series, we knew right away we wanted to tell a magical Old West story that included a diverse cast of characters, a group of resourceful kids who could join forces to fight the Reverend Rose's evil. For us, this meant examining the cultures of 1850s Missouri and Kansas. Our research led us to the *Wah-Zha-Zhi* Cultural Center, where we met the wonderful directors and specialists who would become readers of our story and close reviewers of our cultural content.

All the Osage language and names seen in our series have been directly provided by the Cultural Center and its partner, the Language Department. Though we consulted some written sources in early drafts, such as Carolyn Quintero's *Osage Dictionary* or Francis la Flesche's *A Dictionary of the Osage Language*, the final approval of all words, phrases, and names came from these language and cultural experts who so graciously agreed to help us.

The same holds true for all Osage customs or practices found within the books. Though the Protectors are figments of the authors' imaginations, any Osage customs to which we allude came from extensive conversations with our cultural partners. We also learned a great deal about the traditional clothing, weapons, and traits of Osage warriors in the 1850s. In addition, the center's consultants worked closely with us on the character of Strong Heart, not only providing her name for the series but also guiding her dialogue and interactions. Naturally, any mistakes or inaccuracies in these details are the fault of the authors and no one else.

To learn more about the Osage Nation, please visit https://www.osagenation-nsn.gov.

Throughout our drafting and revision process, our research and discussions of various cultures have included many other experts, from South American contacts to Nigerian American readers. Though some of the information discussed with these kind professionals may appear in our books as only passing phrases or details, we appreciate all the important voices who have spoken with us. Because the Lost Causes are about people coming together for common goals, we hope this series helps to strengthen and contribute to a community of inclusion and acceptance.

With regard to the cryptic Black Verse seen throughout the story, this fictional language is based loosely on the writings of H. P. Lovecraft and not intended to resemble or represent any real language. Any similarities to authentic languages or dialects are unintentional, and as mentioned before, strictly the fault of the authors.

In the end, Legends of the Lost Causes and its accompanying stories are meant to be enjoyed as magical fantasies full of adventure. But it is also our hope that this series grants young readers a larger awareness of the remarkable cultures of 1850s America, as well as a deeper recognition of the country's darker histories of slavery, cruelty, and violence. When we understand where we came from, we can steer the course of our lives into better harmony with one another.

ACKNOWLEDGMENTS

Welcome back to the light, partners! We were certain you wouldn't escape the deep, dark perils that awaited you, but here you stand, undefeated and as strong as ever. Now come on over to the campfire, kick off your boots, rest up your pony, and let the authors say a few final words. We've got a whole heap of folks to thank before this here book closes, and we'd like to start with:

Our agent extraordinaire, Brooks Sherman, who told us long ago to keep steady eyes on the long path to publishing this series. Brooks, thank you for believing we could do that, and for trusting that we could cross the finish line. Simply put: You're the best. The same can be said for our amazing team at Henry Holt Books for Young Readers, remarkable folks like:

The great Brian Geffen, our brilliant editor and fearless leader of the Lost Causes. Brian, you're one of the finest cowboys to ever ride in the saddle, and we're mighty thankful for your friendship and your dedication to Keech's story. Ditto for the incomparable Morgan Rath, our publicist and first-class trail captain, as well as the magnificent Christian Trimmer, editorial director at Henry Holt. We also thank the exceptional Liz Dresner, best book designer this side of the Mississippi, along with Mark Podesta, Katie Halata, and our marvelous Macmillan School and Library team. Friends, for keeping your faith in a pair of old buckaroos, we tip our hats to you. As well as to the wonderful:

Alexandria Neonakis, our interior art and cover illustrator, who has brought the world of the Lost Causes into such breathtaking view. Alex, we're so grateful to have had your imagination and talent on our team.

We also extend our sincere appreciation to the folks at the *Wah-Zha-Zhi* Cultural Center and Language Department in Pawhuska, Oklahoma. Director Addie Hudgins, cultural specialist Jennifer Tiger, cultural specialist Harrison Hudgins, and anyone else at the Osage Heritage Center who assisted on the cultural content of the Lost Causes series—we thank you endlessly for your guidance, assistance, and friendship.

Next, we offer our "much obliged" to Ibeawuchi Travis Uzoegwu, for your patient, eagle-eyed reading of Quinn Revels throughout the series and the excellent notes you provided our team. When you gave advice, Ibe, we paid close attention. Thank you for taking the time to read our novels and providing your extensive knowledge and insights.

We also thank Dr. Beckie Bigler and Reinaldo Sanchez for your amazing assistance and input on the Spanish content of the series. The same goes for Marianne Caron for your kind support with regard to French words and phrases. And a special thanks to our Pawnee contact for a much-needed cultural perspective of Pawnee interactions on the Santa Fe Trail in 1856.

Brad says: Well, Louis, I reckon that just might do it! We best skedaddle.

Louis says: Not so fast, partner. Let me take the reins for a spell. I want to thank my wife, Kimberly, and the pups for being so understanding about my long writing hours and for listening to me work through ideas. Also, a massive thanks to my folks, who continue to be the best, and to my siblings, who make a mighty cool pack. Thanks as well to my wonderful in-laws for all your support, and to my rambunctious nieces and nephews for making me laugh like you do. And a special appreciation to the good folk at Lewis-Clark State College, especially for the support I've received from my chair, Martin Gibbs, and the creative-writing faculty. And to all my students who've read the Lost Causes books, I hope you follow my lead and write some rip-roaring adventures of your own. Finally, I'd like to thank my partner, Brad, who has remained my most loyal companion through this process. Thanks, pard.

Brad blushes. Aw shucks, Lou, same goes to ya! You're the best trailmate a fella could ask for. Now let me take those reins a moment; I reckon I've got a few folks to thank myself. I'll start with:

My amazing wife, Alisha, and stepdaughter, Chloe. You both are my world, and I dedicate every month, hour, and second of writing this series to you. I also send my love and appreciation to my mother, Babs, and stepdad, Joe, for always believing in me and pushing me across the finish line, as well as my pa, Jerry, and my siblings, Missy, Pam, and Greg. I'd also like to thank my friend Brandon Hobson for his continual encouragements and brainstorming sessions over coffee at The Perk. And I'd be terribly remiss if I didn't tip my hat to the various bookstore friends and colleagues I've met on the trail in Oklahoma—folks like Roger and Pat Mullins of Bliss Books & Bindery in Stillwater; Tara Smith and Jerry Brace and all my friends at Brace Books & More in Ponca City; Joe and Nan Hight and Shelbee King at Best of

Books in Edmond; Jeff Martin and Pat Cawiezell and all the good folk at Magic City Books in Tulsa; and, of course, all my exceptional friends at the Woodland Plaza Barnes and Noble in Tulsa. Thank you all for supporting Keech's journey and for sharing the Lost Causes with so many readers.

I also offer a bundle of gratitude to my ever-supportive colleagues at Fire Protection Publications. And a very special shout-out to my debut group, the Electric Eighteens, an outstanding passel of authors who are changing the world one sentence at a time. I also thank the tremendous middle-school librarians and teachers I've met while taking Keech and his crew on the book trail. That goes double for Jennifer Leonard and her eighth-grade English students at Rensselaer Jr./Sr. High School in Rensselaer, New York. Thank you so much, friends, for welcoming this Oklahoma writer into your classroom and letting me serve for a time as your #KidsNeedMentors author.

Louis says: That's a dandy list, Brad! Anybody else to thank before we scoot?

Brad says: I couldn't allow this here book to close before I thank my best friends, Jim Patterson, Michael Armstrong, and Eric Vaughan, for always standing tall with me through sunshine and cloud. Jim, though you left this world far too early, your magnificent spirit endures. Neither death nor illness nor outlaws nor cursed relics can ever stop the power of our friendship. I love you, brother.

At long last, we come to YOU, amazing reader. As we've said before, we couldn't have accomplished any of this without you and your imagination. May you and your pony find all the greenest grasses, may you ride the calmest trails, and may you drink the coolest water. As you gallop on down the path, remember to be good to one another, spread love and compassion to everyone you meet, and live each day with courage. Ride tall in the saddle, friends, and be well.